Praise for Neil Spring:

'Explosive'
Daily Express

A deft, spooky psychological drama based on a true story'
Daily Mail

'Surprising, serpentine and clever'
Sunday Times

'Spooky and tense with a truly horrifying denouement'
Sunday Express, S Magazine

'Close the curtains, pull up a chair, open a book –
and prepare to be pleasantly scared'
Metro

'A sinister tale'
Heat

'A triumph of creativity . . . the conclusion
will shock and amaze you'
Vada Magazine

'A real page turner'
Tatler

Neil Spring writes psychological chillers, many of which are inspired by real events. His debut novel, *The Ghost Hunters*, was adapted into a critically acclaimed television drama for ITV. His second novel, *The Watchers*, concerns UFO sightings during the Cold War. In 2017, he published *The Lost Village*, a ghost story about the haunting of the abandoned Imber Village. *The Burning House*, set on the shores of Loch Ness, is his fourth novel. Originally from south Wales, Neil lives in London and can be contacted via his website, www.neilspring.com, or followed on Facebook at https://www.facebook.com/Neilspring.author, and on Twitter as @neilspring. Neil is represented by the literary agency, Curtis Brown.

Also by Neil Spring

The Ghost Hunters
The Watchers
The Lost Village

THE
BURNING
HOUSE

NEIL SPRING

Quercus

First published in Ebook in 2018 by Quercus
This paperback edition first published in 2019 by

Quercus Editions Ltd
Carmelite House
50 Victoria Embankment
London EC4Y 0DZ

An Hachette UK company

A CIP catalogue record for this book is available
from the British Library

PB ISBN 978 1 78648 886 2
EBOOK ISBN 978 1 78648 885 5

10 9 8 7 6 5 4 3 2 1

Typeset by CC Book Production

Printed and bound in Great Britain by Clays Ltd, Elcograf S.p.A.

For my dear friend, Guy Chambers

PROLOGUE

For sale on Loch Ness: an idyllic holiday retreat. Quiet and private. Period property prime for updating, and offered with no onward chain.

The words were embossed in royal-blue lettering on the cover of a glossy brochure, which Oswald Cattenach held between trembling fingers.

'Prime for updating?' He knew what that meant. The house was probably decorated by someone with spectacularly bad taste. As for 'no onward chain', well, that was easy: someone had probably died, maybe even inside the house.

But of course, Oswald already knew that was true.

The serenity and beauty of the location, framed by the loch, Farigaig Forest, and the mountains, make this a very special part of the world.

The ashy morning light shone on Oswald's angular face and the wind ruffled his shock of blond hair as he lifted his gaze. Some, in fact, may find the landscape desolately rugged, the mountains brooding, the dense woodland, and the loch, sinister. But it stirred Oswald's muse; he had an urge to be amongst his oils and watercolours and charcoals so that he might capture the eerily idyllic view. And certainly, he thought, watching little waves break on the shingle shore, this place was special. Boleskine House was special.

He leafed slowly through the brochure, studying the pictures: four large bedrooms, four bathrooms, a variety of smaller rooms, a dining room, a library and the east wing with the adjoining terrace, where he would undertake his most vital work. The house really was perfect.

'Quiet and private', the brochure promised. It was the privacy Oswald required, and here the estate agent was spot on. Being so isolated on the side of the loch, Boleskine would give him total privacy, especially during the winter. The gales here could be ripping and fierce, the sort that could take a door off its hinges if you weren't careful. And a house with an unsavoury reputation like this wasn't exactly likely to draw many visitors. Local legend had it that the dwelling was built on the site of a church that had burned down, killing the entire congregation, who were trapped inside attending Mass. A tragedy. An accident? Possibly.

But then again, possibly not.

Oswald raised his eyes, gazing over the restless waters at the dwelling he had travelled some six hundred miles to see. A thick mist hung over the loch, but he had a clear enough view of the sprawling, sullen bungalow that stood on the hillside above the cemetery. Even from this distance, there was an oppressive air about Boleskine. Sombre and brooding.

This part of the world, he thought as he studied the opposite shore, grew more intriguing by the second. There was a young woman over there, a girl with ginger plaits, wandering.

She seemed to be carrying something, a large sketchpad, possibly. Who was she? Who, like him, would find anything so fixating in this desolate part of the world? He thought maybe he had seen her once before. This wasn't the first time he had kept vigil here.

Thanks to his tirelessly enquiring mind, he already knew so much about the house's macabre history and the more prosaic details: built in the eighteenth century by Colonel Archibald Fraser as a hunting lodge; six owners so far (one a famous rock star). And now . . . Oswald. He could hardly believe that finally Boleskine would be his – the perfect location for his great operation.

People would wonder, of course: What did he want with the house? What did he do for a living? Why did a single man want to live somewhere so big? Some of these were legitimate questions; he couldn't deny that. Boleskine was built for a family and its staff, but he was just one man on his own, and it had always been that way. The weight of so many long hours passed alone in his London flat threatened to press down on him, but he refocused on the future: the promise represented in the estate agent's brochure.

It did the house proud, and he was smiling as he turned the final pages. Then, when he reached the back page and saw, in a small and delicate font, the price, his smile dropped.

One and a half million!?

The sellers had to be taking the piss, didn't they? What were they thinking?

Okay, he wouldn't have described Boleskine as dilapidated, but it was getting there fast. That roof surely wasn't going to last another winter. And notwithstanding the physical state of the place, there was its reputation to consider. All those gruesome stories? The sellers should have been *begging* for someone to take it off their hands.

They just might beg, too, Oswald thought. *If they knew what had happened within those cracked walls.*

The Highland wind gusted, but Oswald remained rooted to the spot, black overcoat flapping around him, steely eyes trained on the white-stone house across the water, as grim speculations slid through his mind.

The cost was high, beyond his reach. But this property possessed a geographical and spiritual value that was beyond priceless – to him, anyway.

He didn't have the money, but he *did* have the ruthless determination. He had always sought out and followed his true path in life, and that was exactly what he would do now.

Oswald tossed the brochure into the silvery grey waters. As he watched it soak through and drift on the surface like a dead thing, he whispered the guiding principles of his philosophy:

'To will, to wish, to want and to purpose.'

Then, as the brochure was consumed, sinking into the dark depths of the loch, the thought came to him, creeping in slyly and taking refuge in the deepest recess of his mind: Oswald Cattenach would *own* this house. He would inhabit it; possess it. He felt this as if struck by a powerful premonition. Boleskine House would come to him, eventually.

One's destiny always did.

PART ONE

FIRE SALE

There had stood a great house in the centre of the gardens, where now was left only that fragment of ruin. This house had been empty for a great while; years before his – the ancient man's – birth. It was a place shunned by the people of the village, as it had been shunned by their fathers before them. There were many things said about it, and all were of evil. No one ever went near it, either by day or night. In the village it was a synonym of all that is unholy and dreadful.

– William Hope Hodgson,
The House on the Borderland

1

The mist was rising from the surface of the loch and drifting hungrily over the road, blurring the outlines of the gorse and stunted trees that ran alongside it. Although the dull light was beginning to fade, Clara Jones didn't even think about slowing down. She pressed down, forcing the car onward.

Clara wasn't exactly happy to be driving out to Boleskine. In the rear-view mirror, she saw the purple pouches beneath her steel-grey eyes, the grim set to her jaw. She could admit to feeling a little curious about the opportunity ahead and what she would find out there in that lonely spot beside the loch, but mostly what she felt was nervous. Worried. As for the guilt, that was threatening to overwhelm her; it had been for two weeks. She tried to pretend it wasn't there.

Focus, she admonished herself. *And hurry. Can't afford to be late.*

The meandering road ahead veered right. Clara was tensing as she took the turn. Not because she was uncertain of the route; her anxiety was ramping up because the truth was, she knew this route too well. She knew it by heart, even though she had made the journey only once before.

But once was enough.

You did it for your own sake, she told herself. *You had to.* But she would never have to do such a thing again, and she was glad about that. In the same way that she was done with her old life, Clara was done with surprises, especially unpleasant surprises about herself and the crimes of which she was capable. She'd got all the way to the age of twenty-eight without it even occurring to her to set fire to someone's house; but there it was. She couldn't get away from the fact: as of two weeks ago, Clara was an arsonist.

Not officially. It's not official unless you get caught.

But she hadn't been. And if she was going to get found out, it would have happened by now. Wouldn't it?

It's your responsibility. You decided. It wasn't easy, and sure, it wasn't right, but you decided.

The guilt returned in a rush as she remembered making the decision.

She had been sitting at her desk when Gale Kilgour, a leathery blonde woman in her mid-fifties, had bustled into the office fretting about the cooling market conditions. Clara liked her boss, despite her crisp demeanour; Gale was sharp and shrewd; good at selling, and, unlike many estate agents, she wasn't immoral. But business was tough now. Because of the referendum, according to Gale.

'The sellers are on the verge of withdrawing Boleskine from the market completely,' she had said, tugging on the string of pearls around her neck. 'I've advised them to reduce the price, considering its history, but they're not budging. If they don't find a buyer soon, it's us who'll suffer. You know that, don't you, Clara?'

There was a deliberate moment of silence as Gale cast her eyes shrewdly over her employee. Clara, who hadn't completed on a sale in seven months. That made her more than tardy, she knew; it made her downright ineffectual. And broke: with no commission, her salary was miserable, and she hadn't paid her rent for two months.

'We had one interested party from London last week,' Gale went on, all formal and prim, 'but he said he needed to knock the price down substantially.'

The idea had flashed into Clara's head then, from nowhere. A wild impulse too mad to contemplate, too risky . . . too tempting. A victimless crime.

'I'm entrusting the sale to you,' Gale said. 'It's not one we can afford to lose.' She told Clara again how badly it reflected on them to have a house – an expensive house – just sitting on the books or, worse, withdrawn from them. Then, speech over, she peered at Clara and frowned. 'Did you hear what I said, Clara? You look miles away.'

She had been miles away. In London, to be precise. Thinking of her old life, the hellish life that had driven her to drop everything and run. When she hadn't been an estate agent. When she hadn't even been Clara Jones; she had been Mrs Alison Hopkins. Obedient, gullible, weak. She was remembering the early mornings carefully applying make-up to hide her bruises; the anxious hours passed in the doctor's waiting room thinking up excuses that never sounded convincing enough. *Tripped on the rug again, Mrs Hopkins?' 'Caught your hand in the drawer again, Mrs Hopkins?'* These questions put to her as she averted her gaze, looking down at her trembling hands; and then she would apologise in whispered breaths for being so careless, all the while wondering why she endured it.

And then came the day something died inside her, and she found she would no longer endure it. How much time did Karl spend looking for her? Was he still searching? She had no doubt. She remembered only too well the times he had followed her to work, stinking drunk, followed her on a night out.

Karl was that kind of man.

Had it ever crossed his mind to look for her here? She didn't think so. Karl always said he despised the Scots, and she knew he hated wild, craggy landscapes. Which was probably, in part, why Abersky had suggested itself. Coming to the seclusion and wilderness of these parts should have been a tonic. Desolation. Here, at the foothills of the mountains, she could disappear. Begin again. And she had done just that. She wasn't prepared to risk it all now. Which was why she heard herself saying the words that would lead her into unexplored and very dangerous territory.

'You just leave Boleskine to me, Gale. It's old and it has character. If I can't sell that house, I probably shouldn't be working for you.'

That drew a smile from Gale. Being known for her charitable work was all very well, but business was business, and Gale – twice nominated for Highlands Businesswoman of the Year – had a professional reputation to maintain.

'You said you had someone interested last week?'

Gale nodded. 'A gentleman from London, here on holiday. He may even still be in the area.'

'Did he view the property?'

'No, but he came into the office on your day off. Wanted to know why the price was so high.' She tutted. 'Bit demanding, actually. Wilful. Coming from London, you'd think he'd have appreciated that views over the loch come at a premium.'

'Well, quite.'

'I'll dig out his number for you, Clara. It's worth following up. But I suggest you think imaginatively about how to make this sale. Time is of the essence. If we lose that property from our list ...' She trailed off, allowing Clara to imagine the repercussions.

And she had. In vivid detail, she'd imagined losing her job, her home, her place in this tiny village that was overlooked by dark hills, lonely peaks and a vast iron-grey sky. This was a community far from anywhere; a community where superstition died hard, constantly haunted by swirling rumours of 'something' in the loch. Clara didn't quite know why she had been drawn to Abersky, but she did know that she didn't have the energy to start over again. This life was all she had now, and by God, she was going to protect it.

So, I torched the east wing.

The image of the burning house rose before her again. She knew she had done wrong, even as she struck the match and heard the curtains catch with a *foomp!* She had felt the deepest shame as she watched the writhing flames dart and blaze, felt the blistering heat on her face as they ripped through the east wing, and the thought that leapt to mind was: *I won't get away with this. How can I?*

The answer came back immediately: *Because if you want a future in this village, you need to make the sale.*

She had fled then to her car, run as if the devil himself was at her heels, her heart hammering in her chest. Rattling away in her leased Peugeot 308, she had felt a spectre of her former self as the distant wail of fire engines pierced the night air. A glance at the rear-view mirror gave a view of a hellish orange blaze engulfing the east wing; black smoke belching into the starlit sky. She looked away, eyes fixed on the dark road, and, beyond, the twinkling lights of the picture-postcard village.

That had been two weeks ago, and the memory was still

clear and terrifying. But on this darkening afternoon, the task before her was considerably less complicated. She would put on a show. She would flash her best smile and show a house. A house damaged by fire and now priced to sell. And if she was lucky – if her risk paid off – she would make that sale.

The potential buyer who had come into the office on her day off had revealed very little about himself when they spoke on the telephone, but yes, he said, he would like to view the property now the sellers had finally lowered the price (because the last thing they wanted, Clara knew, while living the high life in their Spanish villa, was to worry about the upkeep of a half-ruined property on the banks of Loch Ness).

Mr Cattenach was softly spoken, and seemed intelligent and charming. He was looking forward to meeting her, he had said politely. Clara should have felt the same way. It was completely back to front, unusual, for the estate agent in this scenario to feel nervous. But then, everything about this situation was unusual.

Just act normal. There's too much at stake to make a mess of this.

She was driving so fast she almost missed the turning onto the rugged lane that led up to the house. Braking, she swerved suddenly, and then accelerated again, keeping her eyes on the bumpy narrow track winding upwards through the dark pine trees. Almost immediately, shame washed over her.

As if the house knows I'm coming.

No, that was silly. Probably. But it wasn't the first time she had felt this way.

The night she had come here under the cover of darkness, unlocked a window and set fire to the curtains, she had thought she sensed a presence. As if someone was watching her. The feeling was so powerful that for a moment she had entertained the idea of snuffing out the match and abandoning her mad plan altogether.

Don't be ridiculous, she had told herself. *It's paranoia; there's no one else up here.* Why would there be? Everyone in the area knew to stay away from Boleskine. There were probably a good many locals already wishing that the entire house would be destroyed in a blaze so that the ruins could be demolished and the horrid place forgotten altogether.

As her car rumbled up the meandering track, an imposing edifice rose before her. A long and low U-shaped building; single-storeyed. Dirty white walls, ornamented with Greek columns. It had been a hunting lodge once, she knew, and the centuries had badly discoloured its cracked – and in some places, crumbling – walls.

The car itself seemed to resist the approach as Clara slowed down. A dark discomfort stole into her heart as she took in the house, brooding there on the lonely hillside, squat and sullen, its black shuttered windows like blinded eyes. At the main entrance, stone dogs and eagles stood guard.

For a moment, she felt horribly oppressed by doubt, and she wished she had waited a little longer before showing the house to its prospective new owner. But Clara, the new woman she had created in Abersky, the woman who had struck the match, rose up and demanded that she see sense.

Of course, there were questions about how the fire had started, and the insurance company still needed to complete its investigation. But no one had spoken of arson, and no one had asked about Clara's whereabouts on the night of the fire.

Plus, the blaze had only damaged the east wing, and the west wing was the better part of the house in any case, because it faced the loch. Over time, the house could be patched up. In fact, a new owner with enough time and money might be just what Boleskine needed to cleanse it of its strange and terrible past – the string of gruesome, violent deaths that had occurred here across the years.

Accidents. Suicides. Murder.

So, Clara had struck the match. She had read somewhere that fire gave arsonists power. As she had watched the billowing flames leap and twirl, shooting up through the roof and from the windows, she thought that might indeed be true.

Now, as she had done that night, gazing at the burning house set in these beautiful but harsh surroundings, she told herself firmly that she had done what needed to be done. And something else: she was safe.

She was going to get away with it.

2

'So, uh, do you believe me?'

Six hundred miles south from Boleskine House, in his office at the London Mindfulness Centre on the Vauxhall Bridge Road, Karl Hopkins studied the patient sitting on the other side of his untidy desk: a dark-haired professional, pale, well-spoken and well-attired in an electric-blue suit.

The patient's name was Terry Sanders and he was Karl's last appointment of the day – thank Christ! It was Friday, it had been too long a week, and what Karl really needed was a night on the town. A drink. He could almost taste the double scotch he'd be ordering in The Red Rose in less than an hour.

'You think I'm crazy, right?' Terry ventured.

'Not at all,' Karl said evenly, hoping he looked concerned. He wasn't. As muddled as his mind could become sometimes, Karl was clear on that. His patients' problems helped him enjoy a life of relative comfort; the job of a mental health counsellor wasn't too demanding. Once you learned to shut off, it was surprisingly easy to drown out the moronic voices of the self-obsessed, the depressed, the delusional. If you nodded occasionally, scribbled on your pad, you could take it to the bank that they'd be back next week for their regular session.

'I believe *you* believe what happened,' Karl continued, 'and there's probably a good explanation for what you thought you saw. Let's explore that. Will you tell me again about your experience?'

Terry nodded, looking slightly reassured, but not totally. What came next was the sort of story Karl hadn't heard since he was a kid, drinking with his mates by the campfire: a good old-fashioned, clichéd ghost story. Poor old Terry, still grieving the wife he lost to a car accident two years ago, had come home from work late (of course it was late; why did people never see this shit in the daytime?), tired and agitated with stress, only to find his dead wife waiting for him in the bedroom.

Oh, and what a surprise, Terry had been drinking.

'Had you taken anything else?' Karl asked weightily.

'Only some prescribed medication.'

'I see.'

'I'm not crazy.'

'I'm not saying that you are. But mistakes can be—'

Terry's head snapped up. 'This was no mistake! I always keep the bedroom window shut, but the moment I entered I saw the curtains billowing in and I thought there must be some sort of intruder. But when I turned around, I saw it was her, my Charlotte, her face all bloody and smashed up. Jesus!' He shook his head in horror.

'She was trying to speak, that was the worst part. She was mouthing words at me I couldn't hear. "You'll pay," I think she was saying. "You'll pay for what you did."'

A silence between them. Awkward.

Terry looked fearfully across at Karl and drew a breath. 'Do you believe the dead can return to harm us?'

'You feel threatened by this . . . vision?' asked Karl.

'I'm serious,' Terry said, with sudden anger. 'Do you think the dead can cause us harm?'

Karl remained composed. 'No. I don't believe that, Terry. Do you?'

Terry opened his mouth to reply; closed it. Which told Karl all he needed to know. He'd met men like this before, men who would never believe you could kill a mystery with science.

'It's been two years since your wife passed,' Karl said, checking his notes. 'Why do you think she would want to return to harm you?'

That question made his patient squirm, the fear and uncertainty on his face gradually fading until it was replaced by an emotion that Karl recognised unequivocally as guilt.

Here we go. Scratch the surface and something nasty comes crawling out.

'Why,' Karl prompted, 'would your wife want to come back and harm you, Terry?'

Terry hung his head. Finally, he said heavily, 'I harmed her.'

Karl didn't quite flinch at that, but he did blink.

'I killed her.'

Now Karl did flinch. He put his notepad aside. Terry was either a total screwball or—

'I mean, the car accident killed her, of course, but really it was *my* fault. Before she drove off, we had the most godawful row. She accused me of carrying on with one of our mutual friends and I just . . . lost my patience. Lost control. And she ran from me.'

These words made Karl flash back to the night of Alison's accident.

An accident, that's all it was.

He pushed away the mental images – the stairwell, the puddle of dark blood – and shook his head.

'The car accident would have happened anyway. You can't blame yourse—'

'Except I do!' Terry's head snapped up. 'I hurt her. I mean, terribly.'

He glanced down at his hands as if they were bloodstained daggers. It wouldn't be long now before he needed tissues. Already, Karl could hear the guy's voice was thickening.

'I punched her, get it? Punched her right in the face – oh, her beautiful face. And . . . she was so upset, so frightened, staring back at me like I was some kind of monster. It's no wonder her attention wasn't on the road.'

As Terry babbled, Karl scrutinised him. Clean-cut, well put together. A professional. Yet clearly, he was also entitled and arrogant and clever. In Karl's experience, all abusers were. Abusers were some of the nicest men you could meet – on the surface.

'How could I have done that? I've never laid a finger on a woman before, but . . .'

'I understand,' Karl said. In a strange way, he actually did. Which made him resent Terry a little right now. Karl liked to feel superior to his patients, and his vanity and his pride meant it was hard to entertain the idea that he was anything like them.

'Charlotte suffered because of me.' Terry's voice cracked, and here they came, the tears, coursing down his cheeks. 'I'll never forgive myself for that.' A pause. 'And now it seems, neither will she. After it happened I did a search online on vengeful apparitions. Because that's what this apparition felt like. And you know what I learned?'

Karl tried not to look sceptical. 'What did you learn, Terry?'

'That vengeful spirits occur in every culture, in every age. Apparitions of those who were ill-treated, who died in despair or suffering.'

'Right.'

'You think I'm crazy?'

'Terry,' Karl said in his best reasonable tone. 'Wandering restless spirits are a fiction, you understand that, right?'

'But I *saw* her.'

'I'll tell you what,' Karl said, removing his glasses and setting them down on a pile of paperwork, 'it was late, you'd been drinking, you felt guilty and were missing your wife. Sometimes that concoction of emotions can induce the most vivid and alarming of hallucinations.' His eyes shifted to Terry's hands, which were twisting in his lap. 'I suspect what you saw was a manifestation of your internal grief. Your guilt.'

'You suspect?'

'I know.'

Terry had dropped his head again. 'God. I must be a terrible man.'

Karl pushed away the mental picture of Alison's face. Not how she was at the end, but before. Happy, confident, popular. *That*'s what had made him drink, the bitter self-loathing she made him feel. That's what had made him lose control.

But he was nothing like this pathetic, delusional creature before him. For one thing, Karl only got mad when he drank, and these days that was only occasionally. He'd had to rein in his impulses after Alison left. When he discovered she was gone he'd finished off every bottle in the flat, smashed up the furniture, and done nothing else for days but scour every corner of the net, looking for her. Hunting. He had been adamant: he was going to make her pay for leaving him, he was going to show her who was boss. But he knew now that was just the alcohol, fuelling his obsessiveness, his rage.

It had been scorching him – *them* – for years; he could see that now. There had been days when he had wished Alison not just harm, but wished her dead. On one occasion – he remembered it was the day after he'd tossed a mug of scalding-hot coffee over her – he had come home feeling a weird thrill running through him, an irrepressible delight that she had finally given up trying to make it work. He convinced himself as he took the lift that he was about to find her dead, in the bathtub maybe, wrists slashed. Or maybe she'd overdosed on those painkillers she popped like sweeties. He didn't care. He'd just got to thinking about how he would redecorate as he scraped his key into the lock, but as the door had swung open and he'd stepped into the hall, Alison had been waiting for him.

Ironing.

Ironing his fucking shirts. Worse, she smiled at him then, sheepishly, and apologised for the night before.

She apologised to *him*!

At that moment, he had found it utterly impossible to look at her without feeling small. Pathetic. The purple swelling around her eye was bad; that was one thing. The rest of it was the shirts – knowing he'd be wearing one of those shirts tomorrow as he sat there in his office, listening to his patients pour out their woes. It narrowed the gap between him, the counsellor, and them, the screw-ups. He didn't like that one bit.

In recent weeks he'd been making a colossal effort to cut back; not teetotal, not yet, but he had cut back enough to stop the flames of rage surging up. The job was a part of that; the job helped him focus, and that was good. So long as he had other people's problems to preoccupy him, he didn't have as much time to focus on his own. With Alison gone, the job was all he had left. It tethered him to sobriety – mostly.

'What frightens you more, Terry, the vision you experienced, or the idea that you could ever have raised your fist to your wife in the first place?'

'I think what scares me the most is the possibility that I might do it again,' Terry said, 'to someone else.' He shook his head. 'I guess I have anger issues, yeah?'

'Severe anger issues.'

'Can you help me?'

'I'd like to. If you can accept that your anger doesn't have to be expressed abusively?'

Terry nodded. 'I think so.'

'You can only get better by coming to terms with what you did,' Karl went on, barely aware that he was talking as much to himself now as he was to his patient. 'Are you willing to do that?'

'I can try.' Terry looked hard at Karl, as if his life depended on it, and in a tear-clotted voice he said, 'Sometimes I hate myself. Know what I mean?'

Karl didn't answer. But he did pretend to write a note on his pad.

3

'Hi there!'

Outside Boleskine House, the middle-aged man standing tall in the centre of the driveway was well-spoken and smartly attired in dark denim trousers and a black polo-necked jumper.

'You from Highlands Estates?' he asked as she slammed the car door.

Of course I'm from the agency, Clara thought. *Who else is he expecting?* But she simply smiled brightly and introduced herself. His handshake was firm, his skin surprisingly rough.

He cast a sudden inquisitive gaze over her shoulder, towards the loch.

'What is it?' Clara asked, turning briefly. And her eyes snagged on something that wasn't the loch: an old wooden swing, rotting on a frayed rope that dangled from an ancient cedar tree.

'There's something magical about the mist that hangs over the water,' he said, 'like its nature's giant bathtub.' He smiled. 'For a moment, I thought I saw something out there.'

She turned back to him. 'You'd be amazed how many people

imagine they see something strange in the loch. And most of the guest houses and shops around here are very grateful for that.' She shook her head, smiling. 'Well, I can't tell you how pleased I am to have caught you before you left for London. We've had so much interest in this property, Mr Cattenach.'

'Please, call me Oswald.'

She didn't want to call him Oswald, despite his warm smile. 'Mr Cattenach' was perfectly professional. But the client was always right. And a touch eccentric, she couldn't help noticing.

Oswald was tall and powerfully built, with a shock of curly blond hair – dyed, she suspected, based on the black roots – and a face full of angles. It was a calm face that radiated intelligence. His eyes shone; jewel-like; midnight blue. Over his polo neck, he wore a Trofeo wool jacket of pearlescent grey, with a turned-up corduroy collar. And he reminded her of someone – an old university friend, probably; she'd known plenty with artistic streaks.

He was waiting for her to speak, his crystalline blue eyes fixed on hers. They radiated purpose, and something else – a keen interest, she thought. In the house, she hoped.

'Oswald,' she said with a nod. 'I'm really very sorry to have kept you waiting. We had some unexpected issues back at the office and—'

'Oh, no, no, you didn't keep me waiting. I've been here for a while, looking around, taking in the place. You learn a lot by just watching, I find.'

He smiled as Clara processed what he'd said.

'You've been here a while?'

'Yes,' he said. 'An hour, maybe. I hope that's okay?'

It's a bit unusual.

'Of course it's okay,' she said lightly. She didn't know

whether it was, but she *did* know that she had to sell this house, and she had no desire to put him off by making him feel uncomfortable. 'I'm not surprised you came in advance. This could be your new home, after all. It's a big decision.'

'Well, indeed. I've made a few mistakes in my time and I've no wish to make another,' he said, giving a self-deprecating smile that said, *I may look pretty perfect but I'm very far from it.* 'I wanted to get a feel for the place.'

The low, sonorous quality to his voice, the way he was studying her – she felt odd. Not uncomfortable, exactly, just as if her senses were heightened.

'When it comes to the house,' Oswald went on, 'your colleague probably told you I have some very specific criteria?'

Spot on. Clara could list his desired requirements by heart: an isolated house that was not overlooked; a library facing the loch, with doors opening onto the north; and oh – how could she forget this? – a terrace that could easily be covered with fine river sand.

Maybe that last stipulation wasn't so bizarre. Maybe he wanted to create a play area outside for his kids?

Except, now she thought about it, he hadn't mentioned any kids. Hadn't mentioned any family at all, in fact. So why did he need such a big house?

She flicked a look down at his left hand and noticed the absence of any wedding ring.

'What line of work are you in, Oswald?'

The briefest of hesitations. 'I write poetry.'

'Anything I'd know?'

He shook his head. 'I'm afraid I'm not very good, but perhaps I'll find some inspiration here.' His cool eyes surveyed the craggy mountains behind the house, then returned to Clara's face. 'Did you know that Shakespeare set *Macbeth* not far from here, in Inverness?'

Clara didn't know that, and she didn't much care. Ever since Karl had made her watch the nightmarish Roman Polanski film adaptation, she'd thought of the Scottish play only as brutal and steeped in the sort of superstition that had never held any sway with her.

'One of my favourites,' Oswald went on. 'Anyway, I have other passions. For one thing, I'm a keen climber.'

'You'll be spoiled here then. The forests have some pretty steep climbs.'

'Quite. So much to explore. And there are marvellous caves all over these parts.'

'Oh really?'

'Yes, many splendid natural formations. A few were used as wartime shelters; and I know of at least one, a sacred, secluded cave that was used as a burial ground. I should like to paint it,' he added.

'What do you usually paint?' she asked, her eyes moving to the loch's glistening waters and the raw grandeur of the mountains beyond. In the slanting, late-afternoon light they looked almost ominous. 'Landscapes, I imagine?'

'Mostly. Sometimes I also dabble in life drawing.'

'Oh.' As the word slipped out, Clara hoped she didn't sound too taken aback. Or prudish.

He smiled at her again and said, 'I'm not very good at life drawing either. Still learning to broaden my artistic horizons. I find it relaxes me. Almost a meditative process. Do you draw, Clara?'

Clara. Not Miss Jones. He was watching her shrewdly, anticipating her reaction, she thought. Would she correct him?

She rolled her eyes. 'No, I'm rubbish at drawing.'

'Oh, no,' he protested, 'you can't fail at it. You can only fail to improve.'

He wasn't just looking at her now, he was seeing her with his absorbing artist's eyes. As his gaze settled on her hair, she realised she was fiddling with it – again. A habit that had developed as she'd grown it. She wasn't used to having long hair. Or 'Honey Copper' hair, for that matter. At least her roots weren't visible like his; she was meticulous about keeping on top of them. Maintaining her new persona – her disguise.

'Well, I'm sure Boleskine has everything you want,' Clara said with a confidence she wasn't quite feeling. 'And to be honest, at the reduced price, it's a real steal. You hear that a lot, but truly – this is a bargain. There isn't much work needed, considering the fire. The only room destroyed in the east wing was —'

'The billiard room,' Oswald completed curtly.

Their eyes met.

'I'm aware of what has been compromised, Clara. Painfully aware.' Then, before Clara could wonder about that, he turned his focus to the lodge. 'Boleskine House,' he said with the reverent respect of an atheist who had just discovered God. 'A divine house. It didn't deserve a fire, but as far as I'm concerned, it does deserve a blue plaque.'

That surprised her. *Either he knows nothing about the house's turbulent history or he's ignoring it.* Then again, she struggled to imagine how any sober-minded individual could ignore what had happened in this house.

'Why do you say the house is divine?'

Oswald didn't answer her question. At least not immediately. *He's fallen in love with this house,* Clara thought. It was written all over his face as he gazed at the heavy front door. And people said all sorts of peculiar things when they fell in love. Just look at Karl. He'd said he would make her happy, that he'd give her what she wanted most in this world. And he had, but then – and the memory unleashed white-hot agony – he'd ripped it away.

'I feel like Boleskine has been waiting for me,' Oswald said quietly. 'Sounds silly, but it feels . . . right, somehow. You ever felt that about a place?'

She had, in fact. On the day she had arrived in Abersky, along a winding descent through boggy, heather-sprung moors. That day had been fine and calm, but she remembered the strange mirages warping the distant horizon over Loch Ness, the waves licking the shingle beach. And, of course, she remembered eyeing this house, a fine Georgian villa, brooding over the quiet road on the hillside that sloped down to the shore. Deserted.

Working for an estate agent, she had heard plenty of lurid tales about Boleskine: lights flashing on and off, windows shattering, doors slamming and other sinister nonsense. But until now, she had never heard anyone speak highly of the manor. Perhaps that was understandable, she thought, looking down to the melancholy Boleskine burial ground – notable for the ruins of the original chapel that had stood there, and a squat, round building, strewn with ivy. Clara felt the first drops of cold rain needling her cheek, and she shivered.

'Shall we go inside?' Oswald suggested.

Her eyes shifted to the house. It was U-shaped, like a horseshoe, so from their position, the east wing was out of view. She was thankful for that, but she knew she'd see it soon enough; that was inevitable. She'd see the shattered windows and the blackened bricks. She'd see the rubble and fallen-in ceilings – all the evidence of her dark deed.

'You all right?' he asked her.

She blinked. 'Yes, of course. Please follow me.'

She started forwards, but something made her stop: tyre marks in the gravel. Fresh tyre marks. Clara frowned and asked, 'Did you bring a car up here?'

A brief hesitation. 'There *was* a man who came, an hour ago. He seemed to be inspecting the building. I assumed you'd know about it?'

Clara shook her head and Oswald shrugged. 'I didn't disturb him; he looked busy.'

'Well, what exactly was he doing?'

'Taking photographs of the east wing mostly,' Oswald said. 'Looked like someone official to me.'

'A police officer?'

'If he was, then he was in plain clothes, and the car was unmarked.'

'You didn't think to talk to him?'

He shook his head. 'Kept out of his way. Figured he'd only wonder who the hell I was, snooping around. Hey, are you all right? You look . . . tense.'

Clara *felt* tense. She wasn't aware that anyone else had visited the property today. Who had been here? A local, curious to see the damage for themselves? Unlikely. From what she knew of the locals, they were a darkly superstitious lot who mostly steered clear of the Boleskine estate. An investigator then, from the insurance company? That was more likely, but the vendors had already been in touch to say that the insurance company was close to completing its essential inquiries. It was a mystery – but she was going to make it her business to find out who had been up here as soon as the viewing was over.

Oswald was studying her. His face was creased with curiosity.

Clara plastered on a smile and said brightly, 'Let's go inside, shall we, before it buckets down with rain.'

Oswald's face relaxed and he nodded.

Clara went ahead towards the enormous front door, fumbling in her coat pocket for the key.

But the key wasn't there.

There followed an awkward silence. Turning to face her potential buyer – who was standing right behind her – Clara tried to look unconcerned as she checked her other pockets.

'Everything okay, Clara?'

'Just a sec.'

Hastily, she went to check in the car; but the house key wasn't in there either, and it wasn't in her bag.

She slammed the car door and went to stand beside Oswald Cattenach. He stared at her, a cool gleam in his jewel-like eyes.

'You don't have the key. Do you?'

She shook her head, cringing inwardly. How could she have forgotten it?

'If you're happy to wait, I can go back to the office and —'

'I'm sure there's no need for that.'

'Oh? What do you suggest we —'

His hand reached for the doorknob, and turned it. To Clara's immense surprise, the door slowly swung open.

'Well, we *are* in luck,' Oswald said. 'One of your colleagues forgot to lock up?'

'It would seem so,' Clara said, finding it hard not to show the embarrassment that was warming her face. She felt something else – a knot of puzzlement in her stomach. The truth was, there had been no other viewings. None she knew about anyway.

So why was the door unlocked, Clara? The insurance investigators?

Oswald was looking past her into the gloomy hallway, his eyes alight with interest. Ambition. He wanted this house, and Clara must make sure he bought it.

With sudden decisiveness, she stepped past him and over the threshold – and stopped. Inside, the shutters were drawn so the hallway was pitch black. And what was that awful smell? She had expected the lingering scent of smoke and burned wood, but there was a trace of something else, a fetid odour.

'Clara?'

She tore her eyes from the shadows and beckoned him inside.

'Please follow me, Oswald. I have a feeling your whole life is about to change for the better.'

'Oh, I'm counting on it,' he replied coolly.

4

The pair of them entered a wide, chilly hallway that was at least seventy foot long; stretching horizontally left and right, to the east and west wings.

Leading off the corridor was a myriad of heavy-looking, oak doors, each dressed with tattered tartan drapes. Moth-eaten, dusty drapes; the sort that caught fire easily. Above their heads, a mounted stag's head regarded them eerily.

'Impressive, right? And with all this woodland, it's extremely private.'

She heard him take a short breath. But he said nothing.

'You know, if I lived in a house like this I'd —'

'What?' His eyes flared, full of curiosity. 'If *you* lived in a house like this you'd – what?'

Clara smiled back. It was a gentle, modest smile.

'Oh, in my dreams,' she said, but now her smile faltered, because she heard the lie imbued in those words, and hoped to God he didn't hear it, too. It was vital she performed now. She had to sell.

'You won't be short on entertaining space. This is the dining room,' she said airily, moving to the panelled door facing them, opening it. She flinched backwards as a black beetle scurried out; disgustingly large, with a scorpion-like tail. It was covered with fine dark hairs. Worse, as it scuttled towards her, she couldn't ignore the sudden foul odour, and the first incoherent thought to flash into her mind was that this beetle was alien, beastly, that it somehow meant her harm.

Her left foot came up to crush it.

'Stop!' Oswald commanded.

She jerked her head around; Oswald was already stepping forward, stooping to pick up the winged predator.

'The Devil's footman,' he said lightly. 'You wouldn't hurt it? A beautiful species, common in these parts.'

Her lip curling with disgust, Clara regarded the beetle in his palm; its pincer-like jaws. The pest was still now, oddly pacified. As if his touch had tamed it.

Oswald said: 'Superstition teaches that if the Devil's footman raises its tail, it's casting a curse on you.' And with an odd, analytic expression, he smiled at her: 'Looks like you got off lightly.'

He unclasped his hands and the beetle unfurled its delicate wings, flying away. Towards the east wing.

Clara took a shallow breath; collected herself.

'Shall we go on?'

Oswald smiled; nodded.

As she led him from room to room, she gave him the usual spiel about original features, and the light, and development potential, and all the while she studied him carefully. There was a certain respect in his demeanour, for the space and its history; for the men and women who had occupied these rooms; for the happiness they had savoured and the torments they had suffered.

'I want to do all I can for this house,' he said. 'Strip it back to the bare walls, put a new roof on if that's what it takes. Renew it with new life.'

Life. Sometimes she thought she had seen too much of that, especially its darker side.

Leaving the long, uncarpeted hallway, they entered the living room, and Clara flipped on the light. Spooky in here. A single bare light bulb hanging from the ceiling brightened the space but didn't warm it or make it feel remotely inviting. Clara and Oswald were standing in a nest of shadows thrown by a rickety oak table in the centre of the room. The carpet stank of stale urine, and even if it hadn't, it would have needed replacing, for it was a vile brown colour, stained and threadbare. Black mould bloomed in one corner. Not that Oswald seemed to mind, though, for his eyes were everywhere. Clara felt she was watching a devout Catholic who had just set foot in the Sistine Chapel.

'Boleskine House,' he said slowly, enunciating every syllable. 'You know, there are so many texts that mention this place, so many websites.'

Clara gave Oswald a warm smile. 'I can assure you, this property enjoys pride of place on *our* website. We've had considerable interest.'

He didn't reply, he just looked at her. And the way he looked at her, as if he could see through her lie . . . For no reason she could explain, Clara found herself wishing she had told Gale she was coming here this afternoon.

But that was her paranoia, wasn't it? What reason did she have to fear this man, who was so polite and charming?

Clara remembered the way Karl had made her feel, small and powerless – *'Have you gained weight again? You're letting yourself go'* – and felt rage at him for sparking this irrational wariness of other men. They weren't all monsters.

Oswald brushed past her, a dreamy look in his eyes, and then they were on the move again. Most of the rooms were empty, some furnished to the bare minimum; almost all were smirched with black patches of damp and peeling yellowed wallpaper. Entering the kitchen, coughing against the dust that clouded the air, Clara found herself wishing she had come sooner to get the place in order. Wherever she looked she saw neglect – cupboard doors hanging off hinges and some missing altogether.

He's never going to make an offer when he realises how much he'll need to spend.

'Do you know where the house derives its name?'

'Well . . . I think it has to do with . . .' *No point lying to him. He'll see right through it.* 'You know what? I'm not sure. I can find out, though. Let me do that. Won't take a sec.'

From her bag, she whipped out her mobile phone.

'No, no,' Oswald said. 'Don't trouble yourself.'

She relaxed. He was reasonable, unlike some of the buyers she had to deal with.

Oswald was admiring the ancient beams running across the kitchen ceiling. 'I feel like I know this place,' he said. 'That Boleskine likes me, has chosen me. And you, Clara.'

Clara smiled; as she'd thought, he was a touch eccentric. But she soon lost the smile when he fixed his eyes on her and said:

'Is there anything I should know about this house? Anything you should tell me?'

It was a fair question. And the truthful answer was no, under the Property Misdescription Act (1991), she was under no obligation to mention anything that had happened here at Boleskine. Only public rights of way across the property had to be declared and there were none of those. Even if there were, none of the locals would come near.

'Well, no,' she said. 'I mean, all the information is in the brochure, and if you have questions about anything specific . . .'

He had turned and walked away, moving with sudden decisiveness into the main hallway. When she joined him there, he asked her to take him into the east wing.

'I need to see the full extent of the damage,' he said. His eyes, on hers, were watchful and interested.

She swallowed hard before smiling – again; her cheeks were aching with the effort – and led the way down the long corridor that turned at the end and led to the billiard room, where, just two weeks earlier, she had set the curtains alight. She hadn't even needed to force entry; the window had been ajar. Gale had probably left it open to air the place.

Ahead of her, she saw now the scorched oak door, hanging off its hinges. She halted.

A fierce orange glow, dancing flames, evil-smelling black smoke.

She resisted the urge to cough against the smoke, to raise her arm to protect her face from the heat. *It's only your imagination. It isn't real!*

Turning to Oswald, she said, 'Sure you want to see?'

There followed a moment of silence in which Clara was acutely aware of her breathing. She imagined him agreeing that no, it probably *wasn't* a good idea to see the east wing. If he loved the house so much, he wouldn't want to see the charred walls, would he? Wouldn't want to see the fire-tainted room.

Oswald nodded solemnly, and she had the idea that this was a mark of respect. 'Yes, I want to see,' he said. 'I need to know what I'm dealing with, right?'

'Of course,' Clara said, and she turned back. But she didn't move.

In the billiard room up ahead, the hellish glow was brighter, beckoning to her with a flurry of sparks: *Come and see, Clara. Come and face what you did.*

Tongues of flames building with a roar, leaping and twirling, bursting through the roof, the house ablaze.

Stepping around her, Oswald walked on. She smelt the musk of his cologne, and something else: the smoky odour of her sin. Her victimless crime.

5

As Clara was showing Oswald the house, in London, Karl sat alone at his desk mentally tormenting himself with the familiar questions:

Where are you now, Alison?

Who are you with?

Where are you hiding?

It was twelve months since she had run out on him. No trace of her anywhere online. No trace of her at her aunt's place in Derbyshire, either. He regretted calling there, asking for Alison. Her aunt was bound to have spilled the beans. Now Ally would certainly know he was looking for her.

He didn't have many friends, only a few loyal ones who had stuck with him through the worst bouts of his drinking, but the few he had – the few he trusted – weren't short of their own theories on where Alison had disappeared to. *She skipped the country. She ran off with another guy. Why do you think she left anyway?*

When Karl was sober, he didn't want to think about that, but the desire to know still burned in his soul. If he had a soul. Since Alison's accident, he'd wondered about that more than once: whether he had a soul, and if so, whether it could be saved.

What he needed, of course, was to let her go. Stay well away. It was probably exactly what he would have told Terry if Terry's wife were still alive; and it was good advice, because Karl suffered from 'the cycle'. Thinking about Alison made him sad; being sad made him want to drink; and drinking invariably made him mad.

Furious.

And yes, just possibly, every now and then, dangerous.

When he had discovered her clothes were gone, a small part of him had been relieved. One less liability, and one less miserable cow in his life making demands of him. Then one night, things had got a little heated with Elaine. A little out of hand.

He didn't think it was all his fault, not completely; she had to take some of the responsibility. How many times had he told her that he had no money for the kid, that the kid didn't change anything about them? Their affair was just casual. Elaine just wouldn't see it his way, though. She'd lost it completely. Lashed out. Slapped him hard enough across the face for it to turn numb. Slapped *him*!

How fucking *dare* she hit him?

Karl had raised his hand to retaliate, his whole body trembling with rage, but he hadn't landed the blow.

Something had stopped him. He knew what it was now: Ally would never have fought back. She wouldn't have touched a hair on his head. Why? Because she was afraid of him. So afraid that after her accident, she'd dropped everything and run.

Which was why he tried not to drink as often now. Doing that drove him to the computer, desperately searching for her. Cursing her for running out on him and emptying their joint bank account.

How fucking dare she?

But he had to remember she had her reasons. Misguided reasons – *it was an accident!* But he had been a part of that, and he needed to take some responsibility, come to terms with the fact that she was gone, and get on with his life.

Still, that didn't mean that he didn't sometimes stop and obsess about her betrayal, and so very badly want to get down to business with her again. Make her pay.

You're not that person any more.

Wasn't he? At this moment, Karl wasn't so sure. Terry's little ghost story and his domestic confession had touched him in a way he hadn't expected, touched him in a raw, dark place he hadn't ventured to for many weeks.

He pulled out his desk drawer and gazed down at the hip flask there.

Open me, it whispered. *Drink me.*

He shouldn't. He knew that. But his hand, reaching out, was trembling. Needed steadying.

Just as he touched the cool steel, a knock at the office door made him start. Before he could say 'Come in', the door swung open, revealing a woman in her late fifties, slender, with a crop of brown hair that made her more handsome than pretty.

'Karl, you have a minute?'

He slammed the desk drawer shut. 'Sure, Paula. I've got two minutes for you,' he said with a grin. 'Have a seat.'

Paula ran the Mindfulness Centre, and the authority she exuded was as enviable to Karl as it was irritating.

'Actually, my office is better.' And without waiting for him to reply, she turned and stalked off in that direction.

With a sigh, Karl heaved himself out of his chair and cast a look back at the clock. Four thirty. The Red Rose would have to wait.

This really was proving to be an infuriatingly long week.

*

'Have a seat, Karl.'

He smiled as he sat, asked how her day had been. Without acknowledging the question, Paula, sitting opposite him, slid out a drawer, removed a slim blue file and placed it on her neat desk. She kept her eyes steadily on Karl throughout, causing him to wonder whether this might be a meeting to discuss the progress of one of her patients.

Karl felt a fuzzy glow inside. It always pleased him when his superiors, especially one of his female superiors, asked him for advice.

Then he noticed something else, something that made the breath catch in his throat.

That's my name on the front of the file.

It was suddenly apparent to him that his day was about to get a whole lot worse.

As if deciphering his realisation, Paula said, 'Karl, you need to be aware we have received some complaints.'

'What?' He forced a smile, feigning ignorance.

'I wanted to give you a chance to explain.'

'I don't know what you mean.'

Paula opened the file on her desk, drew out an official-looking form. 'There have been complaints about your conduct. In particular, your temper.'

Karl stiffened. 'Complaints from colleagues, or patients?'

'Both.'

He swallowed. Paula's eyes were fixed on him, cool and appraising. He had been mistaken to think this was a routine meeting. But if he was about to be challenged, there was no way he was giving in without a fight.

'I have to say, I feel a little like I'm being ambushed here.

If you had concerns about my performance then you should have—'

'Come to you directly?' Paula removed the pair of spectacles he always thought made her look more like a librarian than a counsellor and eyed him steadily. 'Well, with respect, Karl, that's what I am doing. Would you like to explain why more than one of your patients have told us they've smelt alcohol on you?'

'Paula, I enjoy a drink at night. You know that. Sometimes I forget to clean my teeth in the morn—'

'One of the secretaries said you were abusive to her. Made threatening remarks.'

'When?'

'Three months ago.'

'Why didn't you raise it with me then?'

'She asked us not to. Anything to say?'

He tried to cast his mind back, but the details didn't come as quickly as he wanted, and he wasn't surprised. Three months ago he had been hitting the bottle hard. Actually, hitting more than the bottle. One of the women he had picked up in some seedy Soho cocktail club could attest to that, and he considered himself damn lucky she hadn't.

'Who complained?' he asked, pulling a bemused face. 'Was it Lucy? I bet it was Lucy, right?' The part-time receptionist. 'You know she's been keen on me for a while now and—'

'That's enough,' Paula cut in. Her voice had turned distinctly sharp. 'You understand, Karl, that I am under an obligation to investigate any and all accusations of improper—'

'Of course,' he said quickly, feeling the sweat beginning to break on his palms. 'I'll do all I can to cooperate. But I'm telling you now, Paula, there's nothing to worry about, okay?

Sure, I was under a lot of stress back when Ally walked out, a lot of pressure, you know that. But I've made a lot of progress since.'

She eyed him dubiously.

'I mean it.'

'One patient has complained you were eyeing her breasts for the duration of a counselling session.'

'What? That's ridiculous! When was this?'

'Last week.'

'No,' he murmured, 'that's just not true.'

'She said she challenged you, and you swore at her.'

'What? No!'

'Are you sure you were sober enough to remember?'

She looked into his eyes with fierce intensity, and all at once Karl's certainty seemed to desert him. He had taken a drink the other week, at work, but he didn't remember getting angry. Perhaps he had said something improper by accident? That seemed more likely. After all, accidents happened . . .

'As I said, I wanted to give you a chance to explain before—'

'Before what?'

Paula matched his glare. 'Before searching your office.'

'You'll do no such thing!'

'I thought that might be your reaction,' she said.

At that moment, as if on cue, Paula's door opened and a uniformed woman stepped in. Tessa, the security guard. She avoided his gaze, looking only at Paula. In her hand was Karl's silver hip flask.

'I haven't touched a drop!' he barked, launching himself from his chair. 'Not a drop, you hear me?'

'I should imagine the entire centre can hear you,' Paula said coldly. She stood and pointed to the door. 'Make this easy on yourself. Go now, and we'll spare you the humiliation of a public disgrace.'

*

Without his job, who was he? A drunk. A paranoid obsessive. A drifter. All of those things. But a voice in his head told him he was something else.

Dangerous. Without that job, you're a dangerous brute.

With that accusation ringing in his head, he decided to walk home, crossing the Thames over Vauxhall Bridge and cutting down towards the Oval through Kennington. He was dimly aware that Charlie Chaplin had once owned a house somewhere around here, to be close to his mentally disturbed mother at Bedlam Asylum. He half wondered how long it would be before he also ended up in a place like that.

When he reached his block and the concrete stairs that led up to his floor and the flat he had shared with Alison, his thoughts drifted back to his session with Terry.

Sometimes I hate myself. Know what I mean?

'Oh, I hear you, Terry old boy,' he muttered to himself. 'I hear you loud and clear.'

Except now that he was out of a job, there would be no helping Terry with his delusional visions from beyond the grave; no helping anyone. The only person in the world Karl now had to think about was himself. And her, of course. Alison.

Always her.

6

At Boleskine House, Oswald Cattenach entered the billiard room and halted in the shadows. Clara hurried to catch up. She closed her eyes for a moment, mentally preparing herself, as she stepped inside. But when she opened them and saw the devastation of the fire, she gasped. 'Oh my goodness . . .'

The once-green billiard table was now an ash-darkened red and yellow. The room stank of burned wood, an acrid, dank smell. The maple flooring was buckled, the wainscoting charred. Shattered glass, soot and rubble covered the floor.

She shivered and wrapped her arms around herself.

'It really affects you, doesn't it?' he said softly.

'I don't like seeing old buildings ruined,' she replied. It wasn't a lie exactly, but nor was it the whole truth.

'Oh, what a woeful degradation,' said Oswald heavily. He bowed his head, and with delicate reverence ran his hand along a charred wall, as if soothing a wounded animal. 'How did the fire start?' he asked.

He was walking across the room, and missed Clara's flinch.

'I'm not sure, to be honest,' she lied.

She pictured the fire's outbreak that night with horrible clarity. Stealthily striding up the winding driveway, head down, her torch off. The dusty, dry smell of the draperies next to the window and how lightweight they looked. The scratch of the match and the way its tiny blue flame flared, guttered, and died. *If at first you don't succeed, Clara!* But she hadn't needed to try again and again; the second attempt had worked a charm.

At first the flame had only singed the curtain, blackening the edge of the fabric, but it had caught within seconds. She'd watched the flames run up the curtains and shoot across the ceiling panels. She'd watched the room blaze, and then she'd hurried away, the fire hot against her back.

She blinked and came back to the present. Oswald had asked her a question and was looking expectantly at her.

He was at the window, she realised. The one through which she had slipped her hand, the match between her fingers.

'Pardon me?' she asked, her voice sounding distant to her ears.

'I was asking you about the burial ground, the one at the bottom of the hill.'

'Sorry, yes,' she said. 'What about it?'

'Is it demised to the property?'

'Um . . . I believe it might be.'

'I would need to know, before I can make an offer.'

All Clara heard were those three beautiful words: *make an offer*. He would buy Boleskine. The agency would get the commission, her job would be safe, she would be safe.

'Of course.' Beaming, she whipped out her phone. 'I'll just call the office and—'

Dammit!

She glanced up at him, brushing a wayward strand of hair behind her ear.

'No signal?' He smiled ruefully. 'You're not having much luck today, are you? Perhaps try in the library. I got a signal in there.'

'Great, thanks. Hang tight, okay? Won't be a sec!'

She headed into the hall and turned right.

'It's the other way,' he called after her.

Stupid!

She turned and faced him.

'Thanks!'

An immense corridor ran ahead of her to an open door, like a dark mouth.

She stepped into the silence of the library and quietly closed the oak door behind her.

Surprise held her for a moment. The room was silent, dust floating in the grey light that slanted in through the shuttered windows, and it was permeated by the distinctly unpleasant smell she had noticed when they had stepped through the front door. Unlike the other rooms, though, this one's potential was easily seen. It was well furnished: an enormous walk-in fireplace dominated the space, a few antique chairs scattered around it, and from floor to ceiling, bookshelves groaned under the weight of leather-bound tomes. At the far end of the room a grand bay window set with double glass doors opened onto a terrace. The paving was cracked, yes, and sprouting riotous weeds – but that view!

The sweeping view of the loch drew Clara across the room. She stood at the doors and took out her phone. There was a signal in here, albeit a faint one; Oswald had been right.

Her body stiffened. Oswald. How had he known? She hadn't shown him this room yet.

She could just about hear him, pacing about in the billiard room at the other end of the house, his polished shoes tapping on the old floorboards. He was humming; 'Quicksand' by David Bowie, if she wasn't mistaken. He was quite at home here.

Now she understood what had been nagging at her earlier: Oswald striding so confidently from room to room, almost as if he already knew the layout. But how could he know the way in a strange house as sprawling as this? How had he already been in the library?

Was he inside before I arrived?

The front door was unlocked. He could quite easily have let himself in. Was that likely, though? Yes, considering his passion for the place, she thought it was – very likely. He had arrived early. Looked about. What was it he said?

'You learn a lot by just watching, I find.'

Clara's heart began to thud, and she grabbed a door handle to steady herself.

That sense of being watched, the night she came here, the night she set the fire. She had seen no one – but had someone seen her? This man, Oswald? And had he been here that night?

But it was dark and I was dressed in black – a hooded jacket. If he was here – was he here? – he couldn't recognise me.

Clara stared out through the glass, over the terrace and garden sloping away from the house and beyond, to the wide expanse of water. Rain was pelting the surface of the loch. A melancholy view, which was how she felt now, returning here. Melancholy – and guilty as hell. And frightened like she hadn't been in so many months.

If she were found out, *if . . .* what would she do?

Tell the truth, Clara. You may as well.

For a moment, she allowed herself to ignore that voice, because it didn't sound like her, Clara. It sounded like Alison Hopkins – obedient and battered. Denial was an option, and plausible. Old buildings caught fire all the time. But then again, weren't there too many loose ends? If they checked her search history, would it throw up 'arson'? She'd deleted her history and the cookies, but was that enough?

No. Somehow, she doubted it was even nearly enough. There

was nothing punched into a computer these days that couldn't be discovered (as Karl was so fond of reminding her). How would she explain her searches? And why had she told Gale to design a new sales brochure for Boleskine even before the fire had taken place? This question swiftly brought her back to the other, less palatable option. Tell the truth.

That was what she ought to do. After all, if Clara were implicated in the crime, so was Gale, and that worried Clara, because Gale was a decent person. Gale had known nothing about her plan, and Gale had her own problems: a struggling business, an adult daughter with learning difficulties. What would Gale think of Clara, if she knew? Gale, who had been kind enough to take a chance on Clara when she applied for the job, with no sales experience to speak of? And what would happen to Gale, Clara wondered, if she didn't tell the truth? Boleskine had been on her books for months; her fingerprints had to be all over this property. What if Gale was unfairly implicated in Clara's crime?

On the other hand, if Clara told the truth, that was the end of her career. The end of her new life here in Abersky. Her crime was certain to be reported on the news, and then what? Karl would find out about it. Karl would track her down.

He'd be mad, outraged. He'd call you a liar and a cheat, because that's exactly what you are, Clara. You're a fraud.

She glared at her reflection in the glass. She barely recognised the exhausted woman staring back at her. With distaste, she looked herself up and down in the glass – and froze. Her breath caught. Every ligament in her body went rigid.

There was someone else in the room with her.

Not Oswald. She hadn't heard the door open behind her. And why would Oswald be lying on the floor?

On the floor!

She spun around, and skittered back, against the glass, her eyes wide.

Beneath a bookcase at the back of the room, in a spot that had been concealed by a couch when she'd entered – was a dark, blackened hump. A heap of filthy clothes. When she saw the charred, gnarled hand, reality struck her like lightning.

She was looking at a dead body.

7

Oswald's head snapped up as he heard the high, startled cry. He closed his eyes and drew a long, steadying breath. *To will, to wish, to want and to purpose.*

The shriek from the library was swallowed by choking sobbing; then all was quiet, except for the wind keening around the manor and the pelt of rain on the windows.

Oswald held back any temptation to smile. He took no pleasure from Clara's fear. Of course, she would be shocked, terrified, and yes, that was partly his fault. But he had no desire to traumatise her – at least no more than was necessary.

He knew it had been a risk, letting her out of his sight to make the phone call. He was a bit surprised she hadn't asked him how he knew there was a signal in the library. She was probably preoccupied. With selling him this house. With the little crime she'd committed that enabled her to sell him the house.

Still, he'd wanted her to experience a few moments alone

in there so that she could properly comprehend the gravity of the situation. A uniquely fortuitous situation to be sure; but just because he saw it that way was no guarantee that she would too. So yes, Clara needed a moment to reflect. After that, he would explain. There would be time to do that, lots of time – after all, there was no one around to disturb them.

To will, to wish, to want and to purpose.

The afternoon had gone smoothly so far, exactly as he had envisaged. Lifting the key from her coat pocket had been easier than he'd anticipated. Throwing one inquisitive look over her shoulder had been enough to get her to look away. Simple but effective; one of the many techniques in misdirection he'd acquired.

But now there was real work to do. What happened next would be crucial. Because the truth was, he needed something from Clara, and unlike the front door key, it was not something he could just take. For his great operation to work, she would have to willingly give him what he desired.

Opening his eyes, Oswald turned on his heel and headed purposefully towards the library, already anticipating Clara's inevitable fear and anger and denial. She might lash out at him. She might even try to get away. But Oswald wasn't worried. In fact, he was smiling.

He had already locked the front door.

8

With slow dread, Clara lowered the hand that had flown to cover her mouth. She was still standing next to the doors leading onto the terrace, but her gaze was no longer on the blackened body. Instead, she was staring at the brass handle of the library door, which was slowly turning.

It clicked; the door creaked open. A familiar figure strode into the room.

'Clara . . .' he said, and then her stuttering brain clicked along a gear.

'Oh, my God, Mr C— Oswald!' She took a few blundering steps towards him, shaking her head. 'We need to phone the police!'

She expected him to ask what had happened, or at least whether she was okay, but Oswald had stopped in the centre of the room and he remained completely silent and still. Rigid, in fact.

Any second now he'll notice the smell, she thought. *He'll see the body on the floor. He'll notice it, and he'll cry out, as I did.*

But Oswald made no sound.

Clara was still shaking her head slowly. What the hell was wrong with him? Why wasn't he saying anything?

Then, as if hearing her mental question, Oswald said reasonably, 'You found him then?'

Clara's stomach dropped like a plunging elevator. She stumbled backwards.

Oswald just stood and watched her. The set of his jaw, the

hard line of his mouth, his cool, obdurate eyes – he reminded her of someone. Memories flashed through her mind: *falling – concrete stairs – blood*. Karl standing over her, watching.

Clara took another step away. Collided with the glass doors.

'It's quite all right,' Oswald said. 'You're bound to be shocked. But I'll help you understand – if you like.'

His smile was perhaps meant to be reassuring, but only induced in her a horrid sensation of vertigo.

He said with soft seriousness, 'We're going to have a little chat about what happens next.'

'What are you talking about?' she said shakily. 'What is this?'

He said nothing, but Clara followed the line of his gaze to the raggedy pile of clothes and bone and blackened flesh. The corpse.

Only once had Clara seen a dead body, after the cancer took her foster father. Those memories were almost comforting. Pressing a gentle kiss onto her father's forehead, she had felt something close to relief. At least he wouldn't have to endure any more pain. The whole experience had been difficult, unquestionably. But it was nothing compared to this, she thought, staring at the body. This was only traumatic.

Horrifying.

For a body that had been ravaged by fire, the corpse was still fairly intact. She noted the wide shoulders and guessed the remains belonged to a man. Other than a pair of burly boots and swathes of blackened fabric, there were no clothes.

Words spilled from her: 'Who is this person? How long has he been here?'

Oswald was still gazing at the body. The expression on his face was all wrong. Not only did he not look surprised that there was a body here, but, disturbingly, he seemed to draw comfort from the remains.

'Two weeks,' he said.

Clara heard these words, but they didn't sink in, because now she was thinking: *There's a dead body in the room with us, and Oswald killed him. That's why he isn't surprised. I'm stuck in here with a bloody murderer!*

'Two weeks,' he said again.

And this time, the words landed in her head like a blow from a hammer. She looked at him, appalled.

Two weeks . . .

He turned to her. 'You look distressed. Are you going to faint? Sit.' He gestured to a pair of high-backed leather chairs near the bay window.

As a swooning sensation overcame her, she sat, sinking into the old, creaking leather. Struggling to breathe.

He came to sit on the adjacent chair. 'I was watching the house two weeks ago, the night of the fire,' he told her. 'I saw what you did. I wonder: What did you do with the clothes you were wearing? Did you dump them, Clara? Or did you burn them as well?'

She stared at him as the room receded and everything became quiet. It was as though she was suddenly seeing herself from outside her body; not sitting here in the library, but outside, two weeks earlier, skulking through the blustery darkness towards the east wing where a pair of dry, dusty old curtains were waiting to be ignited.

'I've no idea what you're talking about.'

He gave her a rueful smile, and Clara felt her heart kick up a gear. *Stay calm,* she thought. *Deny it!*

'You left your car at the bottom of the drive. I made a note of the registration number. It didn't take me long to locate the car, but I must admit I didn't expect to find it parked right outside your office. That felt like destiny to me, Clara. Fate. Do you believe in fate? I do. I believe most definitely that you and I were destined to meet.'

Panic shot through her so violently she thought she was about to throw up. She pressed a hand to her mouth as a voice in her head said, *No, he can't have seen you.* But he had. The knowledge was there in his cold appraising eyes.

He brought his face so close to hers that she could smell the mint on his warm breath. Her heart was thumping as hard as the day she had walked out on Karl, slipping out the front door while he was working late – or, more likely, shagging his mistress.

'Yes, Clara,' Oswald said. 'I was watching.'

With a flush of painful guilt, her eyes shifted to the dead man again. 'Who is this? Oh God, do I know him?'

'You didn't know about the squatters?'

A dim memory surfaced. Gale, in her typically brisk and clipped manner, complaining about the empty beer bottles she had found about the house, the cigarette butts.

Squatters? The enormity of what he was telling her dawned, and a new question, an obvious question, sprang at her.

'How come the police didn't find the body? They've been all over this place! They must have—'

'I moved the body,' Oswald said.

'You what?' Clara stood. Backed away.

He moved the body? That was creepy. Not just creepy, crazy. Bat-shit crazy. It made her doubt him, doubt that she had killed anyone. Because if he was the sort of man who would find a body and move it, he was also the sort of man who was capable of anything – perhaps even killing someone. Perhaps he was the one responsible for this man's death.

Him, not her.

'I can read the doubt on your face, Clara. You don't believe me. So, let me tell you then precisely how it happened.'

He stood, and he didn't move closer, but even a few feet apart, it felt as if he was looming over her.

'Like I said, I've been watching the house. Day and night. I needed to be sure it met my requirements.' He pursed his lips, dropping a look of sympathy to the body. 'Poor guy never stood a chance. You really should have checked the east wing was empty before you struck the match. I'm sorry to say that I couldn't get to him in time. I did try – I tried hard, you must believe that. I entered the property, and found him in the corridor, outside the billiard room. But by the time I got to him, he was ablaze. Screaming. Whether he was high or drunk when the fire started, I don't know, but that seems likely to me, or he'd have got himself out.'

She gaped at him, thunderstruck. It no longer felt as if she was standing in a house, more like a boat; the floor beneath her feet was pitching.

'No, you're lying.'

'Am I?'

'There was no one here.'

'You're wrong about that.'

'But I made sure!' she all but screamed.

Oswald shook his head slowly from side to side. 'I threw my coat over him, did my best to smother the flames, and I got him out. But he died within minutes. He died in my arms, Clara. And I will hear his agonising screams for the rest of my life,' he added, dropping his voice. 'Thanks to you.'

A wave of nausea flooded through her. She sank to her knees. It was obscene, but a part of her suddenly wanted to laugh, to tempt him into admitting he was playing with her, having her on as part of a sick joke. But she already knew that wasn't the case. The truth was shimmering in his eyes. And it lay in a pitiful, charred heap on the floor.

She hunched down, shivering. Horror and disgust rose up, and she vomited.

Curtains smoking and seething, catching fire – black smoke curling up – roaring flames leaping – showers of sparks, like fireflies in the night.

Dimly, she became aware of Oswald speaking to her as if from far away, and then his broad outline as he approached through the haze and stood over her.

'I'm offering you a second chance.'

She was repulsed. 'I don't deserve a second chance.'

She truly believed that. She had taken a life. Was there a family living somewhere nearby, decimated because he would never come home? Did he have children who would miss him?

Her whole being was screaming to put things right, but what could she do?

'I just want to be honest with you, Clara,' Oswald went on in the voice of a neurosurgeon explaining a hideously complex diagnosis. 'It's okay, really. At first I was surprised. Shocked. Well, appalled. Setting fire to a property as special as this? I couldn't just sit back and risk the entire place going up in smoke. So I called the fire brigade. They sent two fire engines. One from Foyers, the other from Inverness. I hid with the body at the edge of the forest and counted four main jets tackling the blaze.'

He surveyed the room. 'You did a good job, Clara. They, thankfully, did a better job. It's thanks to them there's still something left for me to work with. This house has waited too long for my great project.'

Clara was sobbing now. For the dead man, but also for herself. For what she had done, and what lay ahead.

Because two things were crystal clear to her now:

Oswald Cattenach was a cold-blooded sadist.

And she was completely alone out here with him.

9

Karl went out late that afternoon, just as he had planned. The only difference was, he went out big time. Whoever owned The Old Ship on Kennington Road would have been very grateful to his credit card; but whoever owned the strip club down in Vauxhall would have been infinitely more grateful. It was in that club, propped up at the bar, that Karl stared at his reflection in the mirror. His narrow face. His beady eyes swimming in a drunken haze behind the wire-framed spectacles.

Sometimes I hate myself. Know what I mean?

Karl knew.

You're a brute.

His mother's voice. Sometimes it spoke to him.

With a grimace, he gulped another mouthful of vodka, felt the searing heat in his throat as it coursed down. He would have another one of these, he told the barman, tapping the bar with his index finger. Another two. Serve them up!

He took the first drink and hungrily slugged it back as his thoughts returned, inevitably, to his humiliation at work. Just who did they think they were? *Bastards!* Karl may have been drunk at that moment, but his ego was sharply aware of its injuries.

After Paula showed him the door, he had followed Tessa, the security guard, along the Mindfulness Centre corridor, feeling all eyes on him – the staff, the waiting patients. Judging him. As if *those losers* could ever hope to understand the enormity of the pressure he was under. The goddamned *stress* of it all! His investments were fast going down the pan, the bank was chasing his debts, and Elaine was getting needier by the day.

When are we going away together? Why don't you make love to me any more? Is there a problem, Karl? A problem down there?

'Bitch,' he muttered, and took another swig of vodka. Then, staring into his drink, he tried to recall what had happened next at the Mindfulness Centre. He was seeing it in a haze: Tessa had stopped at the exit and held the door open for him.

'What about my things, my files?' he had asked.

'You need to leave. Now.'

That was when Karl's hands had balled into fists, and it had taken every ounce of self-control for him not to raise them.

'But I *need* my papers, and my patients need me.'

'They're not your concern any more,' Tessa said abruptly. 'We'll send your personal belongings on.'

And then Karl *had* raised his fists and raised them high. He had felt the tendons in his neck pulling taut, and for a long, black moment the sounds of the Mindfulness Centre had completely fallen away and he had seen himself as if from outside his body, smashing his fist into her face, taking her down, spitting on the bitch. Then he had it in mind to stride right out that door without looking back, not even for a second.

And then what? Police? Prison? I always said you were a brute, Karl.

'Don't do this,' Tessa cautioned. 'Don't make things worse for yourself.'

He thought he had at last lowered his fists; he hoped he had. He could picture himself blinking, as if startled out of a dream, at Tessa – who just stood there, satisfied and stern, eyeing him in a way that made him feel small, inadequate. And that made him angry again. Furious.

'You'll get yours,' he raged. 'What goes around comes around.'

'Time to leave.' With a scowl bordering on contemptuous, she stepped aside and gestured him out, onto the street.

He remembered stepping onto the Vauxhall Bridge Road; he remembered the traffic roaring past him. He remembered feeling desperate and afraid, and something else: the emotion he feared most of all.

Vengeful.

10

As the sun was going down over Loch Ness that evening, in the library of Boleskine House, Clara's body was shuddering with shock.

'If it's any consolation,' Oswald said, looking down at the

sickening remains, 'I think he would have preferred to die than to live with those atrocious burns. He was in agony. To be honest, I was surprised you didn't hear him screaming.' He regarded her, and said in a smooth and commanding voice, 'You need to calm down now. Look at me, Clara.'

She didn't calm down, but she did raise her head. His eyes were icy and penetrating. As if he could see right into her soul.

'The truth is,' he said, 'I like you. Not despite your sin, but because of it. And how could I have afforded this place if you hadn't summoned the courage to do what you did?'

Hearing that only made her feel worse. She had reached rock bottom. She was the lowest of the low. 'I never meant to kill anyone!'

'I'm sure. But we are where we are, and the problem must be dealt with. I have a few suggestions, and I can make you a promise, Clara Jones: every one of my suggestions will sound infinitely more appealing than the prospect of being blamed for this man's death.'

His gaze shifted from the charred body to the window. Beyond the terrace doors, the sky was streaked scarlet. The library was almost in total darkness

'And if it's any consolation,' Oswald said, '*he* would approve.'

'He?' Clara uttered hoarsely. She had no idea to whom he was referring, but he didn't elaborate.

'You're welcome to go, Clara.' He gestured to the door to the room, still standing open. 'You can walk out of here right now and I won't stop you.'

She stared at the door. At him.

'But if you leave, I *will* tell the police what I saw,' he added. 'I'll tell everyone what you did and I'll make you pay.'

Clara said nothing. She just pulled her legs up to her chest and sat there on the floor, trying to hold herself together as every limb trembled and shook.

Oswald looked down on her and smiled. 'Everything is going to be all right,' he said. 'There's just something I want you to do for me . . .'

At once, her mind conjured the worst possibilities. Would he attack her? Rape her?

Oh God, please, not again.

And then she was on her feet.

'You stay away from me!' she instructed. 'Gale is going to wonder where I am. She'll be calling me.'

'She's not calling you, Clara. She's not thinking about you, and she's not trying to find out where you are.' He almost sounded pitying.

Clara opened her mouth to argue. Realised that was pointless, because this stranger knew the truth. All of it.

'Now,' he said, all business. 'The body can't stay here. We need to move it.'

'Move it? Move it where?'

As he ran his hand through his shock of blond curls, his eyes flicked to the bay window. Clara pictured the view. The ground behind the house sloping down, towards . . .

'No!' she said at once.

Oswald was impassive. 'The burial ground is perfect. It has a mort house. It's where I dumped him two weeks ago. In the old days, that's where they'd lay a body until it was ready for burial, to protect it from the body snatchers. The body will be safe in there. Safe until Boleskine is signed over to me.'

'But . . . but . . .' There were so many buts. In the end, the only argument her shocked brain could form was, 'You haven't even offered on the house.'

'Actually, I offered on it before you arrived.' He grinned at her thunderstruck expression and she registered the perfect, pearly white teeth. 'Gale is so helpful, isn't she? So eager! *She* could answer all my questions about the house. Of course, I was careful to say that you gave a glowing sales pitch. All being well, I'll be in within eight weeks. You know, of course, the vendors are keen to sell. Thanks to you. But there's the small matter of the insurance investigation. It'll probably be fine, right? But you never know! So it's proper that we move the body. Now,' he paused, and added, 'it's proper that you help me.'

In desperation, Clara said, 'You have the house, you have what you wanted – just let me go. I made a mistake, a terrible mistake.'

She expected an ominous look. But he looked . . . wounded, that she would leave.

'You owe me,' he said. 'Yeah, you got the price down, but I did you a favour by not telling anyone how. And I won't tell. I'll protect you. If you help me.'

What he didn't say was what she knew he was thinking: *We're in this together, Clara. You and me. This is going to be our secret.*

The idea made a spider web of horror spin out across her consciousness. She shook her head, hearing her own pathetic murmurs of protest.

'Now, there you go again, Clara. Absolving yourself of responsibility.' He gestured to the body, and in that calm, reasonable voice said, 'You did this. Not me. Sure, I concealed the body and I brought it up here to show you, got it in through the missing window in the east wing – I hold my hands up to that. But now we must put it back.'

His expression reminded Clara of Gale when she was

building up to a sale; it was an eager face, alight with possibility and the promise of a better future.

'I'll bag him up,' he said, 'and we'll carry him down together.'

She was only half listening, because she was thinking: Why did he want to keep the body? Why not dump it somewhere? Why did he have to bring it up here to the house to show her the proof – why not just photograph it?

She knew the answer to every question: he wasn't thinking rationally. He was insane.

'I can't be here,' she said, and she stepped around him, towards the library door.

She half expected his long-fingered hands to reach out and grab her. He was a man of such imposing stature, it would have been easy for him to stop her leaving at any moment. Instead, he allowed her to pass.

Surprised, she paused, hovering on the spot.

'I can't be here,' she said again, putting more conviction in her voice.

She took one more step towards the door, wondering even as she did so why she didn't just burst forward and make a run for it.

'*I'll tell everyone what you did.*'

He would destroy her life here. Everything she had worked for. If she ran out of that door, she would have to keep running, right out of Abersky. For good.

Clara had been running for as long as she could remember. She had run from school when she was fifteen. From her husband, too late.

She couldn't take it any more, the running.

As she stood there, tense, she felt Oswald's steady gaze on the back of her neck, and a voice in her head screamed: *You're not actually contemplating helping him?*

She was contemplating that. Not because she wanted to commit a crime – *another* crime. Because the same need that had driven her to set the fire kept her feet planted on the floor now.

She pictured his hand shooting out from behind her, clamping over her mouth to stifle her scream, trapping her in here with him for ever. He could do it; he could overpower her.

She was helpless.

Slowly, she turned to face him, and made a decision that would alter the course of her entire life.

11

Before staggering home that night, Karl went back to the Vauxhall Bridge Road. It was two-thirty in the morning, and outside the Mindfulness Centre there were no people about and only the odd taxi driving past, which was good.

As he weaved across to the door, Karl saw a new poster had been tacked to the glass. A saucepan on heat, boiling over. 'ARE YOU CLOSE TO BOILING POINT?' it read. And underneath the saucepan: 'DON'T LET ANGER GET THE BETTER OF YOU'.

He pressed his face to the glass door and peered inside, at the line of chairs the patients had been sitting on when he had been led past them in disgrace. Paula had been so adamant about his guilt. It was odd. Made him wonder: Had Alison been in touch with his employers since she ran out on him? Had she confided in Paula about how her accident had happened? He didn't think so, because if she had been in touch with Paula, maybe via email, there would be a link. A trace. He doubted that Alison would take that risk; she knew how resourceful he could be.

Still, she had already fooled him once. Shame on her. Fool him twice? That was on him; which meant he needed to check. He needed to get inside. Right now.

They had taken his keys away from him, but even in his drunken stupor he thought he could still find a way in, perhaps even without being detected. He had counselled many clients less intelligent than him, who had succeeded in similar ventures, so why should *he* fail?

He lurched fifty or so yards down the road to the alleyway he passed every morning on his way to work, and ducked into it. A drug-addled tramp lay comatose a few feet away. Karl edged past him, breathing through his mouth to block out the sour stink of piss, kicking over a discarded bottle with a clatter as he went. He didn't know if he would find what he was looking for, but he thought there was a chance, as the walls that formed this alleyway were filthy and very old.

Ahead of him, at the furthest reach of the alley, was a shattered window. It glinted in the moonlight, drawing him towards it. Beneath the window lay a small pile of rubble, a few dirty, crumbling bricks. Remembering to pull his gloves on first, Karl stooped and grabbed one brick. One was all he needed. He picked it up. The alley took him back to the main road, and from there he returned to the Mindfulness Centre, noticing another new sign in a window as he passed: 'DOING GOOD DOES YOU GOOD'.

Why did you leave me, Ally? Where did you go? I need you.

He needed to see her. To see the fear in her. He needed to taste it on her breath; he needed to see it in her eyes and hear it in her trembling voice. And it was that need that convinced him now, as he raised the brick. He was taking a huge risk, but he was past caring.

It wasn't as if they could sack him again.

He hurled the brick, aimed it right at the centre of that goddamned poster with the boiling pan on the gas hob. The glass door shattered. An alarm wailed; piercing.

Karl froze. Then, quickly, he pulled off his coat and covered his face. He had to have Paula's laptop, he told himself, as he stepped through onto the splintered glass.

I will find you.

If she'd left a trace, that was.

He smiled at the thought of one-upping the devious bitch. All kudos to her, she had surprised him, outwitted him. That was the maddening, inescapable fact. He didn't want to entertain the idea that he had become complacent, lazy even, but wasn't there some truth in that? He supposed so. As long as his shirts kept appearing each morning, hanging crisp and clean in his wardrobe, he had assumed it would always be that way; that she was content with her lot, content to suffer.

As the alarm sounded its high-pitched cry and Karl lumbered down the corridor to Paula's office, he was driven by a single, glorious thought: that the two of them would get down to business again together, and Alison *would* suffer, when he got his hands on her. She would know a whole new world of suffering.

*

The following morning, in his apartment on the fourth floor of a London tower block, Karl stirred, his head thumping and groggy.

Did you throw up?

The lingering sour smell told him yes, probably. But there was another smell, and in this hazy awakening he couldn't quite place it.

Spread out on the sofa, he slowly opened his eyes, only to screw them shut again as sunlight blasted into his throbbing head. If he was lucky, the room would soon stop spinning and he could get back to sleep.

Except he couldn't – because an alarm was ringing. Not in the room, in his head. He had no recollection of getting home, none at all, but he remembered the high-pitched wail, screaming at him.

As he lay there, listening to the rumble of traffic in the street below, he waited for the memories to flood in – of getting home, of crashing out on the couch. It was harder to remain calm, keep his thoughts in order, than it would have been if he were stone-cold sober. Harder to remember the things he might have done, the things he might later regret.

Still, he was in his own flat, and amen to that. Though it didn't feel right to him somehow; the lingering odour from his clothes made him want to vomit, and that pissed him off, pissed him off royally, because he deserved to sleep this off, didn't he? Of course he did, after what his miserable boss had put him through.

Wait, had he taken Paula's laptop?

No, that was just his paranoia, surely. This was the way it was now. Since Ally had left, the line separating reality and fantasy had become increasingly blurred.

He had thought, after all, that he needed that laptop. To find Alison.

Shit, shit, shit.

He remembered now throwing the brick, lumbering out of a shattered door with a stolen laptop under one arm.

So what did you do with it? a voice in his head spoke up. *Where is the laptop, Karl?*

His eyes scanned the room. There, on the floor next to the front door, was his jacket. There, next to it, were his gloves. The coffee table and the floor were strewn with magazines, but there was no laptop in sight.

You dumped it, remember?

He was still drunk, his hands still shaking and his vision swimming, but instead of rage, what he felt now was thumping panic. Because he'd committed a crime and had no idea, yet, how careless he had been. Were there witnesses? Security cameras?

Then he dipped his head and saw the dried blood on his knuckles.

Jerking upright, he shifted to the side of the sofa – and froze. His black jeans were wet, shockingly soaking.

Jesus. He hadn't wet himself since he was a child. It didn't say much for his mental well-being that he was reacquainting himself with the habit as a man approaching middle age. He'd drunk too much, that was all.

But that *wasn't* all, a deeper knowledge told him. For one thing, he knew what pants soaked with piss smelt like, and this odour was different; sweetly metallic, repellent.

For some reason, he didn't want to touch the wet part of his jeans; something told him doing that wouldn't reassure him.

Christ. What had he gone and done?

Maybe nothing. Karl sat there desperately trying to remember. He had drunk too much, that was part of the problem. But it wasn't all of it. The bigger issue was his temper, his *fury*.

Within a few swift moments, he had made it into the bathroom, avoiding his reflection over the sink.

'What did you do?' he whispered, scrubbing his hands, watching the water run red. His last memory was of stumbling out of the clinic with the laptop under one arm. 'What the hell did you—'

Now the memory struck him: a slender young woman in a brown coat approaching him on the Vauxhall Bridge Road; some bystander who had been stupid enough to threaten him with calling the police. He saw her advancing, brandishing her phone.

'Hey! You! Stop! What are you doing?'

For a second there he thought she looked a lot like Alison, and before he knew what was happening he had stepped up to her, one fist catching her on the shoulder, and she had kicked him hard in the leg, shoved him, sending him stumbling a few feet towards the dark mouth of the alleyway, where he had found the brick, where he had kicked that clattering bottle.

The bottle . . . shit!

And now he was remembering picking it up. That worried him, because he was still too drunk to recall exactly what he had done with the bottle.

Karl caught his breath. He remembered yelling at the woman in the brown coat to fuck off and leave him alone. And she said something, something about the police. And his fist connected with her jaw.

Hard enough to split the skin on his knuckles.

Was that when she cried for help, when he snatched the beer bottle? He thought so. But then what? Had she gone to the hospital? Was she sitting in A&E at Guy's and St Thomas' telling some doctor about him? Maybe she'd gone to the police station on Charing Cross Road. These options were possible; but Karl didn't even want to entertain them. What he thought was he'd better not think about last night at all. Not if he wanted to hang on to sanity.

With his heartbeat kicking up a gear, he raised his eyes to the bathroom mirror, a crippling surge of shame washing over him.

Ah, but it felt good, didn't it, you brute.

He picked up the nearest thing to hand – a stainless-steel toothbrush holder – and smashed that disgusting reflection to smithereens.

'FOR GOD'S SAKE!' he shouted, with all his unwanted fury erupting. 'PLEASE HELP ME, PLEASE!'

You can only get better by coming to terms with what you did.

He slid down onto the cold tiled floor, panting and snivelling. A memory of Alison taunted him, screaming at him, a long time ago now, that he would be totally lost without someone like her to push around. Now he saw that Alison had been right. He was terribly lost. But he wouldn't be for much longer.

Alison. That's whom he had to focus on now. Tracking her down; getting her back. In his mind, he pictured her, sleek hair falling around her slender neck, the gleam of adventure in her spirited eyes. He'd show her she was better with him than without him, that they could be a team again. Once she apologised, once he made her pay for walking out on him, they could move on.

He sat there, on the glass-strewn bathroom floor, until his breathing was calm and his head was clear. Not thinking about the blood he had washed down the sink.

Only thinking about his wife, who he was more determined than ever to find.

12

With a gasp of fright, Clara jerked awake, looking around wildly. It took a few strained moments for her eyes to focus on the wardrobe and the sunlight shafting through the small window above her bed. Her whole body sagged as relief flooded through her.

A dream. Oh, thank God! Just. A. Dream.

No, a nightmare.

But the most important thing was that none of it had been real. Not Oswald Cattenach, not the fire at Boleskine, not the blackened body.

The chopping sounds were coming from below again. Loud hammering of a blade on wood. A meat cleaver. Listening to that for too long would give anyone nightmares. Her studio apartment was directly above a butcher's shop in a converted end-of-terrace house. A pleasant young man called Lee who had occupied the flat next door had already moved out because of the early-morning noises – the clatter of knives, the grinding of the sausage-making machine. Lee had demanded that the butcher soundproof his shop. He hadn't. Now the noises seemed to be getting louder and more regular. Clara's own fault, for riling the butcher.

She had been leaving for work one day when he was out on the pavement, cleaning his window. He saw her and asked whether she was feeling okay. She looked exhausted, he said.

How inconsiderate can he be? thought Clara. It was because of him that she wasn't sleeping past five a.m. She found it hard to look his way because to do that she would have to face his shop window – an ordeal for any vegetarian – but somehow, she found the courage.

The butcher was tall and lanky, a fifty-year-old with a mop of grey hair. He wore a white apron that would have looked smart on him – if it hadn't been splattered with fresh blood. Her stomach flipped at the sight of it.

'It's the noise, from your shop,' said Clara coldly.

'Well, this is a traditional butcher's, Miss Jones. We start slicing early.'

'You know there are absorbent mats you can buy, to put under chopping boards.'

'Haven't you ever heard of earplugs?'

He really is oblivious, she thought. She understood he had to make a living, but did he really need to start chopping so early? And couldn't he soundproof the premises?

Reading the hostility on her face, he said with condescension, 'There's been a butcher's here for seventy years. And I'm assuming you knew you were renting a flat above a butcher's shop?'

'Yes, of course. I just didn't expect such noise.'

'Still,' the butcher went on, 'how were you to know the history of the shop?' He let the words hang between them, leaving Clara to decipher the obvious implication:

You're not one of us. And you're not welcome.

She felt that now, with every shuddering impact of his cleaver below.

Sitting up in bed was an effort. Her head was heavy and thick, as if she'd taken a sleeping pill. Had she? It wouldn't have been the first time.

She swallowed – painfully. Her throat ached.

Turning, groggy still, she faced her reflection in the wall-mounted mirror. And saw that her hair was wet. Not just damp, but soaking.

How? Unless, she had got up in the night and showered in her sleep, how *could* her hair be wet?

Gingerly, she reached behind her back and touched her pillow. It was as damp as her hair.

Oh, God, please, no!

Hadn't it been raining when Oswald had asked her to follow him outside and help him with his awful task?

She stared up at the cracked ceiling, her entire body quivering as waking terror slipped in. The gruesome ordeal at Boleskine had *not* been a dream. How could she ever have seriously entertained that idea?

She collapsed back on the bed, remembering.

An innocent man was dead. She'd killed him. And helped to hide his body.

Abruptly, she was right back there, huddled in a chair, back to Oswald as he worked. She heard again the swishing, rustling sound of plastic bin liners, his laboured breaths as he tugged and hauled. Wrapping one bag over the head and shoulders, another over the feet and lower legs; feeding the opening of one bag into the other and tying everything neatly together with string. Was that how he did it? She imagined so, but she hadn't looked, until he said:

'Right, I think that just about does it.'

She turned then and took in the oblong shape wrapped in black plastic and lashed with string, awkwardly bulky. It reminded her of a fat cigar, only wider at one end, where the shoulders lay. She nearly threw up again.

Oswald gestured at her to take the leg end.

There was a long silence in the room.

'I honestly don't know if I can do this,' she said.

He gave her a hard stare. That look didn't say: *You can.* It said: *You will.*

And she knew she would.

Swallowing her disgust, Clara walked to him, and bent down, and gripped the feet. Sturdy boots were hard against her fingers through the black bag.

Looking across at her, both of his hands under the top end of the bag, Oswald said, 'Now lift.'

With revulsion, Clara did.

He had opened the terrace doors, letting in a blast of freezing air. Outside, a fog had descended and it was impossible to see any further than two or three feet ahead of them, with no question of them switching on the outside lights or calling on the aid of torches.

The wind gusted as they edged their way across the terrace and down the bank that sloped towards the burial ground. The grass squelched underfoot, and they moved slowly so as not to slip. She wanted to scream, *I can't do this, you understand me, you sick, twisted bastard? I CANNOT DO THIS!* Instead, she kept her head down, her mind focused not on the grim task but on getting it done.

At last – just when she thought she might collapse from exhaustion and the revulsion she felt – she picked out a solitary gate in the gloom up ahead. Beyond that gate, dark and forbidding, were the jagged shapes of crumbling headstones. She could see, even from this distance, that the burial ground had two distinguishing characteristics: it was small, and it was completely neglected.

'Come on,' Oswald encouraged her, 'almost there.'

Her arms were getting tired now and her neck was aching. Approaching the rusted gate, she felt the house, the dense forests, the mountains, looming at her back, quietly condemning her.

From the dark behind her, a shriek. Her heart squeezed. She whirled, listening hard, but there were no further sounds.

Inside the burial ground, an abandoned-looking structure rose ahead of them, the ancient mort house dressed in ivy. A black, wrought-iron gate separated them from its interior.

Together, under Oswald's instruction, they laid their gruesome burden on the ground. Clara watched grimly as he seized the gate and heaved. With a grating, rusty screech, it swung out on ancient hinges and Clara fell back, bending double and gagging with disgust, as a thick, damp smell wafted out.

'Oswald,' she said. 'We can't . . . it's . . .'

Oswald stood over the body, cool eyes fixed on her.

She desperately tried to think – this was all wrong, but what to do? An idea sparked, and she blurted out, 'The loch . . .'

If they weighed down the body – rocks or something – it would sink to the bottom. Gone for ever.

She had thought she could not be more revolted; she discovered now she could. With herself. She couldn't believe she'd come up with that plan.

'An enterprising idea, Clara,' Oswald said. 'But no.' He heaved the body up over his shoulder and lumbered with it into the mort house, where it was damp and rank.

Clara did throw up then. Again. Until she was retching nothing but vile-tasting bile. Distantly, she registered the scraping sound of a stone slab being pushed into place – a sarcophagus?

She straightened, wiping her mouth with a shaking hand.

She saw a silhouette appear in the yawning entrance to the crypt. Another idea sparked:

Now it's my turn.

She took a faltering step back.

And the man started right for her, seizing both her arms.

There was a moment there, a black moment, when she thought it was Karl, that he had finally tracked her down and was going to make her pay for walking out on him. She blinked, and the mental vision of Karl dispersed, leaving only Oswald, who was gazing steadily at her and . . . smiling? Clara couldn't believe it. The sick bastard was actually *smiling* at her.

'You can go now,' he said then. 'But we're not finished, you and me. We're just getting started.'

'What do you want from me?' she said – sobbed.

And he told her.

She remembered every word now, in the cold light of day. It was enough to make the tears return with a vengeance, and the nausea. It was enough to make her want to burrow under the bedcovers and never come out.

But the clock next to the bed was blinking harsh red digits at her: 10:30. *Get up,* it seemed to be screaming. *You're late, so get the hell up!*

Late. Gale wouldn't be happy. Gale would wonder.

'Clara, where have you been? What's happened?'

With a jolt, Clara realised: she had been here before – she had heard those words before. Years ago, in the early days of her marriage, she had worked as a receptionist at a salon. Her boss, Lisa, had been concerned when she turned up late one day. Out of character for her.

'You look ever so pale, Alison. Is everything all right . . . you know, at home?'

No, was the resounding answer. That was the morning after the first time. Clara had still been in shock. It had happened so quickly; there was barely time to think. They had argued, about Karl's stupid investment, and he'd snapped. Yelled something about getting down to business. Grabbed her arm and yanked her to her feet, pulling a cord that toppled the hall lamp. In seconds, she was in the bedroom, on the bed, her face half buried in a pillow, her head pressed against the headboard. She had tried to struggle as he used the lamp cord to lash one of her wrists to the bedpost, but his fury made him indomitable, and he had forced her legs apart and thrust into her. And all she could think through the pain and his grunts and the *strike, strike, strike* of the headboard against the wall was, *I'll run. I'll run as far as I can, to somewhere he'll never find me.*

But she didn't. Not then. Not for years. She quit that job. She stayed home. Cooked for him, cleaned for him. She still didn't understand why exactly. He had told her she was worthless, that she had nowhere to go, that no one would want her, and she had believed him.

And then, towards the end, there'd been new meaning. A glimmer of hope, even, for their relationship. But he had destroyed that, destroyed all that was good, and she'd been helpless to stop him.

So she'd taken control. Run. Come here, to build a new life. A safe one. Lit a match, to preserve that safe life.

And killed a man.

Killed a man!

'*We're not finished, you and me. We're just getting started,*' Oswald had said. That, and so much more.

The question was, what should she do now? To be safe?

As the clock ticked over to 10:35, Clara threw back the bedclothes and got up to face the day.

13

Just as Clara was getting out of bed, from his perch on a high stool by the window, next to a sign that read 'Ice cream and Scones', Oswald turned the page of the *Inverness Courier* he was pretending to read and took another look outside. The lights were on in the office of Highlands Estates, and he could see Gale Kilgour jabbering away on the phone, but no Clara. Yet.

He had anticipated her showing up late for work this morning, and why not? She had made a sale yesterday; the girl deserved a lie-in! Except Oswald doubted Clara would be feeling anything close to rested. Probably what she felt was frightened to death.

She'd be even more frightened when she saw the police car parked a few spaces down from Highlands Estates. She'd think she was going to get caught, that it was there because of her.

In fact, it was there because of Oswald.

He was on his second cup of coffee, sipped slowly, in the imaginatively named Abersky Tea Rooms. It was welcomingly warm in here, and the fine-netted curtain that separated him from the chilly morning outside provided the ideal level of discretion. Not that he had too much to worry about; the place was close to empty.

At the back of the room, three seventy-something women sat at a small circular table, nattering about the latest album from Michael Ball. None of them seemed to notice Oswald, and he was glad about that, though hardly surprised. If, for whatever reason, these old dears were asked to describe the stranger who sat with his newspaper at the front of the café, they would probably remember the black baseball cap he wore, though they would know nothing of the curly fair hair it concealed. Perhaps they would remember the open-necked white shirt and baggy jeans worn too high around his waist, but if they did, so what? Tourists, especially American tourists, were common in Abersky during the summer, and although winter was already fast on its way, Oswald had spotted enough Nessie hunters armed with maps and cameras to know that he wouldn't look out of place. And that was vital. Because what Oswald needed most now was to observe the people of this village, to understand what drove them. What worried them.

Oswald had been observing Abersky's main street, Glendole Road, for more than an hour, and each minute that crept by he felt increasingly uncomfortable at being away from Boleskine. He had learned it was unwise to be away from the manor for too long. Things ... happened there. Which was why, since arriving in Scotland, he'd spent every night in his Land Rover, parked up, concealed, in the thick glen behind the property. That would probably seem paranoid to some, but Oswald knew better. He knew only too well that Boleskine House had claws; and very occasionally, it slashed you with them.

He would have to tell Clara the truth about the dead man, eventually. His plans required that he be completely honest with her, eventually. And he was at peace with that. More important now was securing her commitment. Clara, the woman with the means to make him or break him. Could she be relied upon to keep silent, about what she had done; what they had done, together?

He took another sip of coffee, watching his hand for any trace of nerves as he slowly lowered the mug. Nothing. That hand was as rigid as the will of his master. Considering the previous night's events, he was holding it together pretty well.

But was Clara?

Last night, he had laid out the path ahead very clearly for her: 'Quit your job. Give up your flat. Come live in Boleskine House, with me.'

She had freaked out then. Shrieking and throwing his arms off her as though he was some lecherous weirdo. So he re-assured her, he was talking about a job.

'You'll be perfectly safe, Clara,' he said. 'You've seen the size of Boleskine. It needs work . . . thanks to you. And I'm going to need some help. You can be my lodge manager.'

'I can't just drop everything – my home and my job. How will it look?'

'Are you honestly telling me you're not screaming to be rid of that poky flat above the butcher's shop?' he said.

He saw it in her eyes, the realisation: *He knows where I live.*

Oswald didn't give her an opportunity to breathe; he launched into a verbal onslaught: 'How do you tolerate that flat, Clara? Contending with that infernal chopping from below, day in, day out, and so damn early. Enduring that stench that makes you want to *retch*. Oh, you've been patient with the butcher, Clara. You've been *more* than reasonable. But why? To save a few quid? When really, all you're doing is putting money in Gale Kilgour's pocket. Does it make you happy paying rent, knowing your employer is skimming a bit off the top every month? Knowing your nearest neighbour downstairs doesn't want you there, the snooty outsider? And you want to run back to all that? You'll sit in that flat and sit at that desk wondering, all the time, if I'm going to tell them what you did. That thought will haunt you, Clara. It will haunt you every second of every day.'

He clearly saw the horror in her flaring eyes. She was swaying on her feet and didn't seem to have noticed he was holding her arms again – holding her up. He made himself relax now and speak more gently.

'Or, Clara, you can do as I instruct: quit your job. Live here. With me. I know what it's like, to want to better yourself. To know what you're capable of, what you deserve, yet to have so many factors pulling against you. Holding you back. But I can make that helplessness go away; I can take the sin away; I can protect you. It won't be for ever, I promise.'

On his lips, the ghost of a smile. She was paranoid and frightened. He was getting through to her. She was asking herself, *How does he know so much about me?* She didn't ask Oswald, though. Maybe she was afraid of what the answer would be. Instead, she said, 'For how long?'

'Winter,' he told her. 'Most of the spring. I'll be done by Easter. Think of it as a prolonged contemplative retreat.'

Oswald looked again at the office of Highlands Estates. Gale was on the phone again – or still on it? – and the policeman appeared to be perusing the property particulars displayed in the window. No sign of Clara. He was sure she would turn up at some point, and he thought he could rely on her to keep silent about last night.

False face must hide what false heart doth know.

She could do it. She was grittily determined, strong. He had an idea that Clara, like him, was a survivor.

Fine. But what about her returning to Boleskine? Could he rely on her to do that? The state of her when she left last night – stinking of vomit, that coppery hair hanging in rat tails, staggering under the weight of her guilt – didn't exactly instil confidence. But perhaps that was all right, for now.

For one thing, he had time to change her mind before the first stages of his great operation. The meditations. The Great Feast. All of that would come, once he had Clara.

He had already planned for the other crucial element of the equation, and it was happening right now, across the street.

A few days earlier, the on-duty constable at Abersky police station had received an anonymous phone call from 'a concerned local resident'. Making that call had been a colossal risk, of course. And Oswald still hadn't quite forgiven himself for unwittingly drawing the police up to the house yesterday. Even though Clara had believed the lie about the plain-clothed visitor snooping about, it had been too close for comfort. But this was the way things had to be now. To will, to wish, to want and to purpose. If his longed-for endeavour were to succeed, nothing could be left to chance. Which was precisely why he had put on the best Scottish accent he could manage, and made the call.

'You say you live locally, sir?'

'Yes.'

It was only half a lie. Oswald would be a resident soon enough, and he was very concerned about Boleskine and his future life there. What he told the constable next, however, was a complete lie.

'You're saying this is about the fire, sir?'

'The fire two weeks ago, yes. At Boleskine House.'

'What do you wish to tell us, sir?'

'Well, it may be nothing and I don't want to waste your time. You know how many sick-minded wanderers you get hanging around that place, so—'

'It's all right, sir. Just tell me what you saw.'

'A young woman, I think, wearing a hooded jacket. She was walking away from the burning house.'

'Where were you at the time?'

'Driving home. There's a quiet old road there at the bottom of the hill, the B852, I think? Runs alongside the water just before the turning splits off, winding up to the house.'

'You've been up there yourself?'

Oswald laughed. 'Years back, as a boy. The kids used to dare each other to run up that rough track and touch the house.'

'I see,' said the constable. 'Anyway, about this woman you saw?'

'I might not have seen her,' Oswald went on, 'but the whole sky was aglow with the fire raging up there, and, well, I was worried about startled animals charging down the hill into the road, deer and whatnot, so I was going slow, you understand? Had my headlights switched to full beam.'

All of this was a lie, but it slipped out easily enough.

'This woman. Did you recognise her?'

'She looked familiar.'

'You think she was local?'

'Maybe. Yeah. Her hair, you know – those ginger plaits. She reminded me of someone I've seen hanging around the shoreline there recently. Young-looking. Almost childlike.'

This happened to be true; Oswald had seen a young woman loitering on the pebbled shoreline a few times; and having kept a watchful eye on Highlands Estates for the best part of two weeks, Oswald now had a very good idea who that woman was.

Not Clara; but someone close to her.

'Sir, who do you think you saw when the house was burning?'

Determined to plan for this day, to make Clara see that she really had no other option than to move into Boleskine with him, Oswald had given the police constable the name he had in mind.

He had been convinced he was doing the right thing.

But at this moment, sitting in the Abersky Tea Rooms and staring at the estate agents' opposite, he couldn't help noticing that as he lifted his cup to drink, his hand was no longer steady, but trembling.

14

Head down, Clara hurried down Glendole Road. She didn't look up to see the pig's head in the butcher's window. She didn't look up to see the autumn sunlight sparkling on the loch and brooding mountains above. She just focused on putting one foot in front of the other as she tried – and failed miserably – not to think about the previous night's events.

She didn't register it at first when someone called her name. Sometimes, even after all this time, it took some adjustment to answer to Clara. But then the call came again – louder, and Clara glanced up.

A heavy-set lady passing on the other side of the street was waving at her. Aggie Blackwood, a middle-aged woman who managed to look sullen even when she was smiling. She was wearing a lightweight black padded jacket, unzipped, with the hood down.

Clara knew very little about Aggie other than that she ran Celtic Crafts, a gift shop at the end of Glendole Road – a shop that, for reasons Clara did not comprehend, managed to keep its doors open even without a steady stream of customers and despite its stock, which mostly consisted of bright green Nessie soft toys that looked as though they had been stitched and stuffed in the 1970s. Clara had only been inside Celtic Crafts once, but it was enough to convince her of two things. The first was that she would never buy anything there. The second thing was that Aggie was the sort of woman who took the Bible at its word. She even had an embroidered sign over the cash register that read: 'Dangerous times demand vigorous faith!' Clara had pretended not to see the sign and fixed her gaze instead on one of the awful lake-green Nessie toys. It had occurred to her in that moment that if Aggie Blackwood did believe in Nessie (which wouldn't have surprised Clara one bit) then it was probably because she considered the monster to be a serpent of evil.

From across the road, Clara threw Aggie a quick smile. On another occasion, she might have stopped out of politeness for a brief conversation about how business was faring, but not now. Not this morning. She walked on, her attention possessed by memories of the night before.

She knew what she needed to do now; it was obvious. Because if she didn't do that, she'd be more vulnerable than she'd ever been when living with Karl.

You thought living with broken ribs and black eyes was hard? Try prison. Try dirty locked cells with buckets to pee in, or performing favours for the male officers. Try slopping out and the daily strip searches. She'd read an article about a woman who had drowned a fellow prisoner in a bucket of pee, about watery soup and black bread, about cold concrete floors, dark-grey walls and nothing else.

And, after all, wasn't Boleskine House the perfect hiding place? Remote. Isolated. If Karl was still looking for her as her aunt had warned. Wouldn't she feel safer at Boleskine, even, than in the heart of Abersky?

Safer with *Oswald*, though? Any sane person would have questions. Who was this man, who wanted to live in a rundown house in the middle of nowhere; who lurked about, watching; who took the fact that *Clara had killed someone* in his stride and helped her cover up her crime?

Whoever he was, Clara had to concede, he wasn't Karl.

I can make that helplessness go away; I can take the sin away; I can protect you, he had said. Maybe part of her needed that protection. To hide. And to atone.

The Highlands Estates office was located at the far end of the street. Clara was almost upon it when she noticed the car parked four cars down from the office, and froze.

She looked in to Highlands Estates. At the window, framed exactly where the glossy advert for Boleskine House had been, Clara could see a man wearing the unmistakable black-and-white chequered hat of a police officer.

Her first thought was: *He knows about the body; he knows what I did.*

Her second thought: *He's come to arrest me.*

Her third: *Run!*

But that would only make things worse, make it look like she had something to hide, wouldn't it?

You know the answer to that. So there's your answer. You deserve this. What would Aggie Blackwood say?

In her mind, she saw Aggie's doughy face, glowering harshly at her from behind her antiquated cash register, meting out her sour judgement:

'*For the wages of sin is death; the soul who sins shall die.*'

As Clara stood there on the cobbled pavement, her eyes still fixed on the police officer, the vision she had built this morning – moving to Boleskine, hiding, safe – disintegrated. She would end up in jail after all.

It was what she deserved. She was guilty. She should answer for her crime. Find redemption that way.

Taking a deep, steadying breath, Clara walked to the office door and pushed it open.

15

The police officer's name was Adam Lake. He was an Englishman, in his late twenties, Gale reckoned, and full of youthful eagerness. But his voice had grit in it and his eyes were sharp and speculating as they flicked between Gale and Clara. They were seated at their adjacent desks, while he sat stiffly on a client's chair, facing them. On his lap lay his hat and a brochure he'd flicked through while Gale finished up her phone call with a potential buyer.

'I'm sorry to have kept you waiting, PC Lake,' she said,

though she wasn't. That buyer had been too good a prospect to cut short.

Adam held up the brochure and jabbed a finger at the cover shot of Boleskine. 'We've had reports that have raised one or two questions about the fire here.'

Clara stared at him.

Gale sighed. 'Except so far the insurance company has found no evidence of suspicious activity. You should have seen the state of the cabling. The whole thing was unfortunate, of course, but an accident. Look, it's been hard enough shifting this bloody house! I hope you're not proposing some sort of criminal investigation, because that could only delay—'

'Please hear me out,' Adam cut in. 'I have a job to do.'

Gale opened her mouth to reply; then, seeing his expression, she snapped it shut. From a sideways look, Clara looked wary and, what – guilty? Perhaps the policeman was just making a routine enquiry here, but somehow she doubted that, which made her nervous. She could ill-afford to lose the commission on Boleskine. She didn't own these premises, and she was a month behind with her rent. That was one of the shortcomings of running a business like this: you were always at the mercy of other people's decisions.

For a moment, she regretted keeping Clara on. If she was honest with herself, the only reason she had done that was because Clara was so good with Inghean. If Gale had an evening engagement, Clara would come around to the house and sit with Inghean, thank God.

Inghean did not cope well on her own.

The property brochure was on the desk now. Adam reached into his inside pocket and drew out a pen and a black leather-bound notepad.

'This is a bit awkward,' he said. 'But we've received a report of a woman leaving the scene of the fire.' He referred to his notepad. 'According to the witness, she was in her late teens or early twenties. Wearing a dark, hooded jacket. With long ginger hair, braided in two plaits.'

Gale looked up suddenly, her eyes wide and hostile.

'Now, listen, Gale—'

'You're implying that my Inghean was mixed up in this? Seriously?'

'Gale—'

'That's completely ridiculous! It could have been anyone. Why on earth would you conclude it was Inghean?'

It was a leap; unless Adam had more to go on, a very great leap. What was he thinking?

'Does Inghean know the history of the house?' said Adam. 'If she'd heard the stories about the place then maybe curiosity got the better of her and she—'

'Ventured out for a midnight stroll?' Gale gave him a withering look. 'Don't be absurd. You know Inghean, she wouldn't hurt a fly.'

It was true. Everyone in Abersky knew Inghean was as gentle and as harmless as a butterfly. Her learning difficulties might make her anxious at times, but that never made her act out. Not any more.

'It's just procedure. We need to—'

'Rule people out, narrow it down . . .'

'Exactly.' Adam nodded. 'So, to be clear, you were with your daughter the entire night? She didn't leave the house at all?'

'That's right.'

'Could she have slipped out without you noticing?'

As Gale glared at him, Clara spoke up:

'There must be some sort of misunderstanding here . . .'

It's about time, Gale thought, turning her glare onto her employee. She was already peeved that Clara had turned up late today, and looking dishevelled – that shirt had been nowhere near an ironing board. The least Clara could do was offer some support now.

'Um . . . I mean, it was dark that night, right?' Clara said. 'So how could someone have been sure the person – if there was a person – had ginger braids?'

Gale found herself assessing Clara's hair, tied back in a messy bun, but long. And with definite red tones. Then she understood the logic of Clara's words. Dark. Impossible to see.

Adam seemed less impressed. His attention focused on Clara, he said, 'And where were you on the night of the fire?'

'I was at home,' she said, 'in my flat.'

He nodded, holding her stare. Then he returned his attention to Gale.

'Inghean,' he began, but Gale cut him off with a hard glint in her eyes.

'Are you for real? Because my daughter's different – an *innocent* – you fix right on her?'

'Look, I know it's not easy to hear,' Adam said. 'But you need to face facts here, Gale. You can't pretend Inghean doesn't spend a lot of time wandering near the water. I've seen her myself. Now, a witness told us they'd seen her out near Boleskine in the weeks preceding the fire. And someone who looks just like her on the night of the fire. I had to check. You understand?'

Gale nodded, but turned her gaze to the shop window and the glossy placards of unsold properties hanging there. She wanted him gone, now. Having a police car parked outside your premises wasn't exactly good for business. And something else was bothering her, something about Clara. Why *had* she been so slow to come to Inghean's defence, for Christ's sake? She would ask her about that just as soon as Adam wished them a good morning and went on his way.

Instead of doing that, though, Adam reached into a pocket, drew out a small Polaroid and said, 'Please don't mention this to anyone, okay? It's probably nothing.'

He raised the photograph to Gale's eye level. 'Do you recognise this man?'

The man in the picture was strikingly handsome, with dark wavy hair, wide eyes and a dimpled chin.

'Never seen him before,' Gale said.

'What about you?' Adam asked, showing the picture to Clara. She shook her head.

'Is he in some sort of trouble?' Gale asked.

'That's what I'm trying to find out. His name is Charles Bartlett. He's a poet from London.' The word 'poet' was pronounced with an unmistakable note of derision. 'Reported missing by his sister a few days ago. Now, he's into drugs. And I don't mean the odd spliff. It's not unusual for him to disappear for days at a time when he's using. But, well, it's been eight weeks now, so I'm curious.'

Curious. That was one word for Adam Lake, Gale thought.

'Why do you think this Charles guy might be in Abersky?' she said.

'Because he told his sister he was coming here,' Adam said. 'Some private research project near Foyers. And as you know, Foyers is the closest hamlet to Boleskine House.'

There was a moment's silence.

'I don't see how we can be of help,' said Gale. 'We don't know this man.'

Adam sat back in his seat. 'What can you tell me about Boleskine?'

'It's a two-acre plot,' said Gale at once, 'giving onto the Loch. Four bedrooms, a kitchen, lounge, drawing room, a library; and there's recent planning permission granted for a three-bedroom log house, which is—'

'I mean what can you tell me about its *history*?'

A long pause followed. It was ironic, given that she was charged with selling the place, but Gale had only a vague idea of Boleskine's past. The gloomy stories. Apparently, a young girl who lived there was found hanging dead from a tree in the garden, and a few years later, in the master bedroom, a lodge manager had blown his brains out with a double-barrelled shotgun. Apocryphal myths? Gale didn't know, and if she was honest with herself, she didn't particularly care. But she figured that if the myths were true, then a policeman like Adam would almost certainly know about them and wouldn't need to ask her.

'Some ridiculous websites make out that the house has a history of black deeds,' Gale said wearily. 'Animal sacrifices to Satan, people claiming they've seen and heard things up there they can't explain. Lights turning off and on, doors slamming, misty silhouettes of people who aren't there. Animal snorting sounds behind locked doors. If you listen to Bat Brains across the road, she'll tell you all about the drugs and sex parties that used to go on at what she calls the "white-stoned home of sorcery". Yes, she'll tell you all that without a shred of evidence to back it up. She'll probably say the lodge is home to the devil himself.'

'I see.'

Gale tutted, to make it very clear that whatever Aggie

Blackwood believed was categorically *not* what she, smart, upright and dependable Gale Kilgour, believed.

'And the house is now sold?'

'Yes, subject to contract.' Gale glanced at Clara. 'We had a sealed bid yesterday afternoon and the sellers have accepted it.'

'Who's the buyer?'

'Oswald Cattenach,' Clara said.

'What's he like?' Adam asked her.

Clara shrugged. 'I just met him yesterday. I know very little about him.'

'Family?'

'None that he mentioned.'

'One hell of a big place for a man on his own.'

'He'll be wanting to let it out to holidaymakers come summer, you wait and see,' Gale chipped in. 'Either that or he'll do it up and sell it on.'

Adam didn't even look at her; he was giving Clara an appraising stare. Clara was smiling, but Gale knew her well enough to recognise how tense she was. She could hardly blame the girl. She herself had the mother of all headaches building.

'How about you?' Adam asked Clara. 'Notice anything unusual at the property?'

She shook her head.

'Any idea how the fire started?'

Clara shrugged. 'Sorry.' She glanced at Gale, and then at the clock. Gale was absolutely on her wavelength.

'Is there anything else?' Gale said pointedly to Adam, rising to her feet.

It was only polite for Adam to stand too. 'Nothing else,' he said. 'For the moment. Thank you for your time.'

She watched him walk to the door. He had a slight limp, and she thought he was trying hard to hide it.

At the door, he put on his hat. 'Can I keep hold of this?' he asked, holding up the Boleskine brochure.

'Of course,' said Gale, noticing Clara's gaze catch on the back of the document, where her picture was discreetly printed.

It suddenly occurred to Gale that she hadn't asked Clara's permission to use that photograph, and she realised, with some mild annoyance, that Clara hadn't asked about it, which either meant she didn't care or hadn't noticed. Both possibilities were equally annoying. Still. At some point she should probably mention to Clara that her picture would also appear on other brochures. And online.

Just then, the phone started ringing again. Gale dived for it. When she looked up again, Adam Lake was gone, but Clara was still behind her desk, as useful and energetic as a statue.

16

Minutes later, as Adam strolled along Glendole Road, his mind ticked over with a mixture of interest and suspicion. He already had it in mind to discover more about the history of Boleskine. He'd heard some vaguely sinister stories since moving to Abersky, but he'd never seriously entertained the idea they were true, and until now, he hadn't had cause to check whether they were.

What he did know was that police officers older and wiser

than him would have the facts written down. Maybe there was a case file back at the station.

Still, he'd never heard his colleagues discuss Boleskine, and he hadn't noticed anything out of the ordinary during his trip out there yesterday. But that didn't mean out-of-the-ordinary things hadn't happened there, did it?

Stepping up to his car, he noticed a short queue forming down the road, outside McHardy's of Abersky. Villagers, women mostly, eager to stock up on their weekend supplies of Shetland lamb and Middle White pork from Islay. Adam had tasted that lamb more than once and he could understand why the villagers were queuing. Murdoch McHardy kept a fine shop; there were more than thirty types of sausage on sale in there, not to mention the homemade black pudding and haggis.

He briefly considered asking some of the customers lining up whether they had heard or seen anything unusual on the night of the fire. But that would hardly be discreet. He had no desire to cause unnecessary concern here in Abersky, and he especially didn't want crazy stories about Boleskine House flying around. Not until he knew more about its history, anyway.

He turned to his car, braced his hands on the roof, and stretched his aching leg. Across the road, a buxom-to-heavy woman armed with an enormous yellow sponge was soaping her shopfront window so vigorously she might have been trying to scrub the soot of hell from Satan's face. It wasn't Aggie Blackwood who caught his eye, though, so much as what was displayed behind the glass she was scrubbing.

Mirrors. Concave and mounted on wheels. The three most ornate and imposing mirrors he'd ever seen.

Adam started to get in his car; paused. Looked back over the road.

Mirrors this grand – wavy, Italian, silver – had no place in a shop like Celtic Crafts; they ought to be in the Royal Opera House.

'Everything all right, officer?' Aggie Blackwood was peering curiously over at him. 'No trouble I hope?'

The cobbled road was narrow – narrow enough, unfortunately, to permit a conversation, albeit one conducted at an uncomfortable volume.

'No, no trouble,' he replied. 'Nothing to worry about.'

'Ah ha. Not turning any blind eyes, I hope?'

'Absolutely not, Mrs Blackwood.'

'It's *Miss* Blackwood. And I'm glad to hear it, because the greatest trick the devil ever pulled was convincing the world he doesn't exist!'

He winced inwardly, for she had pronounced every word with the fanatical, yet farcical, zeal of biblical prophecy. 'Ah, thanks for that, Miss Blackwood.'

'Don't you forget it,' she added piously, the yellow sponge in her hand dripping water as she gripped it hard. 'You turn a blind eye to evil, you become a focus for evil.'

'Right.'

'The only power the devil has is the power we give him . . .'

Aggie was rambling on, but he was looking away, down the street. The queue leading out of McHardy's had grown longer. And standing in that line was someone he hadn't expected to see, someone with protruding eyes and a flat face and fiery hair held back in two neat plaits.

Inghean Kilgour.

Adam thought of the anonymous call he'd received, just a few days earlier – that sonorous voice describing the furtive behaviour of the woman he was looking at now. She looked small, somehow. Lost.

He couldn't question her now, could he?

He certainly wanted to. But it wouldn't be right. Not without Gale's consent. Inghean was not a child, but she wasn't quite an independent adult, either, despite her twenty-two years.

He got into his car, again noticing the giant mirrors for sale in the shop window opposite; noticing Aggie, still planted firmly on the pavement, looking steadily his way. For no reason he could name, Adam's blood was thumping in his ears. Something wasn't right. In Highlands Estates, for sure; those women were on edge. But it was bigger than that. It was the village itself, as if something was hiding beneath the veneer of the prim respectability. Communities like this weren't supposed to have teeth, so why did it feel as if it did?

He registered this mental question and tried to cast it off. He was a policeman. He dealt in facts, not fanciful speculation.

But when he glanced across the street again and saw his own pale face painfully reflected in one of those fancy mirrors, he had the urge to start the car and drive right out of this village and never come back.

17

Inside the Highlands Estates office, Gale stood at the window, her keen eyes tracking the police car as it pulled away. She said nothing. Clara also remained silent.

A thought had occurred to Clara: it was probably Adam

who had been snooping around at Boleskine House yesterday. He hadn't been wearing a uniform or driving a marked car because he was off duty, or because he hadn't wanted to draw attention to himself.

If she was right, it spoke volumes that the constable hadn't mentioned the visit. Showed that he was taking this investigation seriously and wasn't ready to confide too much.

And wasn't it just possible that if the man he was looking for failed to turn up, Adam would return, ask for the keys, to see inside the house? Have a snoop in the library – or, worse, around the burial ground?

In her head, a voice spoke up. It sounded a lot like Alison Hopkins.

Are you just going to say nothing, Clara? An innocent, disadvantaged woman is being implicated here for a crime you committed!

A very small part of Clara was relieved not to be in the firing line herself; the rest of her was worried for Inghean. Seriously, Adam suspected her? A lonely, insecure girl whose greatest distractions in life were her crayons, her sketchbooks and her all-encompassing crush on Justin Bieber? Inghean, round-eyed and trusting? No, it wasn't right. It made Clara angry as hell.

And suspicious. It just didn't add up.

Her gaze dropped to the stack of property brochures on her desk. Boleskine House. Soon to be the home of one Oswald Cattenach.

This was him. Pulling the strings. Using a vulnerable girl as a pawn in whatever manipulative chess game he was forcing Clara to play.

Quit your job. Give up your flat. Come live here, with me.

Oswald had insinuated to the police that Inghean might have caused the fire. Why? She thought she knew: he was prepared to frame Inghean for Clara's crime – if she didn't go to him.

He was a cunning bastard. Not so different from Karl after all, then.

Emotion rose up in her, so strong it was all Clara could do not to shout. Throw something. She gripped the edge of her desk, silently screaming. Across the room, Gale was oblivious, still gazing out of the window. Thinking of her daughter, no doubt.

Dear, sweet Inghean. Clara could not allow her to suffer. She would protect this girl, this *child* – for that was how she saw Inghean. She was so vulnerable. Innocent.

A tear was snaking down her cheek, Clara realised. Her hand was pressed to her stomach.

Empty.

Aching.

Her own child had been an innocent too. And Clara had not protected it. *Him.* She had longed for a boy. He had been so tiny, so helpless.

Karl had kicked her in the stomach when she told him, when she showed him the positive pregnancy test that she'd so stupidly dared to hope would make a difference, would make him look at her as he once had. He'd kicked her, and punched her, and dragged her out of the flat to the concrete stairwell of their building. And even as she begged him not to – '*The baby, please, the baby*' – he had shoved her.

The memories were hazy after that. She remembered the blood – the wetness on her legs, the awful metallic smell. The pain, coming in great terrible waves that dragged her under. A man – not Karl – looming over her. The memory of his face flitted about her. She couldn't clutch it, however hard she tried.

Elusive and maddening. It was as if she wasn't supposed to remember everything of that black moment, and maybe that was for the best. What she knew for sure was that the man was dressed all in green, a figure of hope, telling her to keep her eyes open, to keep looking at him. Reassuring her she'd be all right, she'd be saved.

She awoke in the hospital with a broken wrist, shoulder and pelvis, mild bleeding on the brain and a broken vertebra in her back.

And an empty womb.

The baby – *her* baby, her one precious gift – was gone. And the extent of the scarring meant there would be no more chances, the consultant who'd fixed metal screws to her pelvis explained gently. She would never be a mother.

Clara had lost the will to go on then. She lay in that bed and she planned it: an overdose, or a step off a Tube platform. But at night, while she slept in the quiet ward, she seemed to gather strength somehow. Over the three weeks she spent in hospital, the knowledge came: she must leave London, leave Karl, get far away and do something new with her life. Be, if not a mother, then someone else.

So she had fled. Caught a train to the remote confines of the Highlands and never looked back. She had changed her name and changed her hairstyle, and a year later, she was someone else: an estate agent in a tiny village of twisting roads and gabled cottages nestled on the wooded shores of Loch Ness.

At least, an estate agent was who she had been here.

Clara stood up. She knew what she had to do – even if it meant playing right into Oswald's hands.

'Gale?'

The older woman turned and huffed a sigh. 'What is it, Clara?' she said.

'I'm sorry, Gale, but I need to resign. I'll work my notice if that's what you want, but I won't need my flat any more.'

Silence fell in the office. Clara thought her employer looked surprised, certainly, but not disappointed – which only made Clara feel hollower. Worthless.

'You're sure?' Gale asked.

'Yes.' Clara forced herself to stand tall. To look in control. 'You've enough on your hands with the business and Inghean, without fretting about how to afford to keep me on.'

Gale's face remained impassive, but she didn't argue, and that was good. It made what Clara had to do now that little bit easier.

'You can take the day off,' Gale said, 'if you need to rest. You look like you need it.'

'Thank you, I appreciate that.'

'Wait,' Gale said quickly, 'what about tonight?'

'Tonight?' Clara looked at her blankly. What was tonight? Then, with a jolt, she remembered. *Tonight!*

Of course. Gale was going out, and Clara was supposed to be going around to keep Inghean company. Pizza and a movie. 'Gale, I'm sorry, I can't.'

'You'll have to explain to Inghean. I promised her you were coming.' A pause; a downturned mouth. '*You* promised.'

'I'm sorry, Gale. I truly am.'

With painful regret, Clara crossed the room to the coat rack and put on her long red woollen coat. She tried not to think of how she'd chosen it for this job, to look smart for viewings; the little thrill she'd felt when she first put it on and saw how it offset her new hairstyle.

'Is there anything you want to discuss with me?' Gale called out as Clara walked to the door. 'Anything at all?'

When Clara turned back, she saw Gale was frowning. Maybe she thought Clara was into drugs. Or debt.

Or that she was the redhead who'd set the fire at Boleskine.

'No, thank you,' Clara said. 'I'm fine. I will be fine.'

Without looking back, she stepped out of the office into the crisp morning, her breath pluming out, frosting on the thin air. As she walked, she looked out across the village sloping down to the loch. In the distance, standing before a steep hillside of dense pines and firs, she could just make out Boleskine's blurred edges, its stained white walls catching the morning light.

Some may find the view appealing, romantic even. But not Clara. Her mind was already conjuring an image of the brooding mountainside behind the house; of the tumbledown burial ground, where her shameful secret lay entombed; of the sinister stone dogs and eagles that guarded the entrance to the manor, watching all. She saw the heavy oak door. She couldn't deny it: that was a door she had no desire to step through. But in her waking nightmare it was already opening before her into catacomb darkness. Opening wide, ready to swallow her, like a yawning black mouth.

CAUSE OF *BOLESKINE* BLAZE
OFFICIALLY 'UNKNOWN'

A blaze that destroyed most of the east wing of the historic Boleskine House above Loch Ness has been revealed as 'unknown', the Scottish Fire and Rescue Service has said.

Firefighters from Foyers, Inverness, Beauly and Dingwall battled the blaze at the property near Foyers on 4 October, and initially suspected the fire was suspicious.

However, a report released by the investigating insurance company has concluded that, although the exact cause of the fire could not be determined, it was probably accidental and sparked by overheating and faulty wiring.

Boleskine House was owned by infamous occultist Aleister Crowley and later by Led Zeppelin guitarist Jimmy Page.

It is understood that the property was sold recently to a buyer from London. It is not known what the new owner plans to do with the property.

18

When she got home from her walk late that afternoon, Inghean Kilgour went into the house and straight up to her room without even closing the front door. Over breakfast, Mum had mentioned Clara was coming around this evening for a film.

She sat cross-legged on her bed, excited. Happy. She loved spending time with Clara, who was kind. Never made fun of her. And she enjoyed answering Clara's questions, about where she most liked to walk, and about what she hoped to do with her life when she was older. Open a cosy guest house, maybe.

But what sometimes bothered Inghean was that Clara didn't like answering questions about herself. Whenever she asked Clara about her past, her friend would suddenly look tired and sad, and a wistful expression would cloud her gaze. In so many ways, Clara was a mystery. But now she was coming over and they would have a fun evening. Maybe they'd watch *Frozen*.

As she raised her gaze to the mirror at the end of her bed, gooseflesh sprang on her arms and a familiar tingling began at the base of her neck. Inghean tensed and gave a tiny gasp.

She knew what was happening. How could she not? It had happened so many times. And she had the sketches to prove it.

She squeezed her eyes shut and had a glimpse of what this drawing would be: Clara, again, standing in this very room, wringing her hands sorrowfully.

She swallowed hard; opened her eyes.

And as the sun sank over the loch, the longest shadows began sliding not just into her bedroom but into her mind.

The tingling in her neck intensified.

Almost on impulse, she reached for her nearest sketchpad, took a thick red pencil from the pot next to her bed, and sat perfectly still for a long moment, her heart pounding, the way it always did when she attempted these drawings.

She hated to think that the pictures could show her bad things yet to happen, but nor could she deny that they did. Horrible things. Dark revelations. In school she had got into awful trouble for drawing her friend's parents fighting with each other, their faces a bloody mess.

At first she thought – hoped – her teachers were right; that perhaps she just had an over-active imagination, but when Mary's parents did attack each other – two weeks later – and the matter was all over the local paper, Inghean knew she was different.

Knew her pictures were different, too.

The problem was, once the pictures were in her mind, the only way to get them out was to put them on paper.

Barely aware now that her eyes were rolling back in her head, she took up her pencil and let her hand trail over the paper.

Please let this picture be good, oh, God, please . . .

Breathing deeply, an electrical sensation sparking in her temporal lobe, the pencil flew across the page, forming frantic squiggles that became shapes and numbers. It was a simple drawing, but the mental effort was excruciating. As her hand moved with quick, sweeping strokes, tears pricked the corners of her eyes.

She felt as if her mind was bleeding onto the page.

'Inghean?' Clara's voice, as if from far away, reached her suddenly and Inghean jolted as the bedroom door swung open just as the tip of her pencil snapped, leaving a large dark smudge on the paper. That smudge looked like a crooked scar.

'Inghean? Sorry love, it's only me.'

Without yet turning around, she looked up from her sketchpad and in her reflection in the mirror facing her at the end of her bed, she thought that the odd starburst pattern on her green-blue irises looked brighter than normal. Soulful, and sparking with secret knowledge. Which terrified her.

'Your mother asked me to call in,' Clara said cautiously.

'I know.' Inghean bit her lip as she continued sketching. Tense. Dipping her head, her hair shielding her face from Clara's enquiring gaze.

'Inghean, what's wrong?'

She was suddenly afraid that this would not be a happy evening after all. She didn't want to look at her drawing again. Didn't want Clara to look, either, just in case . . .

'What are you drawing?'

Finally, she turned, greeting Clara with a forced smile.

'Oh, nothing much.'

'May I see?'

Before she could reply, her friend was behind her, looking down over her shoulder at two stick-figure women holding hands in a bedroom. One of the women in the picture looked desperately sad. And a digital clock next to the bed read: 18:42.

Clara registered the digital clock next to Inghean's bed and asked, 'Is this your bedroom in the picture?'

Inghean nodded.

'And this is us, holding hands?'

'Yes.'

'It's lovely.'

'Thanks.' Inghean managed a smile. Not every drawing was as harmless as this one. But still, the picture was sad. And Inghean already knew why. 'You're going somewhere, aren't you?' she said, after a pause.

'How did you know?'

Inghean shrugged, looking glum. 'Mum told me,' she lied.

'I'm sorry, but yes, love. I'm going away.'

'Where?'

'I can't tell you. But I have a job to do.'

'What sort of job?'

'Hopefully one that won't last too long.'

'Tell me, please.'

Clara looked on edge, but her tone was commanding. 'I can't, Inghean. You have to trust me, okay?'

'Do you promise you'll come back?'

If Clara believed she could make such a promise and keep it, she would have done. 'I'll do what I can.'

'Promise,' Inghean repeated, and as she did, she remembered asking her dad the same on the day he left home:

Do you promise you'll come back? Promise you won't leave for good? And her father had nodded curtly, not looking back, just heading for the car in which he drove away.

'We'll always be close,' Clara said, reassuringly. 'Do you believe that?'

Inghean nodded, trying hard not to cry. Then, to her alarm and dismay, she saw Clara's gaze catch on the digital clock in the picture. On the red digits: 18:42.

There was a moment's silence between them.

'Inghean,' Clara said curiously, 'you drew this *before* I came in?'

She nodded.

'But this was three minutes ago.' She checked her watch. 'Almost *exactly* three minutes.' A pause. 'How did you know I'd enter your bedroom, at that exact time?'

Inghean found herself unable to prise the words out. The words her grandmother had whispered and which, when threatened by the doctors, and by her mother, she had promised never to repeat.

Two simple, terrifying words:

Second sight.

In Gaelic: *An da shealladh.*

'Inghean?

Her bottom lip trembled.

'You wouldn't understand.'

'Try me.'

Inghean felt Clara studying her in silence. That she had known Clara would have probably come up to her room wasn't in itself unusual; but that she should have predicted the precise time at which her friend would step into the bedroom? That was downright sinister. How to tell her friend that sometimes the pictures that arrived in her head unbidden, without warning? And that sometimes, often, they came true?

'Inghean?

'The last time I told people about my drawings, I got in a lot of trouble.'

Clara's dark eyes softened. She sat down on the bed next to her friend and stroked the hair from her face. 'Don't you worry. Drawings can't cause trouble.'

But Inghean was shaking her head.

There was a moment's silence. Then Clara, curious, reached for Inghean's sketchpad, which was full of other drawings.

'No, please, give it back!'

'I'd love to see,' she urged, though her voice now sounded slightly less keen.

Tentatively, Inghean watched as Clara flicked through the sketchbook, holding her breath when Clara got to the back page and peered wonderingly at the drawing it bore. 'Hey, you never finished this one?'

Inghean dipped her head, feeling guilty and afraid, her gaze falling sadly onto a drawing of a stick woman floating on a pool of water, hair fanning out around her head in dark streaks.

The face of the figure was featureless.

'Is this me?' Clara asked.

'I think so.'

What she knew for certain was that it was someone very dear to her.

'Why am I swimming? I hate swimming . . .'

'You're not swimming,' Inghean said, tearing the sheet of paper from the book, only to scrunch it up and hurl it towards the wastepaper bin in the corner of the room.

To her frustration, the balled-up paper missed the bin and landed under the window.

Inghean sighed. It was as if the future had just slapped her in the face.

*

Later, when the moon was up and Inghean was in bed alone, she thought about what Clara had said, that she wouldn't be coming around for a while, and the idea crushed her heart and her hope.

She found herself remembering back to her school days,

when she had tried to warn Mary what her parents were going to do to one another. She had seen the tragedy in her mind in vivid colour; she had drawn it, too, and for that she had been punished. It felt so long ago, the day Mary's parents had glassed one another in a drunken rage, but the image of their slashed and blood-spattered faces remained etched on Inghean's memory. She did not think it would ever leave her.

As she lay in bed, longing for sleep, she realised she had snapped every pencil in her bedroom since Clara had gone home.

It had occurred to her that a picture couldn't come true if it wasn't finished.

But the balled-up paper she had aimed at the wastepaper basket remained stubbornly on the floor beneath the window, a drawing half completed. Wanting to be finished.

'Would you like to confide in me?' Clara had asked her before she left. And her eyes had shifted to the crunched-up ball of paper. 'It's only a drawing, Inghean.'

'Except it's not just a drawing,' she had replied quietly, feeling her heart tremble. 'It's the future.'

And it was true, what she had said to Clara. The stick woman she had drawn in that picture was not swimming.

She was drowning.

PART TWO

SECOND VIEWING

The world is full of magic things, patiently waiting for our senses to grow sharper.

– W B Yeats

1

Over the weeks that followed, Abersky gradually came to resemble a ghost town as more holiday cottages emptied out and more shops drew their blinds for the winter. A biting wind came blasting across the loch, whipping its surface into fearsome foamy tips and sending dead leaves, crumpled and brown, whirling down Glendole Road. Quietly, the dark water licked the shingle beach. At any moment, you might think, a wake in the water may draw the eye; a dark hump might appear out there, on the surface of the loch. An eel perhaps, a catfish, an otter . . . or something else.

Instead, a red-haired figure appeared on the shorefront. She hunched down, sweeping her patterned skirt beneath her, and sat on the water-slicked stones, then began making a crayon drawing in her sketchbook, her hand moving jerkily.

In the window of Highlands Estates, particulars of a new property for rent had appeared: a well-appointed studio flat located over the butcher's shop.

Gale was pondering that empty flat as she stood in the porch of her office, drawing on a cigarette. Actually, she was thinking about its previous tenant. Whatever she had going on in her life, Clara Jones wasn't herself. Only the other day, Gale had spotted her further down Glendole Road, standing outside a shop that sold nursery furniture and buggies, staring in. Then, across the street, a young father had begun dragging a wailing toddler away from a sweet shop window. Yelling at him. Clara had watched, and Gale had seen her expression; she looked as if she was doing battle with intense feelings. Jealousy. Envy. Resentment.

Not my concern, Gale told herself, taking another drag of her cigarette. Clara was an adult. Whatever was vexing her, she would have to deal with it herself. She wasn't Gale's problem. Neither, come to that, was some crack addict from London and Adam Lake's bizarre suspicions.

Abersky's local bobby on the beat had come back two days ago asking questions about the missing junkie from London. Was she sure she hadn't seen someone matching his description hanging around near Boleskine House, prior to the fire? Yes, she was sure. It wasn't the answer he had been looking for, Gale could tell, and that bothered her. An earnest young policeman like him, new to town, could be keen to make his mark. To prove himself.

Overhead, the squall of a gull announced worse weather to come. Gale looked towards the tumbling white water and flinched as she saw flaming-red hair. Her daughter. Whom she'd told *very clearly* to stay away from the water's edge. Gale stamped out her cigarette and began walking along Glendole Road. She took deep breaths, trying to lock down her temper. Losing it might upset Inghean, and draw unwanted attention.

'What are you drawing, Inghean?' she said over the girl's shoulder.

'Stuff.' Inghean hunched forwards, covering the sketchbook on her lap.

Gale squatted down to her level. Inghean turned to her. In the daylight, the starburst pattern on her green-blue irises was distinctive.

'What did I say about coming down here?' Gale said.

'You said I shouldn't.'

'That's right.'

'But you didn't say why.'

Gale swallowed. That wasn't exactly true. What Gale had told her daughter was that a man was missing in the area, a man from London, who could be dangerous. It would be better, safer, for Inghean to stay inside, at least until the police found him.

It was a small lie, but a plausible one. She had spoken to Inghean before about her daughter's 'special condition', which made her very trusting towards other people, sometimes even people she didn't know. And those people weren't always good. They could do bad things to people more vulnerable than them . . .

It had happened once when Inghean was growing up. She was by the loch shore, not far from where they were sitting now, eating her lunch, when a stranger strolled up to her, started chatting, and then threatened her and ran off with her watch.

It broke Gale's heart to remember that day, her daughter's normally sunny face flushed and sodden with tears as she threw her arms around her mother, holding on tightly. The anxiety that had been unleashed went on and on for days. And so many broken nights.

Anxiety. Just one of a long list of ways in which Inghean's developmental disorder affected her.

The birth defect was so rare that Gale had never heard of it until that phone call, nineteen years ago, when the genetic counsellor delivered news to crush a mother's hopes: 'I have the results of Inghean's microarray analysis, and I'm sorry: she does have Williams Syndrome.'

Gale's first hint that something might be wrong with her daughter was when Inghean was three. Before then Gale had somehow managed to convince herself that the poor love would grow out of her elfin looks; that her widely-spaced eyes, her slow growth and colonic difficulties might just be coincidental; that her striking broad smile was just an outward sign of the sunshine within. But those lies became harder to believe when, one day, Inghean suddenly stopped playing, got down on the ground and fell asleep. Paul had been the one to say it then: *Something isn't right here.* The doctors explained to Gale that getting down on the ground to sleep suddenly was Inghean's way of regulating her blood pressure. Which was abnormally high. Her aorta hadn't grown since she was a baby.

After all the tears and the anger and the implacable sense of defeat, Gale had surprised herself by accepting the diagnosis. That wasn't a rational decision; it was the instinct of a mother. Her love for her daughter was pure, unconditional. Perhaps naïvely, she had assumed Paul would feel the same. That was her first mistake; her second had been assuming he would stick around and help. But Paul didn't know about special needs, and he didn't want to know, he didn't want the stress, and he didn't want to feel like a failure. What Paul wanted was a daughter who would grow up *normal*, go to college, have a successful career, have a family. Gale had watched him leave Abersky, loving him, wishing him back, and hating him at the same time.

It was fifteen years this winter since he walked out on her, but she felt little anger now. Mostly what she felt was sorry for him; because raising Inghean had been a joy. An unexpected joy, given all the problems the doctors had anticipated. Except for that nasty business two years earlier – the night Inghean lost her temper – her life with Inghean had been the story of a smile; a big, genuine smile that never failed to make others smile, too.

Inghean was Abersky's 'sunshine girl'. Normally. But now, looking at her daughter, Gale worried about Inghean's smile. Because suddenly, it wasn't there any more.

'Can I come back tomorrow?'

Gale was jolted out of her thoughts and reached for an answer. She knew Inghean liked to come to this spot to look at the mountains, and for Nessie, of course. She loved to watch the tour boats ferrying hopeful monster-seekers closer to their wild imaginings. Of course, the ferrymen themselves had heard the old stories too many times now to be anything except cynical, but they would put on a convincing show when the custom was good, and they weren't beyond inventing a few sightings of their own. They did that for Inghean sometimes; and she would listen avidly, watching the water with bright and wondering fascination.

'I don't think it's a great idea for you to be out here alone now, Inghean,' Gale told her. 'Not until the police find the man they're looking for, okay love?'

Her knees were seizing up, squatting like this. She stood up. Inghean remained seated, clutching her sketchbook.

'Will that man in the uniform ask me more things?' she asked.

'No, love. Don't you worry about that.'

Inghean was referring to Adam's visit to the office the other day. Gale had been more than helpful. For a start, she'd allowed him to ask her daughter the one question that was clearly burning in him, and Inghean had answered it: no, she had been nowhere near Boleskine House on the night of the fire.

He had seemed satisfied enough with that, so Gale had helped him out with the photographs and floorplans he asked for, too. What did it matter if she'd lied about one or two small things? She had no desire to tell him about the bottles and used needles she'd found in the east wing while preparing the house for sale.

Was that information even important, really? Abandoned houses often had squatters. No big deal. So, she had cleared those nasty things away. No potential buyer wanted to see that, and Gale had made sure they wouldn't.

'Why did Clara go away?'

The question caught Gale off guard. 'She just needed a change, Inghean. Sometimes people do. You mustn't let that worry you.'

Inghean looked questioningly up at Gale. 'But I *do* worry. I mean, I worry about Clara.'

'Why, my love? Did Clara tell you something?'

Inghean shook her head and her gaze drifted to the dark water, moved along – stopped. Gale followed the line of her sight, to the sprawling single-storey manor. Boleskine House.

She knelt then, heedless of the damp leaching into her trousers, and held her daughter by the arms.

'You would tell me, wouldn't you, darling?' she said, searching the girl's eyes. 'You'd tell me if you were out near that house on the night of the fire?'

Inghean's cheek twitched. She nodded, but her face, normally alive with colourful expression, was a cold grey.

'Come on,' Gale said, gesturing for Inghean to stand. 'Come back to the office with me. We'll have some tea and cake, yeah?'

Inghean rose and took her mother's hand, hugging her

sketchbook tightly to her chest. Minutes later, they had crossed onto Glendole Road and left the water behind. Gale was a touch relieved. She couldn't explain why, but sometimes, especially after dark, she felt that Loch Ness was better left alone. Beyond vast, it had always kept its mysteries.

Now they were approaching the entrance to the office, and Gale was already craving another cigarette, unclipping her handbag for the packet within while inwardly cursing herself for giving in to the habit she had promised herself she would quit. The wrinkles around her mouth had formed long ago; now they were deepening.

Inghean went into the office, but Gale hovered in the office doorway, smoking her cigarette and watching the dark windows of Clara's old flat over the butcher's shop with a mixture of interest and suspicion. Did Clara still have a key? Had she made a copy?

She doubted it; hoped not.

Why had Clara run off in such a hurry? And to where?

Of course, the village was rife with gossip. She'd enrolled at the university in Aberdeen. She'd got pregnant by a secret lover and gone back to England to have the baby. She'd won the lottery and jumped on the first plane to the Caribbean, the Seychelles, Australia – any country without Scotland's incessant rain.

The rumours were complete fabrications, Gale was sure. Still, what *was* Clara doing now? It bothered Gale that Clara had said so little about where she was going. And it bothered her that Inghean was so upset. She had very few close friends in the village, and Clara had been one of them. The best.

Taking another drag on her cigarette, Gale checked on Inghean. She was sitting at Clara's desk, drawing in her sketchbook. Probably the water, or the mountains. Or pictures of Nessie.

The idea made Gale smile and turn her gaze to the murky waters.

As she did that, she could never have guessed that her daughter was working on her fourteenth drawing of the day, a drawing that would certainly have raised the eyebrows of PC Adam Lake, and which was identical in every way to the other drawings in Inghean's new sketchbook. A childlike, jagged depiction of black smoke, belching from the fiery ruin of a burning house.

And lying before it, a dead woman.

2

As Clara stood on the long, tree-lined track leading up to Boleskine, a brisk wind scattered decaying leaves and bent the mature cypress trees that screened the property from the road below. Above the snow-capped mountains, the sky was a brilliant blue, but it may as well have been grey, to match Clara's mood.

This was the day she had been waiting for – and dreading – these past weeks. Her 'employment' commenced today.

While the legal cogs turned to make Oswald the owner of Boleskine, Clara had been staying at a hotel in the next village. Lying low. Though she had come back to Abersky a few times. It called to her.

Moving out of the flat above the butcher's shop had been relatively straightforward, but she had been surprised by the sadness she felt when she closed the door for the last time and handed the main set of keys over to Gale. She remembered when that grim flat and the incessant chopping sounds from below had irked her. It had never occurred to her that the day would come when she would feel an aching to return there.

Now, however, she had a new home to resent.

Head up, shoulders squared, she forced herself to approach the house that, in her mind, would be forever burning. She felt like a woman walking to her doom, and although that wasn't exactly a baseless fear, she wasn't sure to what extent she was exaggerating the danger she was in. It was possible Oswald meant her no harm. Perhaps he was just lonely, an eccentric free thinker. Perhaps he was sane.

Then she remembered how he had concealed the burned body. Kept it. Forced her to help him carry it down to the mort house. No, he had a screw loose, all right.

He wants me here for a reason, she thought. *And I doubt very much that it's a good reason.*

She approached the columned entrance with a heavy sinking in her stomach, looking not at the heavy door but instead at the grey stone Rottweilers on either side of it, teeth bared, eyes boring into her.

'Oswald?' she called, dreading seeing him again. But Oswald did not appear.

Instead of knocking, Clara hesitated for a moment, taking in her surroundings: the untamed garden, the muddy pond choked with green algae, the rotten black fence running around the garden's perimeter. Her eyes soon found the ancient cedar tree off to the side of the house; the wasted length of hanging rope; the rotten plank of wood.

It creaked on a gust of wind. This, together with the twisted trees, heathery knolls and the hard mountain that towered above the garden, contributed to the impression of oddity and macabre eccentricity in keeping with a house known for its troubled history. But beyond what was visible was the *sense* of something. A pernicious presence, cold and strange and menacing.

Evil.

But that was ridiculous. Clara wasn't superstitious and she reminded herself of that fact now as she raised her hand to the black knocker.

An abrupt, hard *thwacking* sound make her jolt. What was that?

She stiffened, listening hard. It seemed to come from inside the house.

She waited, but all was quiet. So she returned her attention to the door knocker. A dull echo resounded within as she banged it, but no one answered.

She waited a while. Maybe he was out. Maybe she could leave?

Thwack!

The sound again. What could it be?

She forced herself to try the doorknob, and to her surprise it turned and the heavy front door creaked open. Stale air wafted out.

'Oswald, are you here?'

No reply.

'Can I come in?'

Nothing.

Clara darted one quick look at the snarling stone canine next to her, took a long breath and entered the hall.

The door swung shut behind her.

It was quiet in the house, and gloomy. The harsh, heavy smell of smoke still hung in the air, making her insides twist. An acrid smell. Would it ever dissipate? She thought of how Oswald had insisted she take occupancy in the house. Maybe one could get used to that odour after a time, the way people living next to a main road adjusted to the noise of traffic, but somehow Clara doubted it. What she suspected – dreaded – was that the smell of the burning house would remain as pungent and offensive to her senses as the sound of the butcher's meat cleaver striking wood.

Breathing through her mouth, she glanced to her left and the long corridor running away from her, left and right, into nightmarish shadows. Strange. Instead of turning into the east wing as it had before, the corridor now terminated in a wall of white plastic sheeting that looked like it had been stapled to the floor, walls and ceiling.

Was that sheeting to keep out the draughts from the east wing? Or was it concealing something?

Either way, it didn't matter, because Clara had no intention of going that way. She couldn't even bear to look any longer, in case the plastic sheeting became backlit by angry flames; or, worse, the sheeting vanished altogether, to be replaced by a gaping hole spitting fire and smoke.

So she turned and moved in the other direction, down the hall towards the kitchen. It was gloomy down here too, but not entirely silent, because somewhere in the bowels of the house Cher was belting out 'The Sun Ain't Gonna Shine

Anymore', singing about loneliness being a cloak and it always being with you.

Karl used to love that song. Not the Cher version, though; he said that was for filthy faggots. But then taste was just one of a long list of qualities he was lacking.

As she walked, Clara's attention was caught by new additions to the flaking walls: elegantly framed watercolour paintings of mountainous landscapes. She paused and looked at one.

She had never been the sort of person to get excited over art, though she had a healthy respect for people who did. Nevertheless, she couldn't deny that the painting affected her in a way she didn't quite understand. The watercolour was faded and old, and depicted a silver waterfall cascading over a high cliff and crashing below into a craggy gorge of foaming water. Evidently, the artist had some talent, but the piece wasn't particularly remarkable. Yet she couldn't shake the notion that it was. As she stared at the scene, she could almost hear the dull roar of the water as it powered over the lip of the fall, could almost feel the weak sunlight that penetrated the great canopy of branches and refracted in the water below.

There was a figure in the painting. Alone, by the top of the waterfall, a hooded figure dressed in black and holding something indistinct that gleamed like a star. The figure's face was hidden, but its silhouette projected an aura that was both ancient and powerful.

Whoever this figure was, whatever it represented, it was entirely alone; staring into the frothing, steaming depths below.

For one wildly disorientating moment, Clara felt she could join that figure. Step into the painting. Become lost in it.

Thwack!

The banging sound jolted Clara out of the scene in the painting. There was nothing to suggest the source of the noise. She had to know what it was.

Thwack, thwack!

Clara turned and followed the sound – a splintery, hard sound – to a room she had no desire to see again. The library.

She spent far too long standing in the corridor, gripping the door handle. Wrestling with herself. Remembering the scene she'd last encountered here. Telling herself the body was gone now – hadn't she moved it with her own hands?

She heard something in the room. A rustling.

'Oswald?' she called.

There was no reply.

Slowly, she turned the handle.

In the blink of an eye the door was wrested from her grasp, blasting open furiously.

And Clara was falling.

3

The door crashed violently into the bookcase on the adjacent wall.

Clara's knees and palms impacted with the wood floor.

She didn't think – her body reacted. She cringed back, into a crouch, her hands flying up to protect her face.

She stayed that way, braced for an attack, for three short, sharp breaths. Then the realisation dawned on her: she was alone in the room.

It was the through draught that had caught the door, she saw now. The doors leading out onto the terrace were wide open, the curtains to each side rustling.

Slowly, and somewhat painfully, she got back to her feet. Took deep, steadying breaths. Told herself, over and over, *He's not here. You're safe. He's not here.*

She didn't take the trouble to identify the 'he'.

Oswald must be outside, she realised, around at the back of the house. Whatever he was doing, the sound had travelled up and through the doors.

She carefully closed the library door and glanced around. There were more books in here now than she remembered, but the same musty smell still permeated, suggesting many of these volumes were very old, perhaps very valuable. She registered the bizarre titles of a couple: *Thought Reform and the Psychology of Totalism: A Study of 'Brainwashing' in China.* Another: *The Rape of the Mind*, by Joost Meerloo.

She looked away from the shelves to the rest of the room. Over the fire, a grotesque painting, stranger than the last. An image of a muscular human body attached to the head of a horned beast: a bull.

Horrifically, the minotaur's muscular arms were cradling a suckling child to its breast.

She turned away in disgust only to see another new addition. On a rickety coffee table was a vintage chess set, the finest she had ever seen. It was the sort of set that would probably be stored in a mahogany box lined with dark-blue velvet. The white chessmen looked handmade, carved in what

Clara assumed was ivory. Yet for all its evident rarity and value, the chess set gave Clara the creeps. Well, not the set exactly, but where it had been positioned.

Why would he do that? Why put it there?

It had been set up exactly where the charred human remains had lain.

Her throat tightened. *The sick bastard. Was that what this was to him, a game of chess? Divide and conquer?*

Thwack!

Startled, she whirled towards the doors. *What was he doing out there?*

Walking out onto the cracked and weed-strewn terrace, she looked around. She expected to see Oswald somewhere in the garden, but there was still no sign of the man who had insisted she come here at this precise time, on this day. His absence was disturbing now, almost as much as that infernal sound.

Finally, she saw where it was emanating from. At the bottom of the hill sloping away from her, at the edge of the loch, was a dilapidated timber boathouse. Its door was hanging open, and as she watched, the wind caught it and slammed it with great force.

That explained the banging sound. The only question now was: why was the door open?

She walked slowly past a small rockery garden, long over-grown with shrubs, and headed towards the boathouse. Once, it had been painted a dark green; now the paint was cracked and peeling. Its entrance was an off-kilter oblong of fetid blackness. It would be dark and mouldy and wet in there; she had no wish to go inside.

But she needed to find the man who had lured her here.

At the entrance to the boathouse Clara saw, lying on the

ground, the rusted chain and padlock that had secured the door. The wind gusted again, catching the door, and she cringed as it banged once more.

'Oswald?' she called.

No answer.

It was a reasonable assumption that he was inside the boathouse. What if he had suffered an accident, needed help?

A part of her knew that was just wishful thinking, and she felt guilty for it. The rest of her was concerned, which was peculiar. Why should she feel concerned for a man who had frightened her, threatened her?

Because I'm drawn to him? Clara wondered. *Is that the real reason I agreed to return? Did I subconsciously surrender to a latent physical attraction to this maniac?*

Her stomach answered that last question, lurching unpleasantly. Since Karl, she had felt nothing for a man, and she very much doubted she ever would again. He had killed that in her, along with her baby.

No, she wasn't here because Oswald was intriguing. Magnetic. She was here because it was the only practical decision she could have made. All that mattered now was getting out of the hole she was in.

Nearby lay an old terracotta planter, cracked and chipped. She dragged it over and wedged the door open.

'Oswald?'

No reply.

She made herself step into the boathouse.

At once, darkness engulfed her. She shivered in the cool air, scrunched her face up against the rank stench of mould and rotting wood. From beneath the creaking floorboards came the persistent lapping of the loch water. The thought of that black, freezing water almost made her turn and leave; instead, she ran her hand down the rough boarded wall for a light switch. Found one. Flipped it. And was rewarded with only a low humming sound. No light.

She eased forward, listening. Terribly aware of her own breathing. To her left, she could just about make out the vague shapes of ropes and boat hooks hanging on the wall. There was a workbench too, and, standing upright on that, a clunky-looking tubular flashlight. It rattled as she grasped it, so badly in fact that she assumed it was very old and wouldn't work, but to Clara's relieved surprise, the torch threw out a trembling spotlight of yellowy light as she clicked it on.

Sweeping the beam around, she saw that there was a boat on the water: narrow, about ten feet long, rotten and warped. The boat was empty. Beyond it were high doors running down into the black water. Those doors would have opened out onto the loch, but they were padlocked shut and they looked as though they had been that way for a long time.

There was no sign of Oswald.

She turned her attention to the workbench, her torchlight bobbing beneath it and illuminating a clutter of tattered and mouldy cardboard boxes. She moved nearer to the workbench and crouched down to see. The boxes looked and smelt damp and old, some of them bulging with whatever they contained, but none appeared breached. She reached for the nearest box, which was open, and shone the torch inside, revealing a stack of mouldy old files and newspaper cuttings.

She reached into the box and took out a faded cutting from the *Caledonian Mercury*, dated 4 May 1822.

She read the article:

> *Romantic Summer Residence in Inverness-shire, to be let, furnished, entry immediately, Boleskine House, within a mile of the Falls of Foyers, the most celebrated of British cataracts, and 18 miles from Inverness, is to be let furnished for such period as may be agreed on. To a family that may desire a few months retreat to the romantic scenery of the Highlands, a more interesting situation but seldom offers. The house is slated, and being situated on a rising ground, commands a complete view of Loch Ness, from east to west. It consists of a spacious public room, of 32 feet in length, two large bedrooms, and two wings, one of which contains kitchen and servant's apartment; the interior of the other wing is not thoroughly furnished. The public post road passes within a few yards of the house, and a steam boat, between Inverness and Fort Augustus, touches at Foyers regularly every day during summer, by which conveyance all kinds of provisions may be depended on.*

A steamboat! Clara could feel the enticing romance of the historic scene. Where did it all go, she mused? The article might as well have been describing a completely different house to the macabre and quaintly grotesque edifice that stood on the plot today. She had a vague notion that the house had changed hands many times over the years, and she was right. She soon found more adverts for the letting of Boleskine. Adverts appeared in the *Inverness Courier* from March to July 1859; June to July 1862; July to August 1865, and April to August 1868.

No one wanted to live here, she supposed. Yet she could only speculate as to the reasons why. It seemed that a property enjoying such an elevated position, private, surrounded by woodland, with stunning views over Loch Ness, should have been someone's for ever home.

She reached back into the box and her gaze snagged on a peculiar headline:

MONSTER HUNTING ON LOCH NESS: EVEN THE POLICE LEND A HAND

The Loch Ness monster becomes more mysterious than ever . . .

While the Daily Mail *mission of inquiry was seeking to pick up its trail, we received news that the creature had been seen disporting itself in the water at Drumnadrochit, five miles away.*

Twenty-nine people witnessed a long, black body with a snake-like head travelling at great speed towards Fort Augustus.

Putting the article aside, Clara couldn't help smiling. The idea of there being some sort of mysterious sea creature roaming these waters was comically absurd to her. Weren't most monster hunters sad, lonely, middle-aged men afflicted by mid-life crises? Probably.

More interesting was the next article in the box.

BOLESKINE HOUSE
Home to the other monster of Loch Ness

Beneath this was a black-and-white photograph of a burly, broad-shouldered man in his late fifties. Entirely bald, with piercing eyes set in a bloated face, he wore a foppish bow tie and a grim expression that hinted at an underlying cruelty. Sinister, his mottled skin accentuating an unmistakably sickly appearance.

The corpulent figure was posing next to a table that reminded Clara of an altar, except it was decorated not just with candles, but with ivy and nettles and animal fur. An italicised quote in larger text appeared next to this picture. It read:

'*The question of magick is a question of discovering and employing hitherto unknown forces in nature.*'

She was reaching for the cutting when she heard a sucking noise behind her. Unnerved, she swung around. In the pool of light thrown by her torch, she saw the bow of the boat bumping gently on the jetty, buffeted by little waves in the slick black water.

Clara turned back to the box of cuttings. Again, this time with a shiver, she examined the faded cutting showing the ugly bald guy, but that wasn't the article she chose to read. Instead, she selected another, newer-looking cutting that was lying immediately beneath. This was from the *Inverness Courier* and was dated 1988, and the headline was even more intriguing than the last. And alarming. It read:

UNHOLY HOUSE
Retired general found dead in suspected suicide

Clara read quickly, and then took a moment, hunched on the old boards, listening to the lapping water, to reflect. She believed there could be all sorts of information about Boleskine House in these boxes. Except she believed a little more than that, didn't she? The article she had just read suggested the talk of tragedy and danger that plagued this property might have some basis. What else would she unearth? More information about the house and the man she had killed? Charles Bartlett?

She was curious enough to shine the torchlight on another mouldy box, and she was about to look inside it when there was a thump behind her again, this time followed by an odd sucking of air. She jumped up and swung around, aiming her torch so that its sickly light washed the boarded walls, floated over the boat and settled on the surface of the water.

She saw the inky, oily blackness. The ripples that buffeted the boat. The trail of tiny bubbles breaking on the surface.

Clara trained the torchlight on that spot.

And saw something in the water.

Someone?

Heart pounding, she dropped to her knees and crawled along the jetty. Then, balancing precariously on the edge, she leaned over far enough until her face was just inches above the water. Without the light shining directly on it, the surface of the water was blackly opaque. But the harder she looked, the more she thought that what she was looking at beneath the water was a human figure. A man.

A dead man.

No, that's ridiculous. Why would there be a dead man in the water?

And then the horrible thought occurred to her: this was *the* dead man, the man she had killed. Oswald had moved the body again.

But why? And why here?

These were questions to which she had no answer, but she did have a torch, and she forced herself now to angle the dim beam straight down, penetrating the murk just enough for her to make out the horrible thing beneath.

She gave a strangled gasp. 'Oh Jesus.'

It was a man. Oswald Cattenach. Immersed in the frigid loch water.

His face was as white as the moon; his hair fanning out around his head in fine golden wisps. His eyes were staring straight up, glazed.

Drowned, she thought. *He must have slipped, fallen in and drowned.*

She shifted even closer to the water, staring into those dead eyes.

Dead. He's dead.

She had barely begun experiencing the heady rush of relief when two hands burst upwards, breaking the surface of the water, and clamped around her throat.

4

'We're doing all we can to find your son, and I promise to keep you informed. Yes, you told me about the other drawings. Twice. Email them over to me. Yes, that same email address. Yes, I certainly hope Charles will turn up. Thank you. Goodbye, Mrs Bartlett.'

At the small, rural police station on the edge of Abersky, Adam Lake dropped the phone onto its cradle harder than he intended. He hadn't meant to sound insensitive or impatient, but since the blaze at Boleskine, he'd spoken to the mother of the missing junkie from London many times, and tried to reassure her that the police were doing all they could to locate her son.

Which was true. Adam was new here, and he wanted to make his mark. More than that, though, he wanted to be known for something other than getting attacked on his last job. He still had the scar over his right eye and the slight limp in his left leg. Permanent, he knew. If anything was going to help the other officers not see them, it would be some sort of local breakthrough, right? Something he could make his name over. And the vast house on the banks of Loch Ness had captured not only his curiosity but his suspicion. The only problem was, so far he'd failed to turn up any tangible leads.

He opened the file that had arrived from the insurance company and flicked through its pages. He had highlighted the passages of interest. The 'severe' fire, it was reported, had ignited next to the window in the billiard room. Officially, the cause was listed as 'unknown', but there was an electrical point in the wall there, immediately behind some old curtains. It had been determined that the internal cabling throughout the house was 'inadequate'. The house had been empty and unoccupied. Case closed.

So why did Adam feel so unsure about that conclusion?

Maybe the pictures Mrs Bartlett had mentioned would prove interesting. She had already sent him one batch she'd found in her son's bedside cabinet. Sketches of a sprawling house on a hillside that looked decidedly familiar. Now she'd found another few drawings while turning the mattress in her son's room; symbols of some sort, she said, that meant nothing to her. Probably nothing, but she was going to take a photograph of them and email it over to him.

He was all too conscious of the different sets of pictures relating to this case, and already his curiosity was reaching for the images he had acquired from the tight-lipped Gale Kilgour.

Although he couldn't quite overcome his suspicion that the sharp-eyed businesswoman was holding back on him, he was pleased she had handed over her photographs of the property. Pleased and frankly a little surprised, because the photographs themselves hardly did the place justice. Amateurish, was the word that came to mind. Unprofessional. He hadn't lived long in the village, but somehow those weren't words he readily associated with the prim and upright Gale.

He slid out his desk drawer, took out a brown envelope, and emptied the contents onto his desk. Photographs of Boleskine House rained down. He laid the photographs out in a collage and studied them. Many were marred by blurs, as though the camera lens had a greasy smear. Actually, it was more like a halo of fog. He started rearranging images, placing the ruined shots side by side. Yes, a fog. And in each photo it was in precisely the same place: the terrace doors at the back of the house.

'Lake?'

Adam started, and turned to see Chief Inspector Val Shawcross standing at his right shoulder. She wasn't looking at him; her hard, inquisitive eyes were on the photographs in Adam's hand. Her face betrayed her disapproval.

'Got a minute?'

Before he could answer, Shawcross was striding towards

her office, leaving him to play catch-up. He followed her in. Behind her desk, Shawcross took a seat, without inviting Adam to do the same. He hoped he wasn't about to get his knuckles rapped. He didn't much like his chances.

'I hear from various sources that you've been asking questions about Boleskine House,' she said. 'That you think there might be a connection with the report of the missing person we received.'

He nodded. 'Still no sign of Bartlett, and it's a reasonable bet he was there.'

'And yet the insurance company's investigation report found no sign of rough sleepers.'

That surprised Adam; he wasn't aware that Shawcross had read the report. Was she checking up on his work?

He had met Chief Inspector Shawcross when she was a guest lecturer at Flint House, the rehabilitation centre in Oxfordshire for injured serving police officers. During a break-out session in the library, he had explained that he could no longer handle the pressures of the Met. She told him life was quieter in Abersky, and as luck would have it, a position had become vacant in her force. It was his, if he wanted it.

It was no exaggeration to say that Adam felt that he owed Shawcross. She had given him an opportunity – hell, a new life. He may have lost his confidence, but he had no desire to quit the police force. But whatever loyalty he had to her was being tested now. The criticism in her tone was worrying.

'I'm going to have to insist that you drop your inquiry, Lake.'

There passed a moment's silence. Stunned, in Adam's case.

'Ma'am, people rarely go missing without a reason. Bartlett was a—'

'Junkie,' she cut in, 'who often disappeared on binges. I

wouldn't be surprised if he turns up dead of an OD in a ditch somewhere.'

'With respect, ma'am, my brother was an addict. I know the pattern.'

'Then you'll know that you can't trust an addict, not ever.'

'I know that when you give up on them, they tend to sink. Without hope.'

Shawcross bristled at that. 'According to Bartlett's family, he mentioned coming up here. Well, who's to say that he actually did?'

'We know he asked his sister for money, to buy a place. We know he disappeared around the same time as the fire at Boleskine. We know he had an interest in that house, because he had pictures of it at his parents' place. Sketches. Which implies not just an interest, but an unhealthy obsession, maybe.'

'Any leads placing him in the area?' asked Shawcross.

Adam shook his head. 'Not yet.'

'Then why are you pursuing this?'

'Given his interest, and given that the house was abandoned, it's not a great leap to suggest that he was thinking of buying it. And perhaps he was squatting there?'

'Then why didn't he simply ask the estate agents to show him around?'

Adam shrugged.

'You think Bartlett started the fire?'

'By accident, perhaps. Sure. Maybe he lit a few candles, got high, passed out and—'

'Except no body was found. Did the agents notice any evidence of squatters?'

Good question. Gale had said no, but then that's what the

estate agent would say, isn't it? She wanted the house off her books. In any event, Adam had a nasty feeling that whatever he told his boss was going to fall on deaf ears, which frustrated him. Why did he feel he could have been showing his superior a photograph of Bartlett's blackened corpse and Shawcross would still tell him he was running on empty, had nothing to go on?

'We've made the Missing Persons Bureau aware. It's their problem now.'

'You think it's coincidental that a missing man drew pictures of a house that was partially destroyed in a fire? What's special about Boleskine?'

'Nothing, it's a normal house. At least, it is now.'

Adam's rigid posture betrayed his surprise at how serious his boss was in that moment. She looked troubled. *Perhaps she genuinely thinks there's nothing to go on here. I shouldn't be so cynical,* he thought. But the way she was looking at him . . . he could have sworn that she knew something he did not. Something she was unwilling, perhaps even unable, to share.

'Ma'am?' he said, and Shawcross fixed him with a sour look.

'This is a small community, Lake. A superstitious community that has no wish to resurrect the sadness of times past. The few who remember would prefer they didn't.'

'Few?'

She bowed her head, only for a moment, but the gesture was not lost on Adam. 'This isn't Tower Hamlets. Here in Loch Ness, people report things that can't be reasonably explained, every month; and I'm talking some weird shit, okay? But the people of Abersky learn to forget, become tight-lipped. Seriously. You could go down to the tea rooms next Saturday, ask those old dears if they remember all that has happened at

Boleskine, and I'd wager you'd see only a few hands in the air. In Abersky, there's a fine line between the infamous and the unremembered. Some villages make what they can from that sort of attention. And we – you and me, Lake – we're walking that line right now.'

He hadn't seen her like this before. She was usually a forthright and commanding woman. Right now, she reminded him of a mother trying to keep her child out of the woods with tales of the bogeyman.

'What are you saying?' he asked. 'Whatever it is, I'd prefer to hear it straight.'

'Your questions are opening old wounds. You must understand, a tragedy occurred in that house, a terrible tragedy that rocked this whole community to its core. Boleskine had a different name back then, thirty years ago. It was known as the Black Lodge. Jeff Ramsay at the paper, he gave it that name. The first suicide was bad enough. After the second, the council hired a PR company to help wash away the stain. Business was drying up, you see. Death, tragedy, they don't attract tourists. At least, not the desirable sort. Boleskine became notorious. We had all sorts of people going up there, wanting to take pictures, poke about.'

'What the hell happened there?'

'The owner, Major General Cornelius Coughlan, took his own life. And then his wife did the same.'

'How? Why?'

'You don't want to know.' Shawcross looked away for a moment, and an expression of sadness crossed her face. Then she went on: 'The house sat empty for thirty years, until it was bought by the owners of the Mortimer supermarket group. They live in Spain now and had managed it remotely, until the fire. They even let it out for a period, which was an achievement of sorts: to move on from all the unpleasantness, the morbid fascination, which wasn't easy. As of last year, there were a few websites about Boleskine, repeating the old legends.'

'Yes, I understand, ma'am, but—'

'People learned to forget, the curiosity seekers went away, the tourists came back. And that's how we need it to stay. And believe me, you do *not* want what happened in that house to be in your head. So drop it, Adam. Do I make myself clear?'

'Ma'am, there's nothing dangerous about the house. It's just bricks and—'

'*Do I make myself clear?*'

'Yes, ma'am.' He couldn't believe the striking intensity on her face, or the volume of those last words.

Seconds later, he was out of her office, pulling the door closed behind him. Two of his colleagues were passing as he did so, and amusement was written all over their faces. One of them eyed the scar over his right eye.

Adam ignored them.

Returning to his desk, he again studied the photographs laid out there, the strange fog obscuring the terrace doors. *What could that be?* he asked himself. *And why is the fog on every photograph?*

He gathered up the photos and was just sliding them back into the envelope when a *ping* from his computer announced the arrival of a new email. He clicked it open.

Dear PC Lake,

Please find attached the photographs I took of Charles's drawings. I have no idea what they mean.

My boy was in a bad way, but he was a good person. A caring person. He was committed to turning his life around. Please believe that.

Thank you,

Diana Bartlett

Adam opened the attached file and an image filled the screen.

'What the hell?'

Surrendering to his curiosity that usually, in some way, landed him in trouble, he clicked through the other images in the set. The shots weren't quite in focus, but the black symbols crudely drawn on the scraps of paper were clear enough. Some looked like signs of the zodiac; the others were a mystery. Overlapping triangles framed within circles, letters arranged in abstract patterns, a five-pointed star within a circle.

He didn't recognise the symbols, and he didn't know where to begin trying to decipher them. But he did think of a man who might be able to help.

It was a long shot, would probably lead to nothing, but still . . .

He glanced up and across at Shawcross in her office.

Adam had always worked best when acting on his instincts; and right now, his instincts were telling him that he needed to find out the significance of these foreboding symbols.

Even if that meant disobeying orders.

5

Inside the boathouse on the Boleskine estate, Oswald Cattenach heaved a colossal gasp as he thrust upwards and his head and shoulders broke the surface of the water.

Clara would have cried out then, but the powerful hands clamped around her throat made that impossible. She clawed at them frantically, ripped at him with her nails.

Suddenly, he let go. And she toppled backwards, her head cracking on the floorboards.

For a moment, the only sound was that of the waves slapping against the jetty.

Before she could even register the pain, he was looming over her, a great black figure – and then she wasn't in the boathouse, she was in a London flat, and it was Karl over her, holding her down, his face twisted with hatred, and he was going to—

The face above wasn't twisted. It wasn't anything. It was totally blank.

It was Oswald's.

That was no safer. He was insane. Despicable. He was going to kill her.

With that thought, she did scream, and thrash wildly as he bent closer. A flailing arm caught him full in the face. He recoiled, and she scrambled back, grabbing the torch, brandishing it as a weapon.

'Clara?' said Oswald, and he sounded unsure.

She turned the light on him. With his matted blond hair

hanging in his eyes, Oswald had a wild look, like a man jolted from a nightmare. Panting, he stared at her. His eyes weren't blank now, but confused.

The two stayed that way for a long moment, a brittle tension between them, until finally the storm clouds blew out of Oswald's face and the muscles that roped his lean body relaxed; first his neck, then his shoulders. His eyes widened, at last clear and comprehending.

'You came back?' he said, almost a whisper. 'You came back.'

He reached for her, but she scuttled back. Reached for the workbench and stood. Swayed. Staggered.

'Clara? Clara!'

The last thing she felt as her eyes closed and blackness enveloped her was Oswald Cattenach's arms around her.

*

A chess set swam into vague focus when Clara opened her eyes. Then a stack of old books. Then a dark figure climbing out of the floor.

A creature ascending from hell.

Dimly, she registered that she ought to do something about the demon. Like run. But her head was hazy and aching, and she was so tired, and her eyes were already closing . . .

*

'Clara, wake up!'

A voice in the night. She heard it, but from a distance. She was trying to focus on what the doctor was telling her at the hospital. *What happened to my baby?*

She heard a soft keening. The baby – was it crying?

'Clara, it's okay. You hit your head, but you're okay.'

Recognition pierced the haze. She knew that voice. She had

heard it before. It was cultured. Concerned. Yet there was a hoarse edge to it.

'You just need to open your eyes. *Open your eyes, Clara.*'

Her eyes snapped open. She blinked as the room swam into focus. She remembered now: she was in the library, sitting on a high-backed armchair beside the fireplace. She looked about. A fire was crackling in the grate. Above it was the grotesque painting of a muscular man with the head of a bull. Off to the left, the chess set was in position. And Oswald was perched on a coffee table at her side.

No demon of hell rising, though. Just how hard had she hit her head?

That appeared to be the question on Oswald's mind, as he fired questions at her:

'Can you turn your head okay? No pain in your back? Your neck?'

'Um ... no, I don't think so,' she said. She winced as she felt the back of her head, the lump there.

'Here.' Oswald handed her a chilled glass of water and popped three white tablets out of a blister pack. He held them out to her, but she took the pack instead and squinted at the writing on it. *Co-codamol.*

'It's just a painkiller,' he said. 'It'll help the headache.'

She badly needed to help the headache. And she knew co-codamol. She'd been prescribed it in the hospital. She took the tablets from him and swallowed them with gulps of water.

He took the empty glass from her and set it on the table. Then he came around the chair and stood before her. All at once she remembered that he had been clad in black the last time she'd seen him – a wetsuit. Now he had on grey jeans and a white shirt, the two top buttons undone. Oswald waited for her to meet his gaze – the anxiety and fear building up in her, would she ever stop feeling unsettled by those crystalline eyes? – and then he said with gravity, 'I'm sorry.'

She'd have stood then, if she thought the room would hold steady. Faced him on the level. As it was, with her pounding head and the sickly churning in her stomach, she had to be satisfied with glaring up at him and snapping:

'You're sorry? What the hell were you thinking? You attacked me!'

'Truly, Clara, I didn't mean to startle you. You've heard, surely, how you're not supposed to shock a person awake when they're sleepwalking? That they can feel threatened and lash out? Well, what happened in the boathouse was something similar.'

'You were under the water; you weren't asleep!'

'Meditating,' he replied. 'You came earlier than I expected. When you found me, I was in a heightened state of relaxation. Mental detachment.'

Her anger dissipated a little, mixing with bewilderment, and, she had to admit, some curiosity.

'You meditate *underwater*?'

He nodded. 'Frequently. I appreciate it must have looked bizarre. Perhaps even a little crazy. But for me, there is no deeper, more intense relaxation than to hear nothing but your own thoughts, to see nothing but darkness. You understand? There can be no greater revelation than to see yourself as you truly are.'

She didn't understand, and she didn't know what she had expected when she came here, but not this.

'I'm not going to harm you,' he said, taking a step closer. Light was streaming in through the terrace doors behind him. She felt a chill as his shadow dropped over her.

'Who are you?'

'Someone who is changing your life for the better.'

'Oh, please, spare me the—'

He actually looked injured. 'You doubt my sincerity?'

'You think?' She gave him a withering look. 'The body – that was you putting a gun to my head, yeah? To get my attention. Well, you have it. So cut the bullshit. What. Do. You. Want?'

Oswald moved to the fireplace. He used a poker to prod a log into place. Her eyes followed his every move. That poker was steel. Sharp.

But he laid the poker back on the hearth, before dusting off his hands and turning to her. 'Your cynicism is understandable, Miss Jones,' he said. 'But when our business in this house is concluded, you'll thank me. For my courage. For the new life you'll have, with your Guardian Angel at your side.'

She squirmed in the armchair; this was New Age bollocks on a whole new level. Just then, her eye caught on the painting behind him: the minotaur cradling a suckling child. God, it turned her stomach.

'Ba'al', he said suddenly and, Clara thought, with an almost whispered reverence. 'An ancient Canaan god represented by the symbol of the bull – the symbol of fertility.'

She felt those brilliant eyes searching her face, and turned away from the picture, partly curious, despite herself, but mostly unsettled. These days, the word fertility only had the effect of dragging her spirits lower.

Abruptly, he got to the question he had been waiting to ask. 'You told no one you were coming?'

She nodded.

'Good. I will permit you to leave the confines of the house

during the day, if you wish to walk in the garden or the forest behind the house.'

The subtext was glittering; she understood. She was to remain in the shadows, maintain an elusive façade.

Fine. Wasn't that something she was accomplished at?

Normally yes, but this was different to hiding from Karl. More oppressive. Intimidating.

'If you do venture out,' he added, 'then I insist you wear your hooded jacket. I think you already have one?'

She nodded grimly as her stomach sank because she could still smell the smoke on that jacket, hadn't been able to wear it since the night of her arson attack; and now, apparently, it was to be refashioned as her unique prison uniform. The idea would have struck her as ironic if it weren't so profoundly degrading. A punishment in itself.

'Stay away from the village until I say otherwise. Got it? No one must know you are here.'

'Oh, come on, I'm bound to be seen by someone.'

A cold glint from Oswald.

'I mean, everyone knows this house. There are websites about it. Someone's going to come here at some point.'

'Then I'll make them leave.'

'Is it that simple? I mean, Murdoch's bound to speculate. Remember? The butcher under my flat?'

'Grim-looking bastard?'

'Terrible gossip. He does home visits all over the area. Now if he should see me then—'

On Oswald's lips suddenly, a tiny morbid smile. 'We take care of him. Scare him off.'

Clara reeled. 'Are you for real? He's a butcher, so maybe you think he hasn't got much of a brain on his shoulders. But that man knows everyone around here. They depend on him for their Sunday roasts, and he knows their kids' names. Get it? They trust him. And he hears everything. Day in, day out. He hears it all! In a small community like this, that means something, Oswald. It means something. You don't mess with someone like Murdoch. I never liked him, particularly. But I respect him. Everyone here does.'

Oswald stiffened. 'If he sees you, I'll deal with him.'

Clara looked grave. 'Don't you think you've done enough?'

Wordlessly, he stared at her.

'If I am recognised then what do I say?'

'As we discussed, you're my lodge manager.'

She summoned some valour. 'Well, if you insist on calling it a job – pay me.'

Their eyes met, her statement suspended in the air.

'Fine, I'll give you whatever Gale was paying. Cash.'

It was an effort for her not to look surprised.

He shrugged. 'To live the lie you have to believe it, right?'

A part of her could actually see the logic in that, just about; even though it disturbed her deeply. For twelve months she had been living a lie, when really all she had done was run and hide. If she had been stronger, braver, she would have faced her demons, banished them. And part of her still believed, hoped, that might one day be possible.

If only, somehow, she could survive this.

'Think you can manage it?' he asked. 'The house, the anonymity?'

Her eyes roamed the ill-lit room, the stacks of old books, the painting of the human body with the bull's head, and a tingle of displeasure ran down her spine.

Unsure, but trying, she nodded and said, 'I can be discreet.'

Her eyes locked with his. 'But you mustn't tell anyone about—'

'Your guilty little secret? Of course not. That is our special arrangement, Clara. Now then,' he turned away from her, 'you were curious about the house, I believe?'

She nodded reluctantly.

'I acquired it to use as my temple. A secluded retreat for intense meditation. I draw power from meditation, Clara.'

'Meditation on what?'

'I know that you resent me,' he said evasively. 'I know that you hate me, that there's nothing you want more than for me to vanish and for you to be free; and you know what? I respect that. Your *will* is strong, Clara. And that's vital. It's the human will that nourishes the soul.'

'Yeah? Well, it's my *will* to leave.'

For a few disorientating moments, she thought she had said those words in her head, because Oswald didn't so much as blink.

'I mean it. I want to leave, just as soon as I can.'

Oswald walked to the terrace doors. He stood there, staring out. At the loch, perhaps, or the burial ground.

'You may leave, if that's what you truly want. But only when my business here is concluded.'

'Your business?' She leaned forwards in her chair. 'What business?'

He turned to her, a dark silhouette against the rays of the setting sun. 'Question. Have you ever been rock climbing?'

'What?'

'Please, just answer.'

She shook her head. 'No, I've never been rock climbing.'

'The idea doesn't excite you?'

'Why should it?'

'To crush the ground beneath your feet,' he said with profound feeling. 'To pound your doubts, your fears, into the earth. To climb higher than anyone else – and be above it all. Until you've climbed, you've never known the hunger, the torment, the anguish.'

'I know anguish,' Clara said harshly. 'Why would I want more?'

'Because you've never climbed high enough. Just think how high we could climb, with power and passion. Together.'

She looked away. Appalled. With herself as much as him, for there was no pretending his words weren't stirring something in her. To feel powerful – when had she last felt that way?

'Climbing is like painting, Clara.' His voice trembled with such fervent, sincere passion he may as well have been giving a sermon from a pulpit. 'It doesn't matter how gifted you are, you can always find ways to challenge yourself. To evolve and grow. These passions fuel the artist, the climber. They will fuel us.'

He came to her then, and knelt before the chair, taking her hand. 'If you're stranded on the side of a mountain and it looks like you're certain to fall, do you look down?'

'Why would I? Why would anyone? To look down would be to contemplate death.'

'You don't think it's important to think about dying?'

'I'm not dying.'

His eyes glittered. 'We're all dying, Clara, some more quickly than others.'

Whatever interest she'd been feeling was quashed by a dread as hot and uncomfortable as his calloused hand gripping hers. Where was he going with this?

'Call me selfish, but when the time comes, I'd rather not be surprised by my own demise. Being diagnosed with a terminal disease? That's sad, sure. But accepting the circumstances of that fate? Giving in to the manner of your demise? That's tragic.'

She wrenched her hand away – saw the flames dancing on the hearth, the chess set right where the body had lain.

'I don't see what the end of your life has to do with my being here,' she said.

Oswald cupped a hand under her chin and turned her head so that their eyes locked.

'The end of my life?' he said. 'Clara, it has *everything* to do with you being here.'

6

The semi-detached cottage in which Gale Kilgour lived with Inghean was hardly the for ever home she had dreamed about when she stood on the shores of Loch Ness and whispered 'I do' to the man who would later run out on her. For one thing, the cottage was too cramped for her taste; for another, it always seemed to need something doing, especially when business was slow. Upkeep. Like the paint peeling around the windows, like the rising damp in the back bedroom.

It was the damp that Gale was attempting to cover with a special paint she'd picked up in the village when she heard Inghean's excited voice calling from the front room.

'Ma, Ma, come see.'

'I'm busy, Inghean,' she called, hastily dabbing at a patch of black mould with her brush. She'd already made a botch of the job once by dripping paint on the floor. Because she was distracted. Only that morning an email from her accountant had arrived in her inbox, kindly informing her that her tax bill would soon be due for payment. Thankfully, Gale would be able to pay it, now the commission had come through from the sale of Boleskine House. Still, with the market as it was, how would she pay the next bill, and the next?

'Ma, come see!'

'I said, I'm busy.'

'But it's the sky!'

'What about the sky?' Gale said, and at last she did put down her brush and go into the front room. Inghean had the window open and was leaning out.

'Careful, love, or you'll . . .'

Gale stopped short, staring past her daughter at the view through the window.

'Oh, goodness,' she whispered, slipping her hand into her daughter's and holding on tight. 'What on earth is that?'

*

In the heart of the village, inside Celtic Crafts, Aggie Blackwood turned the sign on the door to 'closed'. What was the point in staying open all afternoon with no customers to serve?

She gathered up her belongings, pulled on her black padded jacket with the wide hood, and was just stepping out of the door when she froze.

The sky!

What she was looking at gave her a disturbing sense of impending trouble here in Abersky; an ominous prescience that drew the threatening thoughts that had always lain dormant in her to the surface of her consciousness.

And for some reason she couldn't quite put her finger on, Aggie was bound to wonder whether this phenomenon had anything to do with the well-spoken stranger who had come into her shop the other day, marvelling with such wide-eyed wonder at the ornate silver-framed mirrors in her window. He had bought those mirrors, all three of them, which had surprised her, because she had imagined selling them to a collector, an elderly, discerning gentleman perhaps; not a young, powerful man like . . .

What was his name?

It escaped her. Funny. She was normally so good with names. She remembered writing him out a receipt – he had been explicit about getting one – but she couldn't remember much else about their conversation. Something about Gale Kilgour's eccentric daughter? Perhaps. Something else, too; about being somewhere on a particular day. High up. A holy place?

The memory was hazy; it barely seemed real, more like a dream. But what she was staring at now could not be denied. This was as real as the hefty, leather-bound Bible she kept open next to the cash register. Making the sign of the cross, Aggie stared up at the heavens and began reciting verses from Matthew 16:

'*You know how to interpret the appearance of the sky, but you cannot interpret the signs of the times . . .*'

*

'Care to explain what this is, Lake?'

In the Abersky police station, Chief Inspector Val Shawcross stood over Adam's desk, furiously brandishing an article from the *Inverness Courier* in his face.

'For Christ's sake, I asked you to keep this out of the public eye, not blazing in headlights!'

Lake had been scanning his emails when Shawcross jolted him from his thoughts. Now, seeing the lurid headline, he hesitated to answer. He hadn't spoken with the press. Then he remembered the missing man's mother, her dissatisfaction with the pace of the investigation. She must have gone to the paper; but that wasn't his fault.

'I'll speak to the editor,' he said. 'Get them to see that this sort of coverage isn't exactly helpful.'

'Do that,' Shawcross instructed, before turning and striding to her office.

Lake flushed with anger and determination.

Oh, he'd speak with an editor, all right. A former editor. Someone who had covered the Boleskine suicides thirty years ago. Someone intimately familiar with the village and its people – and its secrets.

At that moment, turning to the window, Lake noticed what Gale and Aggie had already seen.

The sky over the village, over Loch Ness, was slowly darkening, he noticed. He'd seen NASA pictures of the Martian sky, and this was very similar; an eerie reddish-brown colour. Strange.

In fact, he had never seen the Highlands sky look anything like it before.

*

In his cottage on the north side of the loch, Jeff Ramsay sat in his favourite overstuffed armchair, one marbled hand gripping his third coffee of the day, the other stroking his black Labrador, whose head rested heavily on his knee. He was reading the newspaper. *His* newspaper, once.

It was getting on for seven years now since he had hung up his journalist's hat, and though he missed the business – the liquid lunches and the rush and fun of it all, the deadlines – he didn't miss what the business had become. Some of the old hacks he'd stayed in touch with only ever seemed to moan these days about how the industry was struggling, which was just another way of saying it was dying on its arse. If the cutbacks were as bad as Jeff had heard, then he felt sorry for any youngster dreaming of a rewarding career in journalism. The *Inverness Courier* wasn't just online now; apparently, you could download it and swipe through its stories on one of those flashy new tablets. His daughter, Katie, had offered to buy him one, even to get him a subscription if he wanted it, and that was generous of her; but the truth was, Jeff would have preferred it if Katie called around more often. He wanted that a lot more than he did an iPad. And besides, he had no interest in reading his newspaper on a screen.

He felt peaceful as he contemplated another day of retirement. After lunch, he might go out and tackle the weeds that were sprouting through the cracks in the driveway, but there was no rush. He wasn't doing anything until he'd finished the newspaper.

He was about to turn to page four when his gaze snagged on the window. When he'd sat down, the sky had been clear and bright and blue. Cloudless. But now, the sky was thick with clouds, teeming with them, and those clouds were tainted with a foreboding reddish-brown hue. Even the murky waters beneath were bathed in a red glow.

Jeff didn't like to entertain superstitions; not like others in the village, like Aggie Blackwood, who were likely to interpret this reddening sky as some sort of apocalyptic omen. Not likely.

A freak weather phenomenon, that was all it was. Dust and sands from a distant desert thrown up by a storm and blown into the country on a hurricane.

Something like that had been the cause thirty years ago, when the sky over Abersky had turned red and freakishly dark at midday; and something like that would be the cause now.

That was what Jeff was telling himself as he turned to page four of his newspaper – and froze, struggling to process the headline screaming at him:

DETECTIVES SEARCH FOR MISSING
MAN WHO HAD 'OBSESSION WITH THE
BLACK LODGE OF LOCH NESS'

Abersky police are searching for a man described as being at risk and possibly danger-ous because of his drug addiction and mental health issues.

Charles Bartlett, a poet from London who disappeared eight weeks ago, was in the area pursuing his interest in occult rituals, it is claimed.

Diana Bartlett, the missing man's mother, said her son was visiting Loch Ness to research Boleskine House, which has a reputation for paranormal activity, and which thirty years ago was the location of several brutal suicides.

The Grade I-listed building was abandoned for many years, during which time it was reportedly used for animal sacrifices and other satanic activities. Seven weeks ago, the house

was damaged in a fire and was subsequently
sold to an unknown buyer.
    Diana Bartlett is appealing for anyone with
any information to contact the Abersky police.

Jeff cast another look out of the window, at the eerie red-dish-brown sky, and took a couple of deep breaths. It was a few seconds before he could look again at the grim headline that was dredging up memories he had long since forced down.

Memories of the suicides, which his paper had covered. Memories of all the horrendous acts that had followed shortly afterwards.

As he closed his newspaper, Jeff Ramsay wasn't peaceful any more; he was in turmoil as he whispered to himself words that every old-time resident of Abersky would tremble to hear:

'It's happening again. God have mercy on us all; it's happening again.'

7

At Boleskine House, Oswald was leading Clara along the main hallway, away from the library, but as they passed the framed painting of the plummeting waterfall, Clara stopped. There was something so powerfully elemental about the artwork, it seemed to speak directly to her consciousness.

'Who's this supposed to be?' she asked, pointing to the hooded figure surveying the pounding water from on high.

Oswald didn't reply; he was already further down the corridor and opening a door.

'Come,' he said. 'This is your room.'

Clara walked to him, but then stopped again, on the threshold. A sour reek assaulted her.

'You don't like it? Larger than your old place, right?'

'It's horrible.'

He looked wounded. She saw that the wild man with bedraggled hair who had lunged at her from the water was completely absent now. The person who had taken his place was the same darkly charismatic artist who had bought the house she so badly needed to sell.

An artist who genuinely adores this place, she thought.

His midnight eyes were already roaming the bedroom in defiance of her judgement. She had to admit that it was impressively large, but easily spoiled by the brown stains on the ceiling and the odour of cat urine emanating from the tartan carpet. The single window looked out over the grounds sloping down to the burial ground, and, beyond that, Loch Ness. But right then it wasn't the water that drew her eye. What did was the darkening sky, the rusty reddish light that was tainting the afternoon.

Oswald saw the bizarre red glow too, and he drew in a breath and whispered reverently, 'It's beginning already.'

'What is?' Clara asked with bewilderment.

Insane, she thought, not for the first time in his company. What they were looking at was an odd weather phenomenon, nothing more; Clara felt sure about that because she suddenly remembered a similar phenomenon happening in London, a few years back; then it had gone dark suddenly in the middle of the afternoon, with street lamps blinking on and off under a weird red sky. It was all because of strong winds blowing in dust from elsewhere, she remembered. But she saw little point in arguing about that now.

'Look,' she said, 'is there another room I could have?'

She was relieved when Oswald blinked and snapped out of his reverie, but hardly reassured by his answer. 'This room will suit you fine.'

Clara gestured, up to the nearest patch of mould on the ceiling.

'I'll sort it,' Oswald said, and there was an edge of impatience in his voice. 'I want you to feel comfortable here, Clara. I need you at your best. Vigilant.'

'Why?'

'Sit down,' he said, gesturing to the rickety-looking bed. She blanched, and seeing that he quickly added, 'I'm not going to harm you. You're tired, and hurt. Sit.'

The late November wind moaned beyond the window as, slowly, Clara sat down on the edge of the bed. Her pulse was thudding in her ears as Oswald came to sit beside her. He left a sizeable gap between them, but still, she felt vulnerable, alone with him here.

As if reading her mind, Oswald said again, not unkindly, 'I'm not going to hurt you.'

She stared at him. Took in his eyes, wide with sincerity.

'You want to know why you're here,' he said. 'Why I need you.'

She nodded.

'Well,' he said, and his tone was all business. 'Someone will need to take care of this house when I'm not here. When I'm gone, Boleskine will pass to you.'

She supposed that made sense; he had employed her as lodge manager, after all. She would manage the estate in his absence.

'You're going somewhere?'

A look of forlorn fragility formed on his face, but it vanished in an instant. 'Clara,' he said softly, 'I'm dying.'

There was a long silence as she processed what he had said. Deliberating, calculating.

'Don't look so cynical,' he said. 'I'm not that good a liar. Now, I ask you again: if you're stranded on the side of a mountain, if it looks like you're certain to fall, do you look down? Do you contemplate death?'

She was shaking her head. 'You look fine to me. Healthy. So, what's meant to be wrong with you?'

'I'm suffering from a high-grade glioma.'

'Cancer?'

'Malignant.'

She didn't know how to respond to that, because she didn't think that she believed him. This was the man who'd essentially blackmailed her to come here: *if you leave, I will tell the police . . . I'll tell everyone what you did and make you pay.* It wasn't as if she was inclined to take him at his word.

'Don't be sorry,' he said, misreading her doubt as sympathy. 'The tumour is too deeply embedded in the brain for anything to be done, and I'm not afraid. Death is a natural process that is rarely considered. Death is merely misunderstood.'

He smiled as he said this, but Clara didn't.

'It may be hard for you to understand, but there's a peculiar peace that comes from finally facing the end. As of this moment, I'm living to die. I have six, maybe seven, months before it becomes ever harder for me to move, to swallow, to breathe. Before I lose every scrap of dignity. So, I need your help.'

His face was lit with a fierce radiance. The radiance of a dying man?

'You and I, Clara, we have business to carry out. Afterwards, the house will pass to you.'

'What?' she said sharply.

'Boleskine will be yours,' he said, as if this were the most obvious, reasonable declaration.

Pain throbbed in Clara's temples. She couldn't keep up with all this – he was dying? He was giving her this house? It was too much. Inconceivable.

'Why the hell would you do that?' she said.

'Your reward,' Oswald said. 'For helping me.'

She didn't like the way he was smiling at her. 'Help you how exactly?' she said.

Oswald stood then and moved thoughtfully to the window – that view of the dark waters seemed to hold a magnetic attraction for him. When he spoke again, he sounded so, so far away.

'Five years ago, in London, I had a neighbour. Mrs Caraway. Dead now, but when I knew her she was a widow. Lived alone. Truly, I was very fond of the old lady. She was good enough to feed my fish when I was away. Indeed, she showed me the deepest loyalty. And during her hour of utmost need, she asked me to repay that loyalty.'

Clara had a bad feeling about where this was going. 'Oswald—'

'Maybe . . . she had taken too many painkillers, or perhaps her dementia had blurred her awareness to such an extent that she no longer knew what she wanted. But that desperate, pleading expression as I wrapped the bag around her head left me in no doubt at all that I was doing the right thing. Ending her agony.'

A strangled gasp escaped Clara's lips. Oswald turned to face her, and one brow arched in question.

'Why do you look so horrified? Mrs Caraway was terribly ill by then. Desperate and lonely. Sick with metastasised throat cancer, severe arthritis, peripheral neuropathy and atrial fibrillation. But in one glorious instant, thanks to *my* intervention, the years of pain she was facing were completely obliterated, and she was set free.'

Clara stared at him, aghast.

'It was a kindness. Mrs Caraway made her final exit with dignity. After my diagnosis, I decided I wanted the same. But it didn't matter which doctors I consulted, they only frowned, shook their heads, looked at me with the most useless, indulgent sympathy. I was beginning to wonder if I'd ever succeed . . . until I saw what you did to this house. The sheer exhilaration of your human will. That's why I've come to you.'

Oh God, she thought. *Oh God.*

He wants me to help him die.

8

'Why are you looking at me like I'm a monster?' asked Oswald, frowning, as he watched Clara erupt off the bed and back away, until she collided with the door.

'Because it's a monstrous suggestion!' she shot back.

Whatever he called it – a kindness, putting him out of his misery, setting him free – he was talking about *ending a life*, something that was completely beyond Clara's comprehension. Every atom in her body recoiled from the thought. *Death comes when it comes.* That was what her foster father used to tell her.

'When the time comes,' Oswald said, 'you will give me a good death.'

'No, Oswald. The answer is no.'

'But this is *my personal will*. And the most powerful forces of the universe will combine to hold me to it. When I am greeted by the gods, it will be at a time of *my* choosing, on my terms. That is why I brought you here, Clara. I need you to help me go. I need *you* . . . to kill for me.'

'I could never take a life!'

'You already have,' he said. 'The blaze you set alight here killed an innocent man.'

Guilt slammed into her, and shame, and remorse. *Death comes when it comes.* But she had brought death to that poor man.

Her legs wouldn't hold her. She staggered to the bed and slumped down, her head in her hands.

She heard Oswald moving nearer. 'Make courage your armour and help me,' he said. 'In return, I offer you the opportunity to discover your true will. Information, guidance, fellowship.'

He could have added to that list 'freedom from punishment for killing an innocent man'; but even if he had said it, there was no guarantee that Clara could bank on the promise.

She felt his hand on her shoulder. 'I know how frightened you must be. But sometimes fear is the worst reason to run.

Sometimes fear helps you find who you are, the person you're supposed to be.'

'Oswald, please.' She looked up at him, feeling the corners of her mouth quivering. 'Whatever you have in mind, just stop this.'

'Don't you think I was afraid when I helped Mrs Caraway to die? I was terrified! That was when I stopped merely advocating assisted suicides and began facilitating them.'

What happened, Oswald? When you killed that old woman. Did you get a taste for it?

That was the thought, the abysmal thought, on a loop in Clara's mind.

She didn't want to ask, but she had to: 'There were more?'

'I have set four people free.'

Insane. Capable of anything. Oh God.

'Oswald, please, I don't feel well.' It was no lie. Those painkillers he'd given her couldn't touch the agony – how had she ended up here, with him? This was worse than being with Karl . . .

No. It wasn't.

'Why do you need *me* to help you?' she said, desperately seeking a get-out clause. 'Why not just end your life now, while you can, if that's what you want?'

'Because it's not my time,' he said, sitting beside her on the bed. 'I still have important work to perform here at Boleskine House. I have come here out of gratitude and regret, to meditate on the past, present and future.'

'But why here?' For the life of her, Clara couldn't think of a house more decrepit and depressing in which to see out one's days. 'What's special about *this* house?'

'You're perceptive. I struggle to believe that you don't feel the magic of this house. This property is sacred, Clara; its fabric is soaked with the blood of mystics. I have spent months, years, searching for the secrets of higher wisdom, to prepare for death. Can you understand? By preparing for your demise, you can confront it. Make peace with it. The house is part of that; the house chose me . . . like it chose you.' His eyes bored into hers, but Clara averted her gaze.

'My last wish is to be at peace with the end that is coming. To do that, what I need is calm and concentration. Enlightenment. And you're going to help me, right to the end.'

Hot tears were coursing down Clara's cheeks, and she wrapped her arms around herself, trying to hold herself together.

'If you knew that you would suffer an agonising, drawn-out death, wouldn't you want the same?' Oswald said.

She pictured herself lying in a hospital bed and wasting away, painfully and excruciatingly slowly. In a very vague and distant sense, she could see where he was coming from. But wanting an end for herself was very far from agreeing to end someone else's life. That was crossing a red line of immorality. It was horrible. Inconceivable. Who was he to ask that of her? She didn't know him; she certainly didn't respect him. Why on earth should she help him?

'I won't do it,' she told him. 'I'll have no part in it.'

'You *will* help me,' he said, and the threat in his tone was unmistakable. He raised a hand and pointed. 'See? From this room, you have a perfect view of the mort house.'

He was right; she could just make out the slanting slate roof that covered her shame. One glance was all it took to unleash memories: striking the match; the sense of liberation, that she was protecting herself, her new life she had built for herself. But then the surging fear of being found out, and the awful certainty that someone was dead, a life extinguished, because of her.

Now she knew why Oswald had chosen this room for her, why the window had no curtains. He wanted her to see what she had done every day. To remind her. What was in that mort house was the secret that made them each other's protectors. Conspirators.

'I'd hate to tell anyone what's hidden down there, or about what you did, Clara,' he said. 'But I can be so terribly loose-lipped sometimes. However, once you do as I say, I'll make sure that dirty little mess you created goes away.'

Again, she contemplated the mort house. The bed creaked as Oswald stood up. He crossed the room to stand before a mirror over on the wall and regarded himself. Then he locked gazes with Clara through the reflection.

'My work requires scrupulous preparation. You will observe my rituals,' he said. 'You will ensure I bathe daily and fast weekly. You will ensure that I abstain from drinking alcohol. All of this is essential, or else I will be deemed unworthy.'

'Unworthy to whom?'

There was a pause.

'Oswald, unworthy to whom?' she asked again. Her mind flashed to the bald, cruel-looking man she'd seen in the faded newspaper clippings; the man posing next to the bizarre altar. 'Is this some sort of religious thing?'

Oswald turned from the mirror. 'Do you know what a living funeral is, Clara?'

'It sounds like a contradiction in terms.'

'A living funeral is a joyous celebration of life. A chance for people to say goodbye. And mine is in a fortnight. You look surprised, but I'm telling you the truth. In two short weeks, a few people will be coming here from London and staying for a day or so. Arrangements will need to be made. I will give you instructions; you will carry them out.'

Clara stared, saying nothing. His face darkened.

'You're committed now, Clara. You will endure. And when the time comes, you will grant me a good death, I guarantee it. You know,' he added heavily, 'you did an awful thing here.'

A horrendous thing, she knew. 'I never meant to harm anyone.'

'I meant the house. You wounded it.'

She stared at him and saw her own trepidation on his face. 'So?' she asked.

'So, for your own safety, treat Boleskine with respect,' he answered, moving to the doorway where he halted for a moment, grim and forbidding. 'Boleskine has been known to exact retribution.'

With that, he pulled the door shut behind him. Seconds later, Clara heard a key scrape in the lock, then nothing; only the sound of his footsteps slowly retreating down the hallway.

9

Clara dreamed she was stranded on a tiny island in the middle of the vast, murky loch, enveloped by a cold drifting mist. There was a boat passing, one of the vessels that took the tourists from Inverness to Fort Augustus to hear the legend of Nessie, but no one on that boat responded when she waved at them. Even when she shouted for help, the boat didn't turn around. Then, on the low wind, words that made no sense: *'You hear me, you little bastards? Get the hell away from my property!'*

Suddenly, her eyes were open, fixed on the window in her room, and she realised that it was morning now and the voice of her dream belonged to Oswald.

Curious, she got out of bed and went to the window.

What? Has he lost his mind?

Oswald was at the bottom of the garden, standing adjacent to the roadside fence. He looked the part of a landowner, in his black cap and quilted green jacket, and he was acting the part too, yelling roughly at some kids who'd apparently trespassed onto the estate. No, not yelling; ranting.

'I said, get away!' he bellowed.

And as Clara watched in horror, he raised the shotgun at his side and pointed it directly at the two little boys.

'No!' She hammered on the window. 'Oswald, stop!'

His face was contorted with such unfiltered anger, she was sure he would pull the trigger.

She had to draw his attention somehow, but the window latch wouldn't move. Lurching towards the door, she cried out in frustration as she remembered that it too was locked.

Frantically, Clara did a circuit of the room, but she saw nothing obvious that would help.

Outside, one of the boys cried out.

No time!

She snatched up one of her high-heeled shoes from the floor and hurled it at the window. But it only bounced off the glass, ricocheting back at her.

Again! Try again!

To break the glass, she needed a different approach. Knowing there was an acute chance she was about to slash her hand to pieces, she stripped the pillow of its cotton case and heavily bandaged her right hand and wrist.

Outside, Oswald was advancing on the kids, who were huddled against the fence. Clara expected a shotgun blast at any second.

Picking up the shoe, she attacked the window pane with all her strength. Cracks spider-webbed across the glass.

Break, goddam you! For Christ's sake, don't let anyone else be harmed because of me.

In that instant, a searing hot pain announced itself in the palm of her right hand, and there was a loud crack as the shoe's heel punched a jagged hole in the glass. She quickly bashed away the surrounding glass and then thrust her head out into the cold morning air and yelled as loud as she'd ever yelled in her life:

'Oswald, *no*! For God's sake, put the gun *down*!'

At the bottom of the garden, Oswald's whole body jolted, and he turned immediately to face her. Even from this distance, she could see the dreamy, flat expression on his face. It cleared like clouds blown away on an easterly wind. He looked at the boys, then at her, and lowered the gun.

Seconds later, when the boys had run off, Oswald began striding purposefully towards the house. Towards Clara.

*

'What? Don't look at me that way. I was just frightening them; the gun wasn't even loaded.'

Her eyes dark-ringed, her hair a tangled mess, Clara was sitting at the kitchen table, keeping her right arm elevated, propped up on one elbow. Blood was still seeping through the bandage Oswald had applied with such delicate attention to her hand.

'How are you feeling?' he asked.

She threw him a glare. 'Spare me the concern, Oswald. For Christ's sake, what were you thinking? They were just children! And I thought you wanted to keep a low profile in the village?'

'I do. That's essential.'

'Yeah? Well, I'm sorry to shatter the illusion, but those kids are going to tell their parents what you did. Maybe they even saw me! Word's going to get around. You'll be lucky if the police aren't here by midday.'

She expected an argument, but Oswald said, 'It was stupid of me, you're quite right.' He sighed heavily. 'Sometimes, Clara, I lose myself. It may seem that I'm not always present, not fully in control, and that's not my fault. It's the tumour, pressing on my brain.'

At that, Clara leaned back in her chair. Glared at Oswald. She was scared of him, yes – all the more so since seeing him terrorise those kids. This man could ruin her. This man was unhinged. But she was not so lost in fear that she couldn't challenge him. And she must. If – God help her – she were even to conceive of helping him as he asked, she had to know he was for real.

'I want proof,' she said. 'This tumour . . .'

He was already striding from the room. When he returned a couple of minutes later, he was laden down. At the table, he let the stash of pillboxes and bottles in his arms cascade down.

Clara stared at the spread of medicines before her. She picked up a box. Read the drug name – didn't recognise it.

But she did recognise the name on the prescription label, and the date was recent. She worked through the pile, checking each label methodically. Clearly, Oswald Cattenach was not a well man.

But was it cancer? And was it terminal?

'Here,' said Oswald.

Clara looked up, and saw that he was drawing a series of X-ray films from a large Manila envelope he'd carried in under one arm. He held them out to her.

'Hold them to the light,' he advised.

She did. And she saw scans of a brain. Lots of them. The large dark mass was unmistakable. As were the dates of the scans – over several weeks – and the patient's name printed on each film: Oswald Cattenach.

'I see,' said Clara, laying the films on the table.

Oswald stood across the table from her. He looked weighed down, vulnerable even, and Clara could not help feeling mildly sympathetic at the fact that he was facing a death sentence so young. She was surprised to feel that; worried a little, too. She didn't want to feel anything for him. She'd heard stories in the news of women imprisoned in basements and attics for years who developed a bond with their captor. Stockholm Syndrome. Was that what she was experiencing?

She had to admit it was possible. But it was so wrong to sympathise with a man who'd lured her here and blackmailed her; who threatened children; who willingly admitted killing people in the name of kindness. Who insisted that she grant him a 'good death' when the time came.

That was beyond her; she knew that. But she'd seen the scans – Oswald was a sick man. Whatever this nightmare was in which he'd trapped her, it would end. A few months, no more, and it would be over. She'd be free – from him, and from what he knew. The dead man. Her sin.

She'd put up with Karl for all those years. She could resign herself to Boleskine and Oswald. For now. It was a matter of survival.

'Well,' Oswald said, 'I must meditate. And you should rest. We only have two weeks to prepare for my funeral.'

Silently, she nodded. As he walked to the door, Clara shifted her gaze to her heavily bandaged hand. She was relieved to see that the cut beneath the bandage had stopped bleeding. She felt calmer.

'You were right though, Clara.'

She looked up to see Oswald standing in the doorway. 'About what?'

'The kids *were* terrified,' he said, his voice suddenly devoid of any remorse. 'One of them pissed his pants. Imagine that.'

Clara saw that the flat, dead expression was back on his face again, and her eyes flitted down to the brain scans on the table. How much could a tumour change a person? How bad could it get? A cold wariness swept through her.

'I suggest you keep a watchful eye over me,' Oswald called back to her as he walked away. 'For both our sakes.'

She waited until he had retreated to the opposite end of the house, to the ruined east wing. Then, feeling thoroughly shaken, Clara walked to her bedroom.

Following a trail of dark blood that led to a discarded shoe.

10

Six hundred miles south, Karl Hopkins was sitting in the harsh, flickering light cast by his computer screen, scanning his search results. Her name had vanished from the lists of all her friends on Facebook. Alison Hopkins might just as well have been dead.

But he hoped to God she wasn't, because he really, *really* needed to find her. To see her.

You can only get better by coming to terms with what you did.

It was good advice. His advice. And over the last few weeks, Karl's uncertainty over whatever had happened on Vauxhall Bridge Road the night he got drunk, whatever he had said – or done – to that innocent bystander in the brown coat, had brought him to understand that if he wanted to get his life back on track, put his conscience to rest, he would need to listen to that advice. He was as sure of that as he was that his investment in the Frank's Pizza start-up business would come good in the end (never mind that the nightclub investment had bombed).

And you know what that means?

He did. It meant atonement. Apologising. Making it up to Alison.

Could he actually do that? Was he capable? The truth was, Karl wasn't so sure; he had been drinking a lot more since he lost his job. But that was only part of the reason for his doubt, and Karl knew it all too well. The rest was because he was afraid of what he might find.

With a single mouse click, he moved to the next page of search results. And saw, finally, a result that gave him hope: *Looking for a missing person? Post their photo here.*

He clicked on the link. The website was scattered with images of missing people uploaded by their family members. There were case studies too. Success stories of people having been found through the site.

Five minutes later, he had created an account. He added the basic information, but hesitated on the section for uploading a photograph.

What if Alison came across the site and the picture he posted? She'd know he was on to her. Perhaps she'd run further away.

Or say the site gave him a lead, and he did find her. Shacked up in a nice house somewhere with a successful, handsome guy; a bigshot capable of satisfying her in ways Karl hadn't been able to. If that's what he found, Karl would only feel inadequate, even more of a failure. And then he would drink; rage would follow.

On the other hand, doing nothing meant everything would stay just as it was. Him, alone in this flat, with only the dead fly on the windowsill for company.

As Karl stared longingly at the screen, his stomach began to feel the way it did when he decided he wasn't going to drink, and yet he found himself unscrewing the cap from the bottle of vodka.

As if operating on autopilot, his hand dragged the mouse to select Alison's photo. And clicked 'upload'.

11

Oswald had covered the jagged hole in her window with a wooden board, which kept out the frigid Highland air. That night, as Clara lay in bed, listening to the vicious wind ravage the bleak landscape, it occurred to her that she had never felt more isolated, or more haunted.

She wondered why Oswald hadn't locked her bedroom door that night. He had made it clear to her that she wasn't to leave her room during the dark hours, and she had agreed. Was this his way of building some unity between them both? A bond of trust? Possibly, but if so, it was a very perverse brand of trust.

The irony was, a part of her would have preferred to know the bedroom door *was* locked, because at night, she had discovered the previous evening, the house . . . changed. Although they were the only two people inhabiting the house, she had the distinct impression that this wasn't always the case. In the darkness, a presence seemed to creep inside the walls of Boleskine, a presence that Clara could not quite define.

She felt it now, as she lay there in the bed, the sense of something other than herself and Oswald inside the house. In her tangled thoughts three questions kept recurring: *What drew him here? What happened here? What secrets does the house keep?*

Then she heard them. Padding, snorting sounds in the main hallway, as if there might be an animal, a stray dog, she thought, out there.

Her nerves taut, Clara got out of bed and went slowly to the door, pressing her ear against it, listening hard.

Nothing. The only sound now was of the blood pounding in her ears to the rhythmic beat of her heart.

Still, she was curious.

Quietly, she opened her bedroom door and peered out. Nothing there but shadows. And, down at the end of the corridor, the very faintest suggestion of light.

She stood there for several moments before she summoned the courage to move cautiously through the house, the floor cold beneath her bare feet, all the way to the tarpaulin that barricaded the east wing. A faint glow was coming from behind it, along with the foul scent of incense, and something else; a thick, noxious smell, defiling the air.

What was Oswald doing in the east wing? she asked herself. And why had he covered the windows of that part of the house with plastic bags?

She hesitated there, a woman who had been on the run from a man for the best part of a year, now standing alone and fearful in the house of another man whose master plan, apparently, was that she end his life.

How did I get here? she thought. *This is madness. A nightmare.*

She should turn and walk out. Run! Get away from Oswald and the body in the sarcophagus. Run from the fear, the guilt. Start again someplace far, far away.

With nothing, said the voice of reason. *You have no money, despite his promise that he would pay you. He hasn't. And he would tell the police, and they would find you, and you'd rot in prison. Or he'd frame Inghean. Imagine her in jail . . .*

She couldn't run. She was trapped. Until Oswald died, anyway. She'd survived Karl. She could survive this. She just had to be the woman who'd walked out on Karl. Who'd changed her name and talked her way into a job in Abersky.

Straightening her back, Clara took a step towards the sealed-off east wing. A muffled cough made her leap back. She spun and padded quickly back to her room, where she shut the door, careful to make no noise, and leaned against it, exhaling a long breath. She did not imagine Oswald would have taken kindly to discovering her out of her room, having disobeyed him.

The wound on her bandaged hand was beginning to throb again. She desperately needed rest. Perhaps she would sleep now she knew there was nothing roaming about in the corridor.

But as she pulled back the duvet to climb into bed, she saw something that made her raise her hand to her mouth to stifle a shocked gasp.

The mattress was covered in hundreds of black beetles, a seething black mass of them, swarming and scurrying over the bedding.

One of the beetles scuttled onto her pillow. With disgust, she registered its foul odour, its appalling size and its fine dark hairs.

You've seen it before, a voice spoke in her head, and she realised with numbing certainty that Oswald had warned her about the beetles on the very first occasion they met:

'*The Devil's footman . . . Superstition teaches that if it raises its tail it's casting a curse on you.*'

As if on cue, the beetle on her pillow opened its jaws, and, in the manner of a scorpion, threateningly raised its tail as if to strike.

Clara stared at the beast in disgust. It took all the strength she could muster not to succumb to her sickening soul, the infection wrought upon her by this wretched house.

12

The following morning, back at Highlands Estates, presiding over a mound of paperwork that had more to do with her own financial affairs than selling houses, Gale kept one eye on Inghean, who was drawing at Clara's old desk, and one eye on the young policeman who had come back with yet another question.

'Clara Jones was a reliable employee?'

'Mostly.'

'I can't find any information on her background.'

'She was secretive that way,' Gale answered briskly, without accusation. 'Why are you interested?'

'Some kids' parents made a complaint about a disturbance yesterday. Not particularly trustworthy kids, I have to say, not the parents either, but there was a description of a woman given that reminded me of your ex-employee.'

'I see. And where was this?'

'Boleskine House.'

'What on earth would she be doing out there?'

He shrugged. 'Working? Or maybe she's involved with the owner in some other way, but I think it's curious that . . . Hey, Inghean! Dear God, is she okay?'

Seeing the policeman's startled face, Gale bolted to her daughter's side and reached for her shoulders.

Inghean's eyes were as wide as dinner plates.

'She shouldn't be there, not at *that* house. We have to get her back!' she cried.

Gale's eyes hardened. She had seen her daughter like this before, when her troubles at school were at their worst. 'Inghean, darling, calm down!'

She stared at her daughter, chilled as she began violently shaking her head from side to side.

Frightened to death, Inghean had squeezed her eyes shut, her mind momentarily blotted with welling darkness. Suddenly, her brain felt as if it was on fire. It didn't make any difference that she had closed her eyes, the low white manor was perfectly visible to her now, etched on the backs of her eyelids. She saw it up close, macabre and brooding over the loch; Greek columns, stone dogs and eagles; echoing passages dressed with tartan drapes; flashes of magical symbols; a damp and dangerous boathouse. And now, in her mind, the building bursting with hellish flames. It was the house she had sketched, over and over, the echoing bug-infested house where magic worked, and atrocities came to life. The death house, where somewhere – in the future she feared – a woman she loved floated under the water, drowning . . .

Clara couldn't be there, could she?

Why?

Her eyes flew open suddenly and she rose out of her chair with a scream, looking around wildly with panicked eyes.

Gale jumped back with shock, one trembling hand covering her mouth as she began to sob with fear for her daughter.

And Adam just stood there, stunned by the terror glittering in poor Inghean's eyes.

Something's wrong here, he thought. *Something's terribly wrong.*

PART THREE

WHAT WE DID AT THE LAKEHOUSE

I looked upon the scene before me . . . There was an iciness, a sinking, a sickening of the heart – an unredeemed dreariness of thought which no goading of the imagination could torture into aught of the sublime.

– Edgar Allan Poe

1

PC Adam Lake sat in his police car, staring through the windscreen at a low bungalow of New England design, all timber cladding, with a pitched, gabled roof. A sign next to the front door indicated that Jeff Ramsay's house was called 'Treetops'. Another sign, fastened to the fence that encircled the front lawn, read: 'It's not Eden but it's my garden. Put your trash in the bin. THANK YOU.'

With the night drawing in, the house looked warm and welcoming; yet Adam had been sitting there for some time, hesitating.

It wasn't only that he knew it was wrong to disobey his boss. Probably Jeff would know all about the history of what Shawcross had called the Black Lodge; but whether he'd be willing to talk was another matter. And as for the peculiar symbols that the missing poet's mother had sent him, he had no good reason to suppose Jeff would understand their meaning. No good reason, but there was a chance, wasn't there?

Eventually, the front door opened. Jeff must have seen the police car through the window. The man stepping out onto the porch was thin and wiry, with short white hair; he wore a brown cardigan and brown cravat. Looking at him, Adam was reminded a little of the eccentric monster hunter Simon

Renwick, who camped out on the shores of the loch. Hopefully *this* man would be rather more reasonable.

Adam got out of the car and approached the porch. 'Are you well, sir?'

'Shouldn't I be?' The older man studied the police officer, then said in a voice that was wary but resigned, 'You know, I had a feeling I'd be a getting a visit from one of you.'

Adam's eyebrows rose. 'How's that?'

'Why don't you tell me why you're here?'

'Sure.' With deliberate care, Adam stepped up into the porch. 'Look, I'm sorry to bother you, sir, but I'm investigating the disappearance of someone I believe may be connected to a story you reported on, some decades ago.'

'A story? I was editor of the *Inverness Courier* for twenty years. You'll have to be more specific.'

'I mean the suicides at Boleskine House.'

Jeff stiffened.

'You *do* remember the suicide of Major General Cornelius Coughlan?'

Jeff said nothing.

'And the death of the major general's wife?'

At that Jeff dropped his gaze. 'Her name was Rebecca.'

Silence.

'Sir?'

'It was a long time ago.'

'Then you do remember. Look. Sir. I haven't come here to upset you, but a man is missing and I need your help.'

Adam pulled out his smartphone and tapped to open the first in a series of badly shot images.

'The family of the disappeared individual found these drawings at his flat, along with all sorts of mind-altering substances.'

He angled the phone so Jeff could see the screen. 'Do you recognise these symbols?'

As Adam began swiping through the set of photos, Jeff's face froze in an open-mouthed expression of distress. He suddenly had the look of a man who was viewing pictures not of symbols, but of some bestial, perverted atrocity. He said heavily, 'it's true; somehow I knew you'd be coming.' Reading Adam's inquisitive stare, he said, 'I may not write them any more, but I still read the newspapers.'

'Of course.' The two men locked eyes. 'I'd prefer that I didn't have to do this, Mr Ramsay.'

'This official police business?' Jeff eyed Adam's uniform.

'Well. Not exactly.'

'Then why should I cooperate?'

'Because I'm worried this missing man's life is in danger.'

'What's his connection to Boleskine House?'

'Seems he was preoccupied with it. I don't know, maybe he was thinking of buying it.'

'Then he could very well be in danger,' Jeff said. He grimaced and took the phone from Adam. His face was drawn and etched with tension; he seemed barely able to bring himself to look at the photographs.

'You know what these symbols mean, don't you?' said Adam. 'You'll explain to me?'

Jeff shook his head. 'I can't say I'm comfortable with doing that. I need to think about it.'

'I really need to talk—'

'No!' Jeff's face tightened; it was stone-grey, his jaw set. 'You can't steamroller me, son. Give me your card. I will think about it. And maybe I'll be in touch.'

Adam dug in his pocket and handed Jeff his card. He opened his mouth to say something polite, anything, to help get the old man onside. But Jeff Ramsay had already stepped back and slammed his front door shut behind him.

2

At Boleskine House, alone in the bedroom she'd come to think of as a cell, Clara stood at the window, watching her jailor push a wheelbarrow down towards the loch's shoreline. His route took him adjacent to the tangled burial ground.

Who did I kill? she thought, her gaze snagging on the crumbling mort house where the charred body was concealed. *Who did I kill, and what was he doing out here?*

She felt a profound duty to answer these questions. How could she not? Seeing the mort house every day, constantly reminded of the life she had destroyed, had imbued her with so much regret and shame that she had taken to washing her hands, over and over. For all the good *that* did. No matter how hard she scrubbed, in her mind's eye the palms of her hands seemed always to be caked in dried blood.

If Oswald had allowed her to check the Internet for local news stories she would have done, but that access had been denied from day one. She still had her old work phone, but she had used all her data before moving here and she had no clue as to the Wi-Fi code.

Staring out onto that chamber of death, Clara told herself that she would atone for her terrible mistake. Perhaps just by being here she was, in a way, because she was protecting Inghean. The thought of her friend made Clara long for her old life – her anonymity, her independence. Would she ever get that back?

One day, was what she told herself, to get through the long days here, and the even longer nights. One day, when her time at Boleskine was over. But how this nightmare would end, she still hadn't worked out. Helping Oswald prepare for a funeral was one thing; helping him *end* his life – giving him a good death, as he put it – was out of the question, no matter how badly he threatened her. Whatever the risks to her own life, she had to find a way out of that.

Her best hope, she realised, was that the tumour would kill him. She'd caused the death of one man, and now she wished for the death of another.

Was it any wonder she saw blood on her hands?

For now, Clara had determined the safest option was to lull Oswald into a false sense of security that she would do as he wished (commanded), so she was trying to shut out all thoughts of her own situation and commit herself fully to assisting him.

The last two weeks hadn't been easy. Her tears – hot, shameful tears – had streamed as she helped him clean out the rubble from the billiard room.

And she had wondered, as she helped him fix curtain rails around its perimeter – not just the windows and door, but every wall – precisely what sort of fabric he would hang in here, and why.

She had never heard of holding a funeral for someone *before* their death, but according to Oswald the practice was a growing trend; a chance for the dying to show their apprecia-tion to those they cared for while they were still alive, and to say goodbye. 'If you're going to have a funeral, you might as well do it right,' he said.

Would there be a casket? she had asked Oswald. Music? Religious readings?

'Yes, all of that,' Oswald had confirmed, his eyes like moon-shine. 'But it will be happier than a regular funeral, more a celebration of life.'

Now the funeral was just one day away, and, as Clara gazed out of the window, watching Oswald at work doing – well, she wasn't quite sure what he was doing out there – she supposed the idea was logical enough, a way of achieving closure in the face of death. Yet she also found something morbid in the concept. Something disrespectful. Egotistical. Was that wrong, or was Oswald genuinely more enlightened than she was?

Most people struggled with the fear of death, but he seemed to be facing the inevitability of his own demise. She almost envied his courage, his resolve. 'I'm living every moment,' he told her. 'Savouring the sheer pleasure of awareness, of being alive.'

Each day with Oswald brought deeper apprehension, yet also, Clara had to admit, deeper fascination. Oswald's purpose – his 'Great Operation' – was confusing to her, and yet at the same time, intriguing. There was some profound meaning she could not quite grasp to the tasks that absorbed him, day and night.

True to his word, Oswald rose at sunrise and meditated underwater in the boathouse for exactly two hours, reflecting on his life and the end of it. He fasted twice a week; sometimes for twenty-four hours, sometimes for as long as thirty-six. At lunchtime on those days, he would insist that Clara eat in the kitchen, and he would draw up a chair and watch her every mouthful with an intensity and passion so troubling it was impossible for Clara to finish her meal. The effect was altogether unsettling – just like his silvery voice, which seemed to speak to some part of her deep inside, a part she couldn't quite access.

His own eating habits were just as troubling. It bothered Clara to observe that he never used a knife and fork, but instead ate with his hands. The fact that he washed them diligently in a silver ritual bowl, before and after, only deepened Clara's unease. And his penchant for cleansing himself did not end there. Every afternoon he went out armed with a towel, to bathe, he told her, at the bottom of a waterfall about a mile away. She'd considered following him there, spying, to better understand. But the thought had occurred to Clara that it was the very same waterfall that featured in the watercolour hanging in the long, dark hallway. And that picture, the effect it had on her, pulling her in – it unnerved her.

What significance did the waterfall hold for him?

What was his religion?

There were clues, but each seemed to contradict the other. Occasionally, Oswald made vague reference to trips to Eastern lands. Sometimes he would allude to Christianity, at other times Buddhism. On one occasion, he referred to 'the sacred work of Abramelin' as pivotal to his mission to discover 'true and sacred wisdom'. Quite how, she had no idea. But the more she observed, the prayers, the daily solemn rituals, the more her discomfort grew – and yet, along with it, her curiosity. Even now, as she watched him push the wheelbarrow back up towards the house, Clara was wondering, *What the hell is he doing?*

She focused her gaze. For the second time that day, Oswald was returning from the water's edge with a wheelbarrow loaded with sand. As she watched, he pushed it out of her line of sight, towards the fire-damaged east wing, where he worked quietly and ceaselessly, always alone.

That part of the house was sacred, he said. Accessible only to him. A zipped tarpaulin secured with a padlock prevented her from getting inside, and black bags taped to the windows denied her ever chancing a glimpse from outside. Sometimes, from that part of the house she would hear incantations, whispered in Latin; incantations that sounded impressive and mystical, and which, for no reason she could account for, made her heart beat faster with anxiety.

And that wasn't all. A few days earlier, she had been surprised to see a small van passing up the driveway. The handyman driving it was delivering three enormous mirrors that Oswald had procured from Celtic Crafts. When the mirrors were safely out of the van, Oswald had moved them into the east wing.

What could he possibly be doing in there?

He doesn't want me to know.

Clara had a vague suspicion that the clues to answering some of these questions might lie in the cardboard boxes she had discovered in the boathouse. But even this was kept permanently locked, which only deepened her frustrations, her suspicions and her curiosity about the impending funeral. 'We're known by the company we keep,' her father used to say. If that was true, then what sort of friends did she expect Oswald to have; what sort of strangers would be coming?

If Oswald was any indication, she could expect the guest list to include a host of unpredictable, threatening and/or dangerous individuals. At the same time, they might also be charming, well-travelled, cultured, intelligent. That Oswald was well educated, Clara was in no doubt. On one of the rare occasions he'd deigned to converse with her over a meal, she'd presumptuously asked, 'Where did you study?'

'Magdalen College, Oxford.'

'Oh, and which degree did you—'

'I never took exams.'

'Why not?'

He had blinked at that, running a hand through his shock of yellow curls.

'What was the point? My closest friend at Oxford taught me about life and self-reliance; gave me moral and intellectual freedom. But a degree?' He shook his head, favouring her with a smile. 'A degree wasn't ever going to help me attain my *true* purpose, now was it?'

For a moment, she was beguiled by his answer, by his smooth, sonorous voice and his unwavering self-confidence. Then, with a peculiar abruptness, he had asked her a question that had made her draw back, uneasy.

'Clara, have you never wanted to hurt yourself?'

'What?'

'Ever imagined yourself hurting someone else?'

The sudden question made her remember the shotgun he'd aimed at the kids, and the flat, vacant expression on his face when he had told her one of the boys was so afraid he'd 'pissed his pants'. The same blank look was on his face now. His tumour, she wondered.

'Why would I wish to hurt someone?' she asked cautiously.

Ever so gently, Oswald got out of his chair and came around the table to stand beside her, placing a tender hand on her shoulder, which made her every ligament tense. 'Because pain is good,' he answered. 'Pain must be cherished; pain reminds us we're alive. You should think about that.'

And she had thought about that. At length. In particular, she'd thought about the pain Karl had inflicted on her.

At least Oswald doesn't hurt me, she thought, watching him steer the now-empty wheelbarrow back across the grass. But as she watched a buzzard soar high above the waters of the loch, there was no fooling her heart that she was any less trapped with Oswald than she'd been with Karl.

3

Later that afternoon, as the shadow of the great mountains was crawling over the stucco mansion and its unkempt grounds, Oswald announced he was heading out. He wouldn't be long, he told her, but he did not reveal where he was going. He did not reveal why.

Moving slowly through the quiet, ill-lit rooms, Clara listened to the roof creaking under the strain of the northerly gales blowing in off the loch, wondering to herself if there could possibly be any truth to the myriad stories of violent deaths associated with this remote estate.

She was at the mercy of her imagination as she drifted from room to room. Passing along the wide, main hallway that formed the backbone of the house, she recalled some of the more lurid stories: a murder–suicide; before that, the housekeeper who inexplicably drowned her toddler in the iron bathtub. And, hundreds of years ago, the congregation burned to death in a church that had stood on these grounds.

Superstition? Or something more tangible?

To Clara, who had never placed much stock in hearsay, it all sounded too fanciful, too contrived. If there had been such a fire here, inside a church, then where was the evidence? Fine, it was possible the foundations of the house had been built on the ruins of the old structure; possible, but likely? Come to think of it, didn't every community with an old abandoned house claim such spurious tales?

Of course they did; those sorts of tales were the lifeblood of school playgrounds the length of Britain. But those stories also got her pondering, made her curious. Unsettled. Part of it was how widespread they were; the rest had to do with the location of the house. It didn't matter how scenic or tranquil others found that stretching pebbled shoreline, here; those freezing waters, all twenty-three miles of them, only deepened Clara's growing sense of imprisonment.

She listened to the punishing wind coming in wild gusts. Unexplained creaks and groans didn't bother her so much; every house in these parts made noises like that. What did bother her was the library door.

It was ajar. And when Oswald went out, that was the one door he normally kept shut and locked.

Fear held her back. Oswald would not like her snooping. But curiosity – the need to understand this place – *him* – drove her forward.

So she entered the silence of the library. What struck her

first, as she saw the wide terrace door that framed the sullen waters below, was a curious realisation:

Windows. The house has lots of windows.

Most of them were large. This meant that rooms like this spacious library should enjoy an abundance of natural light. So why was every room always permeated with a shadowy gloom?

The cold, northern light, perhaps?

Perhaps.

For some curious reason, dwelling on that question touched Clara with a tinge of unease, so she dismissed all considerations of the light, and scanned the room. And saw a large cardboard box resting on top of Oswald's desk. Clara instantly recognised it as one of the boxes from the boathouse, and she frowned.

Why had he brought it inside?

And why had he left the library unlocked? Did he *want* her to look? To learn?

She spun about, heart in her throat, half-expecting to find Oswald behind her. Looming. But she was alone.

Stop it, she told herself sternly. *He's gone. And this is an opportunity. Take it.*

She walked over to the desk. Next to the box was a heavy-looking book bound in red Moroccan leather, edged with silver. It looked dusty and fragile, but, thankfully, still legible. She registered the title: *Publications of the Scottish History Society volume xxiv 1643–1688, with an Introduction, from the Original Manuscript, by William Mackay (Edinburgh 1896).*

Without sitting, Clara opened the book and immediately scented its dusty age. She flipped to the page marked with a bright yellow Post-it note, and her eyes immediately caught the words 'Boleskine House'. She read:

In 1684, the minister of Boleskine reported 'that all persons of all ranks indifferently buried their dead within his church, not only his own parishioners, but some others of the neighbouring parishes, so that several coffins were hardly underground, which was like to be very dangerous.'

She tried imagining that execrable vision: human bones and caskets protruding from the earth; the stench, then thrust the image from her mind.

Reading on:

In June 1670 Mr. Thomas Houston, minister of Boleskine, complained that 'his house had been laitly seized upon by Lochabber Robbers, himselfe threatened with naked swords and drawne durks at his brest, his money and household stuff plundered; and seeing that one of their number suffered death laitly therefor at Inverness the rest of them were lieing in wait for his life, and threatening his ruine and dammage, so that in the evening he is affrayed to be burned to ashes.' Mr. Houston had reason to be alarmed, for his predecessor had been barbarously murdered . . .

Clara lifted her head, staring off. So there had been a church here. And the mention of murder, of a man afraid of being burned to ashes, made her shiver. Was this property destined to suffer a fire? Was catastrophe somehow part of its DNA?

No, that's not reality.

But it's still one hell of a coincidence.

She flipped a few pages on in the book and came to yet another reference to the church:

On a certain Sabbath in the 1600s, the church was torched;
the doors bolted from the outside. A piper marched round and
round the burning building until the flames were no more.

Clara's head jerked up. Was that the front door she heard?
No, couldn't have been. If Oswald was back, she reminded
herself, she would have heard his car.

Closing the book, putting it aside, she reached into the
cardboard box and discovered a sizeable quantity of faded
newspaper clippings. The first one she selected was yellow,
barely legible: a news story dated 23 February 1860, reporting
a man drowned near Boleskine House:

> *At about 5 p.m., James Chisholm, servant to*
> *Captain Clavering, and Duncan Maclaren,*
> *shepherd, went out in a boat to set some*
> *lines, leaving a companion on the shore. On*
> *exchanging positions when about 40 yards*
> *from the shore, the boat upset, and Maclaren*
> *being thrown to a distance struck out for the*
> *land, Chisholm clinging to the keel. The boat*
> *with Chisholm ultimately reached the shore,*
> *but Maclaren must have sunk, overcome with*
> *fatigue and the excessive cold.*

According to the article, Maclaren's body was never found.
Clara felt a chill in her bones as the piece revealed:

> *... the most heartless conduct on the part of*
> *an onlooker; for we are credibly informed that*
> *he actually saw the boat upset and the poor*

> *men clinging to it, and then walked away to*
> *Inverfarigaig, a distance of a mile and a half,*
> *without giving the least alarm.*

She felt a low, aching dread tighten her stomach.

A poor man drowned; and someone just watched it happen?

There was something tremendously callous and cold-blooded about that.

Was it something to do with the house, she vaguely wondered. Could the house change people; appeal to their darker natures; tempt them into committing otherwise unthinkable acts of cruelty?

No, of course not. Houses don't do that.

But houses didn't watch people, either. And it *was* a sense of being watched that Clara felt here, thickening and enfolding around her as the wind cried at the terrace doors.

She gave a small shudder, rubbed at the gooseflesh breaking on her arms, and glanced at the clock on the wall. He would be back soon, but she needed to know more. So she carefully emptied the box of the rest of its cuttings and leafed through them. And the next report that caught her attention – a clipping from the *Aberdeen Journal* – really did make her wonder whether houses like Boleskine brought ill-luck. This one was dated 22 April 1926 and reported an accident that had befallen one Tavish Dunbar of Dunkeld, who was driving to the Boleskine estate when he had swerved his car suddenly, sending it plummeting:

> *. . . sixty feet onto the rocks below. A dog that*
> *accompanied him in the car was thrown into*
> *the water, but swam ashore.*

But the car was badly smashed.

And Tavish Dunbar perished.

Are you surprised Clara?

She shook her head, beginning to wish she had never looked inside this damned box. Despite herself, she reached for the next cutting.

It was dated 12 June 1973:

> ### Teen Dies After Falling While
> ### Trying to Hang Tree Swing
>
> *Police Scotland say a teenager living beside Loch Ness died the same afternoon she fell while trying to hang a swing in a tree.*
>
> *In an official statement it was confirmed that 14-year-old Hannah Goodwin fell Thursday afternoon in the grounds of her parents' Highlands residence, Boleskine House. Police said when she fell, the swing rope was looped around her and tightened around her abdomen, injuring her.*
>
> *Police say Hannah's mother called 999 when she found her. Paramedics arrived and began CPR.*
>
> *Hannah was airlifted to Raigmore Hospital in Inverness, where she died a few hours later.*
>
> *Police called the girl's death a tragic accident.*

Clara put the article aside, trying to resist the sudden image it called up in her memory: a rotten wooden swing outside; the swing hanging from a frayed rope.

She released a querulous breath. Her brain was striving to make sense of this long string of ghoulish events. The likelihood of them all playing out here, on this one property? A story of a horror house in the wilderness, its history saturated in the blood of innocents. The idea that she was now a part of that history, joined with it, was as sickening as it was undeniable.

And again she wondered: why had Oswald left the library unlocked?

Numbly, Clara reached back into the box and found a single black-and-white photograph of the boathouse. No date, but it must have been many decades old; for one thing the boathouse looked brand new. She was about to put it aside when she saw something in the picture that made her throat tighten. It wasn't the boathouse that filled her with fear, it was something *behind* the boathouse, just off to the left side of it. A broad, dark figure. A man, it appeared, wearing animal fur and a bizarre horned headdress, in what she assumed was an imitation of the devil. In the picture, the figure was walking up from the shores of the loch, towards the house.

Her whole body jolted with surprise. *That* wasn't the wind. From the main hallway, a heavy banging was resounding.

Quickly, Clara put the photograph back in the box, and, with fear pulsing through her veins, hurried from the room.

4

As Clara answered the front door, she thought that the man standing on the threshold looked just as surprised to see her as she was to see him.

'Clara?'

Shit. It was Murdoch McHardy, the butcher. Registering his frown, she gave him a quick smile that didn't quite make it to her eyes.

'So this is where you're living now?' he asked, and a flush of embarrassment warmed her cheeks.

'Yes. I'm the lodge manager here.'

'I see,' he said in a tone that said, *I don't see*. 'I'll just leave these with you, shall I?' He held out a plastic container. 'The order came through on email. From you, I guess?'

She nodded, hoping the lie didn't show. Oswald must have placed the order, though he'd never mentioned it.

'Though I don't see why you couldn't have come and collected them.'

'Thank you for taking the trouble,' she said, registering the weight of the container as she took it from him.

What did Oswald order?

Food for his living funeral, probably; steaks perhaps.

'What does he want these for, anyway?'

Clara hesitated. She had no intention of explaining Oswald's living funeral; nor did she want to appear ignorant. 'Well, Mr McHardy, I had no idea that buying meat from you entailed so many questions.' She was smiling as she said this; and he was eyeing her shrewdly.

'I thought you were a vegetarian,' he came back. 'Remember, you told me that was why you never shopped with me. So what are you wanting these for?' He nodded at the plastic container.

'They're not for me. My employer is expecting guests,' said Clara. 'Now, how much do we owe you?'

'You left your place above my shop so quickly,' he probed, his mind clearly snagging on questions. 'My fault, I guess? The chopping?'

'It was a tremendous noise.'

'I remember you saying,' he said, not looking quite convinced that was her reason for leaving. 'I've had a few customers asking after you. People are saying it's like you dropped off the face of the earth. Odd.'

'Not really.'

He looked carefully at her. 'Listen, lass, you sure everything's all right? You look . . . peaky.'

Suddenly, from behind Clara came Oswald's voice: 'She's fine, thank you, Mr McHardy. Won't you come through, please. I'll write you a cheque for your trouble. I do appreciate you coming all this way.'

'Right. And you are?'

Stepping out of the shadows in the hallway, Oswald smiled invitingly at Murdoch, showing those perfect, pearly white teeth. 'Oswald Cattenach. Now please, step inside, follow me to the library.'

Oh hell, Clara thought, where did he appear from? She hadn't heard his car. Where had he been? How long had he been home? Had he been watching her in the library? She regarded him with raging inward displeasure as suspicion and some fear crept over her, but he seemed as cool as the winter breeze.

Murdoch eyed Clara as he stepped past her. She turned and watched as he followed Oswald to the library, and the door clicked closed behind them.

Ten, twenty, thirty minutes passed. During that time, at intermittent moments, Clara put her ear to the door. She heard a voice, Oswald's, on the other side, but she could make out hardly anything of what he was saying. On the chime of the hour, the door opened, and the butcher emerged, looking totally unharmed.

But different, Clara thought. *Serene. Not himself.*

What really surprised her was the smile he gave her as he passed wordlessly by, heading towards his van. Curious, Clara watched him drive off down to the main road.

'What did you say to him?' she asked Oswald, who joined her on the doorstep. With some unease, she was remembering the time he had casually suggested 'dealing' with Murdoch should he ever become a problem.

'Words.'

'Don't be clever.'

Then he said something she hadn't expected:

'Clara, I need you out. I mean, I need you to leave.'

'What? But the funeral is—'

'Tomorrow night, yes. And I need you out. Only for a little while.'

Relief surged through her; she would not have to attend this bizarre event. But it was quickly chased by uneasy curiosity. 'Why?'

'Because you're ... special.'

'In what way?'

He grabbed her wrist, examined her hand.

'Oswald, what are you doing?'

'You have a firm jointed thumb.'

'Why is that important?'

He looked hard at her.

'It indicates you are blessed with a stronger will.'

'Stronger will than whom?'

He shook his head, released her hand, regarded her.

'The shape and length of the fingers have their meanings.'

'Only if you believe in palm reading.'

'And I do.'

She couldn't help noticing that his fingers were long, angular, bony.

'Clara, you must endure.'

'I don't know what that means.'

His eyes on her were cool and meditative. 'It means that if you stay here, your life could be in danger. Leave in the morning, before my guests arrive.'

Not for the first time, she wondered what sort of people they would be, thinking of the old adage: *a man is known by the company he keeps.*

'Where should I go?'

'Anywhere discreet. Do you still have a key to your old flat? It's empty, right?'

She nodded. 'I think so.'

'Go. For one night only, then return. They'll be gone by then.'

'They? You mean your friends?'

Wordlessly he nodded.

Why does he want me out? What doesn't he want me to see?

With these questions churning in her mind, Clara turned

away from him and decided to head down the hall to the kitchen. She was exasperated with Oswald's evasiveness. Exhausted with his dark charisma. She would get something to eat, and then retire to her room, though there was little chance of resting there. At night, her nerves were so taut that sleep was often impossible. As the days had passed and the intensity of Oswald's meditations had increased, Clara had noticed an alteration in the house's atmosphere. A horribly oppressive feeling. The sensation of a storm gathering.

As she entered the kitchen, she thought again of Murdoch. *I wonder what he brought us? And why Oswald made him deliver it to the house?* As she made herself a sandwich, she kept seeing the butcher in her mind's eye, that odd, dreamy expression on his face as he left the house, and she found that after all she had no appetite.

5

Early the next morning, before so much as a single ray of sunlight had touched the horizon, Clara awoke. Her first thought was that this was the day of Oswald's living funeral, and she was to leave the house. She was escaping the prison, for just a little while.

But why return? whispered a little voice inside. *Run, Clara, and don't look back.*

The voice was tremulous, but the idea, seductive.

The thought only lasted for the few seconds it took for her groggy mind to come to and remember why running wasn't an option. Oswald would go to the police. Clara would be hunted down to pay for her crime.

And if not Clara, then Inghean. Sweet, innocent Inghean, who drew pictures with crayons and wore her hair in little-girl braids.

Tears pricked at Clara's eyes at the thought of her friend, and at the thought of her innocence. Once, Clara had been innocent too. Before Karl. Before—

But there was no time to follow that train of thought, however, for suddenly it dawned on Clara that there was a reason she'd awoken so early.

Outside her bedroom door, shuffling sounds.

She shot up in bed. Listened hard.

Silence.

Clara got out of bed, shivering slightly as she reached for her robe and shrugged it on. She was about to open the bedroom door when the noise came again from the other side, louder now. A snorting, snuffling noise.

Oswald didn't own a dog. But it was a dog she could hear; or something very much like a dog, padding around in the hallway. For a moment, she thought she heard it pawing at a door further along the passage. It was a stray, had to be. And she would have to deal with it. That was the thought in her head as she threw open the door and stepped out, looking first left and then right; and then not knowing where to look, because there was no dog in sight – no animal at all.

Stretching ahead of her was the spine of the house, the dark hallway, daubed at its furthest reach with moonlight and shadow. *The east wing,* she thought. *If Oswald's anywhere right now, he'll be in there.*

As she stared into the thickest darkness at the end of the corridor, she thought she saw movement. Then she heard it again, the shuffling sound. It could be an animal, she thought. Perhaps one got in through an open window; certainly she could feel a draught out in the hallway, bringing gooseflesh to her arms.

Clara walked slowly down the hall. She had made it as far as the framed picture of the waterfall when her eyes began to pick out a silhouette in the darkness ahead. Not an animal – too bulky, solid. A man.

'Oswald?' she called hesitantly, coming to a stop.

He took one step towards her, and Clara's heart gave an almighty lurch in her chest. He had stepped into a pool of moonlight cast by a skylight immediately above, and now stood like a statue as she gaped at him.

From the neck down, he was attired in full traditional Highland dress: black jacket with silver buttons, red kilt, tartan waistcoat, sporran with a silver chain and a huge gilt cross that lay flat against his chest. But the head . . . He wore a headdress, like the one in the picture she had found in the box in his library: a stag skull, with huge protruding antlers. A white mask covered the upper half of his face, leaving only the nostrils, mouth and firm chin visible.

Oh, dear God . . .

The skull-faced figure was leering at her. The grim expression stopped her breath and made her hands clammy.

'What's happening?' she whispered fearfully. 'Oswald? Why are you dressed like that?'

The figure made no reply, just stood there like a horned

deity, proud and powerful. And in that instant, a reply hardly seemed to matter, because Clara's questions were already being chased away by another, more alarming observation. Her gaze locked on something he was holding in his right hand, hanging at his side.

A gleaming silver pickaxe.

It's not him. Why the hell would Oswald be dressed like that?

She took a few faltering steps backwards, all the time keeping her eyes riveted on the hulking man. A beast in human form. She told herself she was dreaming. Hallucinating. This was all due to her overwrought imagination.

Except, that's the gleam of light on metal. If there's no one standing at the end of the corridor, then what's causing the moonlight to reflect onto the wall?

It was true. As it caught the silver moonlight, the mountaineering pickaxe cast a shining arc up the wall.

Slowly, Clara turned her back on the form. Kept walking until she reached her bedroom. One hand on the doorknob, she took a long, shuddering breath, and dared to turn around.

The figure was gone.

6

By the time the sun was up and Clara had driven away from Boleskine, Jeff Ramsay was inviting PC Lake into an impressive, open-plan kitchen at the back of his gabled bungalow. As his host filled the coffee maker, Adam sat on a chair before a wide window affording a sweeping view of the loch, feeling ever so slightly relieved that from this angle, Boleskine was obscured from view by the edge of Urquhart Bay.

'I was glad that you called me, Mr Ramsay,' he said. *Relieved* might have been a better word. The days Jeff had taken to consider his position had crawled by at an infuriatingly slow pace.

Three months in a rehabilitation centre had not made Adam a patient man. He'd been going stir crazy waiting on Jeff's call, all the while catching the little looks of his colleagues at his scar, his limp, knowing what they were thinking: *He's not up to the job*. He didn't care so much about them, but he did think he might be able to mine a seam of inner confidence if – *if* – he could unearth whatever perturbing secret this community had so obviously buried. And that meant getting the former editor of the *Inverness Courier* onside. It was imperative that Adam won old Jeff round, if only to prove to himself that he wasn't useless. So he had kept a distance and waited. And the waiting had finally paid off.

'Jeff,' said Jeff.

'I'm sorry?' said Adam

'Call me Jeff. If we're going to be speaking openly, we may as well set aside formality.'

Adam nodded. 'Thank you for agreeing to speak with me, Jeff.' He managed not to add, *at last*.

Jeff said nothing. Adam waited until they were both seated with a coffee before diving straight in.

'What do you know about Boleskine House?' he asked.

Jeff sat back with his coffee and regarded Adam through narrowed eyes. 'You're not from around here, are you, son?' he said.

'Why do you say that?'

'Loch Ness is unique; nowhere feels like this place, so inhospitable, so mysterious, and if you want my view, nowhere should. People may think they know what happened at that house. They don't. Dark magic and danger in Loch Ness? Anyone who grew up around here has heard those stories, but they haven't heard the worst of it. No, they have no bloody idea.'

'You mean the suicides? Wasn't it all in the papers?'

'Isn't it in your files? And yet you don't know much about how they died, or you wouldn't be here. We kept the worst of the story out of the papers. Out of *my* paper.'

'You're saying the press was complicit in the secrecy?'

'Well, I enjoy a good story as much as anyone, but I didn't want my friends' livelihoods ruined.'

'So, what *was* the big secret?'

Jeff fell silent for a moment, looking out onto the dark loch. When he spoke again his voice was unsettlingly quiet. 'Goodness me, I have tried, very badly, to move on. But as ridiculous as this may sound, the only word to describe Boleskine is evil.'

'It's just a house.'

A pursing of the lips. 'It may *look* like just a house son, but take my word, Boleskine has always fostered a culture of untamed, malevolent acts. Anyone who has anything to do with the estate puts their personal safety at risk.' He raised his gaze and added heavily: 'Even you.'

'You speak like a man of faith.'

'Do I?' He took a gulp of coffee. The cup trembled in his hand. 'Well, I suppose faith has helped keep my nightmares at bay.'

'Will you confide in me, Jeff?' Adam asked softly. 'You barely have any reason to trust me, I appreciate that, but I'm a man of principle. Will you tell me off the record . . . please? I need to know. It could be important.'

'I *want* to tell,' Jeff admitted. 'For too long I've kept the demons inside. If it will help others, if it will prevent more suffering, as I have suffered.' He stilled, and a faraway look came into his eyes. Then he said, 'Can you guess why I live up here alone?'

Adam shook his head.

'My wife left me, thirty years ago. There was no way she was staying after what I did. My family was decimated, Adam. I lost everything.'

As Adam was processing this, and wondering how best to phrase the questions burning in him – *Why? How?* – Jeff stood up and went over to the coffee pot.

'More?' he said, holding it up.

'Thank you, I'm good,' said Adam.

Jeff filled his own cup to the brim, then returned to his seat. 'So,' he said. 'You want the story.'

Adam blinked. What he wanted was the *truth*, but it seemed rude to point that out, especially as Jeff was unbuttoning his cardigan and making himself comfortable in his chair, ready, at last, to talk.

'I didn't always want to be a journalist,' the old man began. 'Growing up in these parts was lonely, and most people my age dreamed about getting away, becoming someone. You don't sound like you're from around here, Adam, but if you're not, I have to wonder what would bring a man to live somewhere so utterly remote. Me? I wanted to run away, become an architect, build a city and live there. A kiddie's dream, and in the end, of course, reality bit.

'Turned out I had a flair for writing. So after school, my English teacher secured me some work experience at the *Inverness Courier*, and that's how I ended up writing stories for a living. I stuck with it because . . . well, I suppose I didn't know what else to do. My father died when I was a boy; by the time I hit my teens my mother wasn't in the best of health, and I had to provide. Being a desk reporter for the local paper wasn't exactly thrilling, but the work was steady and I was good at it, and after a time, I discovered I liked writing stories. I met a local girl, married her, and I decided to stay. For a time, life was good. We had three kids.'

Jeff's eyes wandered to the view out of the window. A view of an inky-black lake, shrouded in mystery. 'I grew up with some fantastic stories, Adam. It's fair to say that living here, most children do. It's part of our heritage. You ever heard of Saint Columba?'

Adam shook his head.

'An Irish priest teaching Christianity in the Highlands. Centuries ago.'

'Right.' Adam wondered where this was going.

'Legend has it that when crossing Loch Ness, Saint Columba encountered a man in the water whose life was threatened by a terrible beastie. A monster, rising out of the waters. Saint Columba held up his cross, banishing the serpent, but the rumours of "something" in the waters remained. Something huge, an unknown beast. Rumours that infected the minds of everyone in these parts. Christ, I mean, have you been to the airport? You can't look at a wall or a bus without seeing a picture of that bloody monster. It's like a religion up here, you get me?'

Adam did get him. He had felt it the moment he arrived. A place of wonder and discovery. There was a mystical beauty about Loch Ness, which was also the source of so much psychological uncertainty.

'It's in our heads,' Jeff said, tapping his temple. 'The hoteliers, the restaurant owners – that damned monster is the reason they all get out of bed in the morning. Over 1,500 reported sightings, for Christ's sake! Ah, but I know the truth . . .'

Adam had been watching the old man quietly as he spoke, analysing him. His instincts told him Jeff was speaking honestly. Could he really know something enlightening about this mystery? Then again, Adam reminded himself, Jeff Ramsay was a man who used to tell stories for a living.

'You been down to the Loch Ness Exhibition?'

Adam nodded, visualising the converted Victorian stately home. It was impossible during the summer not to get snarled in traffic on the narrow road running past the place. He had never bothered parting with the entry fee, though. Fifteen quid? No chance!

It wasn't that Adam didn't believe in Nessie; more that, if he was honest, he just wasn't very interested in a cartoon legend. Faint sonar traces cutting through the water? What difference did it make if there was an elusive 'beastie', a creature unknown to science, swimming around out there? As far as he knew, 'Nessie' had never harmed anyone. And besides, wasn't it just a bit ridiculous that in all these years, no one had ever once captured a convincing-looking picture of the thing? Wouldn't the body of a creature that was supposedly so large have washed ashore by now?

Adam decided to keep his cynicism to himself. Better to hear what the old guy had to say before giving him a reason not to say anything at all. For all he knew, Jeff was a card-carrying member of the Nessie Appreciation Society.

'Well, I can't say I've had time to visit the exhibition yet,' Adam said, giving 'yet' a special emphasis. 'Looks interesting, though.'

Jeff acknowledged that with the quickest of nods. 'A good business. Steady trade in the summer. In winter, though, it's mostly deserted. Still, my father should have kept it in the family rather than leaving it to the community. If he'd done that, I'd be living somewhere a damned sight nicer than this.' He gestured around the modest kitchen.

'But that's not the point. The point is, my grandfather got the whole exhibition off the ground, funded it. To say he was totally obsessed with the loch and its monster wouldn't be an exaggeration. It was his life's work. And he did his utmost to ensure that his interest, the fruits of his research, lived on after his death.

'I've visited, of course, but I never needed to look at the eyewitness statements or the huge newspaper archive they keep down there. The stories of how the myth began were in my head, always had been thanks to my grandfather. I can't be sure, but I think those stories of something roaming these waters gave me the flair for writing. You see, my grandfather was one of the first.'

'To hear about the monster?'

Jeff shook his head. 'To *see* it.'

Adam took a quick gulp of his coffee to conceal the smile pulling at his lips. 'Your grandfather believed in the monster?'

Jeff held his gaze. 'In July 1933, he was driving along the road that skirts the loch, very near to the hamlet of Foyers, when he saw something he couldn't explain, something that put the fear of God into him. Now, this wasn't some vague shape in the water, a few humps and a long dark neck. No, no. This was a vivid sighting of a beast, made up-close and on land.'

'Okay, but a sighting of what, exactly?'

Jeff shook his head gravely. 'I was only a boy when he told me, but his story remained etched in my memory. You see, my grandfather was the water bailiff for Loch Ness – a superstitious man, it's true. Believed that Loch Ness, the dark forests, the mountains – the whole goddamned place – was an area of what he called "high strangeness"; a location beleaguered with a supernatural and malevolent danger.' He nodded distantly. 'Even now I can hear him warning me and my friends to stay away from the water's edge in case we were taken by the "bean nighe".'

Adam looked quizzical.

'The *bean nighe*,' Jeff repeated. 'An old hag. An omen of death. According to my grandfather, that's what he saw – not a monster in the typical sense of the word, no dark humps in the water, but something very different. An old hag, ghost-like, shambling towards him from the water's edge.'

'Right. Okay. But he was trying to scare you, yeah? Wanted to keep you kids away from the water's edge?'

'Maybe that's all it was. My grandfather earnestly believed in stories, Adam. Their raw and potent power. After he told me about the water demon, a woman with cloven hooves for feet, a walking corpse carrying the clothing of those soon to die, I began to think about it obsessively. The beginnings of a crazy and delirious obsession, which hounded me. And to be straight with you, that's how it was born, the myth of the lonely loch and its roaming monster. The waters soon became a canvas for the most eagerly tempted imaginations.'

'What are you saying?'

'When my grandfather started telling the locals about a monster in the water, a beastie with dark humps and a long neck, the tourists came in their droves. Soon everyone was seeing it!'

'Wait. Let me get this straight. You're saying the monster myth was fabricated?'

'Oh, yes.' Jeff nodded. 'Why, it was irresistible.'

'But why? Tourism?'

'That was a happy by-product. But no. The myth was fabricated as a diversion. At some subliminal level, we turned the horror of our loch into something we could deal with. Something manageable. Like the sufferer of lung cancer tells themselves they have a mild chest infection or just a bad seasonal cough. We dressed our blackest fear in a disguise that was acceptable to us. We called it Nessie. And we told ourselves it came from the wide and wild waters. When it's real source of origin,' he finished bitterly, 'was Boleskine House.'

7

Clara had driven into the village with no particular destination in mind. It was still early, and a blanket of creeping fog lay over the loch. Very few people were about, and that was good, because the last thing Clara wanted this morning was to be seen – or worse, noticed by anyone who might ask her difficult questions. Murdoch's butcher's shop was a hotbed for gossip, and she had no doubt that by now it was all over the village that he'd seen her up at Boleskine.

So, what does your job entail, out on the estate? people would want to know. Who's Oswald? Why did he move to the area? And hey, tell us, Clara, why does he need such a big house?

Yes, Clara, why?

She had some of the answers. Her 'job' was a fallacy, a cover. Oswald was a maniac. What the hell happened at a living funeral anyway? Whom had he invited, and why was he intent on keeping her away from his guests?

Having parked up outside the Loch Ness Centre and Exhibition, which was shut for the season, Clara got out of the car and gazed across the still waters. There was more than a mythical beastie lurking beneath the surface in this community. She was thinking about the package that Murdoch had delivered, wondering about that distant glazed look in his eyes as he drove away, when a shrill voice pierced her reverie.

She turned around, to the row of shuttered gift shops behind where she stood, and saw the source of the noise: a tall girl, no more than sixteen years old, whom Clara vaguely recognised by her hard, rat-like features and raven hair, shaved on one side and long on the other.

'What have I told you?' the girl screeched at someone Clara couldn't see. 'You were told to stay away!'

As Clara studied her, she saw that the girl wore slippers with her black jeans and black T-shirt, and was holding a white mug that was steaming. She was stepping out of a gift shop that Clara assumed was owned by her parents, and she looked more than angry. She looked furious.

It was not the moment to get embroiled in a local dispute. Could Clara get back in her car and simply drive away? That seemed the best course of action, but no sooner had she reached into her handbag for her keys than another voice – a voice thick with unmistakable fear – called out through the frigid morning air.

'Get away from me, Jenna. Please!'

Clara felt her stomach drop like an untethered elevator. She turned back towards the row of shops, and instantly recognised the distinctive ginger hair, braided in two plaits.

Inghean!

She was standing near the visitors' centre, that spirited and sweet-natured girl, her eyes wide and staring as the other girl – Jenna – approached her, brandishing her steaming cup like a weapon.

No!

Without thinking, Clara marched in their direction. 'Hey! What the hell do you think you're doing? Get away from her! Or—'

Jenna swung to face her. 'Or what? You sad old bitch!'

Clara took a deliberate step towards the teenager, glad she hadn't driven off, thinking there was no way she could leave Inghean to this girl's mercy. She was *not* that person. Not like Karl's friends, who turned a blind eye when he became too loud down the pub, too grabby.

'This is Inghean,' she said firmly. 'My friend.'

'Says something about you,' Jenna shot back belligerently.

'Leave her alone.' Clara stepped nearer. 'That's your *only* warning.'

It happened in a flash. To Clara's horror, the teenager tossed her mug of hot coffee directly onto Inghean's dress. Crying out, Inghean leapt backwards and tripped over her skirt. She landed on her back, hands thrusting out to brace her fall onto the sharp gravel.

'Christ!' Clara said fiercely, reaching for Inghean. 'What the hell is wrong with you?'

'She's always hanging around here, and we've told her to stay away!' Jenna shouted, and she tossed the coffee again, this time in Clara's direction.

Clara leapt a few steps back and stared at the girl. Last year, cowering behind the locked door of her bathroom, Clara had come to realise that it wasn't booze or mental illness that made Karl rain down suffering upon her; it was simpler than that. He hurt her because he was a controller. A bully. So was this Jenna girl.

And Clara would not stand for it.

Inghean's left hand was smeared with fresh blood from her fall, her face contorted with shock. Clara was past the point of worrying whether she would be hurt herself. What she had to do now was defend herself, protect Inghean. She reached into her handbag, pulled out her keys, and stepped forward with the key to Boleskine House brandished like a tiny knife between her thumb and index finger.

'You *stay away!*'

Jenna stepped forward. Instantly, Clara swiped and caught the girl's right hand with her makeshift weapon. With a shriek, Jenna dropped the coffee mug, which shattered.

'Try again!' Clara commanded. 'Just you *dare*, and I'll have your throat, your face *and* your eyes.'

Hunched on the ground, Inghean stared up at Clara, slack-jawed and wide-eyed. Clara was somewhat surprised herself by the authority in her voice. The fury this bully had unleashed in her was unsettling. But liberating too.

Jenna stepped back. 'Both of you piss off,' she said warily. 'Now.'

But Clara wasn't ready to go. She stood directly in front of the girl, key pointing threateningly, her eyes glaring with menace. There could be no doubt: if Jenna hurt Inghean again, there would be blood.

'Never go near this girl again. Understand?'

'Fuck you both!' Jenna growled. 'You deserve each other.' She stalked off, into the shop. As she slammed the door with a crash, both Inghean and Clara flinched.

With the brutish girl gone, Clara released a long, relieved breath, then went to Inghean and crouched down to her level. The girl's broad face was flushed and tear-streaked; it broke Clara's heart.

'Are you okay?' she asked.

In answer, Inghean threw her arms around Clara, and Clara held her, stroking a hand up and down her back and murmuring over and over, 'It's okay. You're okay now. I'm here.'

Finally, Inghean let go of Clara and leaned back to stare questioningly into her eyes. 'I haven't seen you,' she said. 'You just vanished.'

Guilt washed over Clara. Clearly, Inghean had been hurt by her absence.

'Did I do something?' she asked, and Clara's heart broke all over again.

'No, sweetie! No. It's just . . . I've been busy. I have a new job, you see.'

'Is it true you're at Boleskine House?'

'Yes.'

Inghean stared at her, pale as the morning frost.

'Who told you that?'

'The policeman. In the village.'

Clara tensed. She knew the secret could never have been kept, but it was alarming to hear that the police had her scent.

Inghean pulled away and lurched to her feet.

'Inghean?' Clara scrambled up. 'What's the matter?'

The girl shook her head, eyes fixed on the ground.

'It's okay, you can tell me. We're friends, right?'

At that, Inghean looked up, and Clara saw more than the distinctive green-blue starburst in her eyes; she saw love. Concern.

'The house is magic,' said Inghean.

That word again. An image filled Clara's head: the mouldy boxes of old newspapers in the boathouse; the italicised quote that had caught her curiosity. *The question of magick is a question of discovering and employing hitherto unknown forces in nature.*

'The house isn't magic, silly,' Clara said, a little awkwardly. 'Why do you call it that?'

Slowly, Inghean turned her head and gazed reflectively over the loch, into the thick morning murk that obscured any view of the house.

'Can't you feel it?' she said in a low voice. 'The power of the house? Good and bad. It can change people, even us.' Eyes back on Clara, she said, 'Come live with me instead. You'll be safe.'

A shiver ran through Clara. For a moment, she'd felt as if Oswald, or someone else, was watching her. 'I wish I could,' she said. 'But I made a promise and I have to go back.'

'Please don't.' Inghean stared at her. And Clara remembered, with fondness, the times they had shared. The movie nights, the long walks along the loch. The innocence and simplicity of it all.

'You'd tell me if something was wrong, wouldn't you, Clara?'

'I'd do my best.'

'We used to tell each other everything.' Inghean sighed.

Not quite everything, Clara thought. She saw herself lying in a puddle of blood. She saw herself lighting the fire at Boleskine.

'Who was that girl, Inghean? Why are you here?'

'Sometimes I come here to feel safe. The kids who live around here think I'm strange.'

'You have to face up to bullies.' She took Inghean gently by the shoulders. 'Whoever they are, understand me? Whatever Gale – your mum – says, stand up to them. *Fight!*'

Inghean blinked slowly as she thought about this. 'All right,' she said at last. 'I can try.'

Clara hugged her tightly. They had been friends for the best part of twelve months. And while it was hard to interact with Inghean as her equal – there were only so many times she wanted to hear Justin Bieber's greatest hits – watching Disney movies with Inghean and walking with her beside the loch had a way of taking her away from her pain like nothing else.

'I miss you, Clara.'

She smiled tenderly at Inghean. 'Me too.'

8

Oswald Cattenach didn't want to enter the church; it made him feel nauseous just thinking about it. He despised churches. Had done since he was seven. He had a vague sense that he wasn't welcome anywhere near hallowed ground, but thought it best to ignore that feeling. Doubt would do him no good. With the mirrors he needed for his Great Operation safely installed at the house, and his guests from London on their way, all he needed now were the relics:

The silver plates. The crucifix. The holy chalice.

Without those, all was lost.

Which was why, steeling himself, he pushed on the heavy oak door. Frigid air swept over his face as he stepped into the church. His eyes didn't adjust to the gloom immediately. It took a good few seconds before he could make out the rows of empty pews, the cold columns, the baptismal font.

His gaze swept around, taking in the quiet ambience. There was no one here. He could take what he needed quite easily, like he had done all those years ago at Oxford. No one would know.

He walked slowly towards the central aisle, his eyes locked on the elevated chancel area: the communion table immaculately laid with all the essential items for celebrating the sacrament of the Eucharist.

But then, hearing a click behind him, he halted. Turning, he saw that the bullish woman stepping out of the confessional box was Aggie Blackwood from Celtic Crafts. He despised people like her. Earnest, vociferous, puritanical believers who had stigmatised the Old God as the devil.

She was facing away from him, closing the confessional door, then marching towards the exit.

Oswald watched her go, a little smile playing on his lips. He knew she would be useful to him yet. Apparently, Aggie's faith ran deep. Which suited Oswald. In his experience, a person's faith was like a magical shot in the arm. People of faith were always more impressionable, more credulous.

Easier to programme.

In his Oxford days, Oswald's psychology tutors hadn't believed there was any such thing as coercive persuasion: the ability to force one's will upon others, to persuade them into hurting themselves or one another. But Oswald knew better.

He remembered the first time he had tried to hypnotise someone against their will, a faggot chorister boy. It was early on May Day morning. He'd wanted to convince the kid to jump to his death from the top of Magdalen Tower. Once the crowds below had fallen silent and the choir was singing the *Hymnus Eucharisticus*, the boy had got very near the edge of the tower. Perilously close. But he hadn't jumped.

That was when Oswald had pushed new boundaries; that was when he'd turned to his friends reading medicine to get his hands on all those blissful, mind-altering compounds; psychoactive drugs to open a wide new window onto human consciousness. Drugs that affected the brain's opiate system: substances like mescaline, from the peyote cactus; psilocybin, from magic mushrooms; and, most effective of all, a powder called scopolamine. Just a quick puff of that into your victim's face was enough to make them do anything you wanted. Scopolamine – or Devil's Breath, as it was better known – enabled you to completely dominate a person, psychologically and physically. And these days Oswald never went anywhere without it.

The heavy church door banged shut. Now Aggie was gone. From the confessional box, there came the sound of a man clearing his throat. The priest was alone in there. Waiting.

Oswald considered with wry amusement. Why take what he had come here for when he could just as easily *ask* for it?

He slipped one hand into his jacket pocket as he looked at

the dark wooden cabinet. Secret. Ugly. Intimate. He hated to look at it. It took him right back to his Christian childhood.

He pulled his hand from his jacket pocket and looked at the tiny re-sealable plastic bag in his palm. It was filled with that glorious white powder. Scopolamine.

'Do what thou wilt shall be the whole of the Law,' he whispered to himself.

And then he stepped up to the confessional box, and entered it.

9

With a horrid fluttery feeling in her stomach, Inghean Kilgour walked beside her mother – who held her hand tightly – along Glendole Road, towards the corner building where her friend Clara had lived.

She had told her mum she didn't want to come with her to the shops. Not today. Her mum had asked her why, and she'd told her mum why. But her mum had just said she had to 'stop this foolishness'. That nothing bad was going to happen.

Inghean knew her mother was wrong. But her mum didn't realise the pictures were back in her head. She didn't want her mother to know anything about them, in case it meant she'd be taken back to the bad place with the locks, where the nurses were supposed to take care of her. But it was so hard for Inghean to ignore the whispers, because what they were telling her was that Clara, her good friend, was in danger. And not just Clara. Everyone in Abersky.

Because of him.

Because of that house.

Because of what he was doing there.

Inghean had felt this way since the day the man with the yellow curly hair and the black turtleneck jumper had approached her on the loch shore a few weeks ago. He had a memorable smile. Pearly white. That smile was the reason she had ignored her mother's advice about talking to strangers; it was his smile that had captured her gaze when she should have been paying better attention to his eyes and the darkness in them. And it would have been impolite to walk away from him, especially because he said he knew her mother, had done business with her.

The man with the curly yellow hair had a soft, magical voice. It made her think of the bedtime stories she had heard as a child – a gentle voice lulling until she felt tired.

She remembered him telling her that he was preparing for something important and that Inghean should go and visit him sometime in his magical house. She would be perfectly safe. She would know when the time was right to go there, because Inghean was a special girl with special talents.

Was she? She didn't think so. Her drawings were special, maybe; the power behind them. And he had a name for that power; it was a name she had heard before, a name her grandmother had used: *an da shealladh*, the gift of premonition.

The second sight.

It was funny, but Inghean couldn't remember how her conversation with the man on the loch shore had ended. All she remembered was drifting over the loch in her mind, swooping low over the water; then opening her eyes, expecting to see him standing right there, next to her, only to find herself utterly deserted at the water's edge. She couldn't even remember hearing the scrunch of his feet on the pebbles as he walked away. Which he must have done, surely?

Yes, of course, but the fact that she had to ask herself that question was probably part of the reason that Inghean was drawn to the shoreline. Why she kept going back, again and again, to draw, to think, to remember.

On Glendole Road, Inghean walked along with her mother, but she hung back a little, looking furtively over her shoulder as they passed Celtic Crafts. They were approaching the butcher's shop now, and that horrible feeling in her stomach was getting worse. Inghean didn't feel comfortable at all – she felt that the time for her to go and visit the magic house was drawing near, and she was worried, very worried, because she didn't think everything the man with the yellow hair had told her was right.

She didn't think she would be safe in that house, or anything close to safe. But now she knew: Clara was there. Lovely Clara who had rescued her that morning.

And Clara, she felt certain, needed help.

10

In the kitchen of his bungalow, Jeff Ramsay drew in a breath that was as shaky as it was long. 'You have to understand, Adam,' he said, 'because of what happened to my marriage, to my blessed kids, there's a part of me that would rather erase from my mind everything that I know.'

Adam nodded in what he hoped was an understanding way and kept the eager questions from his lips: *What do you know? What happened? Come on, out with it!*

'I told you my wife left me,' Jeff said, 'when I suppose that the truth is, I left her first, for another woman.'

'Honestly, you don't need to go into your personal life. I—'

Jeff held up a hand in a gesture that said: *This is relevant. Hear me out.* 'Her name was Rebecca and she was a typist in our office. Moved here with her sister, then met her husband. An older man, ex-army.'

'Major General Cornelius Coughlan?' Adam asked, thinking, *Now we're getting somewhere.*

'Correct. You've done your homework, I see.'

Adam patted the notebook lying ready on his knee.

'I had very little to do with him,' Jeff went on, 'but Rebecca worked for me. Late shifts mostly. Well, you know how it is. At first it was just sex. Amazing, ball-busting sex. I loved my wife, don't misunderstand me, I truly loved her, but the physical spark wasn't what it had been. I made a mistake – shit, show me a man who hasn't. I'll regret that for the rest of my days, partly because I lost my wife and my kids. But also because getting involved with my secretary was what pulled me into Boleskine's dark orbit.'

'Why did the general buy the house?'

'General Coughlan had lived in London his entire life, a charitable man, a Christian, until he became involved with a spiritual philosophy called Thelema. He called it his new religion, and this worried Rebecca deeply.'

'Why?'

'Because Thelema wasn't a religion, it was a cult. A magical society founded upon a new ethical code: "Do what thou wilt shall be the whole of the Law".'

'What does it mean?'

'Basically? Do what you want, no matter how shameful. Commit any act of brutality, regardless of the consequences, to get what you want.'

'Sounds like New Age crap to me.'

'Yeah, Rebecca thought so, too. I'd laugh about it with her in the office. How her husband was "seeking out his own True Will". Shit, I had no idea.'

He fell silent for a moment, staring into space.

'We began using the house for sex when her husband was out. It was a splendid place in those days, all silky carpets and heavy curtains. But strange too, filled with weird spicy aromas and this unnatural, discomfiting silence. And you know the funny thing? It never felt empty. On several occasions we thought someone was with us, as we were . . . well, you know. But when we turned on the lights, there was no one there.'

Jeff frowned, blinking hard. 'Didn't spook me, though. I was like you are now, curious. About the legends, tales of underground tunnels and all that. I was curious about the cemetery, too. Lying there next to the water. God, it's a desolate, brooding spot. I wanted to go down and explore.'

'What did Rebecca think about that?'

Jeff shook his head. 'We had one hell of a row about the cemetery. I can't remember exactly how we got in, because the gate was rusted shut, but I can remember how angry Rebecca looked when I said I was going to find a way in anyway; probably by climbing over a fence and shredding my hands on barbed wire, knowing me. I wasn't exactly a careful kid. Anyway, I remember her yelling at me not to go in, and asking myself what the hell her problem was.

'But we finally did get inside. Both of us. Maybe Rebecca was afraid of being left alone in that lonely spot as night fell, or maybe my persuasive abilities were a damned sight better than I give myself credit for, but looking back, knowing everything I know, it was bloody cruel to force her. Cruel and reckless.

'We walked around for a bit, reading the names on the mossy headstones to see if we recognised any, but we didn't. There was this old stone building in the far corner, a mort house – you know, where they used to store the bodies waiting to be buried. I wanted to see inside it. As you can imagine, Rebecca did not. Still, I was looking about for something to stand on, so I could peer into the little black window – no glass in it – when we heard it.'

Jeff closed his eyes and mouthed a single word: *Boom*.

'The shotgun,' Adam guessed, and Jeff nodded.

'The sound of the blast came from the house. Which couldn't be right, because although her husband owned a gun, there was no one home. We knew that – General Coughlan was in Inverness, visiting an old friend.'

'Then what was it?'

'An omen,' Jeff said, his face darkening. 'And it put the fear of God in Rebecca. That was the first time I realised just how seriously she'd taken her Bible lessons. The Lord's way had been drummed into her and her sister when they were kids at Sunday school. God, she practically begged me to leave, and I agreed. She pleaded with me never to return to Boleskine cemetery, and I agreed to that too.'

'And did you keep your promise?' Adam asked as Jeff took a gulp of what must by now be at best tepid coffee.

Jeff tapped his head. 'Up here. I couldn't get the place out of my head. Some mornings, I'd wake up in a sweat, still seeing that black window in the mort house, daring me to look, the gunshot ringing in my ears.'

'And Rebecca?'

'Rebecca,' said Jeff, and his voice was heavy with remorse. 'She began turning up late to work, looking grey and drawn. Said it was "that damned house" getting her down. Her husband's behaviour was becoming more and more erratic. He was into drugs by then. He'd barricaded the whole east wing of the house, wouldn't let her near it.

'I tried to put it out of my head. They were offering me more shifts on the news desk. If I focused on my work, put in the extra hours, maybe I'd get a quick promotion. But that house, stuck in my head . . . It was getting to me. So I hit the archives. Research, Adam, a newspaperman's bread-and-butter. And a policeman's, I suppose.'

Adam eyed the notepad on his lap – chockful of blank pages, he knew – and nodded his agreement.

'What did you learn about Boleskine?' he asked.

'That it was built on the site of a tenth-century Scottish kirk that caught fire during congregation. Everyone perished in the fire. Everyone. One of the worst tragedies in Scottish history. But do you think there's an explanation? No. Course not. And that since then, Boleskine had changed hands many times. Various owners suffering strings of bad luck. One sought to build a pig farm on the property. The venture died on its arse, his partner was sent to jail and the animals starved to death. But one owner in particular, around the turn of the last century, seems to have been the catalyst for the worst activity.'

'Who was he?'

'I'll get to that,' Jeff said, a little tersely. Subtext: *I'm the one telling the story here, and I'll tell it my way.*

'Anyway, word started to get around the village that I was interested in the history: who built Boleskine, who owned it, why no one went up there, why so many refused to pass it on foot, preferring to take the old hill paths. But the more I asked, the less people wanted to talk. It was as if the whole community shared some visceral, unacknowledged fear of the place. That's what I thought. I knew I should stop probing. Every time I asked anyone about the site, the warning was right there in their eyes: *Back off. For God's sake, know what's good for you and back off.* But it drove me mad, the mystery of it all. And of course I was as stubborn as they come.'

Jeff cleared his throat a few times and rubbed a hand down it, as if all this talk was physically draining him.

'Take your time, Jeff,' said Adam.

He took a breath, and continued: 'Rebecca's husband, General Coughlan, believed there are parallel planes of reality all around us. He believed that to experience those planes of existence, we need only alter our state of consciousness. Retune the brain. And to do that, he was abusing drugs; experimenting with magical ceremonies, rituals, black masses to invoke spirits he believed would grant him enlightenment.'

'Bonkers.'

'Perhaps,' Jeff said. 'Of course, now you're asking yourself what happened next with me and Rebecca. I'd like to tell you that it was me and me alone who decided to go back to the house, but that wouldn't be completely true. I take responsibility, Adam, hand on heart; but I was acting on the direction – or rather, the misdirection – of someone else. The woman who'd caught God even worse than Rebecca – her sister. Bitter, nasty old cow.

'One night, Rebecca had arranged for us to stay in her sister's spare room. Why the hell we didn't book a room somewhere I don't know. That would have been the sensible thing to do. Anyway, I woke in the dead of night to find that crazy bitch, her sister, standing at the bedside, just staring down at me. The moonlight was bright, and I could see her spiteful face – it was like she was possessed with an absolute hatred of me. For a second, I just lay there, paralysed, thinking, *She's going to pull a carving knife out of her sleeve and lunge for me.* Then I leapt up – but she was already striding out of the room.'

'And *did* you follow her?' said Adam.

Jeff shook his head. 'The next morning, I'd just about convinced myself it was a dream – I'd been dreaming vividly since the cemetery. Disturbing, wild dreams that left me exhausted. But after Rebecca left for work – she was on the early shift – her sister cornered me in the kitchen, apologised for disturbing me during the night, said that she couldn't help it because she was prone to sleepwalking. Blackouts. I laughed when she said that; it was so ridiculous. Pathetic.

'Rebecca and I had argued the night before, and you won't be surprised to hear that what we argued about was the house. My obsession. Her sister must have been earwigging; I don't think for a moment she didn't have a glass pressed to the wall most of the time I was in that flat. Now she told me, "Go back to Boleskine, Jeff. It's all you think about, so go on back."'

'She was that direct?' said Adam.

'And some,' said Jeff. 'She told me by going out there, I'd

see the truth. She knew she was coming off as crazy, but she didn't care. All that mattered to her was getting me away from her sister, for good. I think she knew there was something corrupt about Boleskine House, something dangerous even; she wanted it to affect me. And, of course, it did.'

'One question,' said Adam, flipping open his notebook and clicking his pen to write. 'Rebecca's sister. What was her name?'

Jeff grimaced. 'She runs that craft shop in the village. Maybe you know her? Her name's Aggie Blackwood.'

11

The confessional's confined space smelt of wood and varnish. Oswald Cattenach closed the door and sat down on the uncomfortable bench, keeping his eyes on the silhouette behind the screen.

'My son. How can I help you?'

The priest's voice, dusty and cracked, took Oswald right back to his childhood. Sitting in a low-lit, musty box just like this, talking in low tones to a man behind a velvet curtain.

'How long has it been since your last confession?'

Bowing his head, Oswald said nothing.

'You have been away from your faith?'

In his memory, Oswald saw the quiet, insecure child he had been back then: hands nervously wriggling at his sides as his mother ushered him into the church to meet her new best friend, Father Brown, for confessional.

The first ritual.

'My son?'

Oswald hesitated; to his surprise, his mouth had gone dry. The sensation was deeply unsettling; he wasn't used to feeling intimidated by anything. But he felt a special, vitriolic hatred for the Sacrament of Penance.

How old had he been? Seven? Around that age. Old enough not to understand why he needed to confess his sins like this. Why did confession need to be done in a dark space through the mediation of a stranger behind a velvet curtain? If God was everywhere and always listening, then why couldn't he just confess his wrongdoings from his bedroom?

But such questions had meant nothing to his mother. Her faith had burned like the sun; she had insisted Oswald go to confession. Even when he summoned the courage to tell her what it was really like talking to the priest, alone, she made him go.

'How can I help you, my son?'

Oswald's whole body was tensing now.

'You are seeking guidance in this trusted place?'

Trusted? In that instant, all he could think about were those occasions – how many had there been? – left alone with a man of the cloth, hidden from public view, in a dark, enclosed space just like this. His father was dead by then; maybe things would have been different if his father hadn't succumbed to the liver disease. At least his father, a retired pub owner, had some humanity, some common sense.

But his mother?

Penelope Rose Cattenach was nothing but a brainless

bigot; a cruel fanatic whose every view on life was driven by dogma. As long as Oswald could remember, she'd told him he was a failure in God's eyes; a sinner. After she caught him looking at some porn mags, she called him 'a twisted child', 'a disgusting pervert'. By the time he started secondary school, thanks to her, he was impossibly introverted; a figure of laughter amongst the other boys, his kidneys punchbags for their pleasure.

'My son?'

With a coal-eyed stare, Oswald raised his face to the iron grille.

'You are troubled by something?'

The pit of his stomach suddenly felt hollow. Oswald supposed that yes, he was troubled, very much, by something; but not by the need to avoid purgatory in the next life. What troubled him was the memory of first tasting alcohol in a shadowy box like this. Learning all about mortal sin and the punishment of the eternal fires of hell from a man who discovered Oswald's vulnerabilities and taught him all about the impurity of dirty thoughts. Oh yes, Father Brown had wanted to know all about the sins of a young boy. Had threatened to tell his mother about those sins. Unless . . .

'May the Lord help you to confess your sins with true sorrow.'

Oswald closed his eyes and sat there for a moment, perfectly still, his fist clenching and unclenching around the tiny, powder-filled bag in his pocket. Remembering the shame and the fear. A child penitent in a shadowy space. Where he was encouraged to sit on Father Brown's knee.

Was it any wonder that by his university days, any Christian faith Oswald had held had gone? Replaced by an obsession with magic and hypnosis, with gaining power through any means necessary. Diseases and obstacles could be defeated; even people could be overcome.

'Do you feel it, my son? The call to turn back to God?'

Silently, Oswald fixed his eyes on the priest's silhouette. For a brief moment, he thought about confiding in this old man, telling him about the hurt and the degrading damage he'd suffered because of men like him, men of the cloth. Why not? The stories would never leave the seal of the confessional. And it would feel good, satisfying, to stir this man's guilt. Toy with him a little.

But the throbbing in his head was a reminder of the advanced temporal lobe tumour growing in there; the preparations that needed to be made for his Great Operation. A ceremony of the most arduous undertaking. Time was short, and there was a job to do.

Lowering his voice, he asked a question intended to throw the priest off guard:

'Tell me, Father: is it lonely?'

'I beg your pardon?'

The priest sounded confused, and that was good. There was a knack to bringing someone into a hypnotic trance, Oswald had discovered: induce curiosity first, then introduce the right hypnotic language patterns; words like 'imagine' and phrases like 'have you ever?' That sort of language made the subject reflect. It also helped if you spoke quietly and slowly, to bring the voice right down to the dark basement of their unconsciousness and plant a seed down there. An embedded command that would germinate and grow, until the personality succumbed.

'I asked, is it lonely?'

'I'm not sure that I under—'

'Is it lonely?' Oswald pressed. 'Hearing the messy little secrets of lives you aren't allowed to live. I mean that *must* be lonely, right?'

'Well . . .'

'The more you hear my voice, the more you agree.'

'The more I . . .'

'Agree.'

'Yes,' said Father Allen, in a voice that was suddenly more distant. Lighter.

'I came here for something.'

'Guidance?'

'Not quite.'

Oswald slipped the plastic bag with the white powder from his pocket and opened it. Then he leaned closer to the grille.

'Hey, you know, Father, I couldn't help noticing your silverware out there is looking far from its best.'

'Oh?'

'Yeah, the more I think about it, the more I think you should do something about it. Those are sacred items, right? I mean, the plates and the chalice you use to celebrate the Eucharist. They deserve to be looked after.'

'They *are* looked after.'

'You think I'm lying?'

'I—'

'The more you listen to my voice, the more you feel you can relax and trust me.'

'Trust you?'

'That's right. Every time you take a breath, every time you hear my voice, you'll find yourself relaxing. Trusting me.' Oswald spoke slowly now in a soft, lulling tone. When he used the correct modal operators, the precise tone of voice, few refused him. 'Picture them: the silver plates, the silver chalice. Can you see them?'

'Yes . . .'

'I want you to hold those items in your mind. I want you to notice how badly they need polishing. Do you *see* how tarnished they are?'

'Yes.'

'Do you know what an affront to God that is? Do you know how your congregation will feel on Sunday, when they notice how blackened the silver is?'

'I'll have to clean them?'

'That's right,' Oswald said, his voice light and almost musical now. On his side of the grille, he tapped out a small heap of white powder onto his open palm. He held that powder reverently as he puffed on it.

The priest on the other side of the grille gave a sudden jolt as he inhaled the dust. There was a little crash, which Oswald assumed was his Bible falling from his lap and dropping onto the wooden floor. The priest started coughing. Violently. Oswald listened, smiling. It would take a few seconds, that was all.

Finally, from behind the iron grille, there came only the sound of shallow, slow breathing.

'Are you there?' the priest asked weakly.

'I'm here,' Oswald said, his voice nothing but a soft hush.

And closing his eyes, he reached out, into the old man's mind.

12

'Ah, Ms Kilgour!' Murdoch McHardy said as Inghean and her mother entered his shop. 'I have the steak put away for you out back.'

'Beef wellington again,' Gale said, and Inghean's stomach twisted at the words. Her mum made beef wellington once a month; it had been her father's favourite dish, she said. Inghean didn't really remember her father, or miss him. It wasn't *that* making her feel all wrong.

Murdoch gave a polite smile that said, *Won't keep you long,* then went back to serving Aggie Blackwood her sweated back fat, mixed with onions, oatmeal, double cream and pig's blood. It wasn't as bad as the haggis, with its sheep's liver and lungs and trachea, all churned up together, but Inghean couldn't stand black pudding. Just the thought of it made her feel queasy – which was how she felt now. Not just because of the black pudding, though. Because whatever her mum had said, Inghean was still very sure that something bad was going to happen soon. And that she would play a part in it.

Once Aggie had paid for her pudding and was working on squeezing it into her French-style string shopping bag, the butcher slipped into the back room. He returned a moment later, wiping his hands on his apron, his ruddy face apologetic.

'My mistake, sorry, Gale. I'll need to cut a new piece.'

'No problem.'

'Trimmed to lean?'

Inghean flinched. The horrible feeling in her stomach was growing, threatening to erupt.

'Yes, please.'

'Ma, please, I want to leave. Now.'

'You did say it's beef wellington you're making?'

'Beef wellington . . .' Inghean echoed, the tendons standing out in her neck, her eyes wide. She knew those words. They were in her – *put* in her; she felt that very strongly. And now the next words were burrowing their way out of her mind and into her mouth, onto her tongue. She clamped her lips together to hold them back.

'. . . *with a red wine sauce.*'

The words were out before she knew she had spoken them. Horrified, Inghean slapped a hand over her mouth. But it was too late.

Behind the counter, the butcher had gone very still. 'A red wine sauce,' he intoned. 'Of course. Yes, I remember. Now.'

Aggie Blackwood frowned. 'Murdoch, are you all right?'

Murdoch didn't look all right, not even nearly. It was as if the words 'red wine sauce' had landed in his head like a hammer. His eyes, which before had been bright and friendly, now had a flat, dead sheen to them, as if he wasn't seeing his customers at all.

It was something I said, Inghean thought. *Something the man with the yellow hair made me say.*

'Murdoch?' Aggie said.

'Mr McHardy?' Gale said.

'Ma,' Inghean said, and she tugged urgently on her mother's arm.

'It's okay,' Murdoch said in a tone that suggested nothing about this situation was okay. 'I'll get. Your meat. Now. I'll do it. Now.' As he said this, his eyes were huge and glazed, and he wasn't looking at Aggie or Gale or Inghean. Instead, he was turning slowly to the chopping board behind him.

'Please, Ma. Please, please, *please!*'

13

'I will do as you wish.'

Father John Allen heard himself say those words – words he hadn't anticipated – and registered how weak and distant his voice sounded. A dreamy influence had stolen over him, and he felt as peaceful as a Sunday afternoon.

'Can you hear me?' the penitent on the other side of the grille asked.

'I hear you,' the priest heard himself answer.

But I wish I could see you. Who was this mysterious man who had wandered into his church? He sounded young, well educated. A new member of the congregation, perhaps? He didn't recognise the voice, but he couldn't stop listening to its soothing lull, either. He tried closing his eyes and picturing the man's face, but strangely, all that came was a mental image of the silver plates and chalices he knew he had to clean.

How could he have been so careless, so reckless with such sacred items?

The stranger's voice reached him again, as if from so far away:

'Can you answer a question for me?'

'I can try.'

'What does it feel like when you polish the silver? Does it relax you?'

'When I—'

'Polish the silver. Does it relax you?'

'It does, yes. Very much so.'

'As relaxing as a Sunday afternoon?'

'Quite.'

'And what is it like when you hear my voice?'

'Relaxing.'

'Good. Now then, suppose you entrust the cleaning of the silver to an outside party. Do you remember the last time you trusted someone? Absolutely. Completely.'

'Yes.'

'Remember how good that felt?'

'Yes. It felt . . .'

'What?'

'Reassuring.'

'To have an outside party take away your silverware felt reassuring?'

'Yes.'

'Why?'

'Because I knew they would do a good job.'

'And you would trust *me* to do a good job?'

'Well . . .' Through the grille, Father Allen caught a glimpse of the confessor's eyes; they looked very wide to him, wide and a dazzling, celestial blue. The calmest colour. Serene.

For a brief moment, those diamond blue eyes fastened on his own in an intense stare, drilling right through him. It caught Father Allen off guard.

'Would you trust me?' the stranger asked.

'Yes.'

'You realise that I'm a good, dependable person. You realise I'm the best person to take care of your silverware. Sooner or later, you'll realise I'm the right person for the job. Sooner or later, you'll hand me the plates, the altar crucifix and the chalices.'

Father Allen opened the confessional door, noticing the ornate statues, dark wooden panelling and pews with a new level of detail. It was as if he was seeing the world now through a lens; every colour, every angle, magnified.

He had a vague sense that he should feel frightened, but instead what he felt was intensely relaxed. Cold air was on his face, and he seemed to be moving now, his feet walking of their own accord. Drifting.

Time passed. He didn't know how long.

Then, abruptly, a loud clap jolted him out of his daze.

'Can you still hear me, Father?'

Vague, Father Allen apologised. 'I was miles away.'

As he opened his eyes, the priest realised that the sound of his voice was already fading away, the floor moving under his feet, his vision swaying. An intense weakness in his hands and legs. In fact, he felt sick, and the corners of his mouth were beginning to spasm, as if from a trapped nerve. 'What . . . what's happening to me?'

The stranger's broad figure was facing him now; his eyes so wide and blue. Dimly, Father Allen registered the shock of blond curls; the striking, angular face. The expression it wore was one of sick, satisfied accomplishment.

'Thank you for fetching these, Father,' said the man. 'I'll take good care of them.'

Surprised, Father Allen looked down at the silver plates and chalice in his arms; he hadn't even been aware he was carrying them until now.

'Give me the artefacts.'

That voice, somehow both tender and brutal.

'Give them to me now.'

'Take them,' the priest invited, his vision swimming; his voice no more than a hoarse croak.

And the man did.

14

In the butcher's shop on Glendole Road, Gale couldn't help feeling painfully embarrassed by her daughter's behaviour, especially in front of Aggie Blackwood, but she wasn't alarmed. Inghean often lost control of her emotions. Still, she was sorry to be troubling Murdoch McHardy. He was clearly over-wrought, exhausted.

The butcher was whispering to himself now as he stood over the chopping board. Gale angled her head to get a better look at the steak he had picked out for her. He had never given her a poor cut – only the best for Gale Kilgour, twice nominated Highlands Businesswoman of the Year.

She saw him put his strong hand around the helve of the meat cleaver. It looked heavy, the blade gleamingly sharp.

'Ma, *please*!' Inghean shook her arm.

'If you can't control your daughter, you really should keep her at home,' said Aggie coldly.

'I beg your pardon! Who the hell do you think you're talking to?'

With unmistakable contempt, Aggie raised her chin. 'I'm not sure you'd like my answer to that question.'

The simmering, resentful expression on Aggie's face made Gale realise for the first time that the woman who ran Celtic Crafts really was unhinged. How did someone end up in such a state, alone and embittered and paranoid?

'Ma, Ma, Ma, MA!'

'Not now, Inghean,' said Gale sharply, as Aggie tutted and shook her head, but Inghean yanked on her arm, hard, turning her to face the counter.

And Gale saw the butcher, still whispering to himself, lift the meat cleaver. Her field of vision shrank to the gleaming blade.

'THERE'S NO MEAT!' Inghean shrieked, pointing. 'Ma, there's no—'

The blade came down, slicing through the air, and buried itself in Murdoch's left forearm, a few inches above the wrist. They heard the crunch of blade on bone, the dull thud as the metal embedded in the wooden chopping block, but there were no screams – not even from Murdoch, who stood looking down at the dark blood pooling on the counter.

In horrified shock, Gale grabbed her daughter's arm; Inghean was going to pass out, she was sure of it. Then she saw Murdoch wrench the dripping blade free.

A deluge of blood flooded the chopping board.

The severed hand flopped to the floor.

And Murdoch stood there, his face completely devoid of

expression, the ragged stump at the end of his arm spurting blood – over the counter, the floor, up the white-tiled walls – with an awful pulse.

Then came the scream. It had come from Aggie Blackwood, whose doughy face had turned chalk white with horror and who was stumbling away from the counter.

'Help him, for Christ's sake!' Gale cried, rushing to his assistance – only to jump back, shocked, as Murdoch swiped the cleaver at her over the counter.

Both Aggie and Inghean were screaming now, and scrambling out of the shop.

'Murdoch,' said Gale, edging back, 'please, you don't look so good, and I really think you ought to put that down, now, please, Murdoch—'

'Trimmed to lean,' said the butcher. 'You'll have it. Trimmed to lean.'

'For the love of God, JUST PUT THE KNIFE DOWN!'

But he didn't. And he was no longer frozen, but coming around the counter – *coming for her.*

Now, Gale's only thought was to get the hell out of there, as fast as possible, even if it meant leaving him to bleed to death. She turned in panic to bolt for the door – and slipped on a swathe of blood.

She went down hard, her head landing with a painful *crack.*

From this position, she could see Aggie out on the street, standing beside Inghean, who had collapsed to the kerb.

'Aggie!' she cried. 'Help me, please – AGGIE!'

Aggie Blackwood did not come to help. She just stared back at Gale with a fierce, damning look that seemed to say: *Sorry, but you deserve this, just a little bit. You know that, don't you, Gale?*

Terrified, Gale shot a panicked glance at Murdoch, at the

animalistic sheen in his eyes. He was coming around the counter, moving slowly. As he advanced, the exposed bone where the wicked meat cleaver had severed his wrist seemed to gleam white, and still the fleshy wound was gushing blood.

Gale rolled and began frantically crawling on hands and knees across the blood-slick floor towards the door.

Next instant, her body gave an awful jolt as the butcher stamped on her ankle.

'HELP!' she shouted. 'HELP ME!'

No one came to help.

There was a thud behind. Gale twisted around to see Murdoch on his knees behind her. The meat cleaver clattered to the floor, and his huge, bloody hand reached for her.

She kicked out at him once. Twice. On the third attempt, her shoe smacked him hard in the face.

He cringed back and looked . . . confused? His body stilled, and then a horrible, low gurgling sound arose in his throat. He mumbled something that sounded like, 'What happened?'

Then, bled out and wide-eyed in death, he toppled, face first, onto the floor.

She crawled for the door, pulled herself up on the door-frame, and stumbled out onto the pavement, choking, sucking in the clear air. Her daughter, her sunshine girl, was crumpled up in a ball on the kerb, sobbing. Gale looked at her for a moment as a distant police siren made itself heard, then crouched down beside her, hugging her, holding her close.

PART FOUR

ABERSKY'S HORROR

There is something in my soul, which I do not understand.

– Mary Shelley

1

'So, somehow I summoned the nerve to go back to Boleskine,' said Jeff Ramsay with a sigh.

He and Adam were in the same seats beside the window, empty cups abandoned at their feet. There was no question of another coffee now; no question of a comfort break, even. The words were flooding out of Jeff. He had spent a good ten minutes filling Adam in on the man who owned Boleskine at the turn of the century; the man, he said, who 'unleashed the infernal darkness that has haunted Loch Ness'. Now, he was picking up the story after Aggie Blackwood had told him to go to back to the house, to 'see the truth'.

'Rebecca kept a small dog,' he said. 'A West Highland terrier. Cute little thing. Pickiwig was his name. Well, as I set foot on the driveway, Pickiwig came running up to me with something in his mouth. Dropped it at my feet. I crouched down, picked it up and realised it was a fragment of bone. Now, it's not uncommon to find fragments of animal bone when out walking in these parts, so I thought nothing more of it. I walked on up to the house. And that's when things got weird.'

'Weird how?'

'For one thing, I could smell incense wafting out of the east wing. There was a layer of sand covering the porch immediately adjoining that part of the house. And it was covered with footprints.' He shook his head. 'That's the wrong word. They looked more like animal prints. Hoof prints in the sand.'

Adam stared at him. 'Where did they come from?'

'I know where General Coughlan thought they'd come from. I remember Rebecca telling me about them before, and I'd laughed. The general thought they were the footprints of demons.'

Adam was silent. He wasn't sure he believed in such things.

'When I went in through the front door,' Jeff went on, 'I found another little bone in the hallway. And the dog was at my feet again, licking the damned thing. What would you have done?'

Adam shrugged.

'I took the bone and I threw it outside. Then I went to the east wing.' He paused and passed a hand over his eyes. 'And there he was; Rebecca's husband, sitting in front of an enormous mirror, with most of his head completely blown off – a shotgun at his feet. Adam, his brains and the rest of his skull were splattered all over the wall. And beetles, crawling black beetles. The bastards were everywhere.'

Jeff looked sickened by the memory. There were beads of sweat on his forehead, and his hands were gripping the arms of his seat.

'The pathologist was Harry Kirkpatrick, cause of death: "gunshot wound to head". That's when I remembered the weird boom we'd heard down in the burial ground,' he said. 'Well, what would you think? I'll tell you what I thought, as weird as its sounds; I thought we'd experienced a premonition of the general's death. An omen. That's the sound we heard. His shotgun blast, a week before he actually pulled the trigger.

'I ran then. I didn't stop running until I was half a mile

away. I called the police. And the next day, when they took my statement, I told them all this. They didn't seem very interested in the premonition, but they were interested in the bones I'd found. Turned out they were fragments of the general's skull.'

'Jesus,' said Adam.

'He'd dressed up the east wing like some ghoulish temple. The interior was engraved with bizarre symbols. In every room.'

'Symbols? Like the ones in the pictures I showed you?'

Jeff nodded. 'Exactly like those. Signs of the zodiac.'

Adam shook his head, blinking questioningly.

'If you believe in astrology, Adam – and you may not, but hear me out – you believe that every heavenly body exerts its influence in one way or another, for good or for ill, on the living.'

Adam took a moment.

'*Every* heavenly body? You mean—'

'The sun, the moon, the planets,' Jeff said, nodding. 'Here, show me the pictures again.'

Whipping his phone out, swiping to the right images, Adam did.

'See here.' Jeff pointed tremulously at the phone screen. 'This symbol represents Mars: energy, determination, aggressiveness. And this one' – again, he pointed – 'Saturn. Frustration, gloom, catastrophe.'

Adam processed this as the old man became pensive and said:

'Mars square Saturn is the most sinister sign, I am afraid to say.'

'Why?'

Jeff's eyes, wiser and older, flicked up.

'Hitler had it in his horoscope.'

'Right. But that doesn't mean—'

'There were books, Adam; ancient books, discovered inside Boleskine House, about the general's cult and the inhuman lunatic who started it, the one who owned Boleskine at the turn of the century. A depraved drug addict with a fondness for the dark arts, who used the house as his temple. His lair, would be a better word. And what do you think? The general had followed this wacko's ceremonial instructions to the letter. They found goblets filled with cats' blood all over the house. Can you believe that? And that's not all. In the chimney was a goddamned calf's heart, stuck with thorns. Seriously! The sick bastard had been sacrificing animals in there.'

'No wonder there's a stigma to the place,' Adam said. He leaned forward. 'Tell me something, the symbols . . .'

Jeff nodded. 'Very astute, Adam. Yes, they forebode ill fortune, and yes, they were all over that fiendish house. I heard afterwards that they whitewashed every wall in there, but as the paint dried, the markings just kept reappearing.'

'You're saying it was some sort of black magic?'

'I'm just telling you what I know,' Jeff replied, flinching at the suggestion and looking away. He left a heavy pause. 'Perhaps you can guess what happened next?'

'I'm not sure I want to.'

'My dear Rebecca came undone, bless her soul. The poor love completely fell apart. Couldn't tolerate being in that house on her own after what had happened. She came to me, pleaded with me to leave my wife, my kids, and take her away. I refused.' He swallowed hard. 'I turned her away. Then she really lost it; kept making all these crazy phone calls to my wife, ranting about how her husband's work had set an unspeakable evil free, that it was spreading through the village like a stain, that it would pass down the decades, that others would suffer . . .'

Tears were trickling down Jeff's cheeks now. He didn't raise a hand, didn't acknowledge them. Just continued the story that was riveting and appalling Adam in equal measure.

'Seven days after the general's suicide, I got the second worst visit of my life. It was from you lot. Two officers. I knew Rebecca was dead before they told me; it was in their eyes. But I could never have guessed how she'd done it – the extent she would go to. She took the rope from the swing at Boleskine House, tied one end to a tree and the other around her neck. Then she got in her husband's BMW and floored it, full speed. A deliberate attempt to kill herself, the coroner said. No outside influences, he said. I'm not sure I believe that.

'By the time Rebecca was in the ground, my wife said she was leaving me, and that she was taking the kids with her. But she didn't do that, in the end. Because she couldn't . . .'

He gulped a breath, and it made a horrible rasping sound.

'Jeff?' said Adam, alarmed. 'Are you—'

'No, I'm bloody not all right,' snapped Jeff. 'I saw her. I saw her with my own eyes!'

'Saw who?'

'The *bean nighe*. Remember what my grandfather told me? I saw her, the old hag, the omen of death. It was late on the Sunday evening. I went down to the water's edge and said a prayer for Rebecca. And when I turned around, this atrocious figure was just a few feet away from me. Horrible. The stench' – he shook his head – 'it was like rancid meat. And that face. Christ. I wanted to be sick at the sight of her. Not just because she looked like a rotting corpse, but because of what she was holding, get me? Her hands . . . they were like claws, and hanging from them were these filthy clothes. Two little jumpers my wife had knitted for our children.

'I can't remember how I got home that day. I can't remember if I spoke to the hag or if she said anything to me. Everything's blank. All I know for sure is that seven days later, my ten-year-old daughter died suddenly at her school desk. Two days after that, my fourteen-month-old son died of convulsions on his mother's knee.'

Adam looked on, shocked and horror-stricken, as tremors wracked through Jeff – silent, shuddering sobs. The depth of the old man's burden was painfully obvious. Adam wondered how anyone could endure such tragedy and not lose their total sanity.

Just then, Adam's phone rang.

Both men started.

Adam answered the call, listened to what the caller had to say, and abruptly stood.

'Jeff,' he said, 'thank you for your time.'

'Where are you going?' Jeff called after Adam as he strode as fast as his limp would allow to the front door.

'The village,' Adam called back as he threw open the door. 'There's an emergency in the village.'

2

A small crowd of the curious and concerned had gathered around the entrance to McHardy's of Abersky. As questions were fired back and forth, Gale was kneeling beside her daughter on the kerb. Her dress was dark with fresh blood, her skin the colour of milk, and she was shielding her daughter's sight from the dark, sticky puddle that was pooling at the entrance to the butcher's shop.

'My fault,' Inghean wailed. 'My fault!'

'What do you mean?' Gale cried, mystified, holding her daughter even tighter. 'It was an accident, Inghean, a terrible accident. The shock of it must have . . . I don't know, sent him over the edge. It was nothing, absolutely nothing, to do with you. Understand me?'

'It was everything to do with her,' said an accusatory voice.

Turning, Gale raised her eyes to the woman who had spoken.

Aggie Blackwood stood at the edge of the crowd, and on her face was an expression that had no place at this horrific scene: pious satisfaction. Here stood the disparaged fanatic whose wild beliefs had, she was convinced, been finally vindicated.

'I told you,' she hissed. 'I *warned* you that girl was unstable, and now look, *look* what she made him do!'

A murmur of intrigue rose from the onlookers.

'You're insane,' Gale spat. 'Inghean didn't *make* him do anything! You saw the way he was – berserk! He must have taken something.'

Aggie was already shaking her head. 'He was fine, Gale, completely fine, until your wretched daughter spoke to him. That's what made him snap. Don't tell me you didn't see the dark sheen in his eyes. It's to do with Boleskine, that cesspool of vice. I know it.'

'What the hell are you talking about?'

'Today,' said Aggie significantly. 'I saw Inghean sketching the damned place, earlier today. And I know that just now

Murdoch was bewitched, or possessed, or something! I've seen it before. He did what he did because it was hardwired into him. By that girl of yours.'

Furious, Gale shot to her feet, and the two women faced each other above Inghean. It was all Gale could do not to launch herself at Aggie.

'I warned you,' Aggie snarled. 'I said your girl was different to the rest of us, that she should be locked up. But did you listen? No, you did not. You should remember, Gale: "rebellion is as the sin of witchcraft"!'

'You've lost it!' said Gale, and she looked around the crowd for someone, anyone, to back her up. But no one did.

'I am speaking of the invisible forces,' Aggie insisted, her eyes unmercifully alight. 'Oh, don't look that way. You think you can't impose your will upon another? Shows how naïve you are. Mind control! It's been practised for centuries! Inghean's been hanging around Boleskine House, lured there, I imagine, by temptation, the impulse to do ill. Well, you sold that dia-bolical property, Gale. Who did you sell it to, hmm? WHO?'

Taken aback, Gale hesitated, not knowing that the question of who had taken ownership of Boleskine House was one that Aggie Blackwood had been struggling to contain for many weeks; because just thinking about that property, Aggie's own association with it, years ago, was enough to drive her insane with grief for her dead sister. It was true, Gale thought Aggie was mad; she had no doubt about that. What she didn't know was that Aggie's anger flowed from a reservoir of unfathom-able sisterly grief.

'Oswald Cattenach bought the house! Why do you—'

Aggie was looking at her with desperation. 'What does he look like?'

'I don't see what that's got to—'

'TELL ME!' Aggie bellowed.

Gale looked back at Aggie with a mixture of defiance and defeat.

'Handsome, artistic. Blond curls with dark roots.'

Aggie's face dropped. For a moment, she looked as if she was going to cry. Then her anger returned. 'You realise what you've done, the evil you've unleashed?'

'You,' said Gale, jabbing her finger towards Aggie. 'You *stay away* from me and my daughter, got it?'

She turned to Inghean, but found her daughter was on her feet and pushing clumsily through the crowd, sobbing and gasping for breath.

'Inghean, wait!' Gale called after her, and she started to follow, but came to an abrupt halt as she crashed directly into someone who had lurched out of the crowd before her.

Constable Lake.

'Gale, I came as soon as I heard. You were inside when it happened, I understand?'

'Yes, but I need to get after—'

'I'm sorry, Gale; I need to take a statement. Now, please.'

'But Inghean needs me!' she all but yelled.

Adam followed Gale's frantic stare, but didn't see Inghean. 'I'm sure your daughter will be okay,' he said in a level voice. 'She's probably gone to rest.' Taking Gale by the arm, he began to lead her towards his car. 'I'm sorry, but it's procedure. Come on. We'll get you cleaned up, and a change of clothes. I won't keep you long, I promise.'

She looked at him with desperate eyes, and managed: 'Aggie Blackwood saw what happened too. She was right there, in the shop. She left me with him in the shop! You need to talk to her as well.'

'Fine,' said Adam. But when he scanned the crowd, he found that Aggie Blackwood was also nowhere to be seen.

3

At the far end of Glendole Road, a siren was wailing. Darkness was falling and snow was beginning to drift, and Aggie had the road all to herself, which made crawling along in second gear all the easier.

Knowing that the police would want to interview her about the incident inside the butcher's shop didn't worry her. Why should it? She had nothing to hide, did she?

No. It was Gale's daughter who was guilty of muddying the waters.

Gale's daughter, and Oswald Cattenach.

Aggie hadn't been entirely surprised to discover that man was the new owner of Boleskine House. She supposed that the vague suspicion had been lingering in her mind, just beneath the surface, since he had wandered into her shop and purchased the ornate standing mirrors. (Strange, but in her memory, that whole exchange seemed almost to have never happened now.) What she knew for sure was that the meeting had left her feeling dazed and not quite herself.

She didn't know how Inghean had provoked Murdoch into

behaving like a monster, but she was certain as certain could be that the girl had put the devil into him, and that Oswald Cattenach was involved. Inghean's drawings were a dead give-away; she saw the way Boleskine House transfixed the girl as she sat alone on the loch shore, gazing dreamily across at it, her hand moving jerkily over the paper.

Before today, Aggie had attributed that unusual behaviour to Inghean being Inghean – a simple, strange girl who believed in faeries and water spirits could easily be beguiled by the alluring mystery of a deserted old house. But now Aggie *knew* there was more to it.

Which was why she had followed the girl from the butcher's shop.

Keeping her headlights switched off, so as not to reveal herself, Aggie continued crawling along the road behind Inghean. Another passer-by, less enlightened than she, someone less receptive to the wisdom of God, might mistake the girl's dishevelled appearance for that of someone in need. They might stop and offer a lift to the girl with the broad face and the solemn eyes, who was sobbing into her hands and tripping clumsily over her skirt.

Not Aggie. She would observe, learn. Prepare.

Already, she had noted that Inghean wasn't going home; in fact, she was walking in the opposite direction.

Where are you going, Little Miss Sunshine?

Aggie stared fixedly through the windscreen at the strange girl. How had she provoked Murdoch McHardy into behaving that way? And why?

I'm going to find out. This is a test from God.

In the smudged glow of a solitary street lamp, Aggie saw that the girl was advancing towards a tall, turreted Gothic

building on the opposite side of the street. The Loch Ness
Centre and Exhibition. A sign out front encouraged curious
visitors to 'Experience the magic and mystery of Loch Ness'.

Why on earth was she coming here?

The exhibition was shut, for one thing. Aggie hadn't been
inside for years; all she knew was that this once grand building had been totally gutted inside to produce six separate
elaborately themed chambers, connected with mock tunnels
through which visitors passed, learning the story of Loch Ness
from the Ice Age to the present.

As Aggie watched from the shadows, Inghean, a frail, shivering figure, stood outside the front of the building. She threw
a furtive glance around, as if to check no one was observing
her, and then shambled around to the back of the building
and disappeared.

Interesting, thought Aggie. She had heard Gale complaining
before that her daughter tended to disappear in the evening
hours. Was this where she came? Was this her hiding place?
The exhibition was a sprawling space; it wasn't inconceivable
that Inghean knew of a way to get inside without detection
after business hours.

Behind the wheel, Aggie nodded to herself as a sense of
determination swept through her. She had first-hand knowledge of the horror that visited Loch Ness and the village of
Abersky. If Inghean was consorting with the infernal forces
of Boleskine House, it was most certainly her duty to put a
stop to it.

What would Jesus do? What would Jesus want?

'Micah,' she whispered. '"I will put an end to all witchcraft, and there will be no more fortune-tellers." Revelations:
". . . the corrupt, murderers, the immoral, those who practise

witchcraft, idol worshipers, and all liars – their fate is in the fiery lake of burning sulphur."'

But was that going *too* far?

Aggie considered for a moment, then her mind took her back to the scene inside the butcher's shop: Murdoch's cleaver slashing down, the blood spurting all over. Inghean's fault.

The right thing to do is God's will. Vengeance.

Aggie had scented the sin of the girl, and she knew what must be done.

Resolved, she shifted into first gear and drove away from the visitors' centre – Inghean's secret refuge. But Aggie already knew she would be coming back here.

Soon.

4

Since seeing Inghean that morning outside the exhibition, Clara had driven miles. To Inverness and back, more than once. Thinking about Oswald, his house, his funeral and his expected guests. Now, as she drove back into Abersky village, the flashing blue lights at the bottom of Glendole Road warned against going that way.

Slowing the car, she thought quickly. She still had a spare key to her old flat above the butcher's shop, and thanks to Oswald she had hit on the idea of staying there for the night. Now she would have to find somewhere else to bed down, but where? It was freezing, the snow was falling thickly, and she didn't much relish spending the night in her car, parked up in a lay-by somewhere.

How about the Abersky Hotel?

That was an option. But the proprietor was a nosy busybody who'd no doubt have questions about her new employment at Boleskine House; she would want to know why she needed a room.

Make something up. Say the boiler's blown, anything.

Clara should have turned around and driven to the hotel. But those flashing lights ahead were bothering her.

Something's happened on Glendole Road. What?

She wasn't proud of the fact, but curiosity propelled her to check it out. A few minutes later, she had parked up outside the police cordon and was out of her car. As she got nearer, she saw plenty of other people had come to look too, and that made her feel a bit better – until she got close enough to make out the scene.

In the light cast by the street lamps, she saw a police officer crouched on the pavement, putting something into a plastic bag. A camera crew filming a journalist talking sombrely into a mic. And two paramedics, carrying a stretcher out of Mr McHardy's shop.

'Blood everywhere,' she heard someone nearby say. 'Look, see it all up the window.'

Clara didn't look at the blood. Her eyes were fixed on the stretcher. To be more precise, the body bag on the stretcher.

Who?

Her question was answered in moments, when she tuned into the chatter, and her hand flew to her mouth.

Murdoch McHardy? But she'd seen him just yesterday, at

Boleskine House, when he brought the delivery. It seemed impossible he could be dead. And the blood – how had this happened?

Then Clara saw a face she recognised; it belonged to a man coming out of the shop. Stepping forward, she called out to him.

5

Alone in his London flat, Karl's mind was on Alison. God, he missed her terribly. Needed her.

He weaved out of the bedroom and into the living room and planted himself at the computer. Once the web browser loaded, he logged in to the missing persons' website to which he had uploaded Ally's picture and opened the inbox.

No messages. *Nada.* Zilch.

With a burst of anger, he snatched up a coffee mug next to him and hurled it at the wall. The mug didn't even have the decency to shatter; it just bounced with a dull thud. He pressed his palms against his eyes and gripped the sides of his head.

Where are you?

He typed her name into Facebook. Nothing. Googled her. Nothing.

I will find you.

It was a selfish thought, not exactly altruistic, he knew that, but how could he make peace with his conscience if he didn't find her, if he didn't apologise? It was what he had advised his patient Terry to do; it was what *he* needed to do, wasn't it?

And if he wasn't honest with himself, wasn't he just a little bit jealous at the idea that she had found someone else? Someone better than him?

She's mine.

Karl heaved himself out of the chair and went to the kitchen. The bottle of vodka on the counter was half empty. He was all out of ice and lemon and tonic, but that didn't stop him pouring the vodka neat, a full tumbler of it, and swigging it back. Now, propped up on the breakfast bar, he closed his eyes, distantly wondering where he would be now if he hadn't been sacked. Karl understood that he wouldn't ever be going back to that Mindfulness Centre. Not as a counsellor, anyway.

He drank.

As he dragged a hand across his mouth, he supposed he should probably be grateful the police hadn't come knocking after his drunken break-in. Practising gratitude – that was one of the themes for counselling at the Mindfulness Centre. At least he no longer had to contend with all that crap, along with the rest of the mind-numbing rigmarole of counselling the hopelessly mentally disturbed. Lunatics like Terry Sanders, whose dead wives threatened them with revenge.

Movement caught his eye – the living-room curtains billowing inwards. Strange, because the wind chimes that hung immediately outside that window weren't making a sound. Frowning, Karl peered at the rose petal curtains he had always hated. Wondering at the way the fabric whipped and snapped in a breeze he could neither feel nor hear.

What the hell is making them flap like that?

He thought this reminded him of something he didn't like,

but couldn't quite place. No sooner had the question shrieked through his mind than the curtains stilled again.

He wasn't in the mood for this, and he wasn't going to risk any further disturbance. He would shut the window. But as he trudged across the room, a sound announced itself from the bedroom.

The radio crackled static, then fell quiet.

Karl felt uncomfortable at that moment, though if questioned, he would have struggled to say why. Probably the booze, but he had spent the whole afternoon and most of the evening feeling uneasy, with one eye on his wedding photograph.

He lumbered off to the bottle of vodka waiting in the kitchen. That would calm him.

Just one more drink, he told himself as he unscrewed the bottle cap. *One more, neat, and then maybe a quick bath to help me feel—*

His head snapped up at the faint sound of music. He had turned the radio off before coming to the kitchen, hadn't he? It was possible he had forgotten, but he didn't think that was likely, because he would normally be able to see the radio's flickering LED reflecting in the hallway, and right now the hallway was dark.

Well, when you are drunk, the mind plays tricks, makes mistakes. It was nothing to worry about.

Karl followed the music, which was faint, inconsequential. Only upon entering the bedroom and seeing the radio *was* switched on was he struck with recognition – the fretted guitar and the lyrics.

Yes, the lyrics . . .

Led Zeppelin. How long had it been since he had heard that song? He didn't even want to think about the answer. What good would it do? That song made him remember the dark times, shortly after their wedding, when the bottle first began whispering sweet nothings to him.

He snapped the radio off and was about to leave the room when he halted at the door. He could smell something unusual, something very unsettling. The scent of Sunday morning.

Incense?

It was. He abruptly realised that he hadn't caught that scent since his mother was alive, and felt ashamed. Since she had died he had made a conscious effort to forget her.

A tiny shock of confusion crackled through him, but the sensation was transitory, too nebulous to mean anything. And just as suddenly, the scent of incense was gone.

Karl blinked. Had he even smelt it at all?

He was stepping out of the doorway when he realised that all of this felt too horribly familiar. The billowing curtains, the unsettling sense of intrusion, alone at night – Karl thought of Terry, who had beaten his wife and then seen a threatening vision of her. Terry, who had asked:

Do you think the dead can cause us harm?

It suddenly occurred to Karl that he was afraid. And that made him feel paranoid as hell. With eyes wide and roving, he locked the door and every window in the flat, using the little window key he'd never used before. Then he made himself sit at his desk and reminded himself of his purpose.

Alison. Find Alison.

With the computer screen bathing his face in a sickly yellow glow, he continued searching – unaware that, behind him, at the back of the room, the muted television was showing a news report that should have fascinated him. Unaware that, for the first time in over a year, his wife was, in a sense, right there in the room with him.

On the TV, a woman who now called herself Clara Jones was standing in the cold on Glendole Road in Abersky, looking shaken and frightfully pale as she conversed with a uniformed police officer – right outside a blood-spattered butcher's shop.

6

In the darkness and the falling snow, Gale Kilgour's car screeched into her driveway. Seconds later she was out of it, flying to the front door. Inghean hadn't been in the office on Glendole Road. She would be here at home, she had to be. Gale burst into her house, the front door banging open.

'Inghean!' she called. 'Are you here? INGHEAN!'

Her gaze skittered from the hallway to the living room on her left, to the kitchen up ahead.

All was quiet. Ahead of her, on the right, was the staircase. *She's in her bedroom,* Gale thought. *Must be.*

Gale darted for the stairs, bolted up them, flew into Inghean's room – and stopped. And turned on the spot, taking in the many drawings plastered on the wall over her daughter's bed. Simple drawings, but the subject was clear enough.

Boleskine House ablaze, black smoke belching into the sky. Drawings of stick women, too – floating on water.

Gale's stomach plunged. Why the hell was Inghean drawing such disturbing images?

She had no answer; but perhaps there was a way to find out. Perhaps *that* was where Inghean had gone.

No sooner had the thought struck her than Gale was off again, striding towards the stairs, already calculating the quickest route to Boleskine House.

7

'I don't understand. You're saying he did it to *himself*?'

Horror-stricken, Clara stared at the slick black smear of blood trailing out of the butcher's shop. What PC Lake was saying made no sense.

'According to witnesses, yes,' said Adam. 'Murdoch hacked off his hand, then attacked your old boss.'

'Gale?' Clara's eyes snapped to the policeman. 'Oh, my God, is she okay?'

'She's calmer now. She's gone home to be with Inghean.'

At the mention of the girl's name, Clara felt a stab of guilt. Inghean should be protected, always, at all costs.

'Clara?'

Adam Lake's voice jolted Clara out of her thoughts.

'What?' she said. 'What is it?'

'I had a look at Murdoch's list of recent deliveries. I wanted to build up a picture of where he's been recently, who he's met. His last home visit was to Boleskine House. Is that where you're staying?'

Adam was looking carefully at her – and suspiciously, she abruptly realised. At once, guilt surged up in her and she saw herself carrying the charred body to the mort house. He was right to be suspicious of her; she had blood on her hands.

'You saw him then? Murdoch?'

Clara nodded.

'Yeah.'

'And how did he seem to you? Notice anything unusual about his behaviour?'

'No,' she said at once. But then she realised – with a sickening jolt – that was a lie. Murdoch hadn't been himself when he left. Sort of vacant. After his private meeting with Oswald.

Oswald.

Was Murdoch's death in some way connected to him? But how? It made no sense.

'Sure about that?' Adam asked. He was looking closely at her now as she struggled to banish the mental image of a vacant Murdoch heading back to his meat van.

'Yeah, he seemed fine to me.'

Just then, Adam's phone buzzed in his pocket. He kept his eyes steadily on Clara as he pulled it out and answered the call, his face gradually hardening as he listened to whatever the caller was telling him.

Clara realised – not without a stab of shame – that she needed to get away from here. Now. She was trying not to be paranoid, but she couldn't stop thinking about Oswald. That he had somehow played a part in this bloody mess. She was about to turn away when Adam's hard voice commanded her to stop.

'Just a minute, Clara.'

She grimaced; then, with her heart in her mouth, slowly turned to look at him. 'Something wrong?'

His face said there was, and Clara braced herself for more uncomfortable questions. But the words on Adam's lips were a statement:

'I've got Gale on the phone. Inghean's missing.'

Clara's heart squeezed painfully. The horror Inghean had seen here – it was no wonder she'd gone off.

'She's probably walking along the loch,' Clara said. 'I'll go—'

'No,' said Adam. 'Gale's convinced Inghean went to Boleskine House. She's driving out there now.'

Clara went rigid with alarm. 'What? No. We have to stop her. Now! Oswald can't be disturbed. He gave specific instructions—'

She snatched the phone from Adam and put it to her ear; but the signal was gone.

Adam stared at Clara's horrified face. 'What the hell's wrong?'

Without answering, Clara ran for her car.

8

In the vast and austere kitchen of Boleskine House, Oswald took in the late-evening news report. On the screen, a newsreel showed a dark rubber body bag being carried out of the butcher's shop into a waiting ambulance, while a crowd of horrified villagers looked on.

'Police say the attacker, fifty-one-year-old Murdoch McHardy, had been acting strangely before cutting off his own hand and turning his cleaver on his customers. It is understood that Mr McHardy had been suffering from depression, after neighbours complained of unacceptable levels of noise coming from his shop.'

Oswald moved to the television and snapped it off. Cocked his head, listening.

Was that a car coming up the driveway? He thought it might be.

But that was all wrong. His three very carefully selected guests were already waiting for him in the east wing. So who was this interloper?

Quickly, Oswald stalked to the window and looked out into the black night. The beam of a car's approaching headlights washed the driveway in orange.

More trouble.

He would go to his guests quickly and warn them.

Together, they would take care of this uninvited guest.

9

Adam Lake sat in the passenger seat looking across at Clara so intensely she was finding it hard to focus on the narrow road unwinding before her. She had tried to come alone, *demanded* she come alone.

'You should have listened to me,' she told him. 'This is a bad idea.'

'So you said.'

'I meant it! Oswald's unpredictable. Unstable. And tonight he's in the middle of something . . . important. If I stride in with the police, there's no telling what he might do.'

'What's he got to hide?'

Clara's mind flashed to the mort house, the rotten human remains concealed there.

'Nothing.'

'Clara, what's he doing up there?'

'He's sick. I mean sick in the head. Literally. The guy has mental-health issues, problems with his temper. I'm just trying to help him manage them.'

'Go on . . . explain.'

She realised she would have to give Adam something to go on, if she was to have any hope of keeping him out of the house.

'Today is his living funeral.'

Adam shook his head doubtfully, but she put up a hand.

'I saw him preparing. I've seen his medication, okay? He's dying.'

'Yeah? Well, even if that is true, I'm willing to bet that's no funeral he's hosting tonight.'

She flicked a look at him; saw his face was grim. 'What are you talking about?'

'I spoke with Oswald's old tutors at Oxford, Clara. They were sure he was unhinged. Even as a student he was experimenting with drugs, hypnosis. Something called coercive persuasion.'

Clara frowned. 'Never heard of it.'

'Well, those academics who remember Oswald told me he was learning about neuro-linguistic programming, manipulation techniques, when he should have been studying conventional psychology.'

'Neuro what?' she asked as she steered the car around another treacherous corner.

'Careful,' snapped Adam. But not *slow down*, she noticed; he seemed to accept that time was of the essence.

'Neuro-linguistic programming,' he went on, 'crude mind control; conditioning people to act in a particular way on hearing the right trigger word.'

Brainwashing? Clara shook her head. Was she supposed to believe she had been living with her very own Svengali?

'You don't think it's possible?' Adam pressed. 'Think about it, there's precedent for this. Charles Manson managed to brain-wash his followers into committing murder. Why shouldn't Oswald be capable of something similar?'

Her memory spun back to the books in Oswald's study: *Thought Reform and the Psychology of Totalism*; *The Rape of the Mind*.

Oh God, she thought, suddenly remembering Murdoch McHardy's blank face as he left Boleskine House the previous day. *Could Oswald really have made him chop off his own hand?*

'The human mind doesn't work like that,' she said, answering her own question. 'You can't just reach in and repro-gramme it.'

'No? What do you think ISIS do? Seducing young people, vulnerable people, impressionable people, to commit the worst acts imaginable. I'm talking about the complete annihilation of a person's will, their self-control.'

'Seriously, Adam?'

'Remember Jonestown? 1979. Nine hundred people dead. Cyanide poisoning. Mass suicide, Clara; and all because of one vicious man, who mastered their minds.'

'Yes, but—'

'Listen: Oswald studied these techniques. At Oxford, he had

access to psychedelic drugs like LSD and mescaline, drugs that only made it easier to break minds.'

She flashed back to Oswald raining down medication onto the kitchen table. Proof he was dying. Ever since, there had been bottles of pills all about the house. She'd stopped checking the labels. Were they prescription, all of them?

'I'm telling you, it *is* possible, and Oswald Cattenach is dangerous. A bloody lunatic, I suspect. Just like everyone else who's ever lived in that godforsaken place.'

Taking her eyes off the road for only a second, she looked warily at him. 'What are you talking about?'

'I'm talking about the monster who lived at Boleskine a century ago,' Adam said. 'The maniac who founded the cult.'

'The cult? What cult?'

So Adam told her as quickly as he was able what he had learned from Jeff Ramsay, about the dark cult of Thelema and how it related to Boleskine House, and the beast who had entrapped Clara there.

10

Gale's Volkswagen Golf had barely crunched to a halt before she was clambering out of it, struggling through the driving snow across the driveway to the house, which she now wished had never come on her books.

Inghean must be here. Please let her be here!

Her ankle was throbbing from where Murdoch had stamped on it and her thoughts churned with aching self-reproach. She should never have allowed Inghean to go off on her own.

Neglectful, that's what she was. A bad mother. Wasn't that what Paul had called her all those years ago, when she had sent Inghean to the mental hospital over in Inverness? Neglectful and closed-minded.

She was so sure back then, when Inghean had first started with her peculiar drawings, that she was doing the right thing. But now? Maybe Paul was right. Maybe what Inghean had needed back then wasn't a doctor, but a listening ear. An open mind.

Sinister and leering, Boleskine House rose before her. Only after hammering on the enormous front door did it occur to Gale that something was amiss here. The house was in pitch darkness, but for a dim yellowy light on over the porch – the one light you would leave on when going out – and the grounds, carpeted with snow, seemed to command a perfect and disquieting stillness.

But there were cars parked on the driveway, and Gale could hear a sound, very faint, emanating from the house. What was it? A low, rhythmic drumming.

And she thought she detected a fragrance.

Is that incense?

She banged harder on the door. No answer. The doorknob turned in her grip, and the door swung open. Gale waited on the doorstep, expecting Oswald Cattenach to appear from within. He didn't.

'Mr Cattenach?'

A sudden noise behind her made Gale whirl around.

'Oh, thank God,' she said when she saw the man standing

there; a man in a tartan kilt and black dinner jacket, the finest Highland dress; snow swirling down around him. She noticed at once how still, how watchful, he appeared. Those dazzling, celestial blue eyes.

'Listen, is my daughter here?'

'In *my* house?'

'Anywhere?'

Gale was terrified that her precious daughter was still distressed and in shock at what had happened at the butcher's shop, or worse, that an accident had befallen her Inghean on her way to this blasted place. What if her scarf had come loose and blown into the water? What if she had gone after it? In the darkest corners of her imagination, Gale saw the footprints in the snow trailing to the water's edge. She saw her daughter's still, frail body bobbing gently on those dark waters. She would drown out there, in the loch, without ever knowing how sorry Gale was for not believing in Inghean's gift, for not having faith in her.

Oswald, wordless, tipped his head to one side and simply stared at her. She was uncertain he understood the urgency of her plea.

'Mr Cattenach, is she here?'

'No.'

'Sure you haven't seen her?' She opened the locket around her neck and showed him the photograph of Inghean, angling it to the porch light so he could see.

'No,' he answered. 'Mrs Kilgour, what on earth has happened?'

'An accident in town,' she said. 'God, an appalling accident. Inghean ran off. I thought she must have come here.'

'Here?' He looked quizzically at her. 'Whatever for?'

Heaving a sigh, Gale tried to contain her frustration. She didn't want him to know her daughter was obsessed with his house. He might think Inghean had been involved in the fire, and then what?

'I'm sorry, I should go,' she said quickly, going to walk around him.

'No, wait,' Oswald said. 'Look, we're in the middle of something here, but we'll do all we can to help, if we can.' He smiled at her kindly. 'Come with me.'

She turned to go. But at that moment, Gale remembered her first encounter with him when he came into her office in the village, asking about the house; remembered him also dropping into the conversation that he was from London.

Not Scottish.

She fought her suspicion, but two questions occurred to her. The first was: why was he dressed up like a Highlands laird? It wasn't Burns Night, Oswald wasn't Scottish, so what was with the red kilt, the black jacket, the sporran?

And what, exactly, was he in the middle of?

A formal occasion, from the way he was dressed – but what?

She was sure her suspicions were groundless, but Gale suddenly found herself wanting to see inside Boleskine House; found herself wanting to check for herself that Inghean wasn't here. She told herself she was being silly, paranoid, wasn't she? Probably. But anyway, it wouldn't take a moment just to check, and it would be worth it, wouldn't it, to put her mind at rest?

'Please, do come in.'

Gale hesitated as he led the way through the pillared entrance. Her eyes were on the sinister stone dogs standing guard on either side of the columns. She hadn't liked entering this house when it was her job to sell it, and now he'd taken occupancy it was even less inviting – all shadows and stillness.

'Trust me,' he said calmly. 'We'll do what we can to help. Come in.'

Gale stepped forward, not so much deciding to enter the house as feeling pulled into it. As she crossed the threshold, the shadows within touched her face and scattered her neck with gooseflesh.

'Head down there,' he said, gesturing left, along the main hallway that ran to the east wing, from where a faint spill of red light was seeping around the corner.

Now Gale could hear the murmur of voices from that direction, and that low drumming, like a heartbeat, building and building. Pulsing. She moved slowly through the murk, registering the smell of incense, and something else: a smouldering, stomach-churning odour. Again, she hesitated.

'Don't stop,' Oswald called.

She turned, surprised, and saw he wasn't with her, but was still standing near the front door.

'Go on,' he prompted. 'I'll be right behind you. Promise.'

Doing all she could to remain calm, Gale inched slowly forwards into the east wing, towards the murmured conversation – no, it sounded more like a murmured prayer.

Then she turned the corner and entered the billiard room; and froze in shock.

What in the world . . .

In a second, Gale's eyes darted from the foul-smelling candles, to the three figures, to the strange-looking table . . . to the odious thing upon it.

She had just worked out what that thing was and opened

her mouth to scream when cold, powerful hands clamped around her neck from behind.

'Hush now,' Oswald Cattenach whispered in her ear as he squeezed, and squeezed.

11

Speeding along the narrow road that ran adjacent to the loch, Clara heard Adam's words, but didn't believe them. Even when her mind joined the dots . . . *Oswald's self-imposed fasting* . . . she didn't want to believe what Adam had told her.

'This is the truth, Clara. You must believe me.'

Don't believe it!

The idea that she was complicit in something so nefarious, so obscene, was unacceptable to her. Unthinkable. And yet, deep down, it made sense. It all made sense.

'Clara?'

She held up a hand. 'I can't deal with this now, Adam, okay? It's too much.'

The turning for Boleskine House was coming up. She pulled up at the side of the road and killed the engine. 'I'm going up alone. If Inghean and Gale are up there, then—'

'I'm taking you all back into the village. And you and Oswald are coming with me, to the station.'

'Why?'

'Because you need to start making sense!'

She got out of the car. He did the same.

Clara turned to face Adam, mustered a hard stare, and said over the car: 'I need you to stay here. Please. Will you do that?'

Keeping one hand on the open passenger car door, Adam just stared back at her.

'Oswald's unpredictable. Volatile. He won't respond well to this intrusion. God knows what he'll do!' She remembered her jailer wielding a shotgun at the little boys on his land, and shuddered violently. *Not Gale. Not Inghean.* 'It's safer this way. I think he'll listen to me, okay? He knows me.'

At last, Adam nodded, but the determination still shone from his eyes. 'Five minutes, then I'm coming in. And the two of you will come with me down to the station.'

Clara took this in.

The truth will out?

Murder and madness in Loch Ness?

Well, so be it. As long as Inghean and Gale are all right.

In a way, it was a relief to know the ordeal could soon be over. That whatever happened to her – public disgrace, prison – at least she would be free of the house.

And Oswald, who was, after all, a monster. No better than Karl.

There was no time for that – to process. To feel. She had to go. Now.

She turned back to Adam and said, 'Five minutes then. In the meantime, wait here.'

The freezing wind snapping at her face, Clara passed through the eagle-mounted gates and up the uneven driveway. Only when she saw the three cars in front of the house and the many drawn curtains did she halt. One of those cars was a shiny new silver Volkswagen Golf. It made her recall the early mornings, raring to go; the first viewings; the spiel she had come to know by heart: 'Central, well located, lots of potential.'

For the next few seconds Clara's memory reached back twelve months. She saw herself fumbling with keys, flashing her best smiles at the myriad prospective buyers; ending her days with no commission, cursing herself for her mistakes – like leading the buyers into poky second bedrooms, not letting them wander by themselves. Then she realised why these memories were surfacing now.

The car she was looking at belonged to Gale.

She's here. Inghean too?

Quickly, she trod through the snow to the front door, and used her key to let herself in. She was surprised to find the hall in total darkness. Even before she flicked the light switch, she had a sense that it wouldn't work, and she was right.

A power cut?

Well, that was possible; but what she suspected was that someone, probably Oswald, had deliberately cut the power. Because he wanted to be off grid. Because he wanted no one to know what was going on here.

And what was going on here?

Clara thought at once of what Adam had told her in the car about the house's history, about its previous owner.

'*Clara, the man who owned that house at the turn of the century, the man who gave it its sinister reputation, was a self-proclaimed prophet of a hedonistic new religion. Aleister Crowley. Poet, painter, mountaineer – and occultist. A sadist. Went by the name of the Great Beast. Thought of himself as the devil's chief emissary on earth, you understand? And upon taking ownership of Boleskine, one of the first things he did was to consecrate the north-easterly parts of the house. Those included the billiard room. Get me? The billiard room became his temple. He used it for a six-month ritual to summon demonic forces, with the sole aim of eventually contacting his Higher Self, his "Guardian Angel".'*

In the centre of that wide hallway, Clara was hesitating. She was remembering the masked figure with the horned headdress. Just the mental image of that creature, half-human, half-animal, threatened to weaken her knees.

Maybe it wasn't so wise coming up here alone after all. But what choice did she have? She wasn't going to let anyone else come to harm. Not Gale. And especially not Inghean.

Clara edged forwards, feeling her way along the spine of the house with one hand on the wall. It was icy-cold to her touch, and more than once she nearly shrieked as she became entangled in cobwebs.

Inevitably, she was being drawn to the east wing; that was where she could hear a low, mysterious beat and muffled voices. Someone reciting a prayer?

Oswald must have invited a priest, she thought. That would explain the foul smell of incense, too.

But though she strained to hear, she couldn't understand the prayer. And beneath the overpowering incense, she was picking out another smell. Putrid.

At the end of the corridor, the tarpaulin Oswald had used to screen off this part of the house was gone now. Still, Clara was in no doubt that what lay beyond was out of bounds to her, in Oswald's rulebook.

Pulse quickening by the second, she leaned forwards and peered around the corner into what had been the billiard room. She remembered this part of the house as it had been, after the fire. A blackened ruin, strewn with rubble.

No sign of any rubble now.

What the hell?

12

With snowflakes swirling around him, Adam struggled across the Boleskine estate, the wind crying at his back. More than once he stumbled on the uneven ground – *bloody leg* – but he resisted the urge to use the torch in his pocket. He didn't want to be seen.

He hadn't given Clara five minutes. He'd been out of the car in one. Not following her, though; he'd skirted around to the back of the property.

He could call for backup, probably should do. But if his instincts were wrong and everything here worked out fine, there'd be hell to pay with Shawcross for disobeying her orders. So he was going in alone.

The house loomed above him on the slope. It was engulfed in darkness, but he thought he could make out little slivers of light around windows in the east wing. He knew the layout of the house from when he'd searched it for the missing junkie – who, Adam was now more convinced than ever, had been here. Come to harm here.

Except you searched, and you found nothing.

Adam was about to climb the slope to the house, planning to approach one of those slivers of light and peek in, when a thought stopped him dead. He turned to the gate just beside him.

I didn't look everywhere. I didn't look in there.

The burial ground.

He tried to picture what lay in the darkness beyond that

heavy iron gate. Saw, in his mind's eye, leaning grave markers jutting out of the snow and tangles of weeds. And, in the lowest corner, in a mass of ivy, some sort of dilapidated outhouse. A very good place to hide a secret.

Had he noticed it last time, when he was looking for the disappeared man, before he knew just how evil this location was? He must have glimpsed it, wondered about it. But he had not walked down this slope, passed through this gate, and he had the idea now that fear, innate and primal, had made him turn away.

The thought made him furious. He would not turn away now.

He went to the iron gate, pressed his hand to the cold metal – and it swung open. As he stepped forward, onto marshy ground, a sudden sense of a presence, of being watched, made him spin around, drawing his torch from his pocket and brandishing it as if it were a weapon.

No one there.

You know too much about this place; Jeff Ramsay made you paranoid.

Around him, fir trees whispered. It seemed to him that even the breath of the cold night's wind was soured with evil. Adam looked back towards the house. It was out of sight, from this angle, which meant he was too. He switched on the torch.

You've got this, Adam. Just go slow; keep your wits about you.

As he trudged on through the snow, in the bobbing torchlight the stone structure loomed up before him. It was a macabre, squat, round building constructed from rough granite blocks, with a slate roof. He went towards it. Knowing he had approached more threatening, more intimidating scenes in London's tower blocks was a tiny comfort to him. At least in London he knew what he was dealing with, but this was something new. Was it a tomb? He knew they could be large, but he'd never seen one like this.

He knew one thing, though: he had to see inside.

His spotlight picked out a dark opening fronted with a rusted iron gate. He got nearer, casting the beam from his torch deep within, but it revealed nothing more than a filthy wall and a turning. From this angle, he could see nothing of what lay beyond the bend.

He tried pulling and pushing on it, but the gate refused to open.

Suddenly, his nose wrinkled at an odious smell; it was coming from in there, so foul and fetid he could hardly believe it hadn't hit him earlier.

With mounting dread, he stepped back, then threw himself, shoulder first, at the gate, and with a loud rasp of rusty hinges it scraped open.

Shining the torchlight ahead of him, Adam advanced into the chill darkness, turning immediately right into a room that reminded him very much of a medieval catacomb. The beam from his torch bounced over the earthy floor and the damp walls, and settled on a stone object in the far corner – grey and ancient and mottled with patches of green moss.

A sarcophagus.

He was stepping forward to it – the source of that foul and wretched stench? – when he saw something that froze his blood. The circle of light thrown out by his torch now illuminated a marking on the uneven wall. A symbol he had seen before, in the photographs emailed to him by Charles Bartlett's mother.

A pentacle, a five-pointed star within a circle, pointing downwards.

Aleister Crowley used it for protection, and to signify the descent of spirit into matter, Adam recalled Jeff Ramsay telling him. The official symbol of the church of Satan. And written next to it, in what looked – and stank – hideously like animal excrement, were the numbers 666.

13

In the east wing of Boleskine House, keeping close to the wall, Clara stared into the room that was thickly redolent with her shame and remorse; the room where she had ignited this nightmare by striking a match.

The billiard room was deserted – no sign of Oswald's guests.

Only it wasn't a billiard room, not any more. Clara didn't know what to call this space.

The walls were covered with drapes of black satin. Scarce light was thrown by five guttering black candles that had been placed on the floor in the centre of the room, each candle standing at the five corners of a downward-facing star, which was circumscribed by a circle. It made her think of the old Hammer Horror films in which Christopher Lee would attempt to summon up the powers of darkness. A pentacle, she thought it was called, marked out on the floor with white chalk and surrounded by a scatter of bizarre sigils. The candles created tiny blue flames that pierced the darkness and reflected on the surfaces of six concave framed mirrors on wheels, placed in a circle around the pentacle.

Taking short, shallow breaths, Clara blinked at the eerie tableau, then focused on another oddity.

What sort of table is that?

It stood at the back of the room; a perfect oval supported not on legs but by the moulded, ebony figure of a black man – standing on his hands, on a bloodstained and mottled lambskin, which stretched beneath him. A solitary silver lamp dangled over the table, throwing down a dusty spotlight that illuminated the heavy-looking iron chain running around the table's circumference. The table itself was covered with darkred velvet, and an old silver brazier rested on its surface, along with a tall crucifix that appeared to be made from ivory.

It's an altar, Clara realised.

But like no altar she had ever seen before.

For one thing, the crucifix was standing *upside down.* She had a vague idea that in another setting, an upside-down crucifix was a perfectly acceptable Christian symbol; representing Saint Peter perhaps, who was crucified upside down. Perhaps. But taking in her grimly surreal surroundings, and remembering what Adam had told her, she thought this upside-down cross represented something far more fiendishly sinister. Something abysmal.

The mocking of Christ.

Every fibre of her being yelled at her to get out now, call Adam for help. Scream for his help, if that's what it took. This madness had gone on long enough, and there was no sign of Gale or Inghean. She couldn't stay here; she didn't dare.

She turned to leave, sidled back along the corridor, then froze.

There was movement down at the end of the house, a low murmur of voices. Silhouettes detaching themselves from the shadows, coming this way.

Quickly, Clara ducked around the corner, into the foul-smelling room.

What the hell was she to do now?

As her eyes did another panicked survey of the room, she realised something: the black satin drapes were fluttering in one place. The terrace doors behind the curtains, casting a draught. They were open! She wouldn't have to retreat the way she had come. She started forwards.

Then came to a halt, staring down at the floor.

That belongs to Gale . . .

The gleaming silver locket lay abandoned there. Its chain had snapped. Either by accident or by force.

Gale was in this room. So where is she now?

Voices approaching. No time. Clara desperately needed somewhere to hide.

A large rectangular swing mirror mounted in an antique wooden frame was close by. Crouching behind it, Clara found that the tiniest gap running between the wheeled frame and the edge of the mirror enabled her to peep through into the hellish room. Now she could see most of the space, and anyone who entered it.

She could only pray they wouldn't see her.

14

The sign of the pentacle marked out on the wall of the mort house looked as if it had been there for decades. Adam eyed it, chilled. Then he noticed something else, drawn inside the five-pointed star.

Wait . . . is that a goat?

He thought that was exactly what it was; a crude representation but unmistakably a goat, with its mouth filling the lower point of the pentacle, its ears filling the two lateral points, its horns filling the upper two.

Jeff Ramsay couldn't have been more on the money, he thought. *This property was used for ritual worship. Or someone wanting to make it look that way.*

Sigils like this represented fertility, success, power. Everything Charles Bartlett didn't have. And Adam had an idea that might have been at least part of the reason Bartlett was enraptured with this property.

Outside, the wind moaned low around the mort house, making his neck tense. Adam checked his display of his digital watch. Clara's five minutes had been and gone. Ten. By now, Oswald may even be aware they were both here. Adam might not have much time.

He shone his torch around and noticed two further things that deepened his unease. On a shelf, a few small glass bottles, grimy and filled with a thick, yellowy substance that reminded him of lard or dripping. And at the foot of the stone sarcophagus, a wooden crate. He moved over for a closer look.

Candles? Yes, but what the hell is that stench?

He crouched down next to the crate of candles, scrunching up his face against their putrid odour. That these were black candles hardly surprised him now. What bothered him was whatever these candles were made from. Not wax; they smelt almost . . . organic.

Oh, God.

Quickly, he cast the beam from his torch around, working the scene in his mind – the encircled pentacle on the wall, the 666, the sarcophagus, the bottles of that yellowy, viscous substance.

Horrified, Adam looked at the sarcophagus, awaiting his inspection.

Oh, please, don't let me be right about what's happened here.

Torch clamped in his armpit, he shoved at the lid of the sarcophagus. With a horrible shrieking of stone on stone, it slid across – and the stench of decay struck Adam with full force. He staggered back, retching with revulsion, his face contorting. Then, with a hand covering his mouth and nose, he forced himself to look, peering over the lip of the sarcophagus, shining his torch down inside.

It was like looking down into the mouth of hell; indeed, the awful thing confronting him looked as if it had been created by the devil itself. Ruined flesh, black, yellow and red. Flashes of white bones. Maggots.

What remained of the man Adam had been seeking.

Reeling back, clamping his hand over his mouth, Adam pivoted, only to find himself looking directly at the grimy bottles, the light from his torch lending a faint glow to their gloopy contents. His gaze tracked back and forth between the bottles and the sarcophagus as a horrible realisation arrested him.

'Fat,' he said aloud. 'It's *human* fat. Jesus. The sick bastard made candles out of this guy!'

'Correct.'

The voice, smooth and level, came from behind him.

Adam spun around to see a horrible figure confronting him. A huge, dark figure, entirely clad in the furry skin of an animal. And the head was concealed by a horned headdress; a skull mask.

'Don't move!' Adam declared. 'I'm arresting you under suspicion—'

An enormous curved blade swept up so fast that Adam barely saw it flash.

A *swish* as it cut the air, slashed across his neck.

Adam stumbled back, dropping his torch, and as it clattered to the ground he realised he had been lucky, impossibly so; the blade had missed him, perhaps by no more than a millimetre. He couldn't believe his good fortune; he was still alive.

His attacker was motionless, just standing there. The eyes of the devilish mask – two hollow, chasms of darkness – gazing at him curiously.

Why doesn't he attack?

Suddenly, a line of red-hot pain announced itself across his throat.

Adam clamped his hand there; understanding now, as a gout of dark blood flooded through his fingers.

Not so lucky.

He thumped to the floor and his bulging eyes saw his attacker loom over him, horned head cocked as he watched the blood pump out through Adam's twitching fingers.

His sight was dimming; his eyes closing; memories flashing by.

Before he lost consciousness, Adam's last thought was of Clara and Gale and Inghean – dear, trusting and innocent Inghean – whom he should have protected from this merciless monster.

Who'll save them now?

15

As Clara held herself very still behind the mirror, she watched with dread and some curiosity as Oswald's guests moved with slow deliberation into the room she had begun to think of as a temple. There were three of them, two young men and an even younger woman who barely looked old enough to vote. She was beautiful, though, or had been. That was the second thing Clara noticed about her. The first was that she was holding a knife.

Don't move; don't make a sound. Come on, you can do this. You can stay here until it's over. If you're very careful.

Clara could see that the knife the girl was holding was no ordinary knife; it was more of a dagger, with a red jewel in the base of its handle.

She thought of what Adam had told her about the occult practices carried out long ago here at Boleskine. Was that what was happening now? Judging by the way the room was done out in black drapes and candles, it had to be a possibility; people didn't draw pentacles next to makeshift altars for the sake of it, did they? And the room really did have the feeling of a malevolent temple.

But really, Clara? Satanism? A black mass? Ritual magic? Do you seriously think that's what this is?

It sounded absurd. But then again, every age had its secret societies and brotherhoods concerned with dark workings; desperate wanderers seeking some mystical mental crutch to lean on. Perhaps Adam had a point. When you considered the searing headlines nowadays – religious extremists targeting schools, decapitating innocent civilians on live Internet broadcasts; horrific acts of mass murder fuelled by an ideology that had perverted the name of a peaceful religion – then a group of youngsters worshipping Satan wasn't so far-fetched, was it?

She wasn't an expert on such things, but somehow that didn't fit. Where was the shadowy cabal of evil masked men in ceremonial, dark robes? The three figures slowly stepping into the light cast by the candles weren't like that at all. Not a hooded cloak in sight, just denim and leather jackets; tattoos and piercings. No masks either; these strangers' faces were plainly visible – pale, waxy.

And thin. Terribly thin. Had they been starving themselves?

Drugs, Clara thought. *Addicts, probably.*

It wasn't as glib as it sounded. Karl had treated many addicts, and he'd ranted to her about their faults as if he were a saint standing over them in judgement. What Clara had learned about addicts, apart from the telltale signs of facial wasting, open sores and missing teeth, was that they tended to be insecure and desperate for some understanding or meaning, a sense of belonging.

Oswald's guests had stopped walking now, a few paces away from the pentacle, and they were motionless and silent, their eyes like wide dark discs, staring ahead. As if waiting for someone.

Three lost souls.

Despite her fear, Clara felt a pang of sympathy. Why were they here? Where had Oswald found them? The Internet? Probably. If they were from London, as Oswald had said, they'd come a hell of a way. So what had he promised them? What loathsome, nefarious fate had he reserved for them?

Clara looked again at the youngest of the group, the girl, dressed in an ill-fitting and filthy tracksuit, her coal-black hair scraped back in a messy bun. Her face was painfully gaunt, her skin a leprous white. What worried Clara most was the glazed, drifting look in her eyes. She was submerged in a world somewhere else.

He's broken her mind. Degraded her.

The idea that Oswald could do that, could wield such power . . . Clara's mind screamed, *Impossible!* But the evidence was here, in this room, in these vacant eyes – and in the village, in the monstrous bloodstains on the floor of the butcher's shop.

A distressing idea leapt at her, a question she barely wanted to entertain but couldn't avoid. Was Oswald controlling her? If she accepted that he had controlled others, then surely it was possible?

No, she thought, *I chose to come, to find Inghean and Gale*. Which meant she had deliberately disobeyed his direct instructions.

I am in control. At least for the moment.

She wished she could say the same about Oswald's 'friends'.

Something else worrying: the knife in the girl's hand was trembling; she was quivering uncontrollably. And she wasn't the only one. One of the men – a short, stocky guy with a mop of shaggy brown hair – was suffering muscle contractions in his face, twitches around the eyes and mouth; but his hands were worse, writhing restlessly at his side. And the second man – older, with a shaved, tattooed head – was similarly affected.

Clara was sure that they weren't trembling from fear. This had to be drugs. Pot? MDMA? Something stronger?

Yes, something a lot stronger.

The only thing she knew for sure was that this strange trio were going to have one hell of a comedown. And that was the thought in her mind when suddenly all three of them did something that convinced Clara that what she was seeing had to be some sort of religious ceremony; or a sick interpretation of one. They knelt down before the oval table supported by the hand-standing figure, bowing their heads in worship. It was a simultaneous, fluid motion. Perfectly in unison. As if the action were pre-programmed.

Like Murdoch, Clara thought. *Hardwired.*

And Murdoch had killed himself . . .

Her heart was thumping too fast. She had to get out. Could she slip out, unnoticed, while they prayed?

Not via the way you came in . . .

No, that way they were bound to notice her. But the terrace doors, hidden behind the black curtains, were just a few feet away, and out of their line of sight. If she was quick, then maybe, just maybe, she had a chance . . .

A heartbeat later, that chance of escape was abruptly snuffed out. Someone was parting the drapes, entering the room.

The skull-faced figure with the horned headdress.

Clara's breath caught in her throat and she froze – just as well, because in the next instant the predatory figure was stalking past her hiding place to the altar.

Don't panic, she told herself. *They don't know you're here, and Adam's just outside. Just stay hidden, wait, observe, until Adam comes.*

The horned figure towered behind the altar, facing the others, who were now gazing up at his hellish face with such fervour, they might have been worshiping a god.

What is he holding? Something he carried in from outside?

She peered through the tiny gap in the mirror frame and saw that it was a black cloth bag. Something round and weighty was inside it; something the size and shape of a large melon.

Carefully, the horned figure placed the bag, and whatever it contained, on the altar. Watching, trying hard not to make a sound, Clara waited for *something* to happen.

She did not have to wait long.

16

The two men and the woman on their knees before the pentacle gazed up in dazed wonderment at the horned figure behind the altar.

Peering through the gap in the mirror frame, Clara took in his bizarre appearance: the full traditional Highland dress; the black jacket with silver buttons, the tartan kilt. This time, she didn't think what she was seeing was a spirit or a trick of the light. If only. No, the hellish figure was as real as everything else in this hideous place.

He raised his hands to his head and lifted off the mask and headdress to reveal a shock of blond hair, dazzling eyes; jewel-like eyes, midnight blue.

As Oswald set aside the horned mask, he turned to face the inverted crucifix, bowing his head reverently. Then, with his left hand, he made the sign of the cross, only the wrong way around. The other three watched, and their faces were no longer blank, but enraptured.

Oswald's eyelids slipped closed, and when he opened them again he spoke softly to his companions, coaxing them to repeat after him: 'We are gathered for the convocation of the spirits; let them come, let them tremble before us.'

Slowly, the three youngsters repeated the words, their voices thick, their diction slurred.

'Let us open our minds,' Oswald went on, 'unbowed and unfettered by arcane doctrines born in fearful minds in the dark ages.'

Again, the slack-faced trio repeated his words, as Oswald reverently lifted two objects from the altar: a shallow metal plate and a small silver chalice. Gleaming in the candlelight, they looked like holy items. The Host and chalice. *Had he stolen them from a church?* Clara wondered. Probably.

Carefully, Oswald held the Host and chalice aloft, as high as possible, and in a voice like frosted steel began reciting a rite, which Clara recognised as the Eucharistic prayer. Except it wasn't. The words were in Latin, but it still didn't sound quite right.

He's reciting the prayer backwards.

She understood what happened next as a blasphemous inversion of the Catholic Mass, and she was magnetised by the horror of it.

Instead of placing the Host reverently, carefully, upon the paten, Oswald threw it down upon the altar and spat on it. Then he tossed it to the ground with a clang and stamped upon it, hard.

'My brothers, my sister, tonight we shall satisfy the most hellish thirst of the Most High.'

Slowly, Oswald turned to the black bag, opened it and lifted something out.

It took every iota of physical restraint in Clara not to vomit.

The object in his hands, which Oswald was cushioning on

the altar, was the most sickening thing she had ever seen. A human skull; the flesh horribly decayed, the deep eye sockets writhing with maggots.

Where the hell did he get it?

This question was quickly chased by a more abhorrent realisation: the faceless skull was filthy. Blackened. Charred.

A shock of guilt swept through Clara's frenzied mind as she flashed back to the dismal afternoon she and Oswald had dragged the corpse out to the mort house.

'Shit, man, is that a real skull?' mumbled the man with the tattooed head; but he was dazed still, and his question lacked conviction.

Oswald carefully held up the charred skull, his fingers pressed to its temples, as though it were a priceless religious artefact. And now, before the pentacle, the woman and the two men lumbered to their feet.

'Let us be resolute in protecting the will of the individual,' intoned Oswald, 'and do so with true and loyal hearts. Let us reach for the wisdom of our most Holy Guardian Angel by summoning the superior princes of darkness.

'The sacred Abramelin Operation requires that we ask for their allegiance, their obedience. And we will banish the four princes; but they will always remain close to serve, and they will for ever obey our commands and bring welcome rewards.'

The woman and the shaggy-haired man nodded their agreement.

'My sister, my brothers, this is a house of healings for me, a house of miracles.'

The wrong sort of miracles, Clara thought.

'With the correct magical rites, the house and its energies and the influence of my Holy Guardian Angel can heal me.'

Could a house do that? She had heard all the pseudoscientific theories about old buildings storing negative energies, but was that really possible? If so, could there also be such a thing as positive energies? The idea almost sparked some hope inside her, but it was quickly chased away by the reality of the nightmare in which she was trapped.

'Magical workings require bloodletting,' Oswald went on in a voice that was low but rising by degrees. 'A willing offering to the beings we are calling forth.' He nodded at the young woman, and she returned the gesture. The two of them stood wordlessly for a moment, their eyes locked.

From behind the mirror, Clara stared, dreading what was coming, knowing it wouldn't be good.

Carefully, the girl rolled up a jacket sleeve, exposing her wasted bare forearm. Clara pressed a hand to her mouth as Oswald advanced towards her and held the chalice under the girl's exposed arm. The chalice was ready, waiting for her. And in a moment, she had drawn the knife across her forearm and was watching dark blood trickle into the chalice.

Smiling, Oswald whispered his satisfaction into her ear, then turned back to the altar. When he was standing before it, he tilted the chalice towards the skull and poured the girl's fresh blood into its crooked mouth.

'Hey,' the guy with the tattooed head said falteringly, 'uh, mate. Listen, maybe that's enough, yeah?'

Clara's gaze snapped to him. She realised his eyes were gaining focus; he looked more alert than before. And confused.

Without looking up from the skull, Oswald continued speaking to the girl. 'Angela, cut again, please. Cut *deeper*. Our spiritual entities require blood sacrifice, remember?'

With glazed yet distinctly curious eyes, Angela was nodding, already raising the knife again.

'Mate! You hear me? I said that's enough.'

From behind the mirror, Clara saw that the bald man had moved to the girl's side; had protectively wrapped his fist around her own, so that both of them now were gripping the knife's jewelled handle.

'Angela, please do not delay,' said Oswald softly. 'You know what must be done. It can't be changed; it can't be challenged. Tell me you understand.'

Distantly, her eyes drifting, the girl murmured, 'I understand.'

But the bald man evidently did not understand. He might have done once, far away from this place, under the influence, but not any more. 'I need to know,' he said in a querulous voice, looking from the candles to the inverted crucifix to the bloody skull. 'Why exactly are we here?'

17

Oswald wasn't reassured by the doubt he saw on the junkie's face. It seemed to Oswald that the Devil's Breath he had administered was wearing off.

Earlier that evening, it had certainly been inducing his desired effect. When that stupid estate agent had showed up, there had been no disguising the fact that she needed to be dealt with. So Oswald had told his guests that Gale was an interfering neighbour and explained that she needed to be quietened, before taking her down to the boathouse – and they'd gone along with that. Thanks, in part, to the drug. He knew, from past experience, it turned even the most coherent suspects into zombies; that was its beauty. Sure, its technical name was scopolamine, but really, under the circumstances, Oswald preferred Devil's Breath.

The irony was that it was Bartlett who'd first told him of this drug, so powerful that just by blowing a puff of it, in dust form, in a person's face, you could bend them to your will. For a while, at least. Now, it looked like it might be necessary to treat his guests to a little more. But one had to be careful. In high enough doses, the drug was lethal.

'Did you hear me?' the skinhead said again. 'I want out of this. The others aren't looking so good.'

That did it. There was no getting around it now: Oswald would have to administer more of the drug. Probably not to the girl; she was still drifting in the grip of his will. But the men definitely needed more, to become zombies to do with as he wished; and the best part of it was, they'd have very little recollection of what happened.

'Hey, mate, are you even listening to me?'

At his sides, Oswald's hands balled into fists and he tried to restrain his mounting frustration. They had come this far; the ritual had to be completed. It simply wouldn't do to delay.

He took a step towards the tattooed junkie who had protested. Jack, he thought his name was; but couldn't be sure – in the online chatrooms he would have used a different name anyway. And his name didn't matter. What mattered now was making Jack understand that there was no time for pissing about. He could try overpowering him if it came to it. But this one looked strong.

'You knew the purpose of the ritual before you came here, Jack. You conceded.'

'Yeah? Well, I . . . uh . . . don't think I'm up for this.'

'Let go of the knife, please, Jack.'

'Why are we here again?'

'I'll explain. Promise. When you *let go of the knife*.'

Jack opened his fist. He glanced down at his empty hand, confused, and it was all Oswald could do not to smile. Really, the man had no idea what power Oswald held over him.

Jack looked up, and Oswald could see the question forming on his lips. So, good as his word, he explained.

'Can the mind master the body? It's one of the most profound questions we can ask ourselves. Jack, every morning I wake to the knowledge that my end is drawing near. The cancer growing in my brain will kill me. But there *is* a way to halt death. A man who owned this house a long time ago, a visionary, understood this. He was special, unique. Enlightened.

'Aleister Crowley had resolved to evoke the four great princes of evil and gain control over them. To do this, he undertook the Abramelin Operation, a six-month ritual culminating in the manifestation of the Higher Self. That Guardian Angel would finally grant to Crowley anything he desired. True power; the answer to all things. In this very lodge, Crowley raised demons, but sadly for him, he discovered those demons to be utterly uncontrollable.'

Silence from the room.

'*My* requirement,' Oswald went on, '*my* will, is to survive. And to that end, I am working to communicate with my own Holy Guardian Angel; a being so powerful it can grant any wish, cure the worst sickness, in exchange for blood sacrifice.'

He glared at Jack. 'And *you* are committed to helping me.'

The skinhead looked uncertainly at the other two. They stared back at Oswald blankly.

'Please, Mr Cattenach. This is too much. I want out, now. Yeah?'

'I'm afraid it's not that simple,' said Oswald, running a hand over the skull on the altar.

Jack followed the movement of his hand and frowned. 'Wait . . . man, is that a *real* human skull?' It was the second time he had asked the question and, this time, Oswald answered it.

'It is.'

'Holy shit! You're sure? Where did you get it?'

'An old associate.'

'Wait! You knew him? *Seriously?*'

Oswald checked the other two. No reaction.

'An old friend,' he told Jack.

'Jesus.' The skinhead was, taking faltering steps backwards.

Ungrateful, really, now that Oswald thought about it. The skinhead coming here, accepting his hospitality, only to behave like this. Disappointing. For two years, more, he'd associated with these three on the mental-health web forums. He supposed the police would call it grooming, but that was what paedophiles did to little kids, and he wasn't that sort of man. No, he had offered these losers release from their pain and their miserable lives, to be part of something greater, a religion that granted them power. And this was how they repaid him? It wasn't right.

'Okay,' Jack said, throwing up his hands, 'this has gone far enough. Rituals and prayers, that's one thing. But knives? Blood sacrifices?' He shook his head. 'I thought the rituals were . . . shit, *symbolic* or something! A bit of fun. I think we should all go. Now. Okay? Yeah, right now. I . . . I didn't sign up for this.'

'Oh, but you did,' said Oswald. 'You consented, remember?'

Jack's head was shaking vigorously; his whole body was shaking. 'Yeah, well, I quit, okay?'

'Me too,' said the other man suddenly.

At that, Oswald set down the skull. To free his hands.

'You coming with us?' Jack asked the girl in the tracksuit.

She was silent, still holding the sacrificial knife. Her wrist was bleeding pretty badly, but she didn't look as if she was in pain. Most likely the drugs had numbed her. For the moment.

'Angela! You coming?'

'No,' said Oswald.

The skinhead was sweating, his eyes rolling in his head. Drug comedown. And panic. But still he argued. 'What do you mean, no?'

'You said you quit. You asked whether it was okay.' Oswald ran his tongue over his pearly white teeth. 'It's not.'

He was so profoundly disappointed with the three of them. Shame. Still, needs must when the devil drives.

Beneath the altar, Oswald's reaching hand found the butt of his shotgun.

He was glad he'd already loaded it, just in case.

18

Four miles from Boleskine House, Inghean Kilgour stood in the cavernous blue-lit chamber of the Loch Ness Exhibition called

'The Secrets Beneath'. She liked it here, amid the quiet and the soothing velvet dark. She could almost convince herself she was hiding in a huge dark cavern behind a waterfall, or beneath the loch itself. No wonder this was the most popular room with the tourists. But after hours, she had it all to herself.

She raised her hand to a picture on the wall next to her: an illustration of a wise-looking holy man with grey hair and flowing robes. He was standing in the shallow waters of Loch Ness and making the sign of the cross to banish the creature rising out of the waters before him, a frightful serpent with three humps, a long neck and a horse's head.

Inghean had examined this picture many times; enough to know that the man in flowing robes was Saint Columba, said to have encountered a 'water beast' during his travels in the area as long ago as AD 565. Was this, as many believed, the first recorded sighting of the Loch Ness monster? Or something else?

'Kelpie,' Inghean whispered.

A demon said to haunt the Scottish streams, rivers and lochs. If you believed the legends, the kelpie could appear in any form. An ancient entity of unutterably evil malice that could lure innocent children to violent deaths.

Inghean's mum told her, when she had nightmares, such things weren't real. Maybe that was so.

But what *was* real – what the blood smeared on her shoes told her was real – was the awful occurrences happening here in Abersky. And Inghean had felt they were going to happen for a long time, since even before the fire at Boleskine. By drawing her premonitions, she had been able to keep them at bay, to avoid speaking about them. But now that was becoming almost impossible.

And there was no way what had happened to Mr McHardy

in his shop earlier that day was an accident. *She* had done it to him, she had said those words that had made his eyes go funny. But Inghean knew they weren't her words.

They were his, the yellow-haired man's.

And as soon as she thought of him, she thought of Clara. Inghean desperately hoped her old friend wasn't in trouble, but the idea was there, stuck in her head. She pulled out her phone. No missed calls.

Which was wrong.

Her mother would have phoned her by now, surely? Her mum *always* phoned her. And after what had happened in the butcher's shop, surely she would have rung by now . . .

Inghean considered phoning her mother.

Maybe she's angry with me, like before.

Inghean didn't like remembering that time, when her father walked out on them, but sometimes she couldn't help it. In the same way that sometimes she couldn't help her mind flashing to the future. Glimpsing things yet to happen.

Now, in her memory, she was seeing her mother running after her father's car as he drove away from their house. Her mother screaming, sobbing, as the icy wind whipped her hair around her face. Inghean had seen that in her dreams before it had happened, like Mary's parents, hurting one another. She had drawn it, colouring her mum's face in with a bright-red crayon.

That's what got you into trouble . . .

'That was a long time ago,' she whispered. But she couldn't force out the past. The drawings were part of the reason her mother had become so angry with her; why she had sent her away to the special school where the bedrooms had locks on them and the other residents wept, sometimes even screamed, through the night.

Unfair, sending her there. It wasn't as if Inghean had asked to know the things she knew. She could know things just by looking at someone. Sometimes, Inghean saw a winding shroud flapping around a person, or saw them floating underwater. That's how it had been with Mr Murdoch; he was floating in some murky depths. She'd seen other people like that. Constable Lake, her mother, Clara.

Even herself.

But you agreed with the doctors it was all in your head. You promised Ma the voices were gone. You even promised yourself that if the second sight was real, then you wouldn't use it. Remember?

She did, and she knew it wasn't wise to forget that promise. In the old days, they called women like Inghean witches for dabbling with the invisible influences. Was it so different today? She knew plenty of locals who thought the second sight was a curse. Aggie Blackwood, for one. That horrible woman thought Inghean was wicked. She'd told her mum, outside the butcher's shop, that Inghean should be locked up. Aggie blamed Inghean for what Mr McHardy had done.

Did her mum blame Inghean too? Would she send her back to that school, lock her away – for good this time?

She looked down again at her phone's glowing screen. No, she wouldn't call her mum. She wouldn't go home, either. She would stay here, alone, the whole weekend if she had to.

And in the meantime, she would call the one person who'd never let her down. The sooner she warned her about her visions, about the threat that was coming – about the bad man – the better.

Swiping her phone open, Inghean tapped on her contacts, and keyed in 'C' for Clara.

19

For one hopeful moment, Oswald wondered whether the temptation of more mind-altering substances would stifle his guests' compulsion to leave the house. But the tattooed skinhead seemed pretty determined as he backed towards the exit.

'Come on,' he called to the girl in the tracksuit. 'You're bleeding bad. I'll drive us down to the village.'

'I'd recommend you stay,' Oswald said, his hand gripping the butt of his shotgun, still concealed behind the altar.

'You threatening us?'

Oswald studied them: the skinhead, Jack; the girl in the tracksuit, Angela; and their younger friend – Gaz or Baz, something like that. He couldn't risk them leaving. Not with what they knew. After all they'd seen. They'd tell someone. Maybe not immediately, but in time they'd tell someone. And that was a problem.

Then again, he'd prefer not to take them out: the hassle it would cause him, the attention it might invite from the outside world.

Only if they make me, he told himself. *Only if they run.*

'You don't want a special little pick-me-up?' Oswald asked.

But his words were lost in a moment of surprise: a low buzzing sound that made Oswald snap his head to his left, towards the largest mirror in the room. He thought he knew what that buzzing was, and exactly what it meant.

Decision time.

'Come on.' Jack ploughed towards the door, dragging Angela along with him.

Oswald snatched up his shotgun and swung it up towards them, cocking both triggers.

Click-click.

That sound said one thing:

You want to get out of here quickly? I can make that happen right now. Just one tight squeeze of my finger is all it will take.

His three guests froze, their eyes glazed with shock as they wrestled with the question of whether he had the balls to shoot them.

And Oswald discovered that he did.

KABOOM!

The tattooed bloke's head disappeared in an explosion of gore, spattering the wall. Confusion stole across Angela's face as the realisation of what had happened hit her; then she wiped a trembling hand over her face, saw it streaked with dark blood, and opened her mouth in a shrill scream.

He heard another cry – 'Oswald, NO!'; saw movement out of the corner of his eye; but already he was firing again.

KABOOM!

This time the deafening shot took out two of them at once. Chunks of plaster exploded from the wall as Gaz-or-Baz dropped to the floor and a ragged black hole burst in the girl's back, throwing her forward.

And Oswald swung around and grabbed the woman who'd run at him; seized Clara by the hair, and rammed the barrels of his shotgun into her jaw.

There was a fine hot spray of blood across his face as she caught the blow.

He shoved her, hard, and as she pitched backwards and crashed into the mirror she had been hiding behind, Oswald was already plunging a hand into his pocket. No sooner had she come to a stop, sprawled on the floor, than he blew a cloud of white dust into her face.

He was surprised by how quickly her eyes began to glaze.

She coughed, spluttered; they always did. But sleep would soon take her, and then she would awake, floating, ready to talk. He knew from the way she was squinting up at him that her vision was failing. To her, he must look like a twisting, shimmering mirage.

Oswald knew something else: for the moment, Clara was totally unaware that she had just inhaled a drug that granted him total sway over her mind.

20

As Clara drifted in a drugged haze, Oswald hurried out of the house into the snow and strengthening wind and down to the mort house.

His friendly neighbourhood policeman had left quite a mess down there, and Oswald preferred to have it cleared up right away. The mess inside the main house, too. But that could wait a few hours.

However, the problem inside the mort house was a rather more pressing matter.

The first thing he noticed when he got there, aside from the dark pool of blood and the policeman lying on the floor, was his chequered police hat. The sight of it brought an unexpected

smile to Oswald's lips. He'd never had one over on a policeman before. He decided he would keep it. A memento of this
evening. He would find a special place for it later; that was the
right thing to do. The wrong thing to do was to leave Adam
here. It was only a matter of time before others came looking
for him.

He could, of course, drop the bastard into the loch; that
would certainly be easier than lugging him all the way into the
village, but Oswald had other plans for this guy. More of a long
game, if things did not go Oswald's way. Which was possible,
he conceded. Not likely, but definitely possible.

Standing over the inert form, he regarded his handiwork
with clinical detachment. He felt no sympathy whatsoever.
The officer, pathetically naïve, had interfered. Had needed to
be dealt with, like Gale. And yet, he had surprised Oswald in
ways she hadn't.

Was still surprising him . . .

He dragged the policeman out of the mort house, loaded
him onto his shoulder and got him to his car. That done, he
resolved to check Clara's pockets for the spare key to her old
flat. New to the rental market, yes, but still unlet and hardly
well-appointed. And now with no estate agent able to show
the place. He laughed to himself. Deserted, locked up, empty
for months on end; nobody would ever think to search for
Adam there.

21

Hours later, when Clara opened her eyes, the room was a haze; her mind drowsy, floating.

Is this death?

A voice whispered to her from some place far away: '*I want to live!*'

A faint light was playing at the fringes of her vision. She forced her eyes to remain open, and as they adjusted she managed to turn her head sideways and realised she was looking down on the pentacle and the black candles.

So many more colours than before.

It was true. Now the room seemed to glow with quivering gleams of red and green, and black – in the shadows creeping all over; on the ragged old curtains heaped against the far wall. No, actually, the stains on those weren't quite black . . .

Blood. She could smell it now, metallic and cloying. Her eyes were tracing the bulky – unmoving – human shapes that lay beneath those curtains. Her ears were ringing with the memory of blasts reverberating.

Oh God, Jesus, please no. He killed them all; he killed them!

Her mind began to race. For a moment, she felt the surge of hot panic in her limbs, but the sensation was dampened just as quickly; her central nervous system in lockdown. She tried to move and found that every limb rebelled; she had pins and needles in her hands, legs, feet. Christ, everywhere! Then she felt the muscles around her left eye spasm. Twitch. And she knew then:

Whatever he gave to them, he's given to me.

With almighty effort, she managed to kick out her left foot. It connected with something hard and tall, which toppled over and clattered to the floor. She realised what it was: the ivory crucifix.

I'm floating. No, on a table. The altar . . .

Oh, fuck – fuck!

Clara felt vulnerable to the bone – utterly exposed now, to the house and its power. She understood that Oswald had drugged her. And she understood something else, something that dawned on her in slow, hazy horror: someone was in the room with her. A sound gave them away; a very peculiar sound, which made her think, oddly, of her grandmother:

Clack . . . clack . . . clack . . .

A walking cane, striking the floor in the darkness.

She thought of the first person she knew with an injured leg and told herself this was him, had to be. He moved nearer, and she peered at the dark silhouette, telling herself that the danger was over, that she was about to be rescued.

He's come to get me, like he said he would. And now I'll go with him to the station and be very pleased to do so, thank—

It was not Adam. She saw now that the figure was broader, more corpulent. And not quite . . . solid.

She wasn't fully awake. That was it. The drugs Oswald had given her – she was imagining things.

Clack . . . clack . . . clack . . .

It *was* a walking cane, she saw, but unlike any she had ever seen. This cane was entwined with a carved serpent and topped with the head of a silver skull. Funny that she could make that out quite clearly, whereas the owner of the cane was blurry around the edges.

'Love is the law.'

He spoke. This was madness. She must be totally out of it. Clara took a breath and tried to move. Found she couldn't. Fear pulsed through her. Her bladder felt full, and in her present state she wasn't convinced she would be able to hold it.

With dreadful slowness, the figure advanced, seeming to glide rather than walk. Definitely a man, she saw, shabbily attired in a dark brown suit and a black homburg hat. The hat made her think of the one that Al Pacino wore in *The Godfather*. No one she knew wore a hat like that. It was unusual, certainly; it made her curious, but not unsettled. It was the eyes that made her feel that way. Horrible. Beady and astute and drilling right into her.

'Love is the law,' the voice said again. *'Do what thou wilt shall be the whole of the law.'*

What's happening to me? What does it mean?

'Stop him,' the voice croaked. *'Or you'll never. See her. Again.'*

That was when Clara started to cry. The tears were hot, burning her eyes and stinging her cheeks, and pointless – she knew that. But she couldn't stop them, any more than she could have stopped the drugging, or stopped the man who was not quite a man coming closer, hand reaching—

The figure was gone. So suddenly, Clara had to wonder whether he – it – had ever been there at all.

'Sleep well?'

Clara's whole body bucked weakly as Oswald loomed into view.

'Best not move,' he said calmly, laying a clammy (and bloodstained) hand on her arm. Holding her in place. 'You'll be feeling pretty groggy.'

She stared up at him, eyes wild and bulging. 'Who . . .' Her voice sounded all wrong, thick and garbled. 'Who was that?'

'Who was who?'

'The man . . . the . . .'

'No one here but you and me, Clara.'

'What the fuck have you done to me?'

He held up a hand for her to see, and opened it to reveal a tiny mound of white powdery dust on his palm.

'On the whole, this substance has been more of a friend to me than a hindrance. It comes from a tree called the Borrachero, which means "the drunkard". Insanely powerful. Would you believe that the Nazis used it for mind control? So they say. With this in her system, a woman could be persuaded to confess just about anything. Imagine that.'

Mind control . . .

Clara saw again blood spattering up white tiles; heard a woman screaming.

'Murdoch,' she murmured.

'Putting it together, are you?' said Oswald. 'I did warn you I'd have to take care of him if he interfered.'

He almost made the murder sound reasonable.

'The mesmeric influence was easy to induce. Suggestive trigger words did half the job; the drugs did the rest.' He smiled. 'I'm surprised he got back to the village in one piece, the state he was in when he left here. Do you remember, Clara?'

She remembered.

She remembered Murdoch here at the house, alone with Oswald in the library. She remembered listening at the door, catching muffled words that had made no sense: '. . . *when she comes into your shop . . . trimmed to lean . . . red wine sauce . . .*'

And Clara remembered driving up to the house with Adam Lake – *Where is he? Why doesn't he come?* – to find Gale and Inghean. Now she was petrified for the women.

She tried asking Oswald about them – not very eloquently, it was true; her mouth was desert dry, and in her drowsy stupor she was finding it almost impossible to get her tongue around words. But Oswald seemed to understand.

'Gale came here tonight in a bit of a state, looking for her daughter. Then she left.'

He's lying.

A critical look darkened his face. 'I told you not to come here tonight, Clara. Why did you disobey me?'

She didn't want to answer him, but the answer slipped through her numb lips. 'I was worried for Inghean.'

'Why?'

Don't tell him . . .

'She was drawing this house. Over and over. Gale wanted to know why. Is she here?'

'Who else knew you were coming?'

'Is Inghean here?'

'No.'

'Then where is she?'

'I have no idea.'

'Is Gale okay? Did you harm her?'

'Course not.'

He is definitely lying!

'Clara. Who else knew you were coming?'

'Only Adam.'

'Fine. But why did you bring him?'

Already the question was floating, getting away from her. Momentarily, Clara pictured herself outside in the gusting dark and the whirling snow. She was thinking about Adam in her car; picturing him striding through the snow to her rescue. But wait; he wouldn't stride. He had a limp. That dash of realism cleared a space in the fog in her mind, and she felt the briefest surge of panic.

He knows Adam Lake was here. So where is Adam now?

Her gaze roamed the room, saw the bodies bundled up against the wall.

No sign of any help coming. She was trapped.

She wasn't getting out of this.

Drifting again, floating off . . .

'Clara? Stay with me, please. I need to know: why did Adam come? Did you mention me to the police, my illness? Are more coming?'

With Herculean effort, she managed a slight shake of the head. Oswald leaned over her, so that his breath was hot on her face.

'Did Adam discover why I wanted this house?'

She was silent.

Then she saw his hand reach behind her head; heard the scrape of metal as he picked something up.

'You'll answer my questions,' he said quietly, showing Clara the sacrificial knife in his grip. 'Did Adam relay his suspicions about this house to anyone else?'

Adam had, of course; he'd spoken to Jeff Ramsay. But it wouldn't do to tell Oswald that. He would kill her, and Adam. If he hadn't already.

She looked up at Oswald, at his knife, already darkly stained with blood, and said thickly, 'No more. Please.'

'You'll answer my questions.'

She stared, saying nothing. She was working on something. Working out whether he was right, that the mind could master the body, by willing her fingers to wiggle. Only her thumb and forefinger responded.

But that was something.

'I choose not to answer,' she replied, all the time trying, in her drug-confused state, to think through what Adam had told her about the history of Boleskine House, about Aleister Crowley, the occultist who'd lived here a hundred years ago. A depraved drug fiend and master of black magic. He wasn't that, in Clara's opinion, and neither was Oswald. He was deluded.

And angry, now, at her disobedience.

'Tell me,' he growled, 'who else did Lake speak with?'

Somehow she kept her lips together. Even as he lifted his knife and brought it close to her throat.

22

Clara felt the cold edge of the blade against the skin over her jugular – but no sting.

'You can't do it,' she croaked. 'You can't kill me.'

Oswald tipped his head on one side and gazed mercilessly down at her. 'You know I'm more than capable.'

That was only half true. She knew he could kill. What she didn't know was whether he could kill *her*.

'Who else did Adam speak with?'

Louder now, and with an edge. Oswald was rattled. Which meant, if Clara could negotiate, she might have a chance here.

Oswald's hand tightened around the knife's handle. She felt

a bead of hot blood trickle down her neck. The sensation – and the memories it unleashed – stirred something in her. Spirit.

Are you trying to frighten me, Oswald? Because for too long, I lived with a man far more awful than you. A man who cost me everything. So you're dreaming if you think I'll break now.

Even if he did cut her, hurt her, torture her, he had given her so much of the drug, she doubted she would feel anywhere as much pain as he needed.

But Oswald didn't cut her. He put down the knife, and lifted something else.

'I have some pleasing news for you,' he said. 'Tonight you're going to assist me in completing my ritual. The blood of the worst sort of sinner is required. And you more than qualify. Do you know why? Because you murdered this poor bastard.'

He thrust the charred skull into her face.

A little shriek escaped Clara's lips, and she squeezed her eyes shut.

'Ah, and there she is.' A note of satisfaction in his voice. 'The haunted woman. Tell me, Clara, how does it feel when you look in the mirror knowing what you did?'

Clara said nothing. He was trying to rile her. She had to fight it, she *had* to; she couldn't afford to let the guilt, the self-reproach, overwhelm her now.

She made herself turn her head once again towards the puddles of fresh blood, towards the ragged old curtains heaped against the far wall.

Dead. Whoever they were, those kids were dead. They had friends, families who would spend tortuous nights worrying about them. And grieve.

Was she also responsible for this series of horrible crimes? On the face of it, everything was anchored in her rash, reckless

act of setting fire to the east wing. She thought she was going
to vomit.

'Why *did* you do it, Clara? Because you needed to make
a sale? I get that, but why risk your freedom committing a
criminal act? Why do something so desperate?'

'*I want to live . . .*'

In a white flash of memory, it came to her. The whispered
voice was her own. She saw herself lying like a sad, fractured
doll at the bottom of the concrete stairs, a tousle-haired man
in green leaning over her – a paramedic. Forcing those words
through her swollen lips: '*I want to live . . . Please, help me.*'

She opened her eyes now, sucked in a breath, and, in as
strong a voice as she could muster, told Oswald the truth:
'Because I am a survivor.'

'Yeah? Well, me too.' His voice was low and serious. 'This is
about sacrifice, Clara. Yours and mine.'

The sacrificial knife was suddenly above her again. She eyed
its sheen. Remembered the girl, Angela, holding it, before
making her sacrifice. Her *willing* offering.

Clara felt dizzy then, and not only from the drugs.

'You've already said you're going to kill me,' she said. 'So
what are you waiting for? Go on. Do it, Oswald.'

Silence as he considered this, knife poised.

'But if you kill me,' Clara added, 'I'll be of no use. Because
to make a blood sacrifice, you need my consent, don't you?
To contact your Holy Guardian Angel? You need *my* consent
for *you* to live.'

It came to her then, through the fear and the fog. Her plan
for survival.

Her plan for revenge.

Oswald was glaring down at her, gripping the knife so

tightly his hand shook. Or perhaps there was another reason it shook.

'I want to live, Oswald,' she said urgently. 'That's *my* will. *My* purpose. And you don't have to harm me. Do you know why?'

She saw that he was frustrated; but puzzled too. Curious? Clara hoped so.

He wants to believe me, she thought. *Even if he doesn't yet, he's interested.*

And that was enough for Clara to summon all her strength now to go in harder, to persuade him. However far gone this lunatic was, whatever happened now, she must save herself by appealing to his perverted reason. Even if that meant convincing herself his black magic could work.

And save someone else, she thought cloudily. The drugs fogged her mind again. She knew she had come to help ... *someone.* She thought back to the events in the village, the butcher's shop. She had an idea that she was momentarily overlooking something, someone, vital. And yet her mind couldn't fix on it.

'You said I would endure, that I would give you a good death. Well ... I can.'

Mind mastering body, she lifted a trembling hand and laid it on his arm.

'I can give you a better sacrifice than mine. There is someone looking for me. Oswald, I can give you the soul of the worst sinner I know.'

23

It had been a rough night. Several hours had passed and the sun was almost up. Attired in full traditional Highland dress, Oswald stood in the darkness over his altar. He wasn't praying. He was examining his old university friend's skull, staring, eyeless, back at him; its crooked mouth still darkly stained with the girl's coagulated blood.

Realistically, there had been only one place to dump the shot bodies. And this time, bagging them up had been easier than he thought – although he supposed he had practice to thank for that.

And Clara, of course.

Always Clara.

They'd had a proper heart to heart when he let her up from the altar. It pleased him that she'd been so honest. So forthcoming.

'Your life is upside down because of me,' he'd conceded during their fireside chinwag, and had been surprised by her response.

'My life's been upside down for a long time now. A year. Longer, maybe? Yeah, it's been a whirlwind.' And she'd shrugged, adding: 'You never can tell, right?'

She was right. One never could tell who to trust with something as precious as a human life. Still, that wasn't what he'd said. Instead, he'd played innocent.

'What are you talking about, Clara?'

There had followed a disturbing marital slideshow in her

head. Oswald didn't see this, of course, even though he would have paid good money to do so. But he knew that was where her mind had taken her, because Clara had proceeded to plunge into the story of her husband's long-term abuse. It was satisfying to believe that she had opened up to him in a way she hadn't to anyone else.

And yet, for all that, it struck him as ironic that there was so much she didn't know. About him. About the fire. About the misfit whose life she was implicated in ending. Although she *did* know his name, knew it for certain, because Oswald had confirmed it. Her accidental victim was Charles Bartlett.

She was in her room now, sleeping, and in an hour he would wake her, and they would talk a little more about how they would entrap her husband. But first he was going to smoke a little more skunk and say farewell to the person to whom he owed thanks for the prize of immortality he would soon claim.

Oswald had already smoked four joints since his magical ceremony had ended so disastrously. He had smoked the first joint when Clara told him all about the hopeless, egotistical bastard she'd once been foolish enough to call a husband. And he had agreed; like poor old Mrs Caraway, Karl Hopkins did sound very much like someone who needed putting out of their misery, albeit for different reasons.

Two hours later, he had smoked another joint; just to make the task of cleaning up after the shotgun blasts that bit easier. Scrubbing the walls took longer than he had anticipated; the blood was everywhere. Normally, he was fine with blood. What he wasn't fine with was killing three people. Only the girl was supposed to have died; and the ritualistic killing he had prepared would have been far more satisfying to the Lord than a crude shotgun blast.

If only that skinhead hadn't freaked out over the skull.

Oswald looked down at the blackened cranium, into its yawning eye sockets. 'You old bastard, you always did fuck things up.'

Still, he allowed himself a tiny smile at the efficiency of his clean-up. He had needed to act quickly before dawn came, so he had bagged them up, and then, following the beam thrown out by his torch, he had trudged through the snow-swept darkness around to the front of the house. There was Gale Kilgour's shiny new silver Golf, parked right behind the battered wreck he'd bought for the junkies to drive up in. It wouldn't take him too long to load the bodies into the cars and drive them down to the water's edge; then push them in.

And it hadn't.

At first, the vehicles had just bobbed there on the surface of the water, a few yards apart, and he had felt a surge of panic. But then he had *willed* it to happen, and finally Loch Ness had claimed the vehicles and sucked them down into the blackness.

Was he worried? Not greatly. Since finding the junkies in various chatrooms on the net, he had done his homework; and because of that he didn't think anyone would come looking for them here. Officially, the three of them were already missing persons. Even their own families had given up looking for them.

Still, he supposed he had to be grateful for the black ice that slicked the road, because if they ever did find the cars, there was his explanation, neatly packaged and tied with a bow.

Accidents happened, right?

Now, he opened the terrace doors and went outside. It was still too dark to see his victims' watery grave, but at the bottom of the sloping garden he could hear the waves gently licking the shingle shore. He looked down at his old friend,

Bartlett – what was left of him – and whispered, 'I hope you'll be happy down there with them.'

But when he got to the water's edge, he couldn't do it. Wouldn't do to toss his old friend into the depths without acknowledging his part in all this. So that's just what Oswald did. Standing on the shingle beach, snow swirling down around him, he lit another spliff. Then he whispered a prayer to Satan, his Lord of Misrule, and remembered Bartlett from their university days.

Oswald didn't like to think about Oxford, because it made him sad to remember the great man Bartlett had once been. He frowned, trying to recall what had first drawn him to the poet. Except Bartlett hadn't been a poet in their Oxford days. Back then, he was a medical student: well-travelled, well-informed, hungry for knowledge.

Chess?

Yes, that was it. He remembered Bartlett's intense grey eyes at their first meeting, during a head-to-head tournament at the Oxford University Chess Club. It seemed that every chessboard had fixated Oswald ever since.

Which was odd, because he hated the game.

Perhaps the key to it was the almost omniscient way Bartlett had moved his pieces around the board. Yes, it had to be that, because he remembered being captivated by the way Bartlett could achieve a perfect checkmate with such ease, sometimes without even looking. One time he had triumphed in a match by calling out every move from the bathtub while Oswald sat at the board in the next room. Bartlett said he possessed a third eye, everyone did, and if Oswald wanted, he would teach him to use it.

So Oswald had fallen under Bartlett's spell, and the spell had followed him from Oxford to an apartment in King's Cross. They had become room-mates.

Bartlett soon got a job as a pharmacist; thankfully, the pharmacy had a ready supply of the drugs they needed to explore new planes of consciousness. Particularly the seizure and psychiatric medications. Olanzapine. Quetiapine. Eszopiclone.

After a while, neither of them could function without the drugs. Every high revealed new learnings about the universe. But they were also experimenting with occult practices: clairvoyance, divination, tarot cards. Every evening they knelt together in sacred prayer, drawing on initiated rites handed down from the druids and Crowley's mystical teachings, to embark upon practical experiments with astral visions:

'I conjure and command thee, the most powerful princes, Ministers of the Seat of Tartarus, appear forthwith and show thyself to me, here outside this circle, without horror or deformity and without delay. Answer all my demands and perform all that I desire.'

Sitting in the haze of opium, at first Oswald wasn't sure if the mirror before him had actually brightened with the shape of an indistinct figure; a lean and melancholy figure. And he wasn't sure if the shadowy shapes moving about their apartment were real; but soon enough he could see them better; an endless procession of devils. He knew the risks; that by participating in satanic rites one can become a focus for evil. They were exposing themselves to a terrible force; and if they failed to control that force, it could control them. Destroy them.

But true knowledge, ultimate power, Bartlett reminded him, would come from attaining mastery over those devils, and they would be rewarded by communion with their Holy Guardian Angel, a supremely powerful being who would grant them anything they wanted. Wealth, if they desired it.

Even immortality.

Their cramped apartment, however, was inadequate, unworthy. To conduct the Abramelin Operation successfully, they would need a house that matched its exact requirements; a unique temple, dedicated to the powers of darkness. Self-contained and secluded, with windows facing in all directions to look out on approaching evil spirits.

A house in the mountains, like the one Crowley had used. Boleskine House.

The only problem was that it wasn't for sale. And even if it had been, how would they ever afford it? The drugs were running Bartlett's life, ruining it. It wasn't long before he was caught stealing from the hospital pharmacy – drugs, even patients' medical notes – and he was thrown out.

Bartlett became intolerant, riddled with self-pity.

'Is it any wonder I lost interest in you?' Oswald said, looking down at Bartlett's skull.

No, of course not. Oswald had needed to find others to help him; and he had done so. It was amazing, really, the number of lost souls you could find in railway stations; in doorways; in the chatrooms dwelling in the darkest corners of the web. Even the medical files Bartlett had stolen allowed Oswald to mine a few worthy potentials. Yes, they had come to him, the lost, the broken, begging for salvation.

'But it was you who found the house,' he said to the skull. 'You have my thanks for that.'

The great irony was, by then Bartlett *did* have access to the cash to buy Boleskine House. Outright, if he wanted. His sister was willing to lend him the money. But there was a catch (wasn't there always?). He would have to promise her he would turn his life around. And to Oswald's horror, Bartlett had consented. He would buy Boleskine House as a reminder of the person he had been, and he would run it as a guest house.

Make something of himself.

Even now, the idea sickened Oswald. Of course, he had been all in favour of Bartlett regaining his faculties, going easy on the drugs – but abandoning the ritual? Decimating Boleskine's legacy?

No. All of the house's past owners – the guitarist, the lodge keeper, the general – had detected malevolent presences here. Some thought they had simply been odd people drawn to a place with an odd history, but Oswald didn't buy that. Boleskine was a shrine to Crowley, where demonic presences gathered. A guest house? Hell, no. Oswald could never have allowed that sort of sacrilege.

'Which is why you had to die,' he said solemnly to the skull, and tossed it into the water.

He watched the skull sink into the sullen waters, certain that Bartlett – were he alive – would understand. Of course he would. Hadn't they taken oaths of secrecy and fraternity in their Oxford days? They knew the consequence of breaking those oaths.

A terrible death.

'You got what you deserved,' he said.

Then, inhaling on his spliff, Oswald turned his gaze towards the purpling sky, and it occurred to him that he had been right to take Adam away from here. Gale was out of sight, beneath the boards in the boathouse, but it was likely that soon more curiosity seekers would come. Maybe more police; maybe the estate agent's simple daughter – not that anyone in their right mind would listen to the fantasies of a misfit like her. But still . . . that girl was a funny one, as his mother used to say. There was something about her that creeped him out, because for someone whose perspective on the world was so warped, Inghean Kilgour was a surprisingly intuitive young woman.

Just as well I factored her into the game.

The faintest red glow was creeping over the craggy skyline. Oswald turned from the light, and stalked towards the house, without looking back.

Time to wake Clara. They had work to do.

24

Though she was in her bedroom still, Clara was not sleeping. She was on the edge of the bed, sitting upright, staring at her reflection in the old, tarnished mirror. Haggard, drawn. When was the last time she looked so awful?

In the hospital.

After she lost the baby.

After Karl threw her down the stairs.

Again, the harrowing scenes played out in her head. Karl's furious face in hers. His fists pounding into her – and then dragging her. The cold, grey stairwell steeply leading down. Screaming. Falling, over and over. Darkness. The voice of the ambulance man, reassuring her. She wished she had thanked him; she wished she could remember his face, but it was a blur.

Then, afterwards, the worst of it: a doctor's voice, tragically apologetic, telling her the baby was gone, and she would never again be a mother.

She had wanted to murder her husband then. To torture

him. To watch his face crack and fracture with agony. But instead she had run. To Scotland, to this village.

The reason was no longer clear to her.

Suddenly, staring at herself, she was arrested by a disturbing idea. Someone she was supposed to be helping, who was it? She reached for the memory, but it eluded her. Her thoughts were in disarray, jumbled. Why had she come back to Boleskine House? There had been a reason, she was sure of it; why couldn't she remember?

She shook her head in frustration and listened. She could hear Oswald down the hall in his study, tapping away on the computer. If she slipped out now, there was a very slim chance she might still be able to run from all this. Tell the police what he had done to those kids.

What he had done to *her*.

The woman in the reflection was shaking her head. No more running; no more cowering and hiding. It was time to face her demons – and banish them.

Having to see Karl again wouldn't be easy, but if she was in control of their meeting she could engineer it to her advantage.

Clara got out of bed and went to the window, noticing the deep footprints Oswald had left in the snow earlier that morning. All they needed was Karl's email address, which Clara had no trouble remembering, because it began KarlTheMan. Some man he was. More maniac. They both were, he and Oswald – two crazy, psycho maniacs. They deserved each other. Why shouldn't she lead them both right to one another?

Vengeance.

She dressed quickly and headed for Oswald's study, noting as she walked that the hall was clean of bloodstains.

You can wash it all you like, you twisted sadist. You'll never get it clean.

Because this house truly was evil. Satanic rituals? Demons? She wasn't so sure about that. But could a house change someone, infect a person with the influence of its memories, its history? Inflict its will, its purpose? Yes, she now believed that was possible. Given what she had in mind, she might even be the living proof of that hypothesis. Or maybe she had been influenced by the drugs Oswald had given her. Or maybe it didn't matter either way.

She slowed down as she passed the picture of the waterfall mounted on the wall, and glanced, as she always did, at the mysterious hooded figure. Her whole body shivered; then on she went, alone in the darkness. The study door was ajar, but she didn't bother to knock.

'You're up,' Oswald said, looking up at her over his desk as she entered. 'I was about to wake you.'

'Any luck?'

His face told her yes, they very much were in luck. 'Come and see.'

As she came around the back of his chair, she flirted with the idea of snatching up the paperweight on his desk and smashing his head in with it. The idea was momentarily both tempting and appalling, and she felt its surprise like a hard slap to the face. Sure, smashing his head in would serve him right for what he had done to those poor kids. But exactly when did she become this person? Someone who could so casually entertain the idea of murdering another human being?

And why did she hesitate?

Because I might need him alive to finish this.

And because she had enough blood on her hands. She remembered some of the ordeal – the girl cutting herself, the shotgun blasts. So much of it was a blur, and that was a small mercy.

Peering over his shoulder at the computer screen, Clara couldn't believe her eyes.

Crazy. Fucking. Bastard.

According to the missing-persons website, Karl had posted the advert around the same time she had agreed to come and live here at Boleskine.

'You were right. He has been hunting you.'

'I always knew that.' What she hadn't known was how she would deal with him the day he found her. And now, dropping a vindictive eye on Oswald's face, she had her answer.

'Yeah,' she heard herself say, 'well, two can play that game.'

Oswald minimised the website. Next, he clicked on the draft email he had prepared containing the briefest information about their location. The only missing detail was Karl's email address. A blinking cursor in the 'To' field indicated its proper place.

'It's on his website profile,' Oswald said.

The irony. He'd used the same address as ever. This was too easy.

'Copy and paste.'

He did.

His hand moved the mouse to click 'send'.

'Wait!'

Clara gripped his wrist, and he looked questioningly up at her. 'What is it? Not changing your mind?'

Leaning over him, she put her hand on the mouse. And clicked.

There was a *whoosh* as the email flew into the ether.

With a grim smile, Clara said: '*I* wanted to hit "send".'

PART FIVE

THE GREAT BEAST

Whoever fights monsters should see to it that in the process he does not become a monster.

– Friedrich Nietzsche

1

In London, Karl lay frozen in terror, eyes fixed on the bedroom door. Although his senses were in disarray, the noise, that awful noise coming from the hallway, was unmistakable.

Clack . . . clack . . . clack . . .

It's not the drink, he thought. *There's someone in the flat. An intruder.*

He bolted upright, snapped on the bedside lamp. But the blooming light did nothing to placate his fear. All it did was ignite terror that the light was visible beneath the door and he had needlessly drawn attention to himself. Whoever – whatever – was in the flat with him now, Karl felt sure it meant him harm.

But it could be your imagination, he fought to reassure himself. *It could be the alcohol.*

That seemed likely. He'd spent the entire day drinking. A minor relapse. He wouldn't normally be awake at this time after getting so thoroughly pissed, but normally he wouldn't be cowering from phantom noises, either.

It came again suddenly, that awful sound that made Karl wish he had visited the bathroom instead of waiting for the urge to pass.

Clack . . . clack . . . clack . . .

It sounded like—

It can't be . . .

It sounded *exactly* like a walking cane striking against the wooden floor of the hall.

Beyond the open window, the drone of early-morning traffic, normally one of his chief bugbears, barely even registered with Karl as he leapt out of bed. He ripped open the door to see—

No one.

Just the empty hallway running down to the bathroom.

Karl was alone. The flat was secure. No intruder had gained access. No one with a walking cane.

He dropped a distrustful look onto the empty vodka glass on the table next to the bed, then got into bed again and snapped off the lamp. He lay there shivering a little – from the cold, he assured himself. But within seconds, his entire body went rigid, because abruptly, impossibly, there it was again, the stench of Sunday morning. Incense filling the air. Defiling it.

The wardrobe stood bulkily, brooding, in the corner of the room. He could just make out its door, ajar and crooked, like it was hanging off its hinges. The shadows beside the wardrobe were weighty. Watching him. They had form – hunched shoulders, a head pitched forwards.

What the hell am I looking at?

Very slowly, Karl straightened in the bed and pulled the bedclothes right up to his chin, which had always made him feel safer as a boy. He didn't turn on the light, just lay there, too terrified to move. The important thing now was not to be noticed if there was an intruder, to let the uninvited guest get clean away, without harming him.

Are you serious? said the voice in his head. *There's someone in the room with you!*

He peered hard at the dark silhouette, telling himself that

he was probably imagining the figure. Or dreaming it. Telling himself that Terry Sanders was a nut job and his vengeful spirits were pure fiction.

'Face north to Boleskine,' a cracked voice said. 'Say nothing and listen.'

'*Jesus!*' Karl rasped and threw the bedcovers back, tumbling out of bed and staggering to his feet. He backed up to the wall.

No, he yelled silently. *No, no, no!*

But his eyes continued to contradict his logical mind. There was a man, just visible in the moon's pale glow, standing in the far corner of his bedroom, right beside the wardrobe. He seemed to be leaning on an intricately carved walking cane, and wearing a tattered brown waistcoat and a white shirt, its sleeves spattered with specks of something dark. The dome of his head was entirely bald, his scalp flaking in ragged patches, and his face was bloated and ravished and yellowed. Worst of all were his eyes – small, rat-like, boring into Karl.

Karl had never been so afraid. Not even when Alison fell on the stairs, and there was so much blood and she was so pale. The intruder had not identified himself, but Karl already had a sickening idea that this wasn't his first visit. The smell of foul incense gave him away.

'I have a request,' said the intruder. 'Will you do as I ask?'

What he wanted to say was, *Depends what it is*, but Karl couldn't find the words. Instead, he managed only the briefest of nods. He feared that at any moment his legs would give way from under him. He might fall and crack his head. If he passed out, he might choke on his own vomit.

And something told Karl that this intruder would watch that happen with perverse curiosity.

'Just don't hurt me,' he whispered. 'Please.'

'Stop him,' said the intruder. 'Find her.'

'Who? You mean Alison?'

'She must know that the house is the cradle. Find her soon. Or you'll never see her again.'

2

Stop him; find her.

The voice was back in his head. Invasive. Demanding to be heard.

It was morning. Karl forced himself to sit up. Focus. Although he was pleased his vision wasn't swimming any more, he was curious about the voice – why could he still hear it, even after getting out of bed and splashing his face with cold water?

Find her soon. Or you'll never see her again.

As he slumped onto the couch he tried to forget it. *A dream,* he reassured himself, *that's all it was. Must have been.*

He reached for a half empty vodka bottle on the floor and swigged greedily. Drinking almost allowed him to ignore the ping of the email that dropped into his inbox about ten minutes later. He glared across the room at his computer, not wanting to move. Probably just another message from one of the innumerable adult sites on his favourites list. Probably better to stay on the sofa in the deep, embracing comfort of his vodka.

Probably.

The trouble was, there were other websites, more important websites, he had been using recently; websites for tracking down missing people. Of course, he received lots of useless emails from those sites as well, but he wasn't able to drag them to the trash folder without at least pausing to scan their content. Just to check, just to be sure the backstabbing bitch hadn't slipped up and allowed herself to be noticed somewhere.

So he heaved himself off the sofa and went to his computer. Opened the email.

And stared at the screen.

The title of the email read tantalisingly: 'Boleskine House . . .'

He uttered a sigh of astonishment. He remembered his intruder's prophetic words: *'Face north to Boleskine . . . Find her soon. Or you'll never see her again.'*

It's impossible . . .

He wasn't the sort of man who got lucky, ever, was he? And if this email was a lead, well . . .

Without wasting any time, he punched 'Boleskine House' into Google. The images thrown back at him were of a gleaming white stucco mansion brooding over an expansive, incoherent stretch of dark water. Behind that, an ancient-looking forest and a range of snow-capped, craggy mountains scraping a gunmetal sky.

He didn't know if he would find Alison here, but still haunted by his vision, he had a powerful sense that he should try to learn more about the mansion and its owner. A quick search on Zoopla and the Scottish Land Register revealed when Boleskine was last sold and to whom. One Oswald Cattenach. Nothing about him online. A stranger.

Okay, so how about previous owners?

More images flashed up on the screen.

'Oh my God,' he whispered, 'this can't be happening.'

But it was happening. His pupils dilated in recognition of the face glaring out at him.

'Dear God,' he whispered, 'it *was* him.'

There was no mistaking the domed, bald head, the skin tainted yellow and the eyes that bored right into him. Beside his photograph, there were pictures of Boleskine House, and references to the occult, magical workings, black magic and human sacrifices. There was a name, too. A shiver ran down Karl's back as he processed it:

Aleister Crowley.

A look of disbelief crossed his face. This was impossible. Crowley was *dead*.

Clack . . . clack . . . clack . . .

Karl looked around sharply. That pernicious sound again. Would it never leave him?

Eyes on the screen again; on the image of the man who in life had called himself the Beast. A wicked man. *Stop him; find her*. Who was the 'him'? This Oswald character, maybe?

He told himself to remain calm, not jump to conclusions, trawled yet more search results.

'A mysterious man and his Highlands home' was the head-line of the first of many articles. That was in *The Scotsman*. The piece went on to describe the property as 'one of the most spiritually charged sites in the world, internationally renowned for a dark history of black magic'.

The name that came up again and again was Aleister Crowley. His picture was everywhere: a burly, broad-shouldered brute in his late fifties. Entirely bald, with piercing eyes set in a bloated face.

'According to Crowley's writings,' one article read, 'he bought Boleskine to perform the Abramelin Operation, an ancient ritual to contact one's holy guardian angel.' Apparently, from calling up demons and achieving dominion over them through ritualistic magic, it was possible to command one's angel to grant you anything you desired. To cure disease, even. *Yeah, right.* That smelt like bullshit to Karl, and the more he read the more he was convinced it was bullshit.

Why the hell would Ally be connected to something like this? was the question Karl was ruminating on as he focused on the screen. More links. One of the first was for an estate agency. On first glance it seemed that Boleskine had been on the market just recently.

He clicked through to the website of Highlands Estates and saw that he was right, although the house was now listed as sold.

He scrolled through the website, past the property photo that dominated the screen. And saw that his luck really had come in as he scanned the contact details for the agent.

Shit!

The name given at the agency was Clara Jones.

But the face next to that name . . .

Karl's knuckles went to his mouth in a reflexive gesture of astonishment; his front teeth grazing the skin.

With a few hurried clicks, he saved the picture and magnified it, studying it with ferocious intensity. Oh, that glorious moment – the sweet, hot satisfaction.

It *was* Alison; well, a version of her. Her hair was longer, and the wrong colour. She'd lost weight, and gained lines on her face. But the woman gazing out of the screen at him, challenging him, daring him to find her, was unmistakably his wife.

He became giddy, not from the booze, but from excitement at the thought of seeing her at last, face to face, holding her. The idea was all he needed to begin his recovery. And now she was real to him again, that eventuality was no longer a fantasy; no longer a question of *if*, but when.

He had to go to Boleskine. Now. He needed a map. And he was about to print one, when something made him hesitate. Suspicion crept in.

A location, sent by an anonymous sender – the email address was just a string of random letters and numbers. Whoever had sent this email obviously wanted Karl to find Alison. But why? There was no reward on offer. Were they doing it out of the goodness of their heart? A rare and genuine act of altruism?

Possibly. Not everyone thinks the way you do, Karl.

Certainly, whoever had tipped him off couldn't have known much about the state of their marriage. No one in their right mind would tell a wife-beater where his punchbag was hiding out, would they? Not unless that person harboured some personal vendetta against Alison, and how likely was that? She'd never been the sort of person to make enemies.

No, this had come from someone who had seen the picture Karl had uploaded and recognised her. A neighbour maybe, or just some acquaintance.

What were the chances?

Slim, incredibly slim.

What if it's a trap?

That was beyond Alison. Revenge? It wasn't her style: flight, never fight. A new boyfriend then? Someone she had confided in who wanted to punish Karl? That was possible, and the very idea of it made his blood boil.

Still, what good would it do to question such a stroke of

luck? He imagined this might be what it felt like to win the lottery. And did jackpot winners wait around before booking their round-the-world cruise or buying that mansion they'd always dreamed of owning? No, they did not. This was a lead, and just because Karl couldn't explain where it had come from didn't mean he wasn't going to follow it up. He had to find Alison, to apologise, to redeem himself. To prove to himself he wasn't an inadequate, desperate loser.

Eyes back on the screen. He wasn't normally the sort of man who liked doing research. Too impulsive. Still. He felt that in this case, he didn't have much option. His night-time visitation had scared him witless. A man who, it seemed, was indelibly linked to the house he had now connected with Alison. That didn't seem like coincidence, but it was worth greater scrutiny. If he was going to do this, he needed to know what he was getting into, didn't he? And not just for his own sake.

Stop him; find her.

What had she got herself into?

It was clear to him, suddenly, that Ally could be in trouble. And he was worried for her. Protective. This was a change, he recognised, and a good one. Before, he had wanted to find her to confront his demons by apologising, so that he could come to terms with what he had done and move on. That was still as good a reason as any to find her. But it had little to do with Alison, and everything to do with him – beating the bottle, getting his career back on track. Saving himself. That desire was still inside him, spurring him on, but another desire had stepped in to join it. Help Alison. Make sure she was okay.

You'll never see her again . . .

He needed to know more about his vision – for now, in the cold light of day, Karl accepted that was what it had been;

accepted that poor old Terry Sanders wasn't quite the fruitcake he'd thought him to be.

But what if Karl was being lured towards some dreadful danger? It was a hell of a risk. Why indulge the provocations of a spirit when he knew nothing about its motives?

An idea formed. He went back to the computer and ran another search, this time entering the term 'occult bookshop'. The first result was a shop on Museum Street called Black Sun Books. He clicked.

Established over one hundred years ago, we are Britain's oldest occult bookshop. All of the famous magicians have been customers of ours.

Would they employ anyone with specialist knowledge about Crowley? It seemed likely.

Karl scribbled down the address on a scrap of paper and then headed to the shower to wash away the remnants of the booze, the sweat, the tears – and, he could only hope, the fear of what lay ahead.

3

Black Sun Books smelt strongly of old paper; a woody, smoky scent that was not unpleasant to a man accustomed to smelling alcohol at this time of the day. It was silent as an undiscovered tomb. Motes of dust shimmered in the mid-morning sun.

Karl took some time to browse. The dark bookshelves

groaned under the weight of aged and very fragile-looking titles, many of them bound in leather, with gold lettering, some falling apart. There was a glass cabinet at the back of the shop, locked; inside it, a number of artefacts that wouldn't have looked out of place on the set of a Harry Potter film. From this side of the glass, it was impossible to tell how old they really were, but Karl guessed a few hundred years. Maybe even older. On the top shelf of the cabinet was a twisted willow stick; next to that, some black candles, a human skull and a set of dice that looked as if they had been carved out of bone.

Hocus-pocus mysticism, that's what Alison would call a shop like this. And maybe she would be right. Even so, the shop was famous amongst those with even the most cursory interest in the occult, and Karl had felt drawn here.

'Can I help you?' called the woman sitting behind the sales desk.

Fixing a smile on his face, Karl walked to the front of the shop. The bookseller was painfully thin, and he guessed aged somewhere in her late sixties, her hair an icy white. She had an Ordnance Survey map spread out on the desk and a crystal on a string dangled from her hand. She eyed him, perhaps registering the scent of alcohol on his breath from the night before, and her eyes travelled around the shop, as if she weren't comfortable being alone in here with him. But after a long moment, still clutching that string with the crystal attached to it, she seemed to conclude he meant her no harm, and she regarded him more openly.

'What's with the crystal?' he asked.

'I'm dowsing,' she said in a matter-of-fact voice. 'Selling up here soon. The crystal will show me where to buy the next shop.'

She's crazy, Karl thought. *The one day I choose to do something good with my life, I end up coming to see a crazy person.*

He was about to turn to go when she said, 'You look lost?'

'I am a little.' He hesitated. Then he thought of Crowley's visitation, his warning, and knew he could not leave. 'I'm looking for information about a place. In Scotland. It's called Boleskine House.'

She studied him, leaving the crystal – and him – suspended.

'Boleskine House,' he said again. 'It belonged to Aleister Crowley.'

'Ah, guess you read about the fire?' she said, her eyes keen. 'Not surprised. It was in all the papers. Business in here picked up a bit after that. You looking for a history?'

'Actually, it's Crowley I'm most interested in,' Karl said. 'His religion. I want to know how awful he really was.'

'What do you mean?'

'Well, is it true he sacrificed people for his magic?'

'Sacrificed people?' He saw that she was trying hard not to laugh. 'To be sure, ritual magic was his life's work, but Crowley wasn't a murderer. Wild and uncontrollable? Yes. An attention seeker? Certainly.'

'I don't understand . . .'

'He was a fiend, a mad menace to many, but a killer?' She shook her head. 'He died alone in 1947, a penniless heroin addict, disgraced. And, ultimately, a harmless old man.'

She eyed Karl curiously. 'You look sceptical?'

'Yeah,' he muttered, remembering his intruder with the yellow skin, and eyes that looked right into him. 'You're telling me this guy wasn't threatening or dangerous, but I guess you could say I still need to be convinced of that.'

'Many *described* him as a dangerous satanist,' she clarified, 'but actually there are few satanic elements in his writing. See, Crowley believed in free love, sexual liberation. Above all, the power of nature.'

'But *did* he work magic?'

'Yes, he performed incantations and rites, but all were intended to achieve changes in nature, and often, changes for good. By working through the power of angels and demons. Good and evil. It's a delicate balance, and he acquired Boleskine to use as his shrine. I have little doubt that his work unleashed forces in that house. Transformative powers perhaps. Good as well as bad. As he said himself, Boleskine became the cradle for all that was magical and devious and divine.'

Karl's gaze had wandered. He was looking behind the sales lady, at another glass cabinet of curiosities. This one contained crystal balls, symbolic jewellery and tarot cards. And an African walking stick topped with a serpent's head.

'Are you okay?' said the woman. 'You've turned very pale.'

'I'm fine.'

Karl was not fine. The sight of that stick put ice into his veins and made his stomach flip.

'Sir? What's your name?'

'Karl.'

'Tell me, Karl,' she put down her crystal now and fixed him with a look of fierce intensity, 'what have you seen?'

'Some, uh, some very strange things,' he managed. 'I mean, some serious shit.'

She fell silent, studying him. Then she said, 'You believe you've seen him, don't you?'

He stared back at her, dumbstruck.

'I'm right, aren't I?'

He opened his mouth to reply; closed it.

'You wouldn't be the first,' she said. 'So tell me, has Crowley appeared to you?'

Karl fought his inner cynic and said heavily, 'Yes. I saw him.'

Speaking slowly at first, he told her about hearing the song on the radio and seeing the man in his bedroom. He left out the part about his missing wife. And finished with Crowley's instruction: *Stop him; find her.*

'Do you know whom he was referring to?'

'No,' he said quickly, hoping she didn't see the lie, and judged that she hadn't.

'You're not making this up, Karl?'

'Not at all. Why?'

'Because one of the guitarists from Led Zeppelin owned Boleskine House for a time. It wasn't a coincidence that you heard that song.' She removed her half-moon spectacles, studying him closely. 'If you've seen Crowley, he could be trying to commune with you for a very particular reason.'

He steeled himself. 'What reason? How is that even possible? Crowley is dead.'

'Visions and voice,' she said, and Karl noted the mystical quality that had crept into her voice. Under other circumstances he might have been tempted to smile, perhaps even scoff, but all he felt now was nervous curiosity. 'Do you believe in the human soul?'

Karl shrugged. 'I shouldn't. There's no evidence supporting the idea of a soul that can exist outside of a body. But—'

'For Crowley, the ability to leave the body and project an image of himself was one of his core objectives. He called it a body of light. A double of his own body. An *astral* body.'

'And you think that's what I saw?'

'I wouldn't discount the possibility.'

'Except Crowley has been dead for a long, long time.'

'True, but Crowley believed he could project images of himself into the past, and into the *future*.'

This was too much for Karl. 'Maybe he'd taken too many hallucinogenic drugs.'

'Maybe.' She let that word hang between them for a moment, just long enough for Karl to question his scepticism. He swallowed, shook his head, pressed his index finger and thumb to the bridge of his nose.

'I know how it sounds, and it's good to be sceptical. But if you've had visions of Crowley, you need to be aware that his energy could be working to influence you. Perhaps he's dissatisfied with something in this life, something he wants you to help him correct?'

Karl nodded. 'Thank you for your information.'

'That's why I'm here. I hope you find whatever it is you're looking for.'

'And I hope you find somewhere for your new shop.'

'I have no doubt,' she said, eyeing her crystal and picking it up again.

As he was stepping through the door, the bookseller said, 'You're going there, aren't you? You're going to Boleskine House.'

Karl stopped and stared back at her. He remembered the night he and Alison had shared their first kiss on the Millennium Bridge. He remembered their holiday to the sun-drenched village of Capdepera in the Majorcan mountains. He remembered choosing their wedding rings together. He remembered loving her. Truly. But he also remembered the repellent shame and self-hatred that had ignited in his chest and threatened to consume him as he stood looking down

on her crumpled body at the bottom of the stairs, the blood
flowing out of her; the true impact of his heinous act dawning
on him in slow, black horror.

He had ruined her life.

And now she needed him.

'I am,' he said finally. 'I am going to Boleskine House.'

'Don't take this the wrong way, but would you mind if I
said a prayer for you?'

'Do as you wish,' Karl said kindly, 'but I'm not sure I believe
in the power of prayer.'

'You don't have to believe in something for it to be real,'
the woman said, but already Karl was stepping out of the door.

As he walked along Museum Street, he planned his next
move. Back to the flat and pack a bag. Then a taxi to Euston,
and the Caledonian Sleeper, which would get him to Inverness
for just after breakfast. From there, all he'd have to do was hire
a car and make the eighteen-mile drive south, to the address
that had so fortuitously dropped into his lap.

He had read somewhere once that man's destination is
never a place but a new way of seeing things. He couldn't
remember who said it, and he didn't much care, but it struck
him as thoroughly misguided. Way off the mark. As Karl
Hopkins strode down the pavement in London, he was clear
about his destination.

Boleskine House, Loch Ness.

4

The next morning, Karl steered his black rental car – a Mercedes, if you please – along a narrow, meandering Highlands road at a speed slow enough to brake in good time if a deer should come bounding out of the dense pine woods on his left. Snow was falling thickly now, obscuring any view of Loch Ness on his right, and the windscreen wipers were going at full speed, beating back and forth in rhythm with his own sweeping thoughts.

That morning, he had woken on the Caledonian Sleeper to see a bunch of American teenagers excitedly pointing through the carriage windows at something large moving serenely through the waters. Something odd. True, from that distance the sinuous grey shapes breaking the surface, strangely inanimate, had looked a bit like two dark humps with a long arched neck, but it took all of Karl's self-control not to tell the cretins what they were looking at was nothing more unusual than a tree trunk and a branch, floating in the Moray Firth, not Loch Ness.

Bloody Scottish nonsense.

He could almost understand why Ally had fled to the Highlands. For one thing, she knew he hated the Scots; angry tartan tosspots. For another, so much of it was a wilderness, miles from anywhere. No one would know her up here.

What Karl could not understand was why someone as good-natured and as gentle as Ally would want to live somewhere associated with catastrophe and ceremonial magic.

Maybe she worked at the house. How else could she afford somewhere so grand? But what job could she possibly have? It was maddening not knowing what connected his wife to this location.

He checked the satnav. A mile to go; that was it.

If you've seen Crowley, he could be trying to commune with you for a very particular reason.

The bookseller's words had haunted him all night on the sleeper. Karl had felt the presence of Crowley, and he had surmised, finally, that the old brute must be keeping a watchful eye on Boleskine. The question was why – what was going on there? What sort of trouble had Alison got herself into?

Breathe, he thought. *Steady now.* Then, at once: *How much further?*

The anticipation was just about killing him. The minutes crawled by, the road uncoiled before him, and then he saw, ahead, gateposts flanking a driveway, and the satnav told him he'd reached his destination.

He parked up on the side of the road and got out of the car. He peered through the shrubbery that barricaded the property from the road, but all he could make out was a chimney rising into the sky.

He locked the car and started walking. Then thought again, and returned to the car, popping the boot. Rummaged in his bag. Under the clothes and toiletries, his hand grasped something that did not belong in an overnight bag. He drew out the screwdriver and slid it into a back pocket.

There. Now he was ready for every eventuality.

This time, he passed through the gateposts and strode up the driveway. The further he walked, the more intense his curiosity. The house, he saw, wasn't so splendid after all. For one thing, the east corner looked to be badly damaged as if from fire; all blackened walls and shattered windows. For another, the gardens were utterly neglected. Desolate. Of course, it didn't help that his vision was hampered by frozen flakes drifting all around, but he was sure that beneath the lying snow this whole area was nothing but a barren wasteland of gorse and tangled trees.

It doesn't look magical, devious or divine, he thought. *It looks like a dump.*

Karl arrived at the pillared entrance and stood at the heavy oak door, trying not to eye the two sinister stone dogs standing guard on either side of him.

Remember, stay calm.

Losing his temper was how he had lost his job. Losing his temper was why Alison had run out on him in the first place. This time he would not drink, and he would take things slowly.

But, as he raised his hand to the knocker and banged it, his heart began racing.

What if she answered? He'd have to be as pleasant as possible. Humble as pie, overjoyed to have found her at last; all of that.

But he thought it more likely that when the door opened – if it opened at all – he'd find himself face to face with some privileged Highland arsehole. A friend, or more than that. And then he'd spin a little story about Alison's fragile nature; about her friends who were searching for her back in London, beside themselves with worry about how she was coping after her breakdown, her miscarriage.

Worried about her mental health.

He stood there, tense, watching the door. Waiting.

Then he heard the approach of footsteps on the other side. At his side, his fingers twitched with agitation.

Stop him; find her. Or you'll never see her again.

There was the rattle of a key. And Karl held his breath as the door slowly opened.

5

Karl froze. He couldn't believe it. For a moment he thought he was experiencing some sort of waking hallucination. A vision. *She* was a vision. Hair all long and loose. Lips plump with lipstick. She was wearing jeans with only a bra.

She didn't look in the least bit surprised to see him. It was the exact opposite of how he had imagined he might find her.

'Alison?'

What's wrong with her eyes? he asked himself.

'You were expecting someone else?'

'I . . . well . . .'

'Got my email?'

'*Your* email?' He wanted to ask why she had sent it, what the hell she was doing out here; but it was hard to think past how she looked. 'Where's your top? Jesus, Ally, you always answer the door like this?'

On her face he expected at any moment to see fear, or at least anger; but all he got was that cool, enticing stare.

Something wasn't right here.

'Karl. It's been a while.' She exhaled heavily. 'I've missed you.'

She'd *missed* him? No, of course she hadn't. He'd thrown her down the stairs; she'd blamed him for her miscarriage. Why in God's name would she have missed him?

And yet, the way she was gazing at him with those distant, dark eyes, he wanted to believe that she had missed him. Needed him.

He fumbled for something to say. 'Look, I . . . uh . . . don't understand?'

The moment the words were out, he regretted them. He felt confused, at a disadvantage here. Karl was not accustomed to feeling that way, and he didn't like it, not at all.

'Don't stand there in the snow. Come in.'

'What a house!' he said sceptically as he stepped over the threshold, stamping his feet, looking around at the red drapes on the walls and the high ceiling. 'You renting a room here, or the whole place?'

'Actually, neither,' she replied, closing the door behind him and plunging them into near darkness. 'I'm the lodge manager. For the moment.'

'Enjoying it?' he heard himself ask, but that was the wrong question entirely, and he knew it. The right question was: were they alone in the house?

'I don't want for much,' she replied, keeping her eyes on him, 'and the pay's not bad.' He thought he detected a rueful acceptance in her tone. Then, in a voice that was slow and unusually heavy, she said something he didn't believe, because he knew it wasn't true:

'You look well, Karl.'

A stillness between them for a moment; a silence.

Karl sniffed, wondering about the weird smell in the hallway. Like being in church? Almost, but not quite. And beneath that odour, the distinct aroma of charred wood. For some reason, he remembered the woman in the bookshop telling him that this house stood on a spiritually charged site. That forces had been unleashed here once, good and bad.

'Is your employer here?'

The way she shook her head wasn't quite convincing. And those eyes; the pupils so large and unfathomably dark.

'He's out for the day.'

Karl was suspicious. Inwardly, he didn't trust what he was seeing and hearing, principally because she was acting so unlike the woman he had married and knew. Even in twelve months she can't have changed that much. Nevertheless, there was a hazy detachment on her face, and Karl couldn't help wondering if she really was as confident as she was making out, or whether she was under the influence of a substance, perhaps alcohol; though the woman he knew had never been much of a drinker, and never touched drugs. Alison, he decided, was either up to something here, or was vulnerable. He didn't know which, but he was going to keep his wits about him. Or try to.

'It's freezing. You, uh . . . wanna put something on?' he said.

'Yes. I suppose I should,' she said. Was that a suggestive note in her tone, a hint of flirtation? He didn't think he was imagining it.

This wasn't the Alison he knew. Where was the fear? The vulnerability? He hadn't seen a glimpse of either in her yet. Had she learned to control her emotions? Or to conceal them?

'Come on.' She gestured for him to follow her. 'I'll show you my room, if you like.'

He pondered for a moment. 'I don't want to see your room,' he said slowly, 'I want to talk. I've been worried about you.' He looked hard at her. 'That's the truth. It's been twelve months since you left, and I've done my research on this place. Ally, do you know the history? You shouldn't be somewhere like this.'

'Are you still telling me how I should live my life?'

They stared at one another. 'I'm just very confused,' said Karl. 'You don't seem yourself. At all.'

She regarded him defiantly with shining eyes, and, in a coaxing voice that sounded almost rehearsed, encouraged him to follow her deeper into the house.

Karl didn't want to follow her. He wanted to get the hell out of here before her employer came back. Bad vibes all around. But he wasn't leaving without Ally – and she was already moving away, looking back at him over her shoulder.

Come on, he thought, *she's messing with your head. You're not going to give her that control, are you?*

It seemed that he was, for the moment. With his pulse beating low and steady, he followed her to the dark, panelled door that led into her bedroom, and hesitated before entering, perplexed by her new-found confidence and by the austere scene before him. He hadn't expected such a room: musty, wallpaper stained and peeling. A hulking wardrobe.

He swallowed when he saw that.

'Close the door,' she whispered.

He did, tensing as she drew nearer, raising her hands to his arms, then felt the pressure of her palms on his shoulder blades. She guided him, and he heard the creak of the bed as he sat.

'Relax,' she whispered, and he tried to do that, but he couldn't focus. His gaze kept drifting, over her shoulder, to the wardrobe.

He blinked, and in a white flash of memory he saw the intruder with the yellowy pallor; his serpent cane.

'Karl? What's the matter?'

He shook his head. 'Nothing.'

'Take your clothes off.'

'Ally?' He heard the uncertainty in his voice, the confusion. *She* wasn't meant to be controlling this situation. He felt powerless before her, and that was wrong – but goddammit, she was sexy as hell. The attraction consuming him was like nothing he'd felt for her before.

Magnetic.

Her fingers trailed up his arm, stroked the back of his neck.

Jesus. This is happening. This is really happening.

Surprising himself with his weakness, he removed his shirt, pulled off his jeans. He wanted her; he didn't know if he trusted himself to be gentle, but God, he wanted her. Not in here, though.

'Isn't there somewhere else we could—'

Suddenly, a puff of dust blew in his face.

He coughed, spluttering. And then, before he could form a word, she was pushing him back onto the bed. His head began to float, his thoughts untethering.

'It's all right, Karl, just relax now.'

Although her voice suddenly sounded very far away, the wardrobe behind was closer, much closer, looming over him. He shook his head as she kissed his neck.

'Karl?'

He tried focusing on her lips, but his gaze kept slipping. She had his face cupped in her hands, but her face was hazy, distorted, like a mirage.

What was happening to him? Another blackout? This felt different. He squinted at her, and saw she was backing away, towards the door.

'Ally? I . . . don't feel . . . so good . . . Where are you—'

'Bathroom. Back in a sec.'

Suddenly, all the excitement was gone. Karl was almost thanking his stars when she slipped out of the room and he could have a moment to think. He felt so dizzy. And his vision was distorted – just look at the wardrobe. He had a direct view of it in the mirror opposite him, and oddly, the wardrobe door seemed to be opening. That wasn't right.

He closed his eyes, only for what felt like a second or two, but it must have been longer, because when he opened them again he was on his front, naked. Could hear her moving around, behind him. The wind was raging outside, but he felt oddly serene. He must have dropped off, he realised, and now he felt her touch him.

A finger trailing down his back.

But the finger felt different somehow. Thicker.

A whisper behind him: 'I have something to tell you.'

'What is it, Ally?'

'Can you guess?'

'No,' he said, almost breathless now. 'Tell me.'

He felt a hand cup his left ear. Then a voice hissed:

'I'm. Not. Ally.'

Karl's eyes flew open.

He was facing the mirror, and in its smoky reflection he saw something that made his blood run cold: the wardrobe door was gaping open, revealing empty blackness within. He hadn't imagined its door opening after all; someone had been hiding inside it.

And behind him, grasping his hips, was that very someone.

In the mirror, Karl saw the white skull face.

He saw the antler horns.

He saw the gleaming pickaxe.

And all around Boleskine House, the thickening snow muffled his scream.

PART SIX

DO WHAT THOU WILT

Ordinary morality is only for ordinary people.

– Aleister Crowley

1

Clara was complicit. That was the thought in Oswald Cattenach's mind as he came gasping up for air from beneath the freezing water. The magical invocations directed at her had succeeded. Now she was completely under his spell.

Except for the gentle slopping of the water, the boathouse was silent. The first hues of a purple twilight were visible through a chink in the slatted wall. Night was falling, and soon she would do it; not just because he willed it, but because Karl's demise was her will. And once the sacrifice was made, all would be well.

This insight had been revealed to him gradually through his meditations.

The sacrifice.

He wasn't to forget the intense spirituality of his purpose, how absolutely essential it was to his health. His cure. His life.

He gave thanks, and then heaved himself out of the water. His muscles wanted to shiver involuntarily, but his conscious will defied them. To his immense pleasure, he was learning that his trances didn't just help to strengthen the will, they enabled him to block out physical pain almost completely.

There were moments, submerged under the water, even with Gale's body floating down there with him, when he lost all awareness of his physical state and found a higher plane of existence. Wisdom. Insight. And what that insight told him now was: time was short.

He had been lucky so far, extremely lucky; but Karl was their prisoner, and how many more unannounced callers might they receive? It wasn't as if he could dispatch all of them.

It was going to work.

It had to work.

Stripping off his wetsuit, he thought of the flat he had shared with Bartlett in King's Cross; their own private temple, a hall of mirrors teeming with terrible entities that one had to study, to conquer, to summon one's Holy Guardian Angel. Some would consider that work obscene, blasphemous. Not Oswald. It was essential.

Once, they had very nearly succeeded. It excited him still to think of that unforgettable night, the ceremony: the mystical invocations he had whispered, and the lean, melancholy figure that had flickered into existence, right before his eyes in the mirror, for a second or so, before dissolving. His Guardian Angel? Oswald believed so.

So close . . .

And he knew where had they had gone wrong. Ideally, the sacrificed individual would be a virgin. A male child of perfect innocence and high intelligence. But they had sacrificed a goat. A price had been exacted.

Once summoned, the shadows had a way of hanging around, staining their surroundings. Oswald had checked up on the apartment building and he knew that residents had since fallen ill and died. Committed suicide. He had been too young then, too inexperienced to control what he didn't understand.

But now? Now things were different. He knew what to do.

And Oswald had prepared for the end.

Once he was dry, Oswald pulled on the jeans and thick woollen jumper he had left heaped on the floor.

As he strode out of the boathouse, he fixed his gaze on the lodge looming over him. Crowley's temple, at last. Restored. Behind those walls was an atmosphere thick with the darkest powers, coalescing.

Oswald no longer worried that Clara would try to get away from him. He no longer worried she would turn him in, either. She stood to gain as much as he did from this venture, maybe more. But that would require an act of finality. The ultimate sin to take away Oswald's cancer. In his wisdom, Saint Paul advised: 'Without shedding of blood there is no remission.' And who was Oswald to argue with Saint Paul?

Letting himself into the house, he hesitated, briefly considering checking on Clara, whom he had left in his own room.

No, he would let her sleep for now.

Instead, he moved stealthily to the room he had come to think of as 'the cell'. He pressed his ear to the wood, picturing his prisoner on the other side, handcuffed to the bed: Karl Hopkins, mumbling through his gag, his eyes red raw from crying.

Oswald had resisted looking in on him since he had tied him up, hours ago. But now he was sorely tempted. How badly Oswald wanted to unlock that door and get nearer to the man who would be his salvation. How badly he wanted to smell his clammy fear.

But Oswald did not enter the cell.

Instead he moved silently to the east wing, to his unholy temple. Before the fire, with its glass terrace doors this had once been the sunniest room in the house. Now, even Oswald's muscles tensed against the cool temperature.

Almost immediately, the scurrying sound began. It might have been coming from the walls, the ceiling, or the floor; the point was, the sound was all around him. It was the sound of a teeming mass of insects.

Oswald had no idea yet if he could control the presences that had infected the house, but he was pleased he had come to know them, through meditation.

Now to tame them.

That was up to Clara.

She'd find the sacrifice of blood difficult. Tearing the heart and the liver from a person; devouring those organs while they were still warm? Those weren't acts that anyone unfamiliar with magical rites would perform easily.

But she was up to it. She had to be, because Oswald had sworn an oath to carry out Abramelin's sacred operation. Clara would exact revenge on her husband.

Oswald would make sure of it.

2

Even though her head was fuzzy and light, Clara knew Karl was terrified before she entered the cell. From the other side of the door, she could hear him whimpering like a child, and that was good. The insufferable bastard deserved a little payback.

And Clara was just getting started.

Cold light touched his face as she opened the door. She knew he was afraid, because he wasn't looking her way. Probably he was terrified the sadist in the mask would return. Oswald had been gratuitously cruel to him, and she knew it. She could hear his breathing – harsh, quick. He didn't sound well.

Slowly, he turned his head towards her, bracing himself.

That's right, look at me, you bastard.

'Alison?'

Oswald must have removed his gag, and that was good. They could talk heart-to-heart, at last.

She saw herself in the mirror, and smiled. She was framed in the doorway, eyes glittering – but not with mock desire this time, only intense and visceral hatred. With her hair pulled back so tightly, her face, scrubbed of make-up, milk-pale and lined and haggard, she barely recognised herself.

She had never looked so ominous.

But wait. What was she holding? Some sort of curved steel instrument. A blade? She peered harder at herself.

Yes, some sort of pickaxe . . .

She felt its weight. It looked impossibly sharp.

Strange, she didn't remember picking it up.

Still, it felt good in her grip. Empowering.

'Please, I need help.' She took some grim pleasure in seeing him reduced to this. That his voice was querulous. 'I was sick in the head, Alison, you have to see that.'

Silence. She didn't move.

'I know you'll forgive me. Look how far I came to find you, to bring you back. You're in danger here; can't you see that? This guy's fucking insane! Do you know what he did to me?'

The truth was, she didn't.

Most of what had happened in the bedroom was a blur to her; although she had gone along with the plan to entrap Karl, she had been under Oswald's influence. And if she was being honest with herself, a part of her was glad about that. Relieved.

'We can leave, if you let me go. We can try again, yeah?'

As if seeing herself from a distance, she was moving now, stepping into the room and turning to close the door. The room became pitch black again.

'I'm going to do everything I possibly can to make it up to you,' he said quickly, and she bristled with annoyance. Did he really think she would let him go? Did he think she was that weak?

'I ended it with Elaine. And I've quit drinking.'

Still she said nothing.

'Please, love. Are you listening? I mean it.'

She moved closer to the bed, slowly, hoping he could just about see the curvature of the pickaxe's blade, hoping the blood was fearfully pounding in his ears, as it had done in her own ears for so many years. 'Home just isn't home without you, love. Hear me? I've . . . please . . . I've *missed* you.'

He stank of fear. But as he lay there moaning, she became aware of his natural scent. It took her back to their old life; she remembered how she had feared him, how she had trembled eventually even at his slightest touch. And now, here he was, trying so pathetically to sound like the man she had always wished he would be.

Perhaps, even, the man *he* wished he could be.

'I wasn't responsible, Ally, you've got to see that. I wasn't myself, I was unwell, sick in the head.'

She sat at the end of the bed and he jerked as she pressed the cold, hard steel of the pickaxe's blade against the skin of his leg, just above the knee.

'Please stop.'

She pressed harder, scraping the point slowly up towards his groin. His whole body tensed, his mouth contorting into a grimace.

'Alison?'

She ignored his voice, and in her mind flashed to Oswald's wide, hypnotic eyes, his pupils like black chasms reaching down into her soul. She saw the pills he had tapped into his hand before asking her to get dressed and come in here.

Whatever those pills were, she had a sense they were making this grim task just that little bit easier. Because another part of her mind – that was far, far away – was urgently whispering that this was wrong. That things had spiralled out of control. This was going too far. And that maybe, it would be easier just to turn herself in for the arson. For the murder of Charles Bartlett.

That was the line, but vengeance prepared her to cross it.

Returning to herself, she allowed her hand to move again, and the cold steel scraped ever higher up his leg. Curved, gleaming; a deadly talon.

'Don't you think I've been through enough?' he pleaded, and she smiled as his voice trembled. 'You don't think I'm not fucking terrified? Alison—'

The talon was sharp against his skin. So sharp that if she chose to, she could slash into him as cleanly as if she was holding a scalpel.

'Alison, please.'

Into the tense silence came Clara's voice, firm with new-found confidence. 'I'm Clara now. Alison left when you battered the life out of her. And you're going to pay for that.'

The pickaxe was motionless now, somewhere below his groin, but she was exerting more pressure with its pointed pick. Any firmer and she would draw blood.

'Vengeance?' he uttered. 'No, you're not that kind of woman.'

She inclined her head towards him.

'Don't do that, Karl.'

'What?'

'Don't presume to know *anything* about me.'

'But you're my wife.'

'Your wife?' She let the words hang between them for a moment. 'Your wife, who ironed your shirts and watched the clock, waiting, night after night, for you to just . . . to come home? No, that woman's gone, Karl. Because you killed her.'

With some satisfaction, she pressed the blade harder into his leg. With the pulse of fear came the uncontrollable shaking.

'Listen, Alison . . . sorry, Clara! I know . . . uh, I something must have happened here to make you like this. I don't know what it was and I don't know what control he has over you, but I *do* know we can work this out. Yeah? You don't have to do what he wants.'

The pleading seemed to reach her as if from far away.

Had some of it got through? What? His suggestion that they could work things out, or that she didn't have to do as Oswald instructed?

It had to be that. No way could they patch things up, not after the fall down the stairs, not after losing the baby. Not after this. No, it had to be the other possibility, his only dim chance of survival: that there was still enough of her old self present to know that she didn't have to obey Oswald's wishes. That they could still walk away from this nightmare if they worked together, if not happy, then free. And alive.

Still, she had wanted this, even without Oswald's influence. She had wanted to lure Karl to this place.

'You don't *know* what Oswald wants,' she said.

'Oswald, is it? He must be in love with you, is that it? To want me dead, out of the way.'

'It's worse than him wanting you dead.'

'Worse . . . how?'

'He wants your blood. Your soul. And I don't mean meta-phorically. Do you know why?'

'Because he's a lunatic?'

Silence again. She knew the darkness would make it unbear-able for him.

'Proposition,' she said. 'An occultist who worships Satan requires the soul of a sinner. Conclusion: I definitely wasn't going to allow it to be me.'

She reached past him, snapped a light switch, and smiled gently as he squinted hard against the yellowy light that flick-ered on.

God, he looked ruined, his unshaven face pleading and terrified. Once his eyes adjusted, his whole body became taut. Not because he saw how close she had the pickaxe to his groin, or because its edge had already drawn a bright bead of scarlet blood. She figured that the main reason he was rigid with fright was because he must have recognised her baleful urge to maim him. Punish him.

'I couldn't allow it to be me. And although I'm certainly a sinner, I could never hold a candle to you, you sick bastard.' She nodded. 'Yeah, you'll give him what he needs, Karl. You'll *nourish* him.'

'You're . . . you're not making any sense.'

'You're not listening. To a man as crazy as Oswald, there's nothing more nourishing, more satisfying, than the disgraced soul of a sinner. A man who ripped his child out of the world before it had even been born. That's you.'

Suddenly, she was seeing herself tumbling down the stairs; watching, horror-struck, the dark blood pooling around her legs. Then she was back in the room, struck by the scent of his soiled, damp sheets.

'Oh God,' he said. 'Please. If I could take it back, believe me, I would.'

'You brutalised me. You murdered our child. And now you'll pay.'

'Please! Alison, Clara! Alison. Oh, please, I'm sorry. I am so, so sorry. You have a right to be angry. But not like this, not by giving me to him. Listen! This house has changed you; and if a house can change people for the worse, perhaps it can also change them for the better.'

She stared blankly at him.

'This Oswald is a sadist, an impersonator, propagating a false religion!' His voice was shaking with panic. 'Jesus, what's he going to do to me?'

'Do you have any idea how many nights I asked myself the same thing, living with you?'

Karl was shaking his head furiously. She had to be bluffing, she wasn't capable of this, she *wasn't*! 'Please! You're a good woman. You're not like him.'

'Perhaps you're right about that.' She followed his panicked look and the ghost of a smile touched her lips. 'Perhaps I'm more like you.'

3

Outside the Loch Ness Exhibition, wearing a black quilted, hooded jacket, and keeping away from the street lamps, a buxom-to-heavy figure made its way through the snow, moving slowly, blending with the shadows. When the figure was around the back of the building, it halted at a faded sign ('500 million years of history revealing the unique environment of Loch Ness and the famous Nessie legend'). A hand reached out, found a loose, broken door handle, tried it, and the back door opened sufficiently for the figure to slip inside.

Hardly Fort Knox, mused Aggie. *Typical. Like everything else in this village, the exhibition centre's falling apart.*

She wasn't surprised that a girl who was a detestable slave to the devil would end up seeking refuge somewhere modern like this. Since it had opened, with all its creepy lighting and sound effects, and recreations of what the mythical monster might look like, the venue had practically become a shrine for anyone interested in unusual phenomena.

Unholy phenomena.

Aggie moved closer to the door, opened it, listened. No sound from within. The grand and gothic building was enormous; a network of dark corridors and themed rooms that were usually filled with sound effects and dry ice. As the exhibition was closed now for the season, Aggie didn't think it likely anyone would be coming here anytime soon.

Which was just as she wanted it.

Does she know I'm coming?

She drew back from the door, her feet crunching on the freshly fallen snow. Inghean Kilgour, a grown woman who acted like a girl, had invisible unnatural powers and consorted with the Lord of Misrule. It was possible she was waiting for Aggie in there, somewhere amongst the exhibits; Aggie could almost feel the lurking menace of that demonic witch. But was she powerful enough to have detected Aggie's presence?

Doubtful. Aggie's mind was protected by God. And Inghean was a threat, a diabolical and destructive threat of deviance and heresy. Through consorting with the man who had purchased Boleskine House, she had brought disharmony to the village – chaos. And so she would have to be dealt with.

Aggie would pray to God to purge the evil in the girl.

And if God didn't commit the purge?

Well then; Aggie would.

4

If Karl's wrists hadn't been tied to the bedpost, he would have thrown his arms up in terror as Clara held the silver pickaxe high above him, poised.

A contortion of terror crumpled his face, tears stood in his eyes, but those didn't stop Clara striking him. What stopped her was something outside.

Something moving.

Through the window, just visible in the moonlight, she glimpsed a dark, ambiguous shape in the swirling snow. An animal, a stag perhaps?

On the bed, Karl whimpered.

Clara ignored him, and squinted for a better look. Then staggered back, horrified.

'*Jesus!*'

The pickaxe thudded heavily to the floor.

'What is it?' Karl said.

Clara couldn't speak. Her heart hammered against her ribs as she closed her eyes and confronted the image that flashed up on the back of her eyelids: purple hands, coal-black eyes, breasts hanging like chicken skin off the bone. *An old woman.*

Except 'woman' wasn't quite right, was it? What she had seen, slowly lumbering towards the house on misshapen legs, was a crooked, hunched body clad in sodden rags.

'Alis— I mean, Clara?'

She opened her eyes. Hyper-aware of her own breathing, she dared another look at the window.

And saw the atrocious figure approaching still.

What the hell? It had to be the drugs. Had to be!

It wore a black cap trimmed with ruffles over long, bedraggled hair. A washerwoman who had wandered right out of a Brothers Grimm tale. And what was that it was carrying? Hard to tell, looked like some sort of material . . .

Death shrouds?

Peering harder through the window, Clara told herself not to be ridiculous. There had to be an explanation.

One of the locals?

Maybe. But Clara didn't think so. The nearest house was miles away, and the figure's shambling gait suggested it wasn't even nearly capable of covering that sort of distance on foot. And Clara hadn't seen any cars. Or heard any.

'Clara? For God's sake!'

She turned to Karl, jabbed a finger at the window. 'Do you see that?' she demanded.

From the bed Karl had a direct view out of the window.

'See what?' he said.

'That.' Clara pointed furiously. '*Her*. Tell me you see that!'

'What the hell is wrong with you? There's no one there.'

If Clara had been religious, she might have crossed herself at that instant. With a feeling of utter dread and panic, it occurred to her then what she was looking at.

The *bean nighe*.

A woman with cloven hooves for feet.

Omen of death.

Someone (she couldn't place who, exactly, it was a haze) had told her about it, recently. Very recently. Someone who had heard all about it from a retired journalist. Who? Clara blinked, shook her head. The story had come from a man she knew nothing about. Christ, someone she hadn't even met! Bat-shit crazy for all Clara knew.

And yet, staring at that loathsome wraith, she felt as if she had just received an invitation to her own funeral.

'There's no one there,' Karl said again, and part of Clara wanted to be convinced of that. The rest of her needed to know she wasn't going insane.

An omen of death, or a hallucination?

She closed her eyes. Tried to breathe slowly. Strip away the fear.

'Clara?' Karl croaked. 'Love?'

At that word, her eyes flew open. She cast her gaze all

around the grounds, but saw nothing but pale moonlight spilling over the snow.

She and Karl were alone.

Clara stood there, frozen. Frantically thinking. She felt foolish for indulging superstitions, but she knew she couldn't ignore this. A spectre of death?

The hideous vision had appeared to her, not to Karl. To *her*.

If the myths were true, the *bean nighe* only appeared to those about to die, or whose loved ones were about to die. And Clara certainly did not love Karl. She would never love him. The only possible person it could be was ...

'Inghean,' she said with a start. And at that instant, Clara saw Inghean's wide and affectionate face; the distinctive starburst pattern on her green-blue irises; the fragility in those delicate, trusting eyes. She thought momentarily of the gleaming silver locket she had discovered in the house, the night Oswald had drugged her.

Gale's silver locket ...

'Oh my God,' she whispered.

I came here looking for Gale, so where is she? Where's Adam?

And suddenly Clara had a wretched flash of understanding that brought into clarity what a monster Oswald was; Adam and Gale. They should have been at the forefront of her concerns, yet since the night of Oswald's 'living funeral' she had barely given either of them a second thought.

Why not? She knew the answer to that. She didn't want to know it, but she knew.

Because Oswald had made her forget.

If something had happened to Gale, where was Inghean?

An urgent voice suddenly spoke up in her mind:

Inghean might need you. Find her!

And if she was going to do that, Clara might need help.

With dismay, she looked down at Karl, shaking her head against the strange, dazed state Oswald had induced in her. A madness shared by two, no more.

She stooped, quickly, and grabbed the pickaxe from the floor.

'Please, love, I'm sorry, PLEASE don't hurt me!'

Karl cringed with fear as she moved over to him.

'Shut up,' she snapped; and he did seem to lose the power of speech then, just gibbering and sobbing as she raised the pickaxe and heaved it down, with all her strength . . .

. . . onto the bedpost behind him.

Karl let out a garbled cry.

The wood of the bedpost splintered.

And the leather restraint attaching Karl's wrists to it split apart.

'What?' he mumbled, lifting his bruised wrists.

'Come on!' she said.

Karl stared up at her. 'I don't understand,' he said hoarsely.

'I'm getting you out of here.'

'You're . . .'

'We're leaving.'

5

Karl had to lean on Clara as she helped him, painfully slowly, along the hall.

'Quietly,' she whispered.

'Won't he have the front door locked?'

'We're not leaving via the front door,' she replied, looking straight ahead at the oak door that led into the library room.

She could be making one almighty mistake now. The terrace doors would be locked and shuttered, but she had an idea there would be another way out.

A secret way.

On the day she was knocked unconscious in the boathouse, she'd come to in the library, and an unnatural sight had accosted her: a dark figure climbing, impossibly, out of the floor. A hallucination, she'd thought at the time, induced by a concussed mind. But then Adam had mentioned a rumour about a secret tunnel leading down to the water's edge, and she thought that might actually be true. And if it was . . .

'What are you doing?'

Clara whirled. And her gaze lanced on a fiendish skull mask, antler horns. 'Quickly!'

Karl bellowed with pain as she wrenched him into the billiard room. Clara slammed the door, throwing the bolt.

BANG!

The door shook as Oswald rammed his fists against it.

'Open it!'

BANG!

Again it shook, and they heard splintering.

Karl's eyes bulged with fear. 'That door's not gonna hold!'

But Clara was already hurtling around the room, sweeping her hands across the floor for any sign of a concealed doorway.

Nothing.

Ferocious pounding. Splintering.

Shit, shit, shit, it has to be here somewhere!

On the other side of the door, Oswald was in a frenzy, yelling maniacally, electrified. Galvanised. She thought for a moment she even heard him laugh.

Is this a game to him?

A game!

Clara pivoted, her gaze targeting the chessboard, mounted on a low table in the far left corner of the room. She dashed towards it as the coarse, rage-filled voice in the hall bellowed:

'There's no getting away from what must be done, OPEN THE DOOR!'

Frantically, her hand swept aside the chess pieces, searching the surface of the board for any concealed buttons that might open a concealed exit.

Nothing.

'Hold tight!' the voice bellowed, and Clara found her eyes meeting Karl's as they both heard Oswald running off down the hall.

He's going for his gun, she thought.

'What do we do?' yelled Karl.

Frantically, Clara swept her hands across the underside of the chess table.

Come on, come on . . .

At the door suddenly, more pounding, bellowing:

'LOOK WHAT YOU'RE MAKING ME DO!'

With a cry, Karl threw himself down to the floor, just as the first shotgun blast exploded, ripping a jagged hole in the door and showering the room with fragments of wood.

At that moment, beneath the chess table, Clara's index finger snagged on something: a metal protrusion. Over her shoulder, she caught a glimpse of that skeletal mask leering in at them. It was bone white, fierce and frantic eyes glaring out of black hollows. She felt that baleful gaze with a red-hot intensity, as if it was projected from the eyes of the devil himself.

'Oh, Crowley would have loved this,' Oswald called, his voice thick with demonic fury. 'Yeah, he would have loved to see you both running, like two bleating goats. And you know what?' Stepping back, he raised the shotgun at the door, angling both barrels towards the lock. 'I love it, too!'

BOOM!

Another spray of dust and wood.

Praying that her intuition hadn't deserted her, Clara's fingers pulled on the catch beneath the chessboard.

The click of a mechanism.

And suddenly, she felt the flooring beneath her move. Dropping to the floor, crouching low, she saw that a square of it had come loose, sprung up. In seconds, her fingers were hooking under its edges. Yanking it up. And with a creak, a dark pit below was exposed. Peering into it, she realised this was their way out.

'Come on!' she called to Karl, who was crawling towards her. She seized him and shoved him down into the pit.

'Clara!' Oswald bellowed from the opposite end of the room.

He was clawing his way in through the jagged hole in the door, like a creature bursting out of hell. 'You can't leave now. There's too much at stake!'

She jumped into the pit, pulling the trapdoor closed behind her. As it banged down, her fingers scrabbled on its underside, mercifully finding a bolt. She threw it home, entrapping herself in thick darkness.

With the man who had betrayed her and abused her.

6

Within the cavernous chamber of the Loch Ness Exhibition, Inghean Kilgour stood entirely alone, gazing at the photographs of . . . *something* in the inky-black waters; three dark humps, the long, slender neck. Hoaxes and rumours; truth and lies.

A shock ran through her.

Not once during the countless times she had slipped in here after hours had she been disturbed. This was her sanctuary, where mysteries and possibilities folded around her; kept her believing in something more than her sad little life. She felt safe here. But now she knew there was a risk that her run of good luck was coming to an end.

After a few excruciating moments, she heard the sound again. Footfalls, treading softly, moving slowly through the adjacent chamber.

You need to hide.

There was only one place to hide. Inghean stepped quietly and swiftly across the chamber to a life-sized model of the Machan, the world's smallest submarine, once used to explore the depths of Loch Ness. She climbed on top of it and got inside, pushing herself as far back from the porthole at the front as she could.

Abruptly, the overhead light in the chamber slammed on. Through the tiny porthole, the shape of a woman was apparent, coming slowly into the space, looking behind her and around, then moving forwards cautiously.

'I know you're here, Inghean.'

Oh God, she knew that voice.

There was no mistaking its knowing, judgmental tone.

'Please don't hide from me, Inghean. I just want to talk about what happened at the butcher's.'

Inghean tried not to move; not that moving was much of an option, because there was barely any room for her, squished inside the Machan. It was stuffy in here, hard to breathe. But it had to be preferable to being out there – because out there, in the utter silence of the deserted exhibition, Aggie Blackwood had a plan for her. Inghean knew that in her heart. And whatever it was, the plan was a bad one.

'You're not in trouble, my girl. Well, not much trouble. But you do know things about that house. You know it's evil, don't you, Inghean?' A threatening tone crept into her voice. 'That house is changing you, like it changed my sister; and if we're not careful, it will change everyone in this village.'

Inghean swallowed; she couldn't let Aggie find her.

But she was closer now. Standing right in front of the porthole. Scanning the exhibition chamber.

Please don't turn around.

Inghean sucked in a terrified breath.

And Aggie turned slowly towards the porthole and peered in.

'Ah, there you are.' Aggie beamed, her piggish eyes glinting in the overhead light. 'Now then, my dear, you're coming with me.'

Before Inghean could respond, Aggie Blackwood's hands were reaching down into the submarine, gripping Inghean's arms, painfully hard, and wrenching her up and out.

Outside in the blustery darkness, the snow was thickening;

but that wouldn't deter Aggie Blackwood. The two of them
were going on a journey.

Inghean prayed it wouldn't be her last.

7

Beneath the library, in the filthy pit beneath the trapdoor,
Clara strained to listen. But it was hard to hear anything at all
over Karl's pathetic whimpering.

'Quiet,' she hissed.

Above them, footsteps clumping heavily. The trapdoor
shook and rattled but didn't open.

'We have to keep moving.' She put a hand out, felt a cold,
wet wall. Pushed her hand along, looking for an opening. 'Shit.
I don't know ... I can't see anything.'

To her surprise, there followed a click and a little flame
sprang up from a lighter held in Karl's trembling hand. 'In my
pocket,' he said. He held the lighter up, and his shadow spiked
up the rough rock wall. 'Jesus. What is this place?'

Clara looked around; breathed out in relief.

The rumours were true ...

'It's our way out.'

He shuffled closer to her. 'I'm sorry. I am so, so—'

'Shut up!' She heard her own contempt, and for a moment
the revengeful impulse returned to tempt her.

A dark voice in her head whispered: *He's weak. You could*

overpower him. You know that, right? You could murder him, right here, and no one would ever know.

But no; she needed to stick with her decision. What mattered now was defying that vision of the *bean nighe* and staying alive.

Or keeping Inghean alive.

Her mind flashed again to her memory of Gale's silver locket containing the picture of Inghean. If Oswald had done away with Gale, Inghean would need help. Clara had to find her. And to do that, she needed to keep her resolve.

'So, uh, now what?' Karl asked tremulously.

She gave him a look that said: *You really are as stupid as you look.* Then she gestured behind him, to a yawning black hole made visible by the tiny flame.

'We follow the tunnel,' she said.

'We can get out alive?'

Above them, the clump of Oswald's boots; it sounded as if he was leaving the library.

'We have to try, right?'

Karl stared into the tunnel's abyss. 'But where does it lead?'

That was a good question. A better question was: would Oswald be waiting for them at the other end?

'One way to find out, right?' Clara snatched the lighter from his hand. 'Coming?'

8

Raising his face to the cutting wind, Oswald pushed on through the snow, resolved, his eyes hard with baleful intent.

There was only one place he would go, only one location as sacred as Boleskine House. The only natural wonder in this bleak landscape that wasn't besieged by cheap tourists.

Crowley's hideout.

He had found mention of it in the writings of the Great Beast. The refuge to where Crowley retreated when Boleskine became too troublesome. A spiritual home for sacred moments – a holy temple reserved only for those who believed.

Finding it hadn't been easy, but his rock climbing skills had helped.

'She'll be coming,' he said to himself, his eyes fixed steadily on the route ahead. The biting cold and the thick covering of snow on the heath presented no impediment for him; he had made the trip many times, for his meditations, even in fierce winds and hammering rains. For Oswald was a man who believed in insurance policies. He had made preparations at the hideout so the ritual could be completed there, if necessary.

Now, it seemed, he had been wise to make these preparations.

Because she would be coming; she would be delivered to him. He had arranged it.

Inghean.

The wind shrieked. Oswald's heart sang as he quickened his stride.

Even though Karl had escaped, Oswald was alive with

optimism. Dawn was touching the mountainous skyline, burning orange; and he had never been more hopeful of a good death.

9

'Oh dear God!'

Somehow, Clara stopped herself throwing up; although behind her, Karl was already doubled over, retching at the sight of the bloodstained police helmet.

When they climbed out of the tunnel, the surroundings had been confusing at first. But then Clara had recognised the foul, earthy odour, the brick walls ... They were inside the mort house in the cemetery by the loch. Behind them, on the rise of the hill, was the house.

And Oswald, where was he?

Trying to force him from her mind for a moment, Clara focused on the chequered police helmet lying at her feet. A puddle of blood had pooled around it and dried in a grotesque black halo.

The hat had belonged to PC Adam Lake. The sight of it was appalling to her, not least because she knew the poor guy had come here only wanting to help. He hadn't told anyone he was coming, she knew that; if he had, they would have been out to check by now.

She was suddenly appalled with herself. Utterly appalled.

How could she have forgotten about poor Adam, and Gale, whom he had driven her here to find? They had been at the forefront of her concerns when she had regained consciousness on Oswald's hellish altar. It was evident to her then that they were in danger; why hadn't she thought about them since?

The answer came to her clearly: *after he drugged you. Assaulted you. He made you forget about them both.*

Guilt stabbed at her as she remembered Adam coming into the office, asking questions about the missing poet, about this hellish house, and how unhelpful she had been.

Oswald must have killed him. She felt a flare of rage at that certainty; rage at herself for not questioning Oswald about Adam's whereabouts; rage at Oswald for banishing the policeman from her memory.

Oh God, please, how many more have to die because of what I did?

No, because of what Karl did.

Behind her, Karl vomited again into a corner.

Your monster of an ex-husband began this. You burned the house down because of him. So why are you helping him?

Because I'm not like him, the old her spoke up, the woman who'd once carried a child, a life, in her womb.

Karl straightened up and came to her side, wiping his mouth on his sleeve. 'Crazy motherfucker, he did this?'

She nodded.

'So let's get out of here.'

She hesitated. Something wasn't right.

'What is it?'

'Oswald knows the tunnel ends here, so why isn't he here?'

Perhaps he's outside, waiting.

It was possible; wasn't that his style?

But then, she hadn't heard him enter the mort house when they had been down in the tunnel. Almost fifteen minutes they had waited, crouching in the darkness, shivering, barely daring to breathe. Then they had persevered, pushing on the shabbily bricked-up exit, pushing hard, until it tumbled down in a cloud of dust, allowing them to escape. Into a building that used to be a mort house and was now the tomb of her own misgivings.

She decided they would take the risk, make a run for it. But as she stepped towards the door, she saw something else that made her hesitate, something she recognised.

Cardboard boxes.

They were stacked against the far wall. They looked very much like the boxes she had discovered in the boathouse on the day she moved in. But why would Oswald have moved them? An instinct told her he would have his peculiar reasons, and that she should check.

'What are you doing?' Karl protested as she went to the boxes. 'We need to go!'

Ignoring him, she opened the first box and peered in. She recognised the old newspaper cuttings, stained yellow with age and fetid with mildew; cuttings about this house, its macabre history; cuttings about Aleister Crowley's life here.

But those weren't the papers that caught her attention now. Just visible through an open flap in the next box was a letterhead emblazoned with distinctive blue and white letters: 'NHS: Guy's and St Thomas' Foundation Trust'. She flipped the lid of the box, took out a handful of papers and saw that they were patients' medical records.

The last time she'd seen that letterhead was on her discharge letter, the day she left hospital after losing the baby.

What were these papers? What was Oswald doing with them?

With shaking hands, she rifled through them. So many. Medical cards, prescriptions, patients young and old. No men that she saw; just women and children.

'Hey, we gotta go!' said Karl.

She nodded quickly; then noticed that something had dropped out of the bundle of papers she was holding. An identity badge in a transparent plastic wallet. Holding it up to the lighter's guttering flame, she examined it.

When she saw the picture of the man with dark wavy hair she felt nothing. Did she know him? No. Had she met him? She didn't think so.

But then she saw the name beneath the picture – Charles Bartlett – and felt the wind knocked out of her.

'What is it?' Karl asked.

Clara was looking at the man who had perished the night of the fire. The man she had killed.

'Alison?'

She shook her head, transfixed by the picture.

Bartlett had been a striking, intense-looking man. The cheekbones were high, creating an angularity of the face that was a little severe, but it was softened by the closely clipped beard. Beneath his name, printed in smaller lettering, was his job title: 'Pharmacist'.

Why had he brought medical records here? Had Oswald seen them? She imagined he must have done; but why would such records be of interest to him?

'Ready?' Karl said, standing aside as she stood up and moved to the doorway. 'Come on, the car's not far.'

'Where?'

'Bottom of the driveway.'

Seconds later, they were outside, floundering through the snow. The freezing wind snapped at her face as she plunged through it. A couple of minutes later she arrived, breathless, at the main road. And stopped.

'I know what you're thinking,' he said, seeing her eyeing the black Mercedes that blatantly didn't belong to him. 'But seriously, I want to change, Clara! I can do so much better.'

All she could manage was a pitiful grimace. 'Keys?'

'But where are we going?' he asked.

She looked at him reproachfully. 'I may need you.'

'What for?'

'To help me find a friend. A vulnerable friend.'

Within seconds she was at the driver's side, but when Karl reached the opposite door, she commanded him to stop. No way was she having him ride alongside her.

'Get in the back.'

'Huh?'

'Get. In. The. Back.'

Slowly, reluctantly, he obeyed. Clara slid behind the wheel and started the engine.

I need a phone.

Oswald had found Karl's mobile and smashed it up. But then it struck Clara: Karl always had two phones. At least he used to. One for work; one for his personal, grubby affairs.

She swung around. 'You got another phone in here?'

He shook his head, and she saw the lie; reached over to the glove compartment.

'Ally—'

There was a phone in there, buried under a few maps. She grabbed the device, beeped it on. 'What's the code, Karl?'

'Who are you calling?'

'The police.' She turned to look back at him. 'What's the damn code?'

'You can't phone the police. They may be looking for me.'

There was blank and pallid fear on his face as he spoke. Enough for Clara to wonder if he had done something he bitterly regretted. Perhaps something dreadful.

He said nothing about the woman in the brown coat he had accosted late that night on the Vauxhall Bridge Road.

He said nothing of the beer bottle he had brandished at her.

'I'll try Inghean,' she told him, suddenly thankful she knew the girl's number. 'Just give me the code.'

When he had told her, Clara shifted into gear, but kept the handbrake on as she tried Inghean. And to her relief, like a blessing, the line rang.

10

'Where exactly are we, Miss Blackwood?'

The wind whined eerily as Inghean and Aggie were trudging along the narrow, rugged road in the grey morning light. Off to the left of the road was a sign ('WELCOME TO THE LOCH NESS CAFÉ') and behind that a small shop in total darkness.

There was an air of sombre mystery to this place that chilled Inghean. To the right of the road, shadowy forms of gigantic boulders and gnarled trees were all around, ice-hung and choked by fresh snow.

Aggie had Inghean's hand in a painful grip. She led her steadily towards a black iron gate that bordered the dense forest.

'Please, Miss Blackwood, I want to go back.'

SMACK! Aggie's rough hand left her cheek smarting and her eyes tearing up. Inghean wanted to give in and cry. She wanted her mother; she wanted Clara.

'Stop your moaning! We're almost there.'

Where was *there*? It was hard to see because they were hemmed in by jutting branches. She resisted, but Aggie only pulled harder, Inghean's skirt and coat snagging on a gatepost as they passed. They began descending a steep path that had been cut into the hillside.

'Stop it, please, you're hurting me.'

But Aggie didn't stop. Down, they went, amidst maimed branches bearded with snow, until suddenly Inghean heard a thundering cascade of water.

She knew this place.

She knew it from her dreams.

And she knew it wasn't good.

Winding amongst rocky mounds and frosty pine trees, the path dropped them down to the edge of a craggy ravine. It was barricaded with a rickety fence; a viewing place. And here they stopped – not because of the fence, but because they were arrested by the sight of a natural wonder: across an immense chasm, a fearful torrent of silvery water was cascading down, pounding the jagged black rocks below. Bedraggled and weary, Inghean gasped as she stared down into the crystal spray, the mists rising from the craggy gorge. She had never seen anything more beautiful. Or more terrifying.

A small warning sign advised visitors to keep away from the edge. But Aggie didn't seem to care much about that; she was inching nearer, eagerly craning her bull-like neck as if to scrutinise the unbroken drop. What was she looking for?

Suddenly, Inghean felt the phone in her coat pocket vibrating. Hope flared. Someone was calling her. She couldn't get the phone out; Aggie would see it. But what she might be able to do was answer it, and hope – *pray* – that whoever was on the other end of the line got the sense of where they were.

Inghean shoved her free hand into her pocket, felt for the answer key on the phone with her thumb and pressed it. Then, holding her pocket open, she said loudly: 'Please, Miss Blackwood. Where are we? What is this place?'

'The Falls of Foyers,' Aggie said admiringly.

Please, Inghean thought, *let it be Ma calling. Or Clara. Please let them be coming.*

Abruptly, they were on the move again, along that meandering, uneven trail, descending along the edge of the gorge.

The path split into two. One branch led down through the dark forest to the pebbled shoreline of Loch Ness; the other, the one Aggie chose, narrowed to nothing more than a brittle sandstone ledge that looped around the gorge towards the waterfall itself.

Why are we going this way? Inghean wondered.

The track went perilously close to the edge. But apparently Aggie didn't care. Nor did she care that Inghean was hungry and frightened.

'We're going towards the waterfall.'

'That's right.'

'But it looks dangerous.'

'Yes. But we'll be just fine.' Aggie turned and considered

her with wide, dark eyes. 'I'm taking you somewhere very special, Inghean.'

'Where?'

'Every waterfall hides a secret.'

Inghean nodded, trying to be brave. Wasn't that what Clara would do? She had to be like Clara now, for Clara's sake. Only she wasn't sure why.

They made their way towards a barbed-wire fence, and Aggie helped her climb through it, although she was rough doing that, not caring whether Inghean caught herself on the barbs. The mean old cow really didn't care about her at all; all she cared about was getting to wherever they were going. And she had a weird look on her face. Purposeful. It scared Inghean, because she remembered where she had seen a similar expression: Aggie looked a bit like Murdoch McHardy, the butcher, just after he had hacked off his hand.

Beyond the fence, Aggie led Inghean along the trail that curved treacherously around the gorge. They were only about ten yards or so from the pounding waterfall when the edge narrowed, so they had to press their shoulders tight against the rock, both trying their hardest not to acknowledge the vertical drop. All around them was the thunder and spray of water. Inghean made her way slowly along, doing her best not to peer down into the watery chasm.

Up ahead, she saw a plateau behind the waterfall, and it was towards that jutting escarpment that Aggie led her. As she edged nearer the overhang of rock, Inghean saw that it shadowed what looked like a black seam in the wall of rock.

Aggie swept aside the overhanging ivy to reveal an opening, as dark as the mouth of hell. Narrow; they had to go through sideways. And then they emerged . . .

A cave behind the waterfall! Inghean realised, awestruck.

It was spacious, with slimy, mossy walls, and an uneven floor. Cold, but not entirely dark; a shaft of light dropped onto a five-pointed star within a circle chalked in white on the rock. On the walls, more chalk marks: mystic sigils. The numbers 666. All around was the evidence of sacred ritual. Bones. The remains of sacrificed animals.

'Why are we here?' Inghean asked, hearing her voice echo around the chamber. 'Please, take me back. I'm freezing!'

'Oh, Inghean. I brought you here to bathe you in the waters of redemption, and I can see I was right. Our village is infected once again with evil. Look at these markings. Evil has been done here. You understand there is evil in you, don't you?'

'What? No, please, what are you—'

'You understand you need to be saved, for all our sakes?'

Inghean didn't understand; she began to tremble. She began to cry. 'Please, please . . .' she mumbled.

Aggie slung her rucksack on the ground and crouched over it. 'Nothing to be afraid of now, Inghean. You must be brave and do as I say, okay?'

She rose and came towards Inghean, eyes shining, hand clenched around the object she'd taken from her bag.

'Remember Exodus 22:18,' she said, raising the hunting knife, 'Thou shalt not suffer a witch to live.'

11

'*Stop!*'

Oswald Cattenach threw up a hand as he entered the cave. He stopped at the treacherous edge of the unbroken drop, mountaineering pickaxe grasped tightly in his other hand, and took in the scene.

When he saw the state of Inghean, the cuts on her trembling face, the purple bags under her wide, innocent eyes, he felt a shock of alarm. The old bird had clearly got carried away. Very carried away: Aggie Blackwood had a hunting knife at Inghean's throat. There was a fanatical, manic look on her doughy face that did not fill him with confidence. But she wasn't having the girl. No way.

The girl was for him.

'This where you do your devilry, is it?' Aggie asked him, her nostrils flaring as her gaze flicked down to the pentacle. 'I was right about you; no one believed me, but oh, I was so right. You and Inghean together, cooking up evil.' She swallowed, grimacing. 'I lost my sister to Boleskine. That cesspit infected her husband with its darkness. Boleskine House is the reason my brother-in-law went insane, why he murdered my sister – you know that, don't you?'

'Perhaps,' Oswald said, 'but that's not Inghean's fault.'

You can't allow her to harm the girl.

'Well, here's the way it works in this part of the world, Mr Cattenach,' said Aggie, the cords in her bull-like neck protruding grotesquely. 'People turn a blind eye to the evil. People like

Gale Kilgour, whose pride devours them, they avoid what's staring them in the face; they refuse to confront it. Me? I'm snuffing out the evil for my sister's sake. She deserves that, doesn't she? And Inghean is tainted. What she has; that thing inside her . . . It's abhorrent to God. And in His wisdom, I'm putting that right. Do you see?'

Then she did something Oswald hadn't expected. She made the sign of the cross – and said, 'If I have to take you both, then God help me, that's what I'll do' – and lunged at him.

For a woman of her bulk, she was incredibly quick.

Instinctively, Oswald leapt back from the swipe of her blade, but his right foot hit a mound of rock, which caused him to stumble, and as he did, Aggie's knife slashed his thigh.

'Shit!' he bellowed as pain exploded in his leg and he sprawled backwards. His pickaxe went flying as he went down, and landed near the lip of the waterfall. 'You crazy bitch!'

And he realised something, something that suffused him with a warm inner glow.

He had fallen into the confines of the pentacle.

Which means you're safe. In the sacred name of Abramelin, you're protected.

Despite his predicament, Oswald relaxed, holding faith.

'You shouldn't have come,' Aggie said. 'This doesn't concern you.'

'Oh, but it does,' Oswald said, hoisting himself into a seated position, one hand covering the wound on his thigh, which was bleeding profusely. 'It concerns me very much. How do you think I knew where to find you?'

A little light came on behind Aggie's eyes. 'What are you saying, that God sent you?'

She really has lost it.

'Yes, that's right. God sent me.' For the first time, Oswald was smiling. '*My* God,' he added. 'Not yours.'

The hope dropped from her eyes, replaced with confusion. He couldn't understand how she hadn't worked it out sooner. It was simple really: she had brought Inghean here for one reason: because *he* had asked her to do that.

Although 'asked' wasn't quite right, was it? Rather, he had *suggested* it to her when he had been shopping in the village. The same day he had bought the mirrors. He had been grateful Celtic Crafts was so quiet of custom that morning. Quiet enough for Aggie not to notice him turning the sign on the door from 'Open' to 'Closed'. Quiet enough for him to have a private word with her – just like he'd had a quiet word with the priest; with Mr McHardy; with Inghean.

He had admired Aggie's window display, those wonderful silver-framed mirrors, and bought them, paying cash, insisting she give him a receipt. And that was vital. When practising hypnosis, physical objects could be used to trigger memories at a later stage. Or to automatically trigger post-hypnotic behaviours.

It was a cheap trick – most stage magicians were up to it; but that didn't mean the trick wasn't useful at times like this. Now Oswald's hand was in his pocket, closing around the crumpled, handwritten receipt. Calmly, he held the receipt out to her. 'Aggie, you gave me this, remember?'

She lowered her gaze to the receipt in his hand, puzzled. 'Take it.'

She did. And then the change began; a bewitching transformation he had observed so many times in his subjects. Her bullish shoulders relaxed, her face took on the blank look of the somnambulist. As her ferocious eyes glazed over, Oswald knew she had lapsed into a hypnotic state.

He threw a conceited glance in Inghean's direction. Good, she hadn't moved. Now he was in total control. Aggie Blackwood would be punished. Why not? She had no right to have been so goddamned careless with Inghean; with Clara and Karl gone, Inghean was reserved for the Abramelin Operation. She was his insurance.

He sat there, staring up at Aggie, considering whether to get up, grab her and push her through the waterfall, to plummet to those jagged rocks below. Or . . .

You could let her do it.

Tell her so and she would.

That's right . . .

One word was all it would take.

'Remove your coat, Aggie.'

At first nothing; but then with greater concentration, purpose, Oswald repeated his instruction and watched with rapture as the old battleaxe obediently removed the padded black jacket with the insulated fur hood and discarded it on the slimy floor.

He nodded, allowing himself the smallest smile, thinking of how much Aggie's expression reminded him of the foolish priest; then he saw the other item that needed dealing with.

'Drop the knife.'

She hesitated.

'Drop it, please, Aggie.'

It clattered to the ground. When that happened, he knew the way was clear. Just when he thought he couldn't surprise himself any more with his villainy . . . Oswald found a way.

'You ever been rock climbing, Aggie?'

She shook her head dumbly.

'The idea doesn't excite you?'

'Not really,' she answered flatly. Her trance-struck gaze shifted to the shimmering curtain of water.

Oswald contemplated Inghean, who was cowering against the wall. He smiled with a sort of fiendish delight, and said softly:

'Inghean, my dear. Watch this.'

12

'Sure this is the right place?' Karl asked.

Water thundering down, spray rising up, like tendrils of smoke.

This was the right place.

The Falls of Foyers. The words had been muffled, almost drowned out by the roar of the water, but Clara had heard them clearly enough when her call to Inghean's mobile had connected.

She stared across the immense chasm to the torrent of water plummeting into the black pool below. Her heart was hammering against her ribs. Inghean was here, somewhere.

'Come on,' she said, glancing back at Karl. For someone normally so domineering and confident, he looked distinctly troubled, and if Clara was being honest with herself, part of her felt good about that.

As they descended through the snow-bearded bracken and ferns, she kept her eyes on that cascade of water, steeling herself. Because now she knew why this scene felt so chillingly familiar: the chasm, the waterfall. It was the scene from the painting hanging in the hall at Boleskine House.

All this time, everything that had happened – it had all been leading here.

'. . . *there are caves all over these parts.*'

Was it possible? To the side of the waterfall she could see a cleft in the rock. A dark shadow extending behind the water. It could just be that – a shadow. Or it could be a cavern.

With mounting trepidation, she followed the trail until it branched in two. A few yards beyond the fence was a narrow ledge running along the chasm. Fresh footprints in the snow marked where others had already been.

And as she stood there, gazing across the chasm, confronting the perilous reality of heading that way, her eyes were caught by something.

At first she was afraid it was Inghean she saw, standing so precariously on the ledge next to the falling water and half concealed by overgrown ivy. But no; as she squinted through the misty spray she realised it couldn't be Inghean; the body shape was wrong. This woman was taller, bulkier.

Aggie Blackwood.

What the hell is she doing?

'Who is that?' Karl asked, bewildered.

'Aggie!' Clara bellowed, but her voice was drowned out by the water hammering the rocks below. Water was streaming down Aggie's face, which was drawn and eerily serene. Then it contorted in horror as the bulky woman peered down the sheer drop. So high! A hundred feet or more.

'Is she off her head?' Karl uttered, but before he had the words out, Aggie Blackwood stepped nearer the edge.

A scream from the cave across from her. Clara couldn't make out the words, but she was sure the voice belonged to Inghean. And she sounded utterly terrified.

13

Across the chasm, inside the cave, Aggie Blackwood had turned her blank gaze to the tumbling waterfall just feet away from her. Oswald gathered all his purpose, focused flat-eyed on her and smiled spiritedly. She deserved this for putting Inghean's life in danger. He would not feel guilty about what he was about to do.

'Please,' Inghean spoke up, 'don't harm her.'

Oswald turned his attention to Inghean, who was still against the wall of the cave, shivering and about as afraid as he had ever seen anyone look. But there was something in her eyes – something that wasn't fear – that made him cautious. He suspected that something was a pure and visceral hatred of him. Which was good. Thanks to her heightened state of emotion, if he did take her life in the sacred name of Abramelin, the power her death would unleash was bound to be stronger. And then, finally, he might achieve his coveted union with his Holy Guardian Angel.

It would happen. He would make it happen.

But first, Aggie . . .

He looked back at the bulky woman poised near the edge

of the cave's mouth, the water behind her a glistening silver curtain. She was in his mental grip now.

'Step out,' he commanded. 'Drop.'

Looking on, arms wrapped around herself, Inghean began to sob as Oswald nodded Aggie towards the edge, a grim smile touching the corners of his lips. She shuffled forward. It was this easy. In a blissful moment she would plummet to her death and he wouldn't even need to lift a finger.

'Go on,' he urged, 'don't stop now, Aggie. The Lord is waiting for you.'

Aggie, doing what she was compelled to do, inched nearer the lip of the cave. When she dropped, she might well scream, but he didn't think that was likely. Nor did he think it particularly mattered. Aside from him and the girl, there were no witnesses. They were out in the middle of nowhere. A tragic accident was how it would be reported. One of many in the area.

'Good Aggie,' he encouraged, 'keep walking now.'

Inghean wept harder, so hard that Oswald barely heard her pick up the rock. Instinctively, he ducked as it hurtled close past his head. 'What the—'

The rock struck Aggie hard between the shoulders with a deep thud. With a startled grunt, she lurched forwards, looking so unsteady on those wide feet of hers that for a second, Oswald thought she was bound to stagger in shock over the lip of the cave. But she didn't do that. Instead, she shook her head vigorously, as if trying to clear it of a waking nightmare – which, in a sense, is exactly what this was for her – and turned to look blearily, questioningly, at Oswald. 'Where am I?' she asked, in groggy alarm. 'What am I doing here?'

'You're sleepwalking,' he replied, his face obstinate. 'But soon you'll be with God. Do it,' he said hotly. 'Jump!'

Slack-faced, she turned and stepped pliantly towards the edge, unmoved, unafraid, staring down with eyes like fogged glass at the torrent of water below.

'NO, MRS BLACKWOOD, STOP!'

Inghean, standing tall, so brave, was yelling her warning with a passion that would have made her mother proud. And Aggie heard her. With a jolt, she whirled, blinking madly, shaking her head and coming to. 'What have you done?' she asked Oswald, her voice a slur. 'What's wrong with me?'

He couldn't stop her confusion, her fear, from bringing a grim smile to his mouth.

'Wrong place, wrong time,' he said flatly, then, as her guard was down, he lunged, coming ferociously at her. He had meant to slam into her, knock her over the edge. But to his immense surprise, Aggie threw a meaty fist at his face.

He drew back, dodging her nimbly, lurched up close to her. And spat in her face.

She froze. The shock of it.

His warm saliva sluicing unpleasantly down her left cheek.

Aggie might have screamed then. He really thought she was going to, but just as she was gathering herself, he drew back his arm and threw his right fist hard into her face.

A crack of bone as blood burst from her nose. And just like that – she was gone. Staggering back, toppling over the edge like a dead weight, falling.

Falling, into the abyss.

14

Looking on, pressed fearfully against the rugged cave wall, Inghean stared with full dread at Oswald, who was grinning to himself. With triumph shining in his eyes, he wandered back to the centre of the cave and crouched on the ground within the confines of the symbol marked out there.

The part of Inghean that Aggie Blackwood had feared, the part of her that made drawings of events yet to happen, was whispering two things to her. That Oswald was completely insane. And that he meant to kill her, too.

His head was low; he was whispering incantations under his breath:

'*I do this day spiritually bind myself anew:*

'*By the sword of vengeance:*

'*By the Powers of the Elements:*

'*By the Cross of Suffering:*

'*That I will devote myself to the Great Work: the obtaining of Communion with my own Higher and Divine Genius by means of the prescribed course.*'

As these words came, the monster was regarding her darkly. But the idea of making a break for it, running, didn't even enter Inghean's mind as a serious possibility. Because she had to be here for Clara now. She felt this truth acutely: that as much as she had agonised about coming here with Aggie, this was the way it was supposed to be.

She recognised this waterfall chamber from her wild and anxious dreams. The jagged black walls, the slippery boulders.

She'd sketched it. Even the body, falling to the black rocks below, had made fleeting appearances in her drawings. Weren't pictures like that why her mum had put her in that awful school?

Remember, you have a special condition, Inghean.

Shivering, she dropped her chin to her chest.

Yes, she had a special condition. A special condition that had shown her what was going to happen to the butcher. Just as it had shown her that Boleskine House was going to burn. Only in her dreams and drawings, the house was totally destroyed.

Perhaps her mother was right. Perhaps she really did belong in that school, in a room with a locked door. But Inghean didn't think so. She didn't think she was crazy. She was just different, gifted.

An da shealladh: the second sight.

Grandma had it. I have it, too.

And in that moment, that one horrible instant, something outside her brought the dismal suspicion that her poor mother was freezing cold and alone, somewhere dark and wet. That something, perhaps something despicable, had befallen her. And that soon, someone else would die, right here in the cavern.

'You're very quiet, Inghean,' Oswald said, his voice faintly musical.

She said nothing, and she stayed very still. Because now a prickling sensation on her neck was telling her that, in seconds, they would no longer be alone in the cave.

'Something the matter, Inghean?'

Closer. Closer.

She raised her head to face the hellish man she was suddenly afraid had hurt her mother. He was lumbering to his feet now and reaching for his pickaxe.

This was it.

15

'Inghean!'

The cavern's acoustics threw Clara's voice back at her with hollow resonance. It was Inghean's scream, Aggie's fall, which had helped them find this cave.

A portion of the cave's roof had collapsed long ago, allowing some ashy light to filter through; enough for Clara to see Inghean huddled against a rocky wall. She might have felt a gust of relief at that moment, if it weren't for the monster with the gleaming pickaxe, shambling towards her friend.

'Hey!'

As Oswald pivoted to face her she felt the heat of his gaze and bolted to Inghean's side, throwing her arms around her in an involuntary hug.

'It's okay, love. I'm here.'

Inghean was shivering uncontrollably from the cold and damp. There was a black jacket lying abandoned on the ground, Aggie's jacket, and Clara snatched it up and wrapped it around her.

'I didn't touch her.'

She snapped her gaze back to Oswald, whose form was half

obscured in shadow, his angular face solemn and severe and drawn with exhaustion. He stood there motionless, looking from her to Karl, then back to Clara. 'I don't know how you found us, but we'll finish what we started. Now' – he held out a hand – 'I know you're furious, Clara, but we can make this good. Between us.'

Her temples were pounding with fear.

She glanced at Inghean, who was trembling beside her, and the girl shook her head vehemently.

You'll never. See her. Again . . .

'You should go, Clara. It's over. Leave Inghean here, with me.'

As if Clara was going to listen to this beast. His mind was warped. Depraved.

'If you will it to be so,' Oswald said, 'then you *can* trust me. Love under will, Clara. *Do what thou wilt shall be the whole of the law.*'

'You can quit that shit,' she said bitterly and registered his flinch – and that was good, because now Clara thought this was the moment to hold a mirror to his wickedness.

'Oswald, just think about what you've done.' Bristling with anger, she gathered herself, facing him, so brave. So vulnerable. 'You tried to murder *us*. You understand that, right?' She let out an anguished sigh. 'Good God, those poor kids.'

'I released them,' he said, perfectly calmly.

He's calm for the moment, but not for long, she thought. *That's the way it is with him. First the calm, then the chaos.*

'Didn't I say that if your will is pure, you're capable of changing anything or anyone?' Oswald said, tightening his grip on his pickaxe. 'You should know that better than anyone. Why, look at that magnificent fire you ignited.'

'That was a mistake,' Clara said, stepping forward. 'An awful mistake. But letting you in? *That* was my biggest mistake.'

'We're the same, you and me, Clara. You're a survivor.' He smiled at her proudly. 'Always running and yet, look! Here you are. You could have run far away tonight, but instead you ran here. To me.'

He's going somewhere with this, Clara thought, *but nowhere good and nowhere worth indulging.*

'You're demented,' she said, slipping her hand into Inghean's and tugging her to her feet. 'You're insane, you know that, right?'

'Actually . . .' Oswald looked past her, towards the exit to the cave. 'It's your coward of a husband who's insane. *He* was your biggest mistake.'

She turned to look at the man she despised. He was standing, still and silent, before the roaring cascade of water. Perhaps he thought holding back was his best chance of getting out of this mess unscathed. In Oswald Cattenach he had finally met someone who was more unstable than he was.

But then Clara realised something. Karl hadn't been silent because he was afraid; he had been thinking. Plotting. He had the beginnings of a plan. Or thought he did. She recognised the confidence that was surfacing on his face.

'The police know where we are,' Karl said. There was sincerity and strength in his voice, which saddened Clara as much as it surprised her. He had been a good man, once. She wondered if a part of him might still be.

Oswald remained perfectly still, watching. Waiting.

'I mean it. The police know where we are,' Karl repeated. His hand reached into his back pocket and came out holding a screwdriver. He raised it before him, and Clara willed his hand not to shake. 'They're on their way, and I think they'll be pissed they've lost one of their own.'

'No,' Oswald said mildly. 'For one thing, I don't believe you called them; for another, the young police officer who visited my house is very much *alive*.'

A moment's silence. Clara didn't believe Adam was alive, not even for a second. There had been too much dried blood in the mort house. Furthermore, she had seen Oswald murder three youngsters in one night. The idea that he might have spared a police officer struck her as extremely unlikely.

Oswald was at the edge of the pentacle, peering speculatively at Karl, but he did not look worried. 'Besides,' he said calmly, 'the police have lost control. They've become blind to the black forces unleashed here by Crowley, the influence of his black magi—'

'You really believe that shit?' He looked mockingly at the pentacle marked out on the ground. 'What that's supposed to do anyway?'

'Would you even understand something go sacred?'

'Probably not,' Karl quipped, 'because you're clearly insane.'

Oswald drew his head back. 'The pentacle, representing the earth, offers protection to whoever works magic within it. And the image drawn upon it is the being one seeks to evoke. In this case, my—'

'Guardian angel,' Clara finished bluntly, cynically, and he nodded, as if this was the most straightforward thing in the world. For Clara that nod, that simple gesture, was the most frightening thing about the shape chalked on the floor. Not that it might assist in drawing spiritual powers into this world, commanding nature, or working miracles like curing his cancer.

The most frightening thing was that he believed it could.

Still brandishing the screwdriver, Karl flicked a look in Clara's direction. 'Satanism? Evil? No. It's like I told you, Clara. I did my research before coming here: Crowley fundamentally believed in the power of good. The power of *good*.'

'I'll thank you not to blaspheme,' Oswald replied, his voice a little strained. 'This cave was Crowley's sanctuary.'

'I don't doubt that,' Karl said, remembering his vision of the bloated man with yellow skin. 'What I doubt is your interpretation of his teachings. And I think that if he knew what you've been doing in his name, he'd be outraged.'

Oswald blinked. Karl stepped forwards.

'Maybe he'd be so outraged, he'd lead someone here to stop you. A man like me, even.' His eyes flicked to Clara, then back to Oswald. 'You. You've twisted Crowley's religion into something it never was. You've bastardised it. To convince yourself you can survive your disease.' He shook his head. 'The truth is, Oswald, you're just a murdering psychopath.'

Oswald recoiled at this accusation as if mortally offended. For a moment he looked doubtful, fearful even, as if Crowley were right there in the cave, looking down upon him in furious judgement. Then, recovering himself, he said bitterly:

'You didn't come out here to rescue Clara. You came for the same reason you're lying to me about the police – to rescue your conscience. Why not tell Inghean the truth now? Tell her who you really are, Karl. Tell her how you hurt and abused poor Clara.'

Inghean flinched in Clara's arms. Karl looked across the cave at the women, backed up against the wall, and he felt ashamed. And angry.

'Go on. Tell her. How you drove Clara to complete despair.'

'Stop it.'

'Tell Inghean what you did to Clara's unborn child.' Oswald's mouth twisted with sadistic satisfaction. 'Tell us all how that sacred life just flowed away, because of what *you* did!'

'THAT'S ENOUGH!' Karl bellowed, and his voice echoed back at them from the cavern walls.

'Ah, there he is.' Oswald smiled acidly. 'See, Clara? There's the animal that needs putting down.'

Clara's eyes snapped in his direction. Karl's face was brick-red, his eyes burning with rage. He looked just as he had before he had shoved her down those stairs, before killing her baby.

'You despise him, Clara,' Oswald said. 'You want to make him pay. Don't you?'

She saw, again, the dark puddle of blood at the bottom of the staircase – the life draining away. Saw Karl looking down on her, in horror. And for a moment, Clara did regret helping Karl escape from Boleskine House.

Perhaps Karl saw that too, because he began edging back towards the cave exit. 'Do what thou wilt shall be the whole of the law. That's how this works, right? Well, we're leaving. Now. Clara, Inghean, come with me.'

Clara was frozen. Of course she wanted to get the hell out of this cave – get Inghean to safety. But Oswald was hardly going to let them just walk out.

As if reading her mind, he said in a low voice simmering with anger, 'You can't leave. Where are you taking her anyway? What's she got left?'

Horribly, Clara understood. She thought Inghean did, too.

'Where's Mum?'

The question ricocheted off the cave walls like a misfired bullet. And a part of Clara, fearing the worst, hoped to God he wouldn't answer it.

'Dead,' he said heavily. 'Your mother is dead.'

Inghean froze. It was a few seconds longer before her elfin face crumpled with grief and she fell to her knees, releasing a wail of total anguish and despair. 'No,' she cried, 'please, no!'

Watching her friend's face break up punched a hole in Clara's heart. She didn't know what to say, what to do. She had never seen anyone receive such devastating, sudden news. Just as she was thinking what to say, rage pulled Inghean to her feet. With fury in her eyes, she flew at Oswald, so quickly that Clara almost wasn't quick enough to restrain her. But with a frantic lunge, she did – thank God.

'Let me go,' she wailed, 'please, let me go!'

Her arms were flailing, she was thrashing to get free, until eventually she weakened, and her legs, instead of kicking, became limp, her face draining of colour. The tears came next as she crumpled to the stony ground again, overwhelmed, covering her face, shuddering as she wept.

Oswald stared at her, his eyes gleeful and savage. 'Your mother had to die, or she would have ruined everything.'

There was no trace of a lie in the monster's words; they had been aimed to hurt, each one delivered like a dart with malignant pleasure. 'Oh, but don't you worry, she's in a safe place,' he went on, his demeanour now that of a man revelling in Gale's demise. 'Clara knows where, don't you?' He dropped her a sickening wink. 'One of my favourite places, actually; in the boathouse, deep, deep beneath the water. Remember, Clara?'

Her stomach lurched as she remembered finding him meditating there. And with astonishment she remembered something else, from long ago: Inghean's unfinished drawing, the drawing she had feared so badly. The drawing of the stick woman in the water.

Not Clara; but Gale. Always Gale.

And not swimming – but drowning.

Jesus, she thought to herself, *she saw it coming. She saw all of this.*

Inghean, helpless, rose to her feet with the mournful purpose of a child who understands she is truly alone, and Karl's temper flared. 'We're out of here!' he yelled, stabbing the screwdriver into the air. 'Understand? You have no hold over us.'

With that, Oswald launched himself into motion, hurtling towards Karl like a cannonball.

16

It happened so fast that Clara barely had time to react. In her shock, all she could think was that someone with such a bad wound on his leg shouldn't have been able to move that swiftly; but somehow Oswald had found a way.

Karl stumbled back, treacherously close to the waterfall, and raised the screwdriver in defence. But Oswald just kept coming, driving into Karl and tackling him to the ground. Even from across the cave Clara heard the sickening crack of Karl's head connecting with the rocky floor and the clatter of the screwdriver as it rolled towards the waterfall.

In seconds Oswald was straddling Karl, crushing his throat with one hand and using the other to pull something from his back pocket. A clear plastic bag.

Clara snapped a look an Inghean; saw the desperation and helplessness on her face. She imagined she looked much the same.

Across the cave, Karl spluttered. He rolled out from under Oswald onto his side, retching and coughing, until the fight seemed to go out of him. His eyes drifted, glazing over.

And Clara understood: Oswald had thrown Devil's Breath into Karl's face.

Finish him off! Clara saw the suggestion glittering in Oswald's eyes as he stood and turned to face her. She had been willing to do it before, in the house. It was seeing the old hag that had stopped her. An omen.

'He's sick, Clara,' Oswald said softly. Seductively. 'But we can put that right, between us, now. As we were supposed to before you ran out on me.'

She flinched, and he caught it.

'Oh, don't look like that. I know you're eaten up with guilt over Bartlett's death. You needn't be, by the way. Over that pisshead?' He hesitated, drew a breath, and Clara sensed he was building to something else. And that worried her.

'You do feel guilty, right?' he asked evenly.

'Of course I do.' She waited for a moment, but Oswald didn't say anything. An oppressive silence opened up between them. Eventually Clara broke it: 'What are you getting at, Oswald?'

She watched the monster closely. Some secret, mischievous knowledge glinted in his eyes as he raised his head and said, 'I know about guilt, Clara. If you don't master guilt, it will devour you. And guess what?' He flicked her a strangely confidential look. 'I can make all your guilt go away. If you want.'

She saw the wicked, greedy look in his eyes and shook her head contemptuously. 'I don't want anything from you.'

'Well, we'll have to see about that, won't we? Because the fact is, Clara, there's something you must know about Bartlett. Something vital.'

A silence, more ominous than the last, spread between them. 'What are you talking about?' Clara asked at last.

Oswald stepped away from Karl – lying limp and vacant and useless – and spread his hands like a preacher ready to lay down the path to salvation.

'You didn't kill anyone, Clara. Bartlett died *before* the fire. And I know that' – his eyes narrowed unpleasantly – 'because I killed him.'

Clara didn't move.

'You hear me?'

She stared, utterly dumbstruck in perplexity. Confronted with the same question Oswald's behaviour had always posed. Was he telling the truth? Was he telling her this to win her trust? And if he gained it, whatever could he cajole her into doing next?

'I killed him,' he said again. 'Bartlett wanted to run the place as a guest house, can you believe it? I could never have allowed such a desecration to Crowley's memory.'

Clara just stood there, still as a rock, scarcely breathing.

If this is true . . .

'When Bartlett was contemplating buying the house, I came along, convinced him to get inside, take a look around. That wasn't hard; a window in the back hall had been rather carelessly left open. No alarms, either. And once we were inside, it was even easier persuading Bartlett to get high. A simple matter of reminding him we were in a holy temple – the house of the esteemed occultist and ceremonial magician, *Aleister Crowley*. The place that was the cradle for all that was magical and devious and divine. A curative house of magical power. And there we were, two lowly followers, walking the same corridors! Of course, Bartlett was in awe. Once he got high, he was stumbling around in a haze. Stupefied. And then . . . peaceful.

'Administering the overdose was a risk, but in the end rather successful, wouldn't you say? Your fire was perfectly timed. Destiny. Clara, you were always meant to be there at the house that night. You were *supposed* to burn it, so that I could buy it. Do you see? You were drawn to the Highlands for that exact purpose: to serve me.'

Oswald took a few steps towards Clara, stopping in the pentacle marked out on the floor. 'I have your best interests at heart,' he said. 'This one' – he stabbed a finger towards Karl's pathetic figure – 'this disgusting, cowardly weakling deserves what's coming. Either way, you had nothing to do with Bartlett's death, but your fire set all this in motion. And you can still benefit.'

Clara ran a hand down her face. The idea of benefiting from someone's death was repellent to her. Still, a voice deep inside whispered, *Benefit how exactly?*

'If I am to endure, then, in accordance with the rules of transcendental magic, I must summon my Holy Guardian Angel to heal me. And a worthy offering is required. A sacrifice, hot blood.' Oswald looked contemptuously at Karl. 'He'll do fine.'

Clara's hands were trembling, her breath coming in fitful little gasps. She didn't believe in Oswald's mystic ritual, not for a second. Nor did she believe in the curative powers of the house. But a deep, dark part of her despised Karl, and *did* want him to pay. Wanted him dead.

She had cowered from the act before. But then, she had

thought she might need his help to find Inghean. Did she need him now?

'You lost your baby because of this monster. But you can make things right again. Complete the Abramelin Operation. For both our sakes, Clara. *Kill your husband.*'

When he put it like that . . . 'No,' she said. 'I can't!'

'You can, and you must,' Oswald told her. 'I've already invoked the powers of darkness in this village. If we don't complete the ritual, they will run amok, cause devastation to families here – hundreds of innocents. Those forces must be constrained.'

You can't. There are no demons. He's demented.

'Take his life with this,' Oswald instructed, holding up the pickaxe. 'The Great Beast's own instrument of sacrifice. We must show our deference to the Lords of Darkness. Begin. Make an incision on his chest in the sign of the inverted cross.'

Clara looked at Karl; saw fear swimming in his eyes. He was slumped helplessly on the ground, bereft of any fight, immobilised, but not so drugged that he couldn't understand what they were talking about. What she could do to him. In just a matter of seconds, she could end all those years of suffering. Make him pay.

'Conquest requires sacrifice, Clara, and for life, the price is high.'

There is no truth in magical rituals, Clara told herself.

Yet here, in this cave, she could feel the gathering of shadows, like she had at the house. Shadows that almost possessed shape and substance.

There is no truth in magical rituals.

'Don't think,' Oswald commanded, 'just do it.'

The pounding water echoed sonorously through the cave

as Clara hesitated. She couldn't do it. Certainly not in front of Inghean. Not at all! But as Clara gazed at Karl, lying there, held in place by Oswald's will, she could almost taste blood.

'Why hesitate? Come on, Clara! Revenge. He's a monster. *He murdered your baby.*'

She didn't need reminding of that. Or perhaps she did.

With a colossal effort she pictured the way her life might have been if Karl hadn't thrown her down the stairs, or if she had escaped him before she lost the baby. She saw herself at the hospital, her face suffused with the warm glow of motherhood as she cradled the child, marvelling at the tiny fist curling around her little finger. Saw herself taking refuge at her aunt's house in the Derbyshire Dales. Saw herself bringing home her baby – her *son* – tucking him in his crib, stroking his downy head.

And then she remembered the way it had really been when she had got back to the apartment. Alone, moving through the vast silence of those rooms. Feeling their emptiness. The sheer absence of the boy who had never lived.

The memory ignited fury within her.

She let go of Inghean's hand and allowed her legs to carry her to Oswald's side. She felt as if she was floating above herself. Here, but not here. Even with the waterfall thundering down beside them, every sound in the cave had slipped away.

'You and me, we're survivors,' Oswald said softly, and he handed her the pickaxe.

And as her hand closed around its rough handle, Clara felt the surge of its raw power, its potential to ensure Karl never laid a hand on her or anyone else ever again.

At her feet, her former husband looked up at her and whimpered. His eyes on her were dazed, but tears were collecting in the corners.

She would end it here; she would end it now.

'Clara,' Oswald murmured. 'Give me Karl, then Inghean will go free.'

She thought about that, remembering Oswald torturing those poor kids, gunning them down in cold blood; remembering how he had deceived and entrapped her. With a flash of terrible insight, it occurred to her that Oswald had been right about something: nature was out of sorts.

'One life for another,' he said. 'Do we have a deal?'

A strangled noise from Karl. A plea, perhaps.

'Clara . . .' Inghean's voice, barely a whisper, fearful. Innocence shattered.

Clara looked at the girl, trembling against the rock. She would do anything to keep her safe. *Anything.*

Tightening her grip on the pickaxe, she gave Oswald his answer: 'Deal.'

17

Oswald barely saw the gleam of the axe before his hand jumped with a convulsive jerk to his leg.

His good leg.

'FUCK!' He staggered back, somehow managing not to fall over, and bellowed more in shock than rage. 'Clara, what are you doing?'

He was far enough away from her now for Clara to make

a run for it with Inghean. But that would mean leaving Karl behind; and though she hated him still, she no longer had it in her to let him perish.

As for Oswald, the son of a bitch stood there, his leg bleeding profusely, his face contorted with confusion.

If anyone deserved to die, it was him, and Clara understood this as she advanced. She had to do it; not just for her own self, her own pride and her dignity, but also for the innocents he had lured here, drugged and assaulted and murdered. And for Adam, and Gale, and Murdoch, and of course for Charles Bartlett, whose blood even now stained her hands.

'One life for another, Oswald.'

'*Clara, no! No! STOP—*'

With unleashed fury, Clara charged at him, and she slammed him into the cave wall.

What happened next was a blur for everyone in the cavern, especially for Clara. If she were to live, these would be the moments capable of sullying every dream, splintering every nightmare.

She stepped back, watching Oswald cautiously as he struggled off the floor, driving his body through the pain. He got himself upright and stood, just about, at the edge of the pentacle, panting like an animal.

Leaning in close, her lips at his ear, she hissed, 'So tell me, Oswald, *can* the mind master the body?'

She was raising the pickaxe to finish the job when, behind her, Inghean yelled desperately:

'CLARA! BE CAREFUL!'

Clara snapped her head towards the girl, and in that moment Oswald attacked, seizing Clara's neck with overwhelming force and shoving her sideways, towards the waterfall. But before she reached the rocky precipice, a force brought her and Oswald crashing down.

Inghean. The girl had thrown herself at them.

Clara barely had time to register this before Oswald was on top of her, his face just inches from hers.

'Now you know what it's like, Clara, facing death.'

She struggled, raging against him as he crushed her, straddling her, pinning her arms with his thighs. He grabbed a fistful of hair and with an ear-splitting crack slammed her head against the rock. Pain exploded. The cavern receded for a moment.

Inghean – where's Inghean? She had been right here. Did he have her, Oswald?

No. The monster had *her*. He loomed over Clara, leering down at her. He had no weapon, only his hands. Drawing nearer. Wrapping around her throat.

'You had this coming, you bitch!' Oswald grunted as Clara tried furiously to buck him off. Then less furiously. Then she wasn't fighting at all.

Her eyes drifted past him to focus on the jagged black ceiling above, at the beam of light penetrating through from the sky. Somewhere up there, in the light, did her son exist still? Would she be with him at last?

'Clara!' Inghean cried, and something clattered onto the slick rock at Clara's side.

Even though her brain was screaming for oxygen, it reacted. She angled her head to see what Inghean had thrown.

Karl's screwdriver!

A new determination to survive exploded within her. Straining, grasping, reaching desperately outward. The screwdriver was just inches away . . .

With an unearthly cry of rage, Oswald's hand tightened around her throat. 'This is how you cheat death, Clara. By *becoming* it.'

Clara's vision dimmed as he bore down on her. Her flailing hand knocked the screwdriver – out of reach.

No! she thought. *Please.*

Then, behind Oswald, over his shoulder, she saw something. Hope: in the shape of a figure wielding a rock. Bringing it down sharply, striking the back of Oswald's head.

Oswald's body gave a tremendous jerk. He sank back on his heels, releasing Clara's throat, and his mouth fell open in a gasp of shock that quickly became a roar of bestial agony.

As he reeled, and Inghean – dear, innocent Inghean who was desperate to protect her friend – dropped the bloody rock, Clara gasped in a breath and reached again for the screwdriver.

And this time, it *was* within her reach.

She felt its weight. Light but powerful. Deadly. In an explosion of strength, she angled it towards her attacker. And then – *oh God, please* – Oswald's roar of fury became a gurgling splutter as Clara drove the screwdriver into his throat.

His eyes bulged. He coughed, and blood sprayed Clara's face. As he clawed at his neck, Clara bucked beneath him, throwing him off. Frantically, she stumbled to her feet and backed away.

'GET BACK!' she yelled at Inghean, who was still too close to the monster for comfort.

Oswald was clawing his way, inch by inch, towards the edge of the cave's mouth, the waterfall. The black rock floor was splashed with blood, which was pooling in the pentacle. He moaned, one hand clutching furiously at the screwdriver embedded in his throat, the other reaching feebly for his pickaxe. But Clara saw another hand reaching for it.

And with rising horror, she understood. Clara had got it wrong. Inghean hadn't just wanted to help her. Inghean wanted blood.

'Oh, shit,' Clara whispered, and for a few disorientating seconds she felt the cave spinning around her.

Inghean, no longer the sunshine girl, was standing over Oswald, her face glistening with the spray from the waterfall.

'*Please, no, no, no, no—*'

Inghean raised her face to Clara and sent her a steady, uncomplicated look that said: *I'm doing this for Mum and for you. Because I love you. I must do it.*

Inghean meant to kill Oswald. There was no way Clara could allow that sweet, innocent girl to do such a thing. No way. This was on her.

'*INGHEAN, NO!*'

But Inghean was already striding towards the curved steel. With every last vestige of strength, Clara ran for her. They grabbed the pickaxe at the same moment. Clara wrestled it from her, whether because she was stronger or because Inghean let go, she couldn't tell.

At their feet, Oswald cried out in pain. But Clara showed no compassion for the beast; all her compassion she devoted to her friend.

'Look away,' she said to Inghean, but the girl did not. Would not.

'Clara, stop!' Oswald spluttered. 'Love under will!'

She heard him, but it made no difference. She could think of nothing more appropriate to say to him now, at the end, than his own words:

'Do what thou wilt shall be the whole of the law . . . you monster!'

A flash of silver as the pickaxe streaked down and – *thwack* – plunged into his back.

He shrieked in agony, his whole body arching.

'Clara!' he pleaded, blood bubbling from his lips.

She couldn't look at him. Couldn't stand the blood, the pain and terror in his eyes. The waterfall cascaded down behind him; he was right at the edge.

One hard kick was all it took.

18

When it came to it, Oswald Cattenach made not a sound as his body tipped over the edge.

Both women stood still and silent for a long moment, until Inghean slid her hand into Clara's and squeezed.

Clara edged forwards and peered into the chasm. Down below, the foaming waters were a deep, dark scarlet. Oswald was gone. A surge of energy passed through her body. Not just relief, it was more than that. She was staring down at death, but oddly, she felt *alive*.

'Clara?'

She snapped out of her reverie. 'I'm okay, Inghean. We're okay. Come on.'

She tugged the girl away from the edge, turning to look for Karl. He was in a heap, conscious, but only barely. As she went to his side, his eyes fluttered open and she held his gaze for a second.

'What about him?' Inghean asked.

'We'll send for help,' was all Clara could manage in reply. But she meant it. Because she'd seen something in Karl's eyes that made her glad, in fact, that he wasn't dead. Remorse. A swift death was too good for him. How many nights had she mourned the loss of their child? How many nights had she wished she could go back to the day she first met him, shake herself by the shoulders, and tell that love-struck fool to stay away from him? How many nights had she wished she had ditched him at the altar and saved herself those years of bruises and bleeding? How many? The number was endless and always would be, and it was right that he began counting them too. And perhaps, if he was no longer drinking, as he claimed, that was punishment enough.

'What now?' Inghean asked. She seemed remarkably calm for someone who had just witnessed an atrocity. But that observation was not the one that stopped Clara short and sent a chill shuddering through her; what did that was Inghean's attire.

Suddenly, Clara's mind was filled with an image of a hooded figure standing next to a waterfall, holding something that gleamed.

'Jesus,' Clara muttered. 'I can't believe it.'

Wrapped up in Aggie Blackwood's quilted black coat, hood casting her face in shadow, Inghean looked a lot like the figure in the painting that hung in the echoing hallway of Boleskine House.

Clara stared at the girl at her side.

It was you . . . always you.

The hooded figure in the painting.

Inghean's face was pale, her eyes wide and uncomprehending. Innocent.

'Now what?' she asked.

Clara considered that, looking towards the gleaming water-fall and the daylight behind it.

'Now? Home,' Clara said, thinking of her aunt's house in Derbyshire. Then added: 'With one pit stop.'

Her hand delved into her back pocket, her fist closing tightly around the cigarette lighter there. And as she guided Inghean across the cave, she pictured a tiny blue flame springing up like life resurgent, and nodded to herself.

Because great things grew from tiny things.

'I need to take care of something,' she said, parting the undergrowth so that Inghean could get through the narrow, craggy opening. 'And then we're done.'

And there, emerging from the cavern, Clara paused, gazing across the harshly beautiful landscape towards the hill beyond which Boleskine House lay. Her thumb was on the lighter's striker wheel.

Already she could feel the hot glow of one last fire.

19

In a shaft of sunlight disclosed by shifting clouds, Jeff Ramsay sat in his overstuffed armchair in his timber bungalow on the north side of the loch. He was reflecting on the past; on secrets and lies buried long ago.

Everything surfaces, he thought, thinking of the young

and eager policeman who had visited him, asking all about Boleskine House. PC Lake was out of his depth, to put it mildly. Jeff didn't envy the guy digging into the history of that house.

Still, their conversation had made this old man regretful. He had already decided he would try to make amends with Aggie Blackwood. She wasn't a bad woman. Deluded? Sure. Off her head was probably more accurate. But sometimes it was better to step in and help people like that, before their eccentricities ran away with them. For people living alone, suffering with grief, the religious bug could be hard to shake.

A gust of wind snapped at the window. Jeff got out of his chair, his Labrador following quickly, and went to check he had the window properly latched. Looking out over Loch Ness and the snow-covered mountains beyond, he saw that the skies were clearing now. The morning was crisp and clean.

Maybe today was the day to begin again. Maybe today he would drive into the village and call in at Celtic Crafts. She was a stubborn old ox, though.

Still, even if Aggie didn't want to see him, he could at least leave a note for her. Offer to clean her windows next time she needed them doing, something like that.

He was smiling, having decided he would make the call, when something caught his attention. Something odd that stood out against the blue sky.

Further down the stony shores of the loch, on the same side as his house, was a billowing plume of black smoke. A fire was raging somewhere along that stretch of shoreline, though its origin was out of view from here.

Jeff reached for the tablet his daughter had insisted on buying for him in the end, suddenly grateful she had. His television was always on the blink, but he could check the news any time with this.

With a sweep of his index finger, he unlocked the screen and tapped the app for news. He scrolled, scrolled – and gasped harshly at a photograph. Boleskine, the house of his night-mares. Its windows blown out, a plume of black smoke trailing from orange flames that danced within. Jeff stared, awestruck, and then quickly scanned the article.

FIREFIGHTERS CALLED TO HISTORIC
BOLESKINE HOUSE ON LOCH NESS

Scottish Fire and Rescue Service crews are tack-ling a blaze at Boleskine House near Foyers. Fire engines from Foyers and Inverness were first on the scene. A pump from Dingwall and an incident support unit from Inverness have since joined the effort.

Most of the property has been destroyed. It is not clear yet whether anyone is inside.

Boleskine House was owned by infamous occultist Aleister Crowley and later, for a time, by Led Zeppelin guitarist Jimmy Page. This is the second fire at the property in twelve months.

Jeff put down his tablet and went back to the window. It was quiet in his house, and he could just hear the low drone of an approaching helicopter. Probably the Fire and Rescue service.

Part of him was thankful he couldn't see Boleskine House from this angle; the rest of him yearned to see it – to see it blazing crazily; the raging inferno consuming the rooms; the burning roof collapsing and falling in with a crash; the flurry of sparks as tongues of flame exploded from windows spewing out clouds of black smoke.

In the distance, between the water and the mountains, the air was thick with evil, black smoke. Ash drifted down to the calm waters below.

Ramsay sighed sadly, unburdening himself of thirty haunted years. The horror that had visited Loch Ness and Abersky.

It was over. A hellish history ablaze. Thank God. At last, it was over.

With his eyes riveted on the curling smoke, he pictured Rebecca, the love that Boleskine had cheated him out of, long ago. Then he pictured his kids. Their innocent, questing faces. Their beaming smiles; their little hands in his.

Gazing out at the azure sky smudged with smoke, he sat heavily, mournfully, in his armchair and wept.

PART SEVEN

COVENANT

We must remember that Satan has his miracles, too.

– John Calvin

1

Buxton, Peak District, Derbyshire. One year later.

'Clara Jones to Room Three, please.'

To the other patients in the waiting room, the woman who stood abruptly looked too thin and too gaunt. She seemed tense. Worried. A stark streak of grey through her coppery hair lent her the appearance of a woman old before her time. Still, no one would have denied that there was an inner steel to her as she strode to the consultation room.

As she knocked beneath the nameplate that read 'Doctor Mundey', Clara was thinking of blood. Not, for once, of the nightmare at Boleskine House, but of the stains on her bed-sheets that had brought her to this quiet surgery in the Peak District today. After all this time, her body had bled. Naturally. As a woman should.

'I don't want you to worry unnecessarily,' Clara had re-assured Inghean, who had soon worked out something was bothering her. 'It's just a regular check-up, and then we can do what your mother would have wanted: move on with rebuild-ing our lives.'

Clara didn't know if they would ever be able to do that.

Gale's drowned body had been found exactly where Oswald said it would be and exactly as Inghean's original drawing had foretold: floating under the boards in the boathouse. Afterwards, there had been moments when Clara had thought Inghean wouldn't make it. But somehow, together, they had.

How many long afternoons had they spent talking it over, tearfully embracing? At last, it seemed Inghean was coming to terms with her loss, and Clara owed it to the poor love to try to salvage something from the horror. Away from the wilds of Scotland, they had a chance to begin again. Without Gale, Clara was all the family Inghean had. Clara had to be there for her; a mother at last, in a sense . . .

But then last week Clara had found – upon a bloodied sheet of all things – a glimmer of a promise for *more*. A glimpse of hope, after so many barren years. If you believed the newspapers, medical anomalies happened all the time to other people. So why not to her?

She knocked again, harder, on the door.

'Come in.'

The plump, bespectacled doctor was planted behind a desk strewn with papers. As Clara entered, he glanced up from his notes and smiled.

'Please, sit down, Clara.'

With a racing heart, she did.

'How can I help you today?'

You can give me hope, she said silently.

'Clara?'

'I'm sorry. I'll explain . . .'

Clara summarised her medical background – the 'accident' and the damage wrought on her body – and her current symptoms. With each word she spoke it seemed to her that Doctor Mundey looked graver.

'I see . . .' he said when she finished. 'Give me a moment,

please.' He turned to her notes open on his computer screen and began scrolling through.

Clara sat rigidly as she waited. In her deepest imaginings, this change in her body was a vague sign that she might, just possibly, be able to conceive. A recovery, possibly. The more she thought about it, the more she dared to imagine that the injuries she had sustained when Karl had pushed her down the stairs weren't permanent after all, and that the doctors had got it wrong.

'No. I'm sorry.' Doctor Mundey removed his glasses and cleared his throat. 'Clara, it is very unlikely indeed that you will ever become pregnant.'

She stared at him, the information sinking in, all that was good draining out of her, all the hope, all the expectation; she had never felt it like she felt it then, spinning away from her. Crushed.

'Did you hear me?'

'There must be something we can try?'

'I am sorry,' said the doctor again. 'I know that this sort of news is difficult to accept, and it can take a terrible emotional toll.'

Clara heard this as if from a great distance, yet the words struck like a judgement on her femininity. She thought of other women her age, and felt frustrated, envious, angry.

'The emotions can become consuming. But the sooner you face them, the sooner you can plan for the future.'

She was remembering, with horror, her fall down the stairs; coming to; the awful sensation of precious life flowing away.

The ambulance man looming over her.

So much pain endured, all for nothing.

Now, was she failing again?

'Clara?'

Groggily, blinking away the nightmare memories, Clara came back. To reality.

Still infertile.

Doctor Mundey was regarding her with compassion. 'I was explaining that resuming a normal menstrual cycle doesn't mean that you are ovulating,' he said quietly.

The destruction of hope. Never to become a mother. The failure consumed her in a foaming torrent.

'I know it's not the answer you wanted.'

She shook her head, unblinking, calm. The doctor pushed a leaflet over the desk towards her. Beneath an illustration of a tree were the words *Time to Talk – NHS Counselling Services.*

'Clara, at this point it may be best for you to work on coming to terms with what happened. With what your husband did to you.'

She looked back up – and froze.

Doctor Mundey had vanished. And in his place, sitting at his desk, wearing his very same white shirt and tie, was Karl. Not the snivelling, apologetic Karl she had abandoned at the cave in Scotland, but Karl as he had been before she walked out on him – his fists clenched, his face contorted with rage. There was coagulated blood on his knuckles, and his lips were stretched in a grotesque leer.

'*You want a family, do you, Clara?*' he hissed at her.

Her chair toppled over as she leapt out of it. Swiftly, Karl was on his feet, gripping her wrist, thrusting his face so close to hers that she reeled from the stench of booze. From the threat of his vile lust.

'*You want it?*' he bellowed. '*You want it? YOU WANT A FUCKING—*'

She wrenched free, twisting away from him, slamming back against the door. 'You're gone, Karl, you are NEVER coming near me again!'

A barked instruction, fearful, shocked: 'Clara, Ms Jones, *stop it!*'

She blinked, exhaling the longest breath.

'Control yourself!'

No one else in the room now. Just a stunned Doctor Mundey, his podgy face drained bone-white. He was afraid, she realised to her shame, and he had one shaky hand poised over his telephone. If he hadn't already called reception for help, he was surely about to.

'Clara, please, put the scalpel down.'

The scalpel?

Following his gaze, Clara saw the razor-sharp steel between her fingers and jolted with shock. It was only a matter of seconds before shame and a palpable sense of inadequacy washed over her. Jesus. She had no memory of snatching the scalpel from the medical trolley!

'You had an ... episode. It's not uncommon in victims suffering from anxiety, or shock. Now you need to put the scalpel down. Please.'

Barely able to control her shaking hands, Clara set down the scalpel with a clatter. Appalled by her own behaviour, she couldn't even bring herself to look at the doctor.

Get a grip! Karl promised to leave you alone.

He had. After his hospitalisation, after his questioning by the police, almost miraculously, Karl had accepted that she did not belong to him. She had faced her demons and she thought probably he respected that, her new-found strength, because his desire to pursue her had faded.

He gave you his word that he would never come looking for you again.

Except in your nightmares.

Oswald was gone, too. Except, of course, in a more permanent way.

A little shakily, the doctor ambled to the sink and poured her a glass of water. He got her to sit down, and he stood beside her, watching her take slow sips.

It was a few minutes before she was feeling calm enough to continue the conversation, and Doctor Mundey was apparently reassured enough to resume his seat behind the desk.

'As I was saying, the emotional toll—'

'I'll be fine.'

He studied her with acute uncertainty. And whether he believed her or not, suddenly Clara just wanted out of there.

She thought of Adam.

She thought of Aggie Blackwood.

She thought of Gale Kilgour.

And as she felt her world crumble, she thought of the baby, never born, that had haunted her.

For one fleeting, dark and shameful moment she wanted to end this life. Escape. Then, just as suddenly, reason and love broke through her thoughts. How could she think that? How could she possibly, when she had Inghean to care for? Inghean, who relied upon her, needed her.

Inghean, whom she loved like a daughter of her own.

Doctor Mundey was still regarding her with concern.

'Actually,' she said. 'You're right. I do need to find a way to cope. In fact it's vital I do.' She held up the counselling leaflet. 'I can try this. But also . . . I want a prescription for antidepressants.'

The doctor frowned.

'I wouldn't ask for medication unless I felt I needed it,' she added hastily.

Now she saw in his eyes that he understood: her use of the word 'please' had been entirely perfunctory. He gave her a long stare; then came the questions. Did she isolate herself socially? Did she eat too much or too little? Did she have problems sleeping?

'Of course,' she said. 'That's why I want the pills.'

The irony was, this was true; but Doctor Mundey was obviously a more conscientious doctor than she had given him credit for. Clearly, he wasn't worried *just* about her mental state; he was worried she was a risk to herself. Or others.

'One more question.'

'Okay.'

'Don't be alarmed; don't take offence.'

'I won't.'

'Okay then . . .'

She waited.

'Do you ever hear voices?'

'Voices?'

'Yes.' He shifted. 'Or see things that . . . aren't there?'

Clara's whole body tensed as she fought to hold back the memories of that figure in the black homburg hat carrying the walking cane with its serpent head.

She shook her head. 'No, nothing like that.'

'You're sure?'

Tap, tap, tap . . . the figure, inching nearer.

'I'm sure.'

After a long moment, Doctor Mundey nodded, apparently satisfied. He turned to his computer, punched in some details, and the printer whirred. A quick scrawl of his pen, and he handed over the prescription.

'I suggest you get some rest, Clara, and that you see someone who can help you with the sort of outburst you exhibited just now. You're clearly overwhelmed, and it would be in your best interests to—'

'Thank you, Doctor,' she said, and whatever well-meaning guidance he spouted next was lost in the dull *thunk* of Clara closing his door behind her.

2

Clara's breath came in sharp, short bursts as she stepped out of the doctor's surgery onto the cobbled grey-stone street. There were other young women out here, going about their day. Happy. Seeing them, Clara couldn't help but compare herself.

She felt dizzy. Sick. The low dry-stone wall outside the church took her weight. She sat there, arms wrapped around herself, and shut her eyes for a moment.

A part of her soul – the hopeful part that had never given birth and yearned to – was crushed; because now she knew she was still barren. And that hurt like hell.

She swallowed her grief, clutching the prescription slip in her pocket. Perhaps the pills would help, but in her heart she knew she could cope without them.

She opened her eyes and stared at a woman who looked a

little like her, and smiled. It wasn't as if she couldn't bring a unique perspective to other women in a similar situation, was it? She would help them, if she could.

She raised her gaze to the car parked up on the edge of the market square and stared at it for what felt like five minutes. Her infertility would not prevent her being a mother. She had to be strong now. For Inghean's sake. Perhaps she would get halfway to the chemist and decide she didn't need the pills after all, and would be better off calling the number on the counselling leaflet that was also buried in her pocket.

She tried to imagine sitting down before a complete stranger and spilling her darkest innermost secrets.

The house. The fire. The body.

Bartlett's death wasn't her fault; she knew that now. Yet so much of the ordeal *was* on her. The striking of the match. The burning. There could be no doubt, *that* was the sin that had let the monster in.

She remembered her first visit to Boleskine. The sense of strength and power emanating from the house. The idea that a damaged house, forced down in price, would make her safe, solve all her problems.

What nonsense that seemed now, far away from Loch Ness. What fiction.

Gathering herself, she stood and wandered towards the car, one hand clenching the prescription note once more. She had stopped shivering. In fact, she was smiling with resolve. Above all, Inghean was the one who mattered, and Clara would be there for her, as she always had been. No matter what.

3

Inghean had her sketchbook open on her lap and was drawing a picture of herself and Clara side by side on a sunny hilltop. Clara glimpsed it as she opened the car door and slipped in behind the wheel.

'All fine. Clean bill of health!'

'Sure?'

Come on, Clara. False face.

'Sure.'

Inghean gave her the sunshine smile, and Clara tried to match it. She started the engine and was about to pull away from the kerb when her attention was stolen by an elegant Manila envelope tucked behind the gearstick. She killed the ignition, staring curiously at the envelope.

'Where did this come from?'

'A man brought it,' Inghean said innocently. 'He tapped on the window.'

'Jesus! What have I told you about talking to strangers?'

Inghean's smile wavered. She went back to her drawing.

Eyes on the envelope again. Clara hadn't even picked it up yet, but everything about it looked wrong. Felt wrong. There was no name on the front, no address.

'What did he look like, Inghean?'

'His face' – the corners of her mouth turned down unpleas-antly – 'oh Clara, his poor face, such a mess.'

'You mean he was scarred, disfigured?'

She nodded. 'He reminded me of someone.' A detailed

description eluded her, for now. 'He said to give you this when you came back. Said he would try to be in touch again, when you've had time.'

Someone's watching us, Clara thought, lifting her head and looking both ways down Market Street. She saw no one of interest, just people going about their business.

Unsettled, she reached for the envelope. Who would hand-deliver an envelope *to her car*, for Christ's sake? She knew the answer to that, though, didn't she?

Someone who wanted to intimidate her.

A controller.

It's from him. It's from Oswald.

'Inghean,' she whispered. 'Are you absolutely sure you didn't recognise the person who brought this?'

'I need to think,' she replied, gazing at the envelope, her eyebrows furrowing in concentration. 'He did look familiar, but so, so different.' She shook her head in confusion. 'Do you know what's in the envelope? Is it important?'

'Yes,' said Clara without thinking. For she knew, somehow, that this was true.

For one insufferable moment, she stared hard at the envelope, no longer feeling unsettled, but instead perturbed. She knew she should probably wait until she was alone to read whatever the monster had wanted her to know, but her curiosity already proclaimed that waiting wasn't an option. Not today. She cleared her mind enough to know she should open the envelope outside the car.

'Wait here, Inghean.'

She threw open the car door and got out, not quite swaying but still feeling the need to grip the top of the vehicle for support. Leaning against the car, Clara opened the envelope and slipped out the note within.

When she unfolded it and saw the handwriting, the dread froze not just her body but her every thought. For a long moment nothing would compute except the colour of the ink – jet black – the strong shape of the letters, the smooth confidence in those vertical strokes.

This was cruel. Someone's idea of a sick joke.

Except it wasn't a joke.

The familiar, arrogant handwriting confirmed that.

It was from *him*. A letter. From Oswald Cattenach.

Clara's mind reeled as she pictured the monster's gaunt, resolute face, and her whole body went cold as if she were standing not in a market town in the Peak District but in the midst of an Arctic landscape. Finally, with a sinking heart, she forced herself to gaze at the paper and read. Horrified. But not without hearing Oswald's soft, silvery voice in every sentence.

> *Dearest Clara,*
> *If you are reading this, I am almost certainly dead and you probably far away from the shores of Loch Ness. Safe, I am confident, but not forgotten.*
> *Not by me, and certainly not by Boleskine House.*

Again, with trepidation, she glanced curiously around. Who had brought this note? Who knew Oswald well enough to do his bidding after his death?

She was torn, in that moment. Wanting to be invisible; yet wanting to know the messenger. Face to face.

And, as she read on, all she could think was, *Oswald's still with me, still with me, still with me.*

Oh, that magnificent house. How I regret not telling you the meaning of its name. I think once you learn it, you'll wonder about your future, which is right. You deserve that much, Clara, because you are a survivor.

You always were.

I wonder, Clara, how well you remember the night of your tumble down the stairs? When they wheeled you into the hospital on that stretcher? I wonder if you remember the ambulance men who took pity on you? One in particular. His hair. Those blond curls.

Remember?

Clara looked up from the letter, her eyes huge, her vision swimming. For the first time since leaving Scotland she fully comprehended the vicious deviousness of the Beast; fully understood her experiences in Abersky.

He had always been with her; since before Scotland, all the way back to the night of her miscarriage – the night he marked her as another of his victims.

Why did she pick Scotland, why Abersky? Why become an estate agent?

'*You were always meant to be there at the house that night. You were supposed to burn it, so that I could buy it. Do you see? You were drawn to the Highlands for that exact purpose: to serve me.*'

She did see. Now, devastatingly, it was clear to her. All this time, the paramedic who'd talked her through the pain, promising her she'd survive: Oswald, planning a black magic ceremony he imagined, fantasised, would be his salvation.

Had he come to see her afterwards as she lay in the hospital? Was that when he had whispered his dark influences? Or had he done that in the ambulance?

She couldn't stop herself from glancing around at the market square again, wary. Just a few locals nearby; a teenager walking her German Shepherd; an old man with a shopping bag heading into a corner store.

No one she recognised. Yet she was horribly afraid that at any moment the watcher who had delivered this disturbing missive would pounce and surprise her. It was that paranoia, that doubt, which made hatred and vicious rage swell in her gut; so much so that she needed to steady herself against the car again, and it was a good minute longer before she could summon the strength to focus back on the vile letter:

> Perhaps, indeed, you think of me as the true monster of Loch Ness? A depraved man who took possession of a magic house. Truthfully, Clara, I have felt since my teenage years that I was born with the devil in me.
>
> Yet, know that my crimes were not born from deviant pleasure alone, but from my true will to survive. A will that you share.
>
> Bole-ess-kine. Did you know that the word 'Bole' is an ancient Scottish form of the word 'bull'? The Bull's House.
>
> Remember that name. Respect it. Be thankful to it. Because its power will endure in you.
>
> Think of that as your magical inheritance.
>
> Goodbye, Clara.

Clara looked up from the letter, her limbs like stone, hot, salty tears coursing down her face. She stared out at the market square, seeing not the charming stone buildings, but the intruder at Boleskine House. The one with the snake cane and the black homburg hat. She heard in her mind something Oswald had said: *a house of miracles.*

She remembered what Karl had told her:

'*Crowley wasn't the monster history records. His rituals impregnated the house; not just with evil but with magic. Dark magic and good magic.*'

She remembered that nefarious ritual at the house, Oswald claiming: '*This is a house of healings for me.*'

She knew the idea was fantastical, a product of his drug-induced fantasies. Even so, could her horrendous experience in that house have unleashed positive energy?

She thought, *No! I won't contemplate this nonsense, not for a second.*

But her mind was already flitting to the next memory. Oswald assuring her, just before his death, that Boleskine was the cradle for all that was magical and devious . . . and divine.

Then she remembered the monstrous painting in his library of the man with the bull's head. Remembered the child that grotesque figure was holding to its breast. Remembered Oswald explaining its meaning:

'*An ancient Canaan god represented by the symbol of the bull – the symbol of fertility . . .*'

For a moment, time stood still as Clara's entire mind was consumed by an astounding thought.

It had worked? The Abramelin Operation had succeeded? Only to my benefit and not to his!

Of course not. That was impossible.

Wasn't it?

Her period had come back. The doctor had told her it was very unlikely she would ever conceive again. One of those statements was certainly true; but 'very unlikely' didn't mean impossible, did it? Clara had no way of knowing. Unless someday, somehow, she was able to trust a man again and—

No, this was insanity. Oswald was playing with her, taunting her, because he had been certifiable. Psychotic. Believed impossible things.

'. . . *a house can change people for the worse, perhaps it can also change them for the better . . .'*

'*A curative house of magical power . . .'*

But Clara didn't believe a house could have healing energy. Not *that* house. Maybe there were precedents for this sort of thing. She had heard of the shrine in Lourdes, with its reputation for miraculous healings of incurable diseases, but that was different. Lourdes was a holy site, and as far as she was concerned, any reports of miraculous healings there were probably psychosomatic or misdiagnoses, or simply cases of outright fraud, not the hand of God. And anyway, Boleskine was just an old hunting lodge; it wasn't a site of pilgrimage, it wasn't a holy site.

Except it was, whispered a voice inside. *Centuries ago, there was a church on that plot of land. Remember? A church that burned down . . .*

'Oh God,' she said, and the thought – the name – brought her to her knees right there on the cold, hard pavement.

Despite her scepticism, despite her fury, one emotion above all others was cutting through, taunting her: hope.

She knew it was impossible; still, there it was, the flicker of hope in her soul, and that was good. There was no life without hope, her father used to say, and hope was better than fear. True, but as Clara regarded the letter between her fingers, she was equally sure of something else: it was not Oswald she had to thank for that spark of hope, not even partly. In no way would she permit the idea that that depraved, brutal psychopath could have left her with anything good. He was in no way her saviour.

It was Boleskine she had to thank for the little flame inside.

Suddenly, Inghean was out of the car, having noticed her hunched on the ground. She helped Clara up and back into the car. Slipping in behind the wheel, Clara felt the warmth of the girl's uncomplicated love, and, with effort, slowed her breathing, focused.

'I remember,' Inghean gasped. 'The man who brought the letter, his face was a mess. Mutilated, I think, but I remember who he reminded me of.'

'Who was it?'

'I think it was the man who asked me all those questions.'

'Which man?'

'You know, the policeman.'

Clara, wordless, stared at her.

'Adam Lake.'

Clara found this bewildering. Adam was dead. Wasn't he?

'PC Adam Lake? You're absolutely certain?'

Again, Inghean nodded, and Clara was stunned into silence. Eventually, she exhaled, staggered, and shock, a great swelling wave of it, swept through her entire body.

Why hadn't she followed the news in Loch Ness? Why hadn't she pressed to discover how exactly Adam had died?

The answer came back immediately: *Because you wanted to move on, to put the ordeal behind you.*

Suddenly Clara's memory flashed to Adam's chequered police hat. She was remembering seeing it for the first time in the estate agency; remembering it discarded and blood-stained on the floor of the mort house; remembering Oswald at the cave insisting he had allowed the young man to live. He had mentioned nothing of mutilating Adam's face, but she wouldn't have put it past the monster.

Her eyes searched Inghean's, then shifted away to scan the street, left and right, but there was no sign of Adam.

A long silence. Clara's face reflected conflicting emotions. On the one hand she was startled. On the other, ever so slightly relieved. And surprised.

'Oswald told us the truth, Inghean. He didn't kill Adam.'

The girl, diminished by grief, focused on her.

'I don't care about that. He murdered my mum.'

Hearing that was heart-wrenching. She had to think about what she was going to do, for Inghean's sake. They were family. She reached into her coat pocket for a tissue. Her grasping hand found the prescription for the antidepressants.

She couldn't look at Inghean; not then. The girl, knowing something was wrong, went back to her sketch pad. Her drawing.

It was a good five or ten minutes before she was able to think clearly again, her tears stemmed, if only for a little while. To distract herself, she clicked on the radio. The news was saying something about another far-off storm that could change the colour of the skies over Britain; air and dust sweeping in from distant deserts in southern Europe. She snapped the radio off, started the car and pulled out into the traffic.

She wasn't driving with any particular destination in mind, because she was still dazed with shock, rearranging her thoughts, realigning them. What preoccupied her most was the time. Two o'clock. That's when the nearest chemist opened after lunch.

'Are we going home?' Inghean asked, looking up from her sketchbook.

They were held up at a traffic light. Clara glanced over and saw that Inghean's drawing was complete: a sketch of the two of them, her and Clara, standing together in the sunshine, smiling happily.

'Clara, are we going home?'

Clara considered. The dashboard clock said it was eleven-thirty. Home was half an hour away, in the sleepy village of Hartington; a small stone cottage with an annexe that belonged to Clara's aunt. A kind woman, who was only too happy to let them stay. She could never have taken sanctuary in Hartington when Karl was hunting for her; that would have put her aunt at unacceptable risk. But now her aunt's home was a base from which to rebuild her life. She even had a job, serving in the village cheese shop. Comfortable. Safe. Inviting.

But why go home only to go back out again? The chemist would be open soon enough.

'Fancy some lunch?' Clara asked.

Inghean nodded, but she didn't look happy. 'And after that?' she said, her tone almost pleading. 'Straight home?'

Clara didn't answer. Her heart was thudding heavily with indecision. What she needed now was wisdom. Courage.

Faith.

Eventually, she said, 'Let's see how the day turns out, yeah?'

Inghean gave a little nod.

What am I thinking? She needs me and I need her. New beginnings.

That was right. So long as she had Inghean, there was no room for depression or despair. Perhaps she could even find Adam.

Clara glanced again at the drawing on Inghean's lap. A pink squiggle caught her eye, crayoned in just between the stick figures of Clara and Inghean, like a third entity. An indistinct smudge that may have been a cloud, or a puff of candyfloss – or hope itself.

The traffic lights turned green; the sky curving above the grey-stone village darkened to a reddish hue.

Some places stayed with you for ever. And as Clara put the car into gear, it struck her that perhaps she would be grateful after all if Boleskine House were one of them.

ACKNOWLEDGEMENTS

My deepest thanks to:

My family and friends for their continual support and encouragement.

The indefatigable team at Quercus, in particular, my editor, Emily Yau, for helping me make the book everything it needed to be.

My agents Cathryn M Summerhayes and Luke Speed at Curtis Brown, who always shoot straight with their valuable guidance.

The village of Abersky as written is fictional, but on a map you'd find it very close to Fort Augustus, in the parish of Boleskine, at the south-west end of Loch Ness. Thanks to the Lovat Hotel, which was my base for researching this story; and to the Loch Ness Centre and Exhibition, both of which are well worth a visit.

And thank you to the following, all of whom made their contributions in their own way: Stephen Volk, Charlotte Webb, Guy Chambers, Tobi Coventry and Owen Meredith.

I'd also like to thank my mum, Pamela Spring, for her valuable suggestions.

Finally, thanks is due to Boleskine House itself, for the inspiration for this story. The property really did suffer a mysterious fire in 2015, and the burned-out shell still stands, lonely and brooding on the shores of Loch Ness. So do the cemetery and mort house, which feature in this book, and the beautiful waterfall at Foyers.

I don't recommend anyone visits Boleskine; the ruin stands on private land and is too dangerous to enter. Perhaps one day it will be restored, but as an edifice to the macabre and all that is mysterious, there are few locations in Britain to equal it.

The cause of the mysterious blaze at Boleskine House is officially unknown, but I feel confident that, were he alive today, Aleister Crowley would take some grim pleasure in knowing that people still tell stories about his wild and magical house.

Neil Spring
September 2018